ADAM PULLED HER TO HIM. "DOES THAT BRING BACK MEMORIES, MISS ASHTON?"

Charity tore her eyes from his and sought to quench her body's recollection of his embrace. He pulled her hands up to his chest and she tried to push him away. "Adam, please." Even through his waistcoat she could feel the hard muscles of his chest against her fingers.

"Charity, look at me," he commanded. She felt suddenly helpless as her strength drained from her as though he were truly a magnet. Slowly, she lifted her head.

As his mouth covered hers, the shock went through her entire body. Slowly, insistently, he kissed her, still holding her hands....

FLAME OF TOURNAY

by

Lisa Beaumont

FAWCETT CREST • NEW YORK

FLAME OF TOURNAY

Published by Fawcett Crest Books, a unit of CBS Publications, the Consumer Publishing Division of CBS Inc.

ISBN: 0-449-24397-4

Printed in the United States of America

First Fawcett Crest Printing: September 1981

10 9 8 7 6 5 4 3 2 1

PART ONE

Chapter 1

"Nooo..."

The agonized wail came through the very walls of the library. Charity Ashton dropped her book and jumped from the window bench. She tugged ferociously at her skirts and ran across the room to the paneled doors. Her hand reached for the curved iron latch just as the door swung open and she met Charles's ash gray face on the threshold. The slave's large eyes were rolling, the whites looking enormous and nearly blue against his paling black skin. Her own sea green ones widened in reaction.

"Maman?" she breathed.

Charles shook his large head. "Monsieur..." he choked.

Charity was past him and running for the wide stairs. Snatching at her skirts she jerked them above her knees and took the stairs two at a time, allowing only a split second for the thought that her mother would swoon if she saw her.

Servants were milling in the upstairs hall, but they parted at the sight of their young mistress charging down upon them. They nodded toward her father's room and she streaked past without a word. Around the corner there was more confusion. Her mother, supported by Marie, was weeping before the high mahogany door. Two field hands were shuffling their feet in consternation, and a footman was staring blankly at the barrier before him. Charity ran up to the group.

"Maman," she said softly, touching her mother's shoulder.

Tear-filled eyes lifted to meet hers, and the shapely mouth moved, but no sound came out. Charity looked at the maid.

"The master took a fall," Marie said simply. "They just carried him in."

The girl nodded, feeling her stomach lurch. She turned to the two field hands. "You brought him in?" she asked in Creole.

Dumbly they nodded their heads, then moved their feet again. Summoning up a smile, Charity thanked them and dismissed everyone.

"Come, Maman." She took her mother's free arm and helped to guide her the few paces to her own rooms. Gently she settled the collapsing figure on a satin divan.

"Can you bring her something, Marie?"

The woman bowed her head and left on silent feet. Charity sat down beside her mother and smoothed black hair from her brow. She took one of the delicate pale hands in her own and squeezed it gently. The dark eyes refocused slowly.

"Ah, *chérie*. He has done what I have always feared." The lilting voice was barely audible.

Charity leaned closer. "What happened?"

"That horrible great horse of his…" A shudder ran through her mother's body. "They practiced for a wager." A small hysterical laugh bubbled up and ended in a sob. "A wager," she repeated. "He was so proud of that awful horse."

Charity's staring eyes bored into the overflowing ones before her. "He fell at a fence?"

Her mother nodded, then turned her head again, her eyes beginning to focus on the distance once more.

Charity wanted to jump up and run to her father's room, but she sat still, holding her mother's hand, waiting for Marie.

Oh, Father, how could you? her mind kept repeating. Of course he would be all right. Nothing ever kept Mark Ashton down for long. But at this of all times. Just when no one knew what to do; when half the planters on the island were beginning to fear the possibility of a slave revolt and to whisper about sending their families abroad, or at least into Cap Français.

Publicly, Mark Ashton had raised no voice of alarm. But Charity knew he was worried. And had been making contingency plans to get his family away from the island at a moment's notice if need be. By her own methods, Charity was aware that the slaves were meeting more than anyone guessed, and that something was in the air this summer of 1791. Tonight she had hoped to find out more.

Tonight! She started. Tonight she and Jacques were to have gone off again to watch a *vaudun* ceremony. She glanced at her mother, sitting so motionless beside her. Émilie Ashton would never survive the shock of discovering that her gently bred seventeen-year-old daughter was slipping out of the great plantation house in the company of one of the *gens de couleur*, the son of their own overseer, to watch the black slaves dancing in ancient rituals and new ceremonies. She found it hard enough to deal with the wayward girl who insisted on riding a horse like a man; who preferred books to the company of demure young girls of her own age; who made friends with the slaves and played with their children; and who insisted on learning any business of the estate her father would teach her. No, Charity would never let her mother know anything about her rare nighttime escapades with Jacques.

Interrupting her thoughts, the door opened quietly and Marie's strong form slid easily into the room. A silver tray held two icy mugs. Putting them on a tiny inlaid table, she patted Émilie's hand and called on her to refresh herself after the shock she had sustained. The beautiful woman on the couch sighed and nodded. Slowly she took the mug. Charity smiled gratefully at the slave.

"There's a drink for you too, *chérie*," her mother said softly, indicating the second mug. "You will need it also."

Charity pushed down her impatience. "Yes, Maman." She gulped at the cool lemony drink, wondering what was in it. Then she rose. "I am going to try to see Father. I'll be back with whatever news I can get."

Her mother sighed again. "Yes."

Charity all but ran from the room. At her father's door she skittered to a halt. Gently she pushed down on the latch and felt the door move before her. Like a wraith she slipped through the narrow opening and stopped. The room was shadowy, the tall, green shutters nearly closed against the afternoon sun. But on the great bed she could make out the large, inert form of her father. Her frightened eyes flicked to his face and saw such a pallor that she winced. Surely he wasn't dead!

Slowly she approached him. The only other person in the room was Henri, her father's overseer and friend. The mulatto looked nearly as pale as his master as he stood beside the bedpost. He glanced up at the soft rustle of her skirts and met Charity's eyes. His head shook slightly.

"I don't know, Mistress," he answered her unspoken question. "It was a bad fall. But I have seen worse."

Charity nodded. Their silence was broken by the sound of voices at the door as Charles escorted a panting doctor into the chamber. Then orders were being barked and the room was filled with movement as the doctor stripped off his light coat and approached the bed, motioning everyone away. Charity retreated outside to the hall, where she sank into a delicate chair to wait.

Some time later, the doctor emerged to find her sitting, back straight, hands folded, eyes steady. Trying to sound brusque, he told her only that her father was unconscious and would likely remain so until tomorrow. He had had a bad fall, and had broken his arm. But the blow to his head was perhaps the worst of his injuries, and that, with care, would heal.

"Perhaps?" Charity spoke quietly, but the doctor winced as though he'd felt her lunge at his unguarded word.

"I do not know if that is the only injury we cannot see," the man said slowly. "His fall was over a stone fence and he hit some of the dislocated stones. You understand, there may be internal injuries...But we cannot know yet. I am hoping not." He looked at the wide eyes and wished he had comforting words for the beautiful girl. "Tomorrow will tell us more." He shrugged and tried to look sanguine.

Dinner was a strained affair. Charles, in darkest maroon livery, presided over serving the several courses in the elegant paneled dining room just as efficiently as ever. But the ash gray pallor had not left his face, and Charity knew the servants were as worried as she.

Émilie had recovered enough to sit with her husband for an hour, and then to come downstairs for the meal. But she seemed to be quivering on the brink of hysterics every time her eyes encountered the empty chair at the end of the gleaming table, and Charity noticed that she only toyed with the food. Charity, herself, was sunk in thought and so had little cheer to offer her mother.

She'd spent the past hour pacing in the long gallery on the second story, staring out its high windows at the lush bushes surrounding terraces below, the barns and pastures in the near distance, and the great spread of waving sugar cane beyond. From that height she could even make out the flickering lights of ovens and stacks at the boiling houses far across the fields by the creek, where the sugar cane was refined.

When she wasn't looking out the windows, she was studying the portraits hanging on the marble and panel walls across the long room. Some indistinct sense of foreboding made her look at these pictures more closely than ever before, as though to memorize the faces and lines for all time. They were all Tournays but her father, and his firm face and pale hair stood out as much in that line of dark heads as his English blood stood out in this French colony of Saint Dominque.

Charity started down the gallery, looking first at the stern, dark face of the original Tournay to come to the Caribbean, the great-grandfather sent by the French crown to help administer its new half-island colony ceded by the Spanish in 1697. Guillaume Tournay had been one of those Frenchmen who helped to establish the vast plantations on the fertile Plaine du Nord, and to make Saint Dominque a rich colony for the crown.

Guillaume's wife, the sharp-featured Madelaine, had accompanied him here to bear five sons in this house. But Louis, Charity's grandfather, had been the only one to live, to marry in France, and return to take over when his father died. It was to Louis's unending sorrow that his son, the pale, effeminate-looking boy beside him on the wall, had died in adolescence. That left him with only his daughter, the exquisite, raven-haired, and delicate Émilie, to leave his vast empire to. And Émilie had driven him half mad by falling in love with an Englishman.

Mark Ashton may have come from an excellent family, and may have arrived armed with letters of introduction, but it was early evident that he was not an eligible suitor for Émilie. Older brothers stood between him and any large share of his father's fortune. And even though he spoke French fluently, had the manners of a courtier, and obviously loved Émilie as she loved him, he was after all, *English*. Émilie was sent packing to France to forget this madness. But Mark Ashton stayed on in Saint Dominque, learning the ways of the island and making himself indispensable to the planters in a myriad of ways. Before Émilie returned in two years' time, her resolve to have Mark as great as ever, the Englishman had won a place in the world of the plantations, and her father's objections had softened. Tournay had eventually become Mark's.

Charity had smiled to herself as she stood before the glowing portraits of her parents, painted just two years ago. She thought of how bravely they had defied the conventions of Émilie's world, and she was grateful for their courage.

Now, seated at the table, she realized her own courage at defying convention was wavering. What was she to do tonight? If her father's condition remained the same, could she safely choose to go off in the dark with Jacques? Charity's appetite, usually lusty, was dimmed by worry and indecision. She began to push the food around her plate.

"Charity, you do not eat." Her mother's soft voice held mild reproach.

The girl smiled at her. "Nor do you, Maman."

"But you always eat well. You must not let worry keep you from your food, child."

Charity didn't answer, and her mother went on. "You are looking tired and strained. You mustn't look like that in a few nights. The ball..." The voice trailed away. Charity's social success and eventual marriage were never far from the front of her mind. But tonight things were different. Unless her beloved Mark recovered...

Charity knew what was going through her mother's mind. "I'm really quite all right, Maman. I will get plenty of sleep before the ball."

A delicate frown appeared on the ivory forehead across from her. "Yes." Then the woman fell to musing again.

An hour later the two ladies repaired upstairs to return to their vigil. Charity finally left her father's side with the decision that she would risk going out tonight. His condition was unchanged; for now, there was nothing more she could do.

Dusk had long since slipped over into dark when she sent her maid away and listened carefully to her shuffling retreat to the back stairs. Then softly Charity lifted the latch and opened the door. A candle burned in the hall by her father's room, its flickering light casting wavering shadows over the white and gilt walls. All was silent.

The girl backed into her room and crossed to the doors onto the balcony. The thinnest sliver of moon was riding a crested cloud low on the horizon. There would be little light to show them their way this night. Nodding to herself, Charity extinguished all her candles but one. This she carried to her wardrobe and set it on a slipper chair nearby. Rummag-

11

ing through the depths of the great closet, she pulled out a homespun shift, a slave garment Jacques had procured for her months ago. It was dark and lightweight and loose, a garment good for walking, for riding, for hiding. She threw it onto her bed and searched in a drawer for her plainest underthings.

Then standing before the mirror in her wardrobe door, she slipped out of her nightdress. For just a moment, as her mass of golden brown hair tumbled about her shoulders and down over her breasts, she allowed herself to appraise her ripe young body. Vaguely she wondered if it was as good as other girls her age. Then she shrugged and her full lips curled into a small smile. At least in Jacques' eyes she seemed to be all right.

Quickly now she took the candle over to the balcony door and set it on a stand so its flicker would show on the drive below. Then, in the dim reflected light, she scrambled into the shift and tied her hair back with a ribbon.

A soft clucking sound floated up to her straining ears. Smiling broadly, she snuffed the candle and groped her way to the door. Silently, on bare feet, she slipped along the hall and down the wide marble stairs. At the bottom she paused to listen. Still no sound. Tiptoeing, the lithe figure circled the great front hall and turned down the carpeted passage, past library and morning room and office. Beyond, a small door gave easily at her touch and she stepped out onto the sultry night air heavy with the scent of oleander, jasmine, and hibiscus.

The grass was thick and soft under her feet as she began to follow the line of the drive toward the stables. Crouching, she crossed the broad ribbon of white and ran for protective shadows. Only then did she pause and look back.

The house stood silent and dark but for a faint glow at the corner window toward the back. That would be her mother's room, where a candle had been left for Émilie's vigil. The mellow brick of the high walls and the darker tile roofs above seemed to shimmer in the thin moonlight. From the kitchens nearby she could hear the familiar clanking sounds of the last cleaning up for the night.

She gave one short, painful thought for her father lying unconscious on his bed at the back of that great house, then she turned her back and cut diagonally away from the stables, giving a wide circuit to the slave compound with its long rows of huts. She wondered if Jacques had their horses

12

out yet as she groped past high walls. In a moment she could make out the line of the first pasture fence. As she climbed over it, a shadow detached itself from the railings and a muscular form came toward her.

"Jacques," she breathed.

He took her hand, giving it a quick squeeze. "All is well, *ma petite.*"

Charity could make out his long, oval face with its high cheek bones and black eyes. She smiled, returning the pressure of his hand. "The horses?"

"Beyond the fence. No saddles again. I couldn't risk the noise of tacking them up."

"Good." Charity loved riding bareback anyway. Especially in this lovely loose shift. It gave her a wild, free feeling.

The two moved quickly along the fence and Jacques helped her mount the wiry little horse, his hands lingering on her waist longer than necessary. She smiled at the gesture, then gathered up the reins, threw back her shoulders and breathed deeply. "Where do we go tonight?"

Chapter 2

The faintest breeze stirred the sugar cane on either side as the two horses picked their way along the narrow track in the darkness.

"Soon we will be on the road and there will be more light. The moon is rising." Charity had to lean across her horse's neck to catch Jacques' words. "We must go far, to the hills. Once there, the drums will lead us. There was an excitement tonight when the men came in from the fields. I think this is no ordinary meeting."

The girl felt a small shiver run through her. She pictured the dark forms around the small central fire, writhing and stamping in their dances to their African gods. Perhaps tonight would be a Petro ceremony, reputed to be the most frenzied, occasionally the most violent, of the *vaudun* cult.

"How long will it take us to reach the foothills?"

"Less than an hour, I think."

"That is far for the men to go. This must be something special. I wonder why?"

"I wonder also. But I think this is not just a meeting of the slaves. It is so far, I think it must have been called by one of the escapees—perhaps Boukman."

Charity's eyes widened in the darkness and she sat up straighter. The tiniest feeling of apprehension tickled at the base of her neck. She tried to remember what she'd heard about Boukman. She knew only that he was a Jamaican slave who had escaped several years ago and had been living in the hills ever since. Stories of the maroons, or fugitive slaves, filtered through the lives of the landowners even to the ears of the ladies. Charity remembered snatches of tales about the leaders of these men practicing sorcery in their mountain valleys. Some were said to be giants who could cast spells on any blacks who came near, and order violent acts to be done in their names.

Mark Ashton tended to make light of any stories that reached his family's ears, but Charity knew he and the other owners worried about these daring men. The thought of them spreading insurrection among the thousands of slaves on the plantations was too grisly to bear. And this *vaudun* cult that was taking strong hold among the slave population was something to be watched. Charity had seen enough to know that *vaudun* was a weird mixture of African rites, Catholic teachings, and local imagination. Although all slaves, under the *Code Noir,* were baptized and received instruction in the Catholic church, everyone knew there were few convinced Catholics in the lot. Most seemed simply to adapt newly learned rites and beliefs to their native African religions.

She pushed her little horse up beside Jacques'. There was no use speculating. She'd have to wait to see. They were on a good, wide road now and the scant moonlight was sufficient for them to urge their horses to a faster pace. Their eyes and ears strained for any chance encounters, but no one was abroad this hot August night, and they made good time across the plain.

To Charity's eager senses, it seemed a long while before Jacques turned off the high road into the underbrush and began picking his way over rocky ground toward a line of low hills just before them. Soon they were lunging up steep embankments and crossing tiny valleys in the foothills. The purple-black humps of rugged mountains stood outlined against the inky sky ahead.

Several times Jacques halted and listened and Charity caught her breath at each stop. At last they heard the insistent staccato of a single drum in the still night air. Jacques pulled up short. Nearby, a shallow ravine offered a dense cover for the horses. The two dismounted and led the animals forward. Tying the horses loosely to some satinwood trees, they turned and scrambled to higher ground once more.

Jacques reached for her hand, and demurely Charity gave it to him. His teeth flashed in a smile. "I am not asking you to dance, *petite*. This is in case you stumble."

Tossing all ladylike manners over her shoulder along with her heavy plait of hair, Charity stuck her tongue out at him and tried to tug her hand away. She got only a low chuckle for her gesture and a firmer grip around her fingers.

"Come, we will find them this way." And he pulled her gently forward.

It was hard to move silently through the underbrush, but Jacques went slowly and carefully. Crouching, the two inched forward until they reached a thicket of bushes in front of a clearing ahead. Charity felt her pulse quicken with excitement as she settled herself behind her leafy screen and parted a section of branches. Before her, the central fire of the clearing glowed brilliantly. Dark forms moved slowly around it, throwing huge shadows across the assembled worshippers, most of whom sat or squatted in a ragged circle just outside the firelight. The drums were silent now, and an air of anticipation hung in the smoke above the gathering.

Jacques leaned close, touching her shoulder. "This is a large group," he whispered against her ear. "They've been collecting for some time from the looks of it, and have already made their food offerings to their personal *loas*. Smell the roasted pigs?"

Charity nodded. She knew this was an interval of quieter ceremony before the primary gods of the evening were called upon.

"Here we go." Jacques' whisper was barely audible as a slow drum beat began somewhere on the left of the circle.

A man had appeared beside the fire now. He was a large, square form, clothed in red rags, and in his powerful hands he carried a pot. Charity knew this vessel would contain ashes and that the man was a sort of priest who would now dance around the fire, sprinkling the ashes in patterns or pictures called *vevers*. This ritual would summon the *loas* to the ceremony.

After a time the priest moved to the edge of the circle and a chorus of voices began to rise and fall in a repetitive sing-song as other forms appeared. A deeper drum joined the chorus, and dancers began to shuffle and stamp toward the fire, beginning the ceremonial obliteration of the *vevers*.

"What gods are they calling?" Charity asked, her voice low.

"I'm not sure. I thought I heard the name Kita. So I think they call on the *loas* of the Petro family."

"Oooh." Charity shivered and moved a little closer to her companion. Jacques put his arm around her shoulders in a gesture of casual protectiveness.

The drum beat became more insistent, and others joined the circling dancers while those who remained seated took up the singing refrain. On and on the dancers went, building momentum slowly until the drums suddenly fell silent.

The priest reappeared, a scarlet kerchief on his head now, and nodded twice. The drums began a slow booming and suddenly somebody yelled—a frenzied, drawn-out sound that made the hairs on Charity's neck stand up.

Into the firelight jumped a nearly naked woman, a magnificent young slave whose ebony body glittered in the flickering light. Charity gasped as she recognized this proud creature strutting before the crowd. It was a serving girl at the LaRoche plantation whom Charity had seen many times. Ursula was her name, and always she had looked demure and had served with grace and humility. Now she wore only a kind of loincloth around her hips and a wide, carved bracelet on one arm. Bits of colored cloth were twisted into her short hair, and they bobbed crazily as she threw back her head and posed for an instant, her high breasts thrust forward and her hip cocked to one side. Charity caught her breath as the rhythm of the drums changed and the woman began to move slowly around the circle, her eyes unfocused, her arms describing graceful arcs.

Jacques' arm tightened across Charity's shoulders and his hand gripped her arm. She pressed against his side. Something about the pulsating drums and the movements of the dance made her breath come unevenly.

The lone dancer paused now, her legs bent, her arms akimbo on knees, her head nodding from side to side. Strange sounds seemed to be coming from her throat. It was hard to tell if it was Creole, or indeed any language at all. Charity looked questioningly at Jacques.

"Not Creole," he said, reading her mind. "It's *langage*, some speech from the land of her origin. She must be a *serviteur*, one now possessed by the god she is serving."

Charity shuddered. She wondered what it would be like to be possessed by a *loa*, to be caught in a religious ecstasy that dominated one's whole being, even gave one the ability to speak in a language one didn't know.

Just then, the woman nodded and the drums changed once more, working a sultry beat. The dancer straightened and thrust her hips forward toward the fire. Slowly she bent backward, her hands behind her back, her breasts reaching high. Flinging her arms out from her sides, she began to writhe in suggestive circles.

Charity stared. Never had she seen anything so sensual and explicit. She squirmed, feeling Jacques' hard body next to hers. His hand was beginning to hurt her arm, and the coarse cloth of her loose shift seemed to prickle her skin. She wished she could look away from the scene, but she was mesmerized by the vibrating drums and the undulating body now moving nearer.

Jacques made a small noise, but Charity ignored him.

The woman was past them now, still circling and beginning to go faster. Throaty voices had joined the drums, and a swaying motion had begun in the crowd, like the tall cane waving in tropical breezes. The dancer threw up her arms, stamped one foot and began to undulate with a quickly mounting tension.

So riveted was Charity, she hardly noticed the priest catapult through the air and land on his knees near the fire. He seemed to circle something on the ground, touch his forehead to the earth, then, bent over, whirl around the circle. Two more men joined in. The woman seemed oblivious of their movements, writhing in some private ecstasy of her own. Someone at the edge of the circle fell prone in the dust as the priest turned to meet the woman coming around the fire.

Their bodies paused for a second, then leaned toward each other and began a weaving dance of desire.

In a trance, Charity watched more dancers enter the fire-light and approach the writhing pair. The drums made the earth and sky vibrate to their rhythm. Her whole body was taut and her eyes were beginning to burn with the strain of staring.

Suddenly she felt a hand pass over the small of her back and travel down toward her thighs. Then she was being turned over and Jacques was kissing her. Feeling the rhythm of the drums in her whole body, she responded to his kiss, wondering at what was happening. She felt her breast being cradled in a strong hand, and his body pressed against her, hard and urgent. The deep drums boomed on through the earth. Strange prickly sensations crept through her. She began to feel frightened.

And suddenly there was silence. The drums had stopped.

Charity opened her eyes. "Jacques," she whispered.

He raised his head and tried to cover her mouth with his. She twisted aside. "Jacques, listen. Something's happening." She pushed at his broad shoulders.

He pulled her closer. "Charity," he breathed huskily.

She started to say something pleading, but her voice was drowned by shouts and calls from a hundred throats.

Startled, Jacques loosened his grip and looked up. Charity scrambled out of his arms onto her hands and knees. The beautiful slave girl was still in the circle of firelight, her body pressed to that of the priest. He held her to him with one arm, and with the other shook his fist to the sky, shouting something Charity couldn't understand. Men and women were on their feet calling and gesturing too. They all looked angry. A single low drum slammed at a rhythm as the calls began to settle into a deep chant and men shuffled their feet and stamped in place.

"What are they doing?" Charity, wide-eyed, tugged at Jacques' sleeve.

He shook his head. "I don't know. But that priest is working them up to a frenzy."

Arms were waving now, fists clenched. Lines of men began stamping around the fire as the drums beat a sort of martial rhythm. Charity shrank from the sight. What had started out as an innocent and exciting adventure was becoming a frightening experience.

The circle widened. Women moved back clapping, shaking, and chanting. Men danced and prowled angrily in ever-increasing arcs, some with clubs or stones upraised. Their threatening gestures made her cower in her hiding place. She tugged at Jacques' sleeve again. "Please," she whispered.

The boy nodded and began to back very slowly from their nest. Once clear of the little thicket, he pushed her to the ground and showed her how to slither on elbows and knees. Desperately, Charity worked along beside him, but her loose shift kept catching on rocks and twigs. The fearful sounds behind her made her feel like a hunted animal. She only prayed she could keep going without being seen.

Her elbows were raw, her legs scratched, and her garment nearly in rags by the time Jacques halted and lifted himself to his knees. "The horses are down there," he said, nodding toward a deeper darkness ahead of them. "Come, hold my hand."

Crouching, the two moved forward as quickly as they dared. The frenzied sounds behind them still sounded very near, and Charity had to fight her own panicky impulse to run crashing through the jungle growth in the ravine. When they reached the horses she nearly fell on the neck of her dark little beast. But still they must be careful. As silently as they could, they led the animals along the ravine, then tugged them up a steep bank through tangled vines and bushes. At long last the sounds of the excited crowd and the beating of the drums were beginning to fade.

Jacques halted then and nodded. He turned to help her up, but Charity's fear had already flung her onto her mount's back. Jacques was beside her horse, looking up as she tried to drag her tangled hair together with her trailing ribbon. She heard his sharp intake of breath and glanced down. Only then did she realize that her shift was in tatters, split nearly up to her waist on one side and rent down her shoulder, leaving her bosom almost exposed. Instinctively, she pulled the shift closer around herself, hiding what she could.

"Can we go straight to the road?" she asked, trying to keep her voice level.

Jacques straightened his shoulders and swallowed. "No. I think many of that gathering were fugitives, not slaves. That priest has them all in a wild frenzy now, and there's no knowing where he will choose to lead them. The road may be dangerous until we are well away from here."

He swung onto his horse then, and looked up to the sky. Small clouds drifted lazily near the partial moon. Stars twinkled cheerfully all around. Charity wished fervently that she were looking at them from the terraces at Tournay instead of from a hidden valley in the foothills miles from home.

Their progress seemed painfully slow at first, and Charity expected any moment to hear the sounds of the hundred *vaudun* worshippers pounding down upon them. Biting her lip, she clung to her horse, keeping her eyes always on Jacques' back before her, never looking behind. And at last she was rewarded with the sight of the road ahead of them.

Jacques halted in the trees and went forward on foot to listen. Within moments he was back. "I hear nothing behind us on the road, *chérie*. I think we now use it as fast as we can." With those words he was on his horse's back and away down the track, Charity hard on his heels.

The little animals' flanks were heaving before the two finally reined them in and allowed them to walk the last two miles through the fields. Once near the borders of her familiar land, Charity breathed more steadily and her mind cleared itself of the fog of fear that had gripped it. She knew only that this was the last *vaudun* ceremony she'd witness. The forces in that clearing back there were too sinister and too far beyond her comprehension to allow a repetition of tonight's adventure.

At the edge of the stableyard, Jacques grasped Charity's reins. "Go now. I will watch that you get in safely."

"But I will help with the horses. I always do."

"That is my job." His voice was very low, but Charity thought she detected a strange distance in it. She dismounted and put her hand on his arm, but he moved gently away. "You'll need both hands to keep your shift together."

Charity flushed and put her hand obediently to her neck. Memory of his kisses returned and she stepped back a pace, flushing more furiously.

The young man before her was looking at her feet, and his hands holding the reins were very still. "I am sorry it turned out so tonight, *ma petite*," he said softly.

"Jacques...I don't know what happened back there, but..."

"I know you don't, *chérie*." He made a small gesture with one hand. "It was my fault for taking you out there, for..."

"Oh, no. I made you promise to take me."

"Yes, but you did not know what it might be like." He reached out a hand as though to touch her face, then withdrew it. "You are becoming very beautiful, Mistress Ashton, and there is so much life in you... You must be careful with yourself as your maman now looks for a husband for you."

"But I don't want a husband," Charity said indignantly. "I just want to go on here and remain friends with you."

Jacques looked at her for a long moment, then hunching one shoulder, he turned toward the stables. "Good night, Charity."

The girl stood where she was, feeling his abrupt dismissal like a slap. He had withdrawn from her and she was sure it was her fault. Perhaps she should never have allowed him to kiss her that way. Puzzled, she walked despondently toward the house and tiptoed through the silent halls and up the stairs to her room. There the violent emotions of the evening began to take their toll and she started to shake. Fighting off sudden tears, she slipped into her nightdress, then thought of her father. Picking up the candle, she stole down the wide corridor. Her father's door stood ajar and she tiptoed into the room. Marie sat by his bed, her heavy, graying head nodding near the flickering candle on the bedside table. In the dim light, her father looked as pale and still as she'd last seen him.

Feeling suddenly chilled and lonely, Charity fled to her bedroom. She was grateful for her body's insistence on the need for sleep, for she feared she was going to cry in earnest, and she didn't really know why.

Chapter 3

Mark Ashton regained consciousness at noon the next day, and the effect of the news on his household was dramatic. Instead of moping about in the corridors, the indoor servants were suddenly busily at work, and loud voices were heard once more outside as activity resumed its normal pace.

Contrary to his doctor's explicit orders, the master of the house had himself propped up in bed and sent for his wife, his daughter, and food in that order. When Charity's turn came, she bounced into his bedroom, her heart lighter than it had been in twenty-four hours. Restraining her impulse to throw herself at him, she leaned over and gave her father a light kiss on his cheek. With his good arm he pulled her down and hugged her, but then winced in pain.

"Oh, Papa, is it hurting very much?" she asked, leaning back to give him ease. She spoke in English as he insisted she do when in private. Her native French gave to his language a lovely lilt that always pleased him.

"Never felt better," he lied, his face ashen with pain. He did allow, however, that he'd better not hug her for a few days. She smiled at that and settled into the chair by his bed. His first question then was about his horse. Charity was able to assure him there was nothing to worry about.

"Good," was the reply. "But I fear I've lost my wager that Cloud could clear that fence with feet to spare."

"It was a silly wager. You could have died."

The two beamed at each other in fondness and understanding. "Well, I'll have another chance when I'm ready to ride again."

"Another chance at what?" Émilie entered the room looking fragile and beautiful in a rose lawn dress. Charity marveled, not for the first time, at her delicate mother's lovely elegance, wishing she too had the pale, creamy skin and raven hair that had made Émilie the belle of all the plantations in her youth. Not a few hearts had been broken when she married Mark Ashton.

Her husband looked at her fondly. "Another chance to ride soon, I hope," he said with a gentle smile, and held out his hand to her.

Émilie arranged herself on the edge of the bed and took his hand between both of hers. "You will not be riding very soon, I think." She too spoke in English though more haltingly. "You will rest in this bed and recover from your oh-so-foolish fall." They smiled at each other. Émilie kissed him quickly and stood up again. "I only wanted to see you again. Now I must go and greet more callers. Oh, yes," she said to his raised eyebrows, "the word went out yesterday that you were injured. We have already had inquiries after your health. But today *you* see no one."

The figure on the bed stirred. "But I . . ."

"No one," Émilie repeated with gentle firmness. "Come, Charity. You may assist me in the drawing room."

Her daughter wrinkled her nose, but stood obediently. Patting her father's good arm, she turned reluctantly to follow her mother.

In her elation about her father and her consciousness of duties to be performed, Charity managed to submerge memories of last night's adventures as she sat through the formal calls. But when Madame Lamarque mentioned that the Moreau plantation south of here had sustained considerable damage in a raid made on it in the middle of the night, she was forced to remember her own outing.

"They are saying that it was that awful Boukman with a large band of followers who carried off livestock and burned the barns and outbuildings before anyone could stop them," the visitor said.

Émilie looked shocked. "That is closer to us than any before," she answered, not noticing Charity's wide-eyed silence.

The two women nodded and clucked their way to the door.

Charity stood where she was, unwelcome memories of the *vaudun* ceremony flooding her brain. So it *was* Boukman

23

they'd seen. One of the fierce leaders of the maroons now dared to come to the edge of the plain and call plantation slaves to his band. She wondered what it meant, and wished she could talk to her father about it. But she knew she must wait till he was stronger. Her mother would allow nothing to interfere with his recovery, no matter how long it took.

As it was, Émilie did not have her way. Although Mark Ashton conceded that he could not immediately leave his bed, he had his secretary bring a desk and two more comfortable chairs into his room the next morning, and then closeted himself with his overseer for an hour before lunch. Émilie wrung her hands to no avail.

In the afternoon, Charity went up the wide stairs to see if he would like her to read to him while he rested. Not wanting to knock if he were asleep, she pushed gently on the massive door to his room. She stopped as her father's voice rumbled across the Aubusson carpet toward her.

"You are counted among my oldest friends, Hercule. And your father before you. Your property adjoins Tournay. It would seem fitting if, when my daughter's thoughts turn to marriage, she should choose Paul. But they are young yet, eh? And need time to try their wings. Charity is to have her first season this year. I would wish her to enjoy it thoroughly, to be brought into the fashionable world of adults with gaiety. After that, who knows..." His voice trailed away.

The listening girl let go her breath. So Hercule LaRoche would see her marry his son! No doubt he'd broached the subject on behalf of Madame LaRoche, an ambitious and self-important woman who would rub her hands with glee at the thought of joining the LaRoche lands to Tournay. She wondered if their son had had any say in this scheme and wrinkled her nose. Paul LaRoche, whom she'd known since childhood, was not the sort of man she thought of as a future husband. In her eyes he was still the rather nasty little boy who used to pull her hair just when he knew she couldn't cry out and bring adult attention to them. For the past two years Paul had been traveling for his father, and she'd scarcely seen him, but she doubted he'd changed so much she would view his suit with favor. For that matter, there was no man she knew of whose suit she would consider encouraging.

Charity was so lost in her thoughts it was with a start she realized the two men were bidding each other farewell.

Quickly she pushed the door open and stopped in seeming surprise.

"Oh, pardon. I had not realized you had another visitor, Father."

Mark Ashton's pale face lit up at the sight of his daughter. "Come in, come in, Charity. Monsieur LaRoche was just leaving."

Charity turned wide eyes and a light smile on the thin, elegant figure who advanced to take her slender hands in his. A narrow smile split the swarthy features as he bowed, murmuring good-bys. She inclined her head and he walked languidly out the door. Charity watched him leave with arched brows, then looked down at her father's laughing eyes.

"I know, I know. A bit foppish for my taste too. But he's a smart man and has done well by his lands. Made quite a fortune."

"Perhaps." Charity's tone was dubious. "But I have to confess, Papa, that I heard the last of your conversation, and was glad you would not wed me to his son before I even have my first season."

Her father smiled thinly. "You have time yet. But you might do worse than Paul."

Charity plopped unceremoniously into the recently vacated chair beside the bed. Pouting slightly, she considered this. "Well, I suppose he's attractive enough," she said judiciously. "But I don't think his famous swordsmanship qualifies him as a husband. I suspect winning those two duels has been his only real accomplishment. Besides," and she frowned, "Jacques has told me that Paul has a bad reputation with the slaves. I don't know just why, but it doesn't make him sound appealing."

"Oh?" Her father raised a querying eyebrow as he cautiously turned his head on the pillow the better to see her. "What else has Jacques been telling you?"

At the question, Charity forgot M. LaRoche and his son. She thought of the ceremony she'd seen and of the raid which followed it. Her face became grave. "Have you heard, Papa, about the destruction on the Moreau plantation two nights ago?"

Ashton tried to nod and winced at the effort. "Henri told me."

Charity continued slowly, picking her words. "There was a *vaudun* ceremony that night. It is said that it was led by

Boukman himself, and that many slaves attended. It is thought that he led his followers on that raid."

Her father's eyes narrowed, and a large hand tugged at the thin sheet covering him. "Boukman grows bolder," he said at length. "Too bold. Now the authorities will be after him in earnest."

"You don't think this is the start of something bigger?"

Mark's laugh was a weak version of his former heartiness, and Charity thought she detected a hollowness in it. "Hardly, my dear."

He coughed then and slowly turned his head away from her, wiping his mouth with his good hand. After a space he resumed. "There is little chance that anything will happen, daughter. But I want you to know that if anything should, I have made some preparations."

The girl tensed. "Preparations?"

"Of course." Ashton's voice was casual. "A poor husband and father I would be if I didn't plan for even the most remote possibilities." He paused and his jaw clenched once. "LaRoche and I have spoken of the chance of slave unrest. An uprising is unlikely, but we would not have our families subjected to even the slightest unpleasantness. Should anything occur, we will take you into Cap Français. My agent there will see you are cared for. There are several merchant vessels... Should things get out of hand, one of those vessels, whichever is first in port, will be ready to remove you from Saint Dominque."

"Remove us from Saint Dominque?" Charity gasped at the thought. "And what of you?"

"It depends on the situation." Her father tried to laugh again, coughed once and then closed his eyes. "If anything happens to me, Charity, Henri will see you and your mother are taken care of. If there's trouble he'll contact LaRoche and get you to the port."

"If anything happens... But Papa, you are recovering now." She tapped his arm lightly. "And Maman and I expect to be under your care for many years yet."

Her father opened his eyes and she saw they were smiling. "Yes, I expect so too, little one."

"Anyway, where should we go without you?"

His face turned serious. "I have given that some thought, and wonder how you would like England. After all, it is the home of your grandfather."

"Yes, indeed. That charming man who threw you out of

his house after you and your eldest brother quarreled. Thank you, Papa, but I think not!"

Her father sighed. "I hardly see many choices. You couldn't go to France with all the turmoil there. We don't even know if your mother's relatives still live."

Charity gave him an impish look. "We could go to the north, to the United States and live among the savages. I'd look very smart dressed in animal skins, don't you think?" She dimpled as her father chuckled. "Well, it's all beside the point, since Maman and I will go nowhere without you."

The man on the pillows looked long and thoughtfully at the girl until her smile began to waver. Then his eyelids dropped again and the corners of his mouth twitched. "I suggest then, that you *do* begin to think about marriage." His voice became very gentle. "I won't always be here to protect you, Charity. Some day you will need the strong arm of another. You may find that Paul's fearsome reputation with a sword could stand you in good stead."

Charity jumped from the chair. "I can quite well look out for myself, thank you. And Maman too," she said with spirit. Then her tone softened. "I've stayed too long and tired you too much. It is that that makes you talk so." She patted his hand lovingly. "Rest now. We will look in again later."

For the next three days Émilie made careful and cautious preparations for the upcoming ball. Mark Ashton had decreed that the ladies must attend, though they both protested at leaving him even for one evening. He was recovering, but slowly, and they wished to see he had proper care every moment until he was on his feet once more. But he assured them he would prefer to know they were having a change of view from the sickroom, and in the end they chose to humor him.

When Charity went to see him now, she took care not to tire him too much, and not to raise any more disturbing subjects. He was always cheerful when she was there, and she told herself that if he didn't chafe to be up and around it was only natural after such a hard fall.

She had other worries on her mind too. She had not seen Jacques for several days now, and she could not help but realize he was avoiding her. She felt hurt at his aloofness, but deep inside she was aware of a tiny flicker of relief, too. Guiltily she reflected that she had been using her childhood friend this summer to test her powers, to see if she was capable of arousing a man. She'd proved all too well that she *was* capable, and had nearly gotten burned for her pains. She wanted to seek Jacques out and apologize to him, but some newfound instinct warned her to leave well enough alone.

Her father's words about marriage had made Charity uncomfortable. If she were to marry Paul LaRoche, she would retain her pampered life of luxury, and would satisfy her mother's desire to see her wed to a member of an old aristocratic family. But she felt a restlessness grow in her at the thought. As much as she loved Tournay and Saint Dominque, she would like to see some of the world beyond these shores. She craved excitement, even romance. Never before had she given thought to her future, but the sensations evoked by Jacques' kisses and then her father's talk of her marriage, made her try to marshal the prospects. She knew only that she would not settle for Paul LaRoche before she'd had a chance to see what alternatives were open to her. Beyond that she could hardly think. Surely her father would not force her to marry a man she did not love! But there were others, and the coming season would give her an opportunity to see if there was someone who might touch her heart. Meanwhile, she must try to please her parents at the upcoming ball.

On the afternoon that Charity swept across the broad veranda of the LaRoche mansion, the soft, pale green skirts of her glazed chintz gown billowing gracefully around her long legs, the darker, vine-like embroidery outlining her full breasts and nipping to the tiny waist before twining down the length of the skirt, she was a vision of demure loveliness. Her gold-streaked hair shimmered in loose waves behind her ears and down her back, and her large, blue-green eyes sparkled with anticipation. Unconscious of the picture she made, she smiled a greeting at the round figure of her hostess at the great door. Beyond she could see a cluster of elegant women, wide skirts swishing deliciously as they moved in the vast hall. Charity's eyes widened and she felt her first small twinge of uncertainty. Never before had she been in the uncomfortable position of being judged against other girls for the favors and attentions of eligible young men. As the girl's steps faltered, her mother's small hand squeezed her arm gently and she knew her parent understood. She remembered her father's broad smile of approval when she'd gone in to say good-by, and she took heart. After all, she was here to do some judging of her own. This preseason dance would give her an opportunity to see what the months ahead

28

might bring. As she drew nearer, her smile broadened at the quick look of amazement in Madame LaRoche's pale brown eyes.

Hugging Émilie swiftly, Madame's darting eyes glided over Charity in an appraising manner. "My, don't you look lovely today," she said in her throaty voice.

Charity laughed aloud. "Why, thank you, Madame. I always seek to pass inspection."

A look of puzzlement crossed the fleshy face and Charity fluttered her lashes innocently. The old cat, she thought, she's evaluating me like a brood mare for her son.

Her mother's hand tightened warningly, and rather breathlessly Émilie filled the awkward pause with light chatter as they all turned to the cool spaciousness of the indoors. Soon the incident was forgotten in the rounds of introductions and the sudden interest of the men who were privileged to be among the first presented to the dazzling Mademoiselle Ashton of Tournay. Quickly she was separated from her mother and led through the house to the terraces at the rear where groaning tables and steaming pits were labored over by a score of servants. To her delighted surprise, she was promptly surrounded and pampered by young gallants vying for the privilege of serving her the dinner that followed. But it was not until she came slowly down the grand staircase that evening, dressed in a thin silk gown of palest rose, that she saw the object of many of her thoughts these past days.

Standing at the base of the wide stairs, his swarthy features arranged in a sardonic look, Paul watched her descend with a quickening of his pulse. So this was what little Charity Ashton had grown up to be! His parents had certainly been right about her beauty. He studied her cool composure carefully. There was nothing there to show him the excessive independence and outrageous behavior they also decried. But the spark in those lovely big eyes warned him there might be a deal of spirit that would need harnessing. His mouth lifted at the prospect and he stepped forward, deftly cutting off the advance of a stocky young man who looked as though he would faint at the sight of the gold and pink confection.

"So little Charity Ashton has grown up to capture the hearts of all who are unwary." He held out his hand and Charity put her own slim fingers into his palm.

"I cannot imagine you ever being unwary," she said frankly, meeting his eyes with a dimpling smile.

"Ah, but you are a vision to make even the sternest of resolves crumble to dust tonight, *chérie*."

Charity flushed at the extravagant compliment, and willed her fingers to stay still in his hand. He seemed taller and more darkly handsome than she recalled, and he looked resplendent in a wine-colored coat that seemed like a second skin on his long, slender frame. She was aware of the stares of envy from other girls in the hallway and was suddenly glad she had tugged the lace neckline even lower than intended. What fun it would be if she could make a conquest of Paul tonight, too. The fact that she had never cared for his manner, and that she could not now like the way his eyes slid past her as he spoke, did not matter. She was discovering a new game she could excel at—that of collecting beaux for the season to come. She gave Paul her most dazzling smile and moved forward to the door on his arm.

Despite its small size, the ball was a glittering affair; a perfect setting for a girl on the brink of ripe womanhood who was looking for her first male attentions. A myriad of candles twinkled in the gilded sconces, their brilliant reflections illuminating the room through high panel mirrors. The gentle breezes wafted over balconies through open doors, aided on their way by small black slaves waving huge palm frond fans. Silks and satins rustled deliciously to the soft strains of a small orchestra as dashing men in tight coats and high cravats paid court to the beauties of the seasons past and of the one to come.

Never lacking for partners and attention, Charity whirled through the ball in a daze of newfound emotions. Always before, she had disdained the niceties of the carefully orchestrated manners that marked formal occasions. But tonight she felt for the first time her power as a beautiful woman, and she drank deeply of the heady wine it represented. For one brief moment only, while she was trying to decide which of two importuning young men she would dance with next, she thought of Jacques. Here in this glittering room she understood at last his sudden distance from her. They were of different worlds, and she was growing up. Jacques knew, after that strange, frightening, wild night at the *vaudun* ceremony, their old easy friendship could not continue. He had released her to go to her own destiny among the people of her world, and she was grateful to him. What a contrast this gay dance was to the furtive scurrying under bushes, afraid of people locked in a power she didn't understand!

To her secret amusement, Paul paid her as much attention as propriety allowed, and she wondered if his parents had requested him to do so. But she found his dark eyes followed her wherever she was, and his long jaw tightened when she danced with another. Flattered, she flirted lightly with him, enjoying herself immensely.

As he led her from the dance floor for the third time, she smiled at the thought of the season to come, and he looked at her quizzically. "What is it that puts the enchanting dimple in your cheek, Charity? The heartbreak we are causing that group of young men?" Paul's eyes scanned the room and returned to survey her face before moving down her throat to rest on her swelling breasts.

Too flushed with success to be embarrassed at his scrutiny, Charity dimpled even more. "I have enjoyed myself so much tonight, Paul."

"Good. I trust you will enjoy yourself even more in the future." He cocked one roguish black eyebrow at her as she smiled again. "But not so much that I cannot keep watch over you." Deftly he was guiding her to the end of the room where massive potted palms bowed gracefully in one corner. Behind their leafy screen Paul's face took on more warmth. "You have begun truly to grow up, *ma petite*," he said, and his voice had a huskiness that made Charity look at him sharply.

She started to reply lightly, but his hand came out to trace the line of her face and throat. His fingers felt cold and she jerked away. Paul smiled, but his eyes glinted. "I will be with you this season, my beauty. So do not capture too many hearts, as they will all have to break for you." As he spoke, Charity edged past him into the light. But his voice followed her. "They will break, for if all goes as I hope, by this time next year you will be mine."

She looked around, pretending she hadn't heard him. "Oh dear, I see Maman signaling to me. You'll have to escort me to her, Paul, and make my apologies to Henri Moreau for the next dance."

Paul's hand was under her elbow as she began to move away, and his head bent near. "I'm only pleased that mine will have been the last arms to hold you tonight, *chérie*. Perhaps you will dream of them when you are safe at home in bed."

31

This time Charity did blush at his intimacy and turned her face away without comment.

The high leather seats of the carriage felt good after hours of dancing, and Charity leaned back contentedly, wriggling her toes in her thin slippers. Her mother smiled as Justin turned the team out of the high gates onto the road.

"You enjoyed yourself tonight, *chérie?*"

"Oh, yes, Maman. It was wonderful."

Charity dimpled and her mother patted her cheek with a gloved hand. "Ah, you will have a fine time this season, just as I did when I was your age. And this year...or perhaps next...you will find a man worthy of you. Perhaps Paul, no? Though there are many good men on Saint Dominque."

"But you didn't marry one of them." Charity leaned forward earnestly. "You chose a romantic outsider instead of one of the 'worthy' men of the island."

It was her mother's turn to smile. "Yes, indeed! But I met your father at an oh-so-proper party. And it was never a question that his family was good."

"Well, I don't care so very much about being proper," Charity said, sitting back again and clasping her mother's hand. "But I think I would like to fall in love with a dashing stranger." She stared into the dark night, watching the glow of small torches that seemed to be crossing a side road. Vaguely she wondered who was about in the middle of the night. Then her mother's voice pulled her attention back.

"It is very rare when a girl has her white knight ride up, *chérie*. Most of us must settle for more mortal men. And very well they do, too, I assure you." Her laughter tinkled, and Charity had to smile, even though her thoughts were rebellious.

As much as she'd liked this evening, she'd seen no one who could capture her full attention, let alone her heart. Certainly not Paul LaRoche. She found his thin-lipped scrutiny of her—as though she were an objet d'art to be appraised for proper value—and his furtive fondling vaguely repellent. But there was time yet...The carriage was turning up the avenue to home now, and Charity began to think longingly of her bed.

A muffled *"mon Dieu!"* from the driver brought both women upright. The slave reined in the horses and Charity half stood in her seat to see why Justin had stopped. Her gasp made the driver turn, his frightened face blank of thought.

"Lord. Drive on, Justin. Hurry!" Charity's voice broke on the command as fear welled up inside her.

"What is it, Charity?" Émilie tugged at her daughter's skirts. Then her cry pierced the air as the carriage moved onto the open drive before the huge house and a dull orange glow could be seen rising from behind the roof. Just then a single tongue of flame shot out from the corner near the stables. Tournay was burning!

Chapter 4

The house was ablaze with lights, and through the open windows, shadow figures could be seen darting among the rooms of the far wing. From the barns the shrieks of terrified horses mingled with shouts and cries of men. On the portico two black shapes moved stealthily toward the doors to the study. The sight of the sneaking figures made Charity's blood pound in her temples. With a howl of rage she jumped from the carriage, heedless of her gown tearing on the narrow steps. Only her mother's terror-stricken voice stopped her from hurling herself across the drive to the front door. She paused for a second, then reached up and grasped Justin's trembling arm.

"Back the horses down the drive to the shadows," she shouted at the immobile slave.

His eyes rolled in his head, but he made no move. Émilie was struggling to reach the carriage steps as the vehicle jerked and swayed. Charity turned back and shoved her mother into her seat again. "Stay there, Maman. You'll be safer." Her voice rang with her father's authority and Émilie could only stare wide-eyed with shock from her crumpled corner.

"Justin!" The girl stamped her foot, but the slave didn't seem to hear. Wild with fright and fury, Charity snatched the whip from its holder beside the driver's seat. Flinging her arm back as she clung to the carriage side, she brought the whip down across the man's shoulders and head. Instinctively he threw up an arm to ward off the blow and cowered away from her. With an oath she brought the whip down again.

At last the frightened eyes focused on her. "Back," she bellowed and waved her arm. To her relief Justin nodded and began to gather in the reins.

Charity snatched up her skirts and began to run. Her mother's scream followed her across the wide drive, but she didn't glance backward as her feet found the wide stairs and she started up. At the top she paused. The silent figures were gone from the veranda. Almost she turned toward the stables, but flames were climbing high in the air now, and she could see that the outbuildings were burning and bringing the fire closer to the house itself. She threw herself at the front door. Her father lay in the wing nearest those buildings and she must get to him.

The tiered chandelier in the front hall was fully lit. She blinked as she crossed the threshold, unable to comprehend what the light illuminated. By the curved stairs two field hands were lifting a massive porcelain vase. They looked up as the heavy door thudded back against the wall. The sight of the golden-haired young mistress standing there with huge fierce eyes and a long whip trailing from her hand seemed to throw them into a panic. With a crash the big vase splintered on the marble floor as they turned and fled down the hall.

Charity wiped her eyes with the back of her hand. The world must be going mad. What were field hands doing in the front hall at this time of night? She stared at the fragments of porcelain littering floor and carpet. Her mother would never get over the loss of one of her favorite antiques. Dully she wondered how she would break the news.

A scream from overhead recalled her to her senses. Father! She hurled herself toward the stairs and started up. Above her a gigantic man blocked the top of the stairs. Charity shrank back, then saw a hand shoot out from a pillar by the

34

stair and drag the man sideways. He stumbled into the hall and there were sounds of a scuffle, a crash, and an oath. Clinging to the banister and fighting down her own screams, she saw the figure of her mother's maid standing against the far wall. The slave woman sobbed her name, and Charity started toward her. As she neared the top of the stairs, the men hit the balustrade and began to bend over it above the hall. She gasped as she recognized Henri, her father's overseer, bending backward, fighting for his life against the huge black man who was choking him.

Half blind with her own fear and anger, Charity rounded the wide pillar at the top, shoving Marie's outstretched arms away. Grasping the butt of the big whip in both hands, she rammed it as hard as she could into the lower back of Henri's opponent. The man grunted and jerked backward against the pain, loosening his hold on Henri's neck. It was all the mulatto needed. Twisting away, he grabbed the big head and smashed it sideways into the pillar. Arms flailed out, but the giant was dazed, unable to aim his blows. Ducking, Henri grabbed a leg and heaved. The great body lifted off the floor, teetered on the lip of the wide balustrade, then slowly toppled over the edge. It hit the marble hall with a dull thud.

Sobbing, Charity fell backward into Marie's arms. Henri leaned against the pillar gasping. They stared at each other.

"Get out," he said hoarsely.

Marie tugged at Charity's arm, but the girl jerked away. "Father?"

Henri slumped further. His head shook. Suddenly feeling white hot, Charity stepped up to him. Henri's breathing had slowed. He raised his head and looked her full in the face. "He is dead, Mademoiselle. He tried to get up. He must have been bleeding badly inside. He didn't even make it to the window."

"Papa!" It was a piercing wail which froze the blood of the two who watched her. Before they could react, Charity was running down the long hall, her suddenly ashen face twisted with pain and frenzy.

Henri bounded after her, snatching her arm as she rounded the corner to her father's room. She twisted, clawing at him to get free. Without hesitation, he brought up his hand and slapped her hard. Her head snapped back and her body went rigid in his grasp. Dulled eyes stared at him.

"We are in the middle of a slave revolt," he shouted into her lifeless face. "We must get out of Tournay!" Charity tried to back away from him as though to put all his horrible words as far from her as possible. "The slaves are burning and looting the plantation," he shouted again.

This time life sprang into her eyes. With a snarl she snatched her arm from him. Quickly he went on. "Marie and I laid your father out. He is at peace, Mademoiselle." He took a tentative step toward her.

Just then the door to the back stairs opened and two howling figures hurtled through into the hall. Stunned, Charity stood and stared as they advanced on her. With a great leering grin, the first man lunged toward her. His body slammed into hers, flattening her against the paneling. For a brief moment she struggled, then went limp. The man relaxed, just that trifle that allowed her to bring up her knee smartly into his groin. As he doubled up, she whirled. Snatching up the delicate chair she'd used only days before, she brought it crashing down on the man's head. And they think women are the weaker sex, she thought hysterically as she saw a knife flash in Henri's hand. Then the ugly attacker lay sprawled on the carpet. His companion was running for the stairwell. To Charity's stricken gaze came the fresh horror of flames licking up the back banisters. The man, caught between the raging inferno below and the maddened pair behind, chose the flames and jumped down the burning stairs three at a time.

Still clutching a splintered piece of chair, Charity found herself being pulled back along the hall toward the main staircase where a terrified Marie still waited. Charity was in shock, but Henri's words about what was happening were beginning to sink in. She saw him pick up her discarded whip and heard him drag something from one of the rooms, but her attention was caught by a fresh danger.

Coming slowly and carefully up the curved stairs was one of her father's trusted foremen. One look at the glint in his eye showed her he was no longer her father's man. A huge sickle for cutting cane dangled from the man's hand, and she stared at it as though mesmerized. He was nearly upon her when a burst of heat and orange light down the hall made her flick her eyes. The man turned his head. It was the only moment she'd have, and she reacted without thought. From behind the tattered folds of her skirt she brought up the broken chair piece and with all her strength she drove it straight for the slave's face. The jagged wood caught him on the cheek and glanced along the side of his head. With a howl of rage he flung up his arm, the huge sickle pulling the wood from Charity's nerveless fingers. But the blow had caught him unprepared. He careened backwards, clutching at the banister.

The force of her thrust had carried Charity nearly down to the man. She kicked out wildly, and her foot caught his arm where he held the railing. Shouting an oath, the foreman lost the last of his balance and toppled crazily backward down the long staircase.

Charity felt her legs begin to crumple beneath her. But a strong hand gripped her elbow, holding her up, and Henri's voice steadied her.

"His neck may not be broken, alas. We go." And he shoved her stumbling down the grand staircase, past the slumped form and toward the door.

The sounds of bedlam were all around them now. The roar of hungry flames was suddenly punctuated by the crash of heavy timbers falling at the far end of the house. Marie stood by the wall, keening. In the main parlor, glass shattered as plunderers flung furniture aside in their search for treasures. Charity put her hands over her ears.

A hand tugged at her arm. She looked up to see Jacques, his face smeared with soot and grime.

"Oh, God, where have you been?" was all she could say.

"Cutting loose the horses and trying to find you," he panted. "You've got to get out. The whole back of the house is in flames."

She nodded dumbly and let him half carry her across the veranda. "Your mother, where is she?" he demanded.

Charity pointed toward the gates. "I told Justin to back the carriage that way."

Jacques nodded as his father and a tearful Marie joined them. Henri was carrying a small trunk. There was a hasty consultation in low voices, then Jacques turned to Charity.

"I'm going back in for the papers my father couldn't carry. You must lead him and Marie to the trees and find your mother. I'll catch you. There's no time to spare."

"Jacques, where are the others?"

"Either killed or fled, *ma petite*. Now go."

A sudden rending crash from inside the house made them all jump. Shouts and curses could be heard above the raging of flames, and black smoke was beginning to billow from a front window.

"You can't go back in there!" Charity looked wildly at Jacques.

Gently his hand touched the side of her face and her tangled hair. More shouts were heard inside. Jacques reached out and spun Charity around, facing the driveway. "Go," he shouted in her ear, and shoved her down the stairs.

Grasping Marie's quaking hand, Charity pulled her onto the drive. Now that they were in the open, they could see the sky was an eerie rust color. Charity ran like the wind, tugging Marie along like a large puppy.

Not until she was under the trees did Charity pause to look back. Then she shrank from what she saw. The fire had marched across the house to the central hall now, and the door through which they'd come only moments before was a solid sheet of flame. Bright tongues of fire were beginning to eat through the roof and columns of smoke rose like a screen behind.

Charity gnawed on the back of her hand as she thought of her father lying amidst the wreckage in the inferno of his room. "A pyre fit for a king, Papa," she said aloud and felt as though she were strangling.

"Mademoiselle!" Henri's sharp voice made her bite her lip. But she couldn't tear her eyes from the corner of hell that had been her home. "Mademoiselle, the carriage." In his urgency, Henri thumped her side with the trunk.

The girl's eyes blinked. Maman! She turned and sped over the dry grass beside the drive. Far down the avenue between two trees the bulk of the carriage loomed. But the small figure beside it, holding the horses' heads was not Justin. Charity ran until she could see it was her mother's pale face beside the team, then sobbing, she threw herself into Émilie's arms. Almost immediately Henri was hissing they must hurry. Reluctantly Charity drew away from the encircling arms.

"Where is Justin, Maman?"

Even in the dark she could see her mother's fine eyes were wide with shock and fright. "I don't know. Gone."

"You mean he just ran off and left you here?"

Her mother nodded, but her eyes were not on her daughter. They were looking beyond her, back up the drive where the glow of the conflagration illuminated the grounds before the house.

Charity's own tears threatened again as she watched her mother's anxious gaze. Gently she pulled Émilie to the carriage steps where Marie waited to help her mistress. "No one but Jacques is coming, Maman." Charity spoke softly, and attempted to put her arms around the fragile figure.

Stiff fingers held her off as wide glazed eyes continued to stare past her shoulder. "Mark." The whispered word bore an ocean of feeling.

"He died before the fire, Maman." The twisting pain inside the girl felt as though it would tear her apart.

Émilie gave no sign that she'd heard the words. She swiveled her head once, taking in all that could be seen of the devil's work that was being done. "Tournay," she whispered then.

Charity held her mother's arm helplessly.

"Madame, we must move quickly." Henri peered into his mistress's face, but the wide eyes did not even blink in answer.

"Come, Maman." Charity turned the now unresisting body to the carriage and between them they pulled Émilie into a seat. Silently Marie took the place beside her beloved mistress.

The girl stood alongside her father's overseer. "Where can he be?" she cried.

The man shrugged. "He may have had to run. We will have to go without him."

"Go without him?" Charity's voice broke.

Henri nodded. "He will survive, Mademoiselle. There is not a path or a bush he does not know around Tournay. Do not fret for him. But you must get away." He pulled off his tattered lightweight coat. "Here, you may need this."

For the first time Charity became aware of her own appalling condition. Her ball gown hung in shreds, one shoulder nearly gone and her bodice only barely together. Thankfully she slipped into the large garment. She was beginning to shiver uncontrollably. When she took a step, her legs felt like broken twigs. She was grateful when Henri's strong arm helped her into the well of the carriage and she could sink onto the tufted leather seat and try to still the trembling that seemed to make her teeth rattle.

As the coach rumbled out to the road, she looked down at the small trunk and the several boxes at her feet. Had Henri gotten the strong box from the safe in her father's room? Her father's room... her brain repeated "father" over and over as though stuck in a deep rut. She shook herself and leaned back. She wouldn't try to think now. First they must get away. Concentrate only on that, and watch for any movement along the road that might be Jacques.

Because she was peering intently into the night, Charity saw the single torch and the running figures at the same instant as Henri. Spinning onto her knees on the seat, she watched dark forms jumping about crazily before them, making the horses plunge in their shafts.

Her cry of alarm was bitten off by the sharp crack of a pistol as Henri discharged it at the nearest man who clung to the lead horse. Then he threw the weapon into the face of another leaping for the carriage side. An animal whinnied in fright, and a feeling of hopelessness swept over the girl as she watched the horses being subdued and two burly figures approach the steps. But suddenly from the roadside another shadow sprang up with a yell. A long knife flashed and one of the broad shapes clutched at an arm as he fell onto the road.

"Jacques," Charity cried. "Jump in."

But already the others had left the horses and come at Jacques in a yowling pack. With his back to the carriage and his knife cutting the air in arcs, the young man held them at bay until one man launched himself on the driving board and dragged Henri from the high driving seat. The carriage jerked and tilted, throwing its occupants across each other. The women on the rear seat screamed, but Charity's throat was closed with fright.

How she kept her wits about her, she couldn't tell, but the next lurch of the carriage brought her to her feet, her skirts held high in one hand. Then she was scrambling forward and up to the driver's seat, grasping wildly for the trailing reins. Sprawling over the back of the seat, she caught the leather thongs before they could slide down between the shafts. Frantically she pulled them up, trying to exert a steady pressure on the sensitive mouths of the terrified beasts. Praying Henri or Jacques would leap to her aid, she looked around. But the only face she could see in the human maelstrom below was a dark snarling visage climbing a wheel.

Her hand groped blindly for the whip holder and miraculously her former weapon was there. Never taking her eyes from it, she brought up the whip and smashed at the enraged face with all her might. With an unearthly yowl, the man fell back to join other figures sprawled all around the carriage. The girl looked for her protectors as she fought to hold the horses. From below, Jacques' hoarse voice rose up to her.

"Charity, whip the horses. There are more coming over this field. Father and I will lead them off. You must get away."

"Jacques," she cried. "Get in."

"Go, girl. Stop for nothing. You'll make it to Cap Français. Go." And he slapped at the nearest horse.

It was all the overwrought animal needed to send him plunging in the shafts again. His panic infected the other, and the two bolted for freedom down the dark ribbon of road. It took all of Charity's strength just to stay on the swaying seat at first, and without a firm guiding hand, the horses ran helter-skelter, jerking the carriage dangerously. In a minute they would overturn the precarious rig and pull themselves down with it.

Years of careful schooling in horsemanship came to Charity's aid as her half-numbed brain issued vital commands to her trembling arms and hands. Dropping the whip on the seat and focusing only on the horses, she worked on the reins, trying to control rather than halt the frenzied energy in those powerful shoulders. Slowly the animals responded to the familiar pressures, and when they discovered they weren't to be balked in their headlong flight, they settled into a ground-eating stride.

Minutes passed before the girl dared take her eyes from the road before her. They were running along within sight of the sea now, where moonbeams blended with rolling waves, unconscious of the mayhem being inflicted on the land they were visiting.

In another few miles they would begin the gradual descent into the valley where the harbor town of Cap Français nestled. Easing the terrible strain on her shoulders, Charity shifted in the seat and turned to look down into the carriage. Her mother sat slumped onto a wide-eyed but silent Marie. Émilie looked as though she'd fainted, and for a second Charity envied her her oblivion. Then she returned her attention to her task and tried to recall all that her father had taught her about handling a team.

Long after their fright had been left behind, the horses from Tournay found they were being urged at a slower but relentless pace by a skilled hand and an iron will. By the time they entered the streets of the town and turned toward the main square and its harbor beyond, only the repeated lashes of the long whip kept them moving at all.

Cap Français was not asleep this night. Usually quiet

41

streets were alight with swaying lanterns and bobbing torches. Glazed eyes inside crested carriages showed the slave uprising was not only at Tournay, and the tight-lipped, wild-haired girl in torn skirts and a man's jacket who drove her own team was hardly noticed in the confusion.

The normally tranquil square of pastel façades and shaded porticoes was a whirling mass of shrill humanity. Bracketed torches cast eerie light across angry men, sobbing women, and snarled vehicles. If she got her team caught there, it would be hours before they could make their way through. Already there was barely room to manoeuvre on the feeder streets. Fighting off a renewed sense of panic, Charity thought of her mother slumped in the seat behind. She must get to the side of the square nearer the warehouses.

Gritting her teeth, she slid down from her seat, ignoring the length of silk which ripped from her hem. Grabbing the bridle of the near horse, she tugged and cajoled the reluctant team into a side street to another turn toward the harbor. Down darker back streets she led the stumbling animals, crooning and calling to them to keep going. Until at last she spied the pale yellow front of the neat little house she sought.

At her first tap, the white door swung open and she nearly fell into the arms of her father's agent, Esteban duCrot.

Stuttering with agitation and relief, M. duCrot held the girl upright. "Wh-where are the others?"

"Maman. In the carriage."

The balding little man stepped outside his doorway. "And your father, no?"

Charity's throat closed. She could only shake her head against his shoulder. She felt the soft, round body go tense beside her.

"*Mon Dieu,* child. Who brought you here?"

"We...we came alone. Tournay has burned." Charity pulled herself up and faced the little man. "We need your help, monsieur."

Nodding and bobbing, M. duCrot peered with narrowed eyes into the dark. Since he seemed to be shocked into silence, Charity continued. "Maman has fainted. She is in there with her maid. We have very few things. Do you know where we could go?" She looked dubiously at the small house which doubled as duCrot's offices.

The agent was muttering now, wringing white hands against his chest. "Ah, he knew this might happen. He knew." Then he shook his head and looked at the girl before him.

"Mademoiselle, we must get you away from here. My only spare room has already an entire family in it. The slaves have made chaos of Saint Dominque, and it is no place for females alone. Wait."

Before Charity could protest that a corner of his hearth would be all they required, he darted back into the house. Desperately she wished she had somewhere else to turn besides this scared little man. An honest and astute businessman she knew him to be, but not one on whom she cared to rely in a time of emergency.

Almost immediately he reemerged, carrying a small leather bag. Looking more decisive now, he took her arm and steered her back to the carriage. "We will go to the docks, Mademoiselle," he said as he gathered up the reins and clucked at the horses. "You are in luck. Captain Winslow is still in port with his brig. Your father knew him well. He will carry you away from the danger here."

Charity's eyes widened as he talked, but she offered no resistance to this bizarre suggestion. She felt as though her life had already ended. Without Tournay and her father, what did it matter where they went? She turned to look at her mother. Still leaning on her faithful maid, Émilie was awake now, sunken eyes regarding the passing buildings dully. Charity shut her own red-rimmed ones and tried not to think of what lay ahead. If only she hadn't lost Henri and Jacques, she'd feel safer now. She rubbed at her eyes with a dirt-smeared fist. She thought of Jacques' face turned up to her on the road, and prayed that he and his father had gotten away to safety.

A sudden jolt and the wagon came to a stop. Charity forced her eyes open as she felt the reins being pressed into her hands once more.

"You must wait here, Mademoiselle. I think I have seen the men we need. But it is dangerous on the docks. Wait." And he slipped from the seat to disappear into the milling throngs ahead.

They were halted in the shadows of a warehouse and the darkness around them seemed alive with ominous specters. Before them Charity could see the end of a dock where barrels and boxes were stacked and where swarthy seamen held at bay a throng of men. Suddenly afraid of the shadows and of losing M. duCrot forever, the girl jumped down and ran to the front of the team. She tugged at the off horse's bridle, but the frenzied press of people ahead had frightened him and he refused to move. Angry now, as well as scared, Charity tore Henri's jacket off and threw it over the horse's eyes. Then, with her hand beneath his chin, she urged him forward.

As they rounded the corner of the warehouse, Charity could see the bedlam that was fast threatening to engulf the dock area. Vehicles of every description jammed the quayside as drivers lashed out at blockading teams; women and children sobbed with fear and men shouted to be heard above the din. Charity led the team into a gap at the edge of the dock and stood on tiptoe to spy M. duCrot. He stood only yards from her, waving his hands and slapping the leather bag as he faced a haggard-looking man in shirtsleeves and dark knee breeches. The girl waved, trying to get his attention.

"Ya' beckonin' to us, lassie?" A broad form appeared beside her and slipped a familiar arm around her waist. "Lookee here, mates. Found me a beauty, an' her wavin' me to 'er side at that."

Letting go the horse, Charity twisted wildly as she saw two more leering faces approach. But the man beside her held her tight and she gagged as his rum-soaked breath bathed her face. The tumult beneath their noses was too much for the team of horses. Now that the jacket had slipped from his eyes, the horse Charity had been leading took fright again, and with an unrecognizable whinny, he reared in the shafts, hooves slashing. The sailors tangled and fell as they tried to get away and Charity screamed, beating on her assailant.

The man stumbled backward away from the crazed horses, lost his footing, and with a crash he and the girl landed amidst trunks and barrels at the water's edge. Bruised and dazed, Charity lay over the end of a barrel, wondering if she'd ever get her breath back, and thankful only that the hateful arms were gone from around her. Sounds of a fearful fight were all about her now and she tried to sit up.

Suddenly strong arms were lifting her and a hand brushed the tangled strands of hair from her face. She looked up and met a pair of steel gray eyes beneath a shock of black hair.

"Mademoiselle, can you get up?" The French was heavily accented, but understandable.

She nodded, still gasping for breath. The wide, grim mouth moved to a tight smile as the glittering eyes surveyed her bedraggled form. She clutched at her shredded bodice, hating the blush she knew must be rising from her neck, and pushed herself upright.

44

"DuCrot!" The black-haired man straightened too, looming over her. "Take her down the dock."

Charity closed her eyes so she wouldn't see him staring at her ruined clothes and matted hair. "Maman," she breathed.

"We are getting everything from the carriage now," the deep voice assured her. Then she felt a strong hand push her forward. "And Mademoiselle, try not to faint before you are in the boat."

Her eyes flew open at that and forgetting to clutch her bodice, she whirled on him. But he was already moving away and M. duCrot was tugging her free of the overturned barrels.

A few yards away the shirtsleeved man awaited them at the top of a ladder. He shouted to two seamen in an open boat and they began casting off lines. Then with a slight bow, he acknowledged Charity. "Miss Ashton," was all he said, and looked beyond her.

Moving swiftly toward them were several swarthy seamen, carrying the little trunk and the boxes from the carriage. Behind them the black-haired man carried Émilie Ashton as Marie dogged his heels.

The man at the ladder narrowed his eyes. "No slaves."

M. duCrot looked startled. "But that is Madame Ashton's personal maid."

"I can't help that. The captain said only essential passengers."

"But she is essential," Charity cried. The group had joined them now, and men were lowering the boxes into the boat as her mother was gently set onto her own feet. "Marie has been with mother since they were girls. We would never leave her behind."

"Sorry, Miss, but captain's orders." The man looked surprised at her perfect English.

M. deCrot stepped between them. He tapped the leather bag the man now held. "There is more than enough money for all their passages there," he said.

"It's not money, man. It's space. We're a merchant ship. We haven't much room for passengers."

Charity looked at Marie whose tearful eyes showed she understood what was happening. Then she saw her mother's fragile hand grope for Marie's.

"Marie must go," she shrilled.

The man shrugged helplessly and looked around, appealing for masculine support.

45

"Then we do not go on your ship." Charity flung up her head and turned, reaching for her mother.

But the tall, gray-eyed man stepped up and grabbed her arms. She jerked away, feeling if one more man touched her tonight, she would go completely mad. He reached out again, and this time she lashed at his face. He snatched her hand, and she began to kick him, sobbing and snarling like a wild thing. Suddenly, paralyzingly, a ham-like hand came out and slapped her. For the second time tonight she'd been smacked like a slave for her hysterics. This time she crumpled under the blow and slowly she felt dark oblivion engulf her.

Chapter 5

Something was piercing Charity's eyelids and she threw up an arm in defense, moaning aloud. Immediately a cool hand touched her brow and a soft voice called to her. Lowering her arm, the girl turned her head. The narrow bar of sunlight that had waked her fell on Marie's troubled face. Charity smiled tremulously. Where was Sylvie? Her eyes slid past Marie's face and fell on rough timbers beside a low door. The room moved gently, and she frowned. Something was very wrong. She looked up and saw a lantern swaying from a beam low overhead.

With a jerk she sat up. "Where are we?"

"On the ship, my little one." Marie straightened and put a hand out to steady herself. She watched memory flood back through the girl's mind, and shuddered as she saw the beautiful pale face begin to crumple in pain.

"Oh, *mon Dieu*," Charity wailed. "Then it was no dream after all."

Marie shook her head then gathered the slender form to

her as great racking sobs shook the young body.

It was some time before the storm abated, and minutes more before Charity could bring herself to begin facing her new reality. The scenes at Tournay she pushed to the farthest recesses of her mind, trying to concentrate on the present. Although sore in a hundred places, she realized she had no broken bones or permanent damage from her ordeal. She rubbed the slight swelling on the side of her jaw, and her eyes grew dark with remembrance of that final blow on the docks. That terrible man! But at least she seemed to have won her war, if not the battle, for Marie was here beside her. She could recall nothing of the journey they must have made out to the ship at anchor offshore, but she did have dim memory now of swaying lights, rattling chains, shouts and orders, before she was carried below.

She swung her legs off the narrow bunk, noticing for the first time that she wore one of her cambric nightdresses. "Maman, Marie. How is she?"

"Resting peacefully at last, *petite*." Seeing the color returning to the girl's face, Marie smiled and began the long process of brushing the tangles from the thick, tawny hair.

Charity sat stoically enduring the agony of the brushing as her eyes roved the tiny cabin. "There is a pallet at the foot of this bunk, Marie. You slept here last night? Why not with Maman?"

"She shares a cabin with Madame LaRoche."

"Madame LaRoche!" Charity jerked and flinched at the added tug to her aching scalp. "Did all the family make it aboard?"

"Not Monsieur. He was lost in the fighting."

"So, M. LaRoche too," breathed the girl.

Marie nodded. "But Madame and Monsieur Paul came just as the anchor was being pulled from the water. It was very dramatic. The dark-haired one, the man who saved you from the ruffians on the dock..."

"You mean the one who beat me senseless," Charity interrupted with venom.

Marie smiled. "That one, he went over the side on ropes and brought Madame LaRoche to the deck slung over his shoulder. Madame, she kicked and screamed, but she could have gotten here no other way."

For a moment Charity savored the picture of the fat matron being handled like a sack of grain. But then she scowled. "It seems that brute enjoys his role as molester of women."

Her lowering thoughts were interrupted by a knock.

"Who is it?" Charity called.

"Paul. I came to see if you are all right, and would care to walk on deck."

"In a while, Paul. Thank you." Charity cringed from the thought of facing Paul. But she knew she had to do it. Besides, she'd never been on a ship before, except in port, and she thought she might like to glimpse the open sea. "Marie, have I any clothes?" She surveyed her reddened eyes in the fragment of mirror that dangled from a bulkhead. A tiny basin of water stood beneath it, and she splashed some on her hot face.

"A few things, Mademoiselle." Marie was the efficient lady's maid once more. "We saved some clothes in those boxes. Yours are here." She stooped in the corner of the tiny cabin and began pulling garments out for inspection.

Charity wrinkled her nose. Two of her primmest dresses. But at least one of them was dark blue, the closest she could come to the black she should be wearing for her father. She knew Mark Ashton would not have her dress in mourning for him, but she felt she owed him somber colors for a while at least. The green glazed chintz, left in the carriage after the ball, would have to wait.

As Marie dressed her carefully, Charity plied her with questions about the ship. But the maid had seen little more than she'd already related. Her impression, she sniffed unhappily, was only of cramped space and hordes of evil-smelling men.

Charity smoothed the folds of the full skirt and nearly smiled at the descriptions. Behind her Marie's voice was soft. "There is nothing left for any of us on Saint Dominque, *ma petite*."

"Marie, do you think Jacques and Henri are all right?"

"Those two, yes. They are survivors."

And so am I, reflected Charity and squared her shoulders. She allowed one quick thought for all the dead they'd left behind. Then she shut that door in her mind. "What was in that trunk you and Henri saved?"

"Things from your father's room. You will go and see later. I think some money, a few papers perhaps. I filled the rest with things for you and your mother."

"Oh, Marie," Charity's shoulders slumped, but the maid's

brisk voice didn't allow her time for thought.

"Now you need food, Mademoiselle, and I shall see you get it."

It was not very long afterward that Charity, led by Marie through the narrow passageways, made her way up to the quarter deck. The tropical sun, now high overhead, made the very air shimmer in the glare and the girl paused to adapt her eyes before venturing to the rail. She was all unconscious of the picture she presented as she swayed prettily, trying to plant her feet against the roll of the deck. Sun glinted on the waving brightness of her drawn-back hair and her full lips pouted into roundness as she shielded her eyes with one slender hand. The few seamen who were privileged to witness her emergence into the golden day gaped openmouthed at the vision. Marie, determinedly by her side, set her mouth in a disapproving line at this display of appreciation, but her charge had noticed nothing, staring instead beyond the rails to the rolling expanse of turquoise water. Far above her the great sails billowed and stretched taut with erratic breezes. The creaking of timbers and the rush of wind in the rigging made a new music for her ears. Entranced in spite of herself, she made her way across the deck. Marie, who was not at all taken with the view of the open sea, stayed where she was, watching through narrowed eyes.

Charity leaned on the wide rail and looked down. Far below her, rushing foam curled away from the ship's side. Her eye traveled over crested waves to where, in the dimmest distance, hazy blue water met hazy blue sky in a shimmering dance of undulating line. It was a dizzying view, and she clutched the rail, wanting reassurance of the solidity of the brig in this endless vastness.

"Does the sight please you, Miss Ashton?" The deep voice spoke so near, Charity started. She looked up to see clear gray eyes regarding her steadily. "I asked if the sight..."

"I heard what you asked," she snapped and saw a dark brow rise. More softly she added, "But I cannot imagine that my views of the sea would be of any great interest to you."

"Oh? On the contrary, your views are of definite interest to me. Or I wouldn't have asked." The tall man leaned negligently on one elbow and regarded her with eyebrow still cocked. His mane of dark hair was pulled back today, clubbed neatly at his neck, though one unruly lock fell forward above his eye to give a slightly quizzical look to his face. His white

49

shirt, stretched tight across broad shoulders, was open at the throat, revealing dark hair on his chest. Charity quickly averted her eyes, finding his nonchalance irritating.

When she didn't speak, he stood straight. "I see you haven't forgiven me for slapping you back from the brink of strong hysterics, Mademoiselle. May I beg your indulgence to do so now."

Out of the corner of her eye Charity saw him bow slightly from the waist, and she lifted her chin, turning toward him again. "I...I suppose I must thank you for saving me from the drunken group of your fellow seamen, Mr...."

"Fellow seamen? Ah. Yes. The name, Mademoiselle, is Adam Crandall. At your faithful service." He was grinning as he bowed once more, and Charity had a sudden mad urge to slap him for it. She saw nothing funny in the services he had done her last night, and she said so rather waspishly.

"No indeed," he agreed, his face sober once more. "There was nothing at all funny about any of the events of last night. May I offer my condolences to you on the loss of your father, Miss Ashton. Indeed, on the loss of your home."

Charity held the rail tightly. "Thank you, Mr. Crandall," she said stiffly. "I'm sure you have duties to perform. Don't let me detain you."

The gray eyes were alight with appreciation as they regarded her slowly. And for a moment she was glad she wore a high-necked dress that concealed at least some of her rounded young figure. She kept her chin up and returned his stare as coldly as she could, trying not to notice how very handsome he was.

After what seemed an endless minute he smiled lazily. "Yes, of course, Miss Ashton. I do indeed have, ah, duties to perform. And you would like to be alone with your thoughts. We will meet again later."

In a few quick strides he was gone, leaving Charity to mutter, "Oh, will we?" and to wonder vaguely why a common sailor should have the speech of a gentleman.

Her reflections were not long, however, for Paul LaRoche was soon at her side, bending solicitously over her hand and inquiring how she did.

"Well enough," she answered. "And grateful to you for suggesting that I come up on deck. The sun and fresh air help to chase away the shadows."

"I had hoped so, Charity," he said gravely. "We all need it now."

"Oh, Paul, it's all so awful."

"All of it." His thin mouth was set in new, harder lines, and his usually languid expression was a scowl. With an effort, he relaxed his face. "But we have to be thankful for getting away at all. In fact, we received enough warning to save a great many things. But father wanted his papers..." Paul spread his hands in a helpless gesture.

"I know," Charity said softly, and a tense silence fell between them.

Tactfully, he didn't go into any details of their flight and Charity was glad of that. She didn't think she could bear to discuss the horrors they'd lived through. But as he grasped her arm and walked her down the deck, Paul was all solicitude and she found herself relaxing slowly. The pains inside her were settling to a dull ache, and the tension she'd felt on seeing Adam Crandall was subsiding. It was good to be with a familiar person now, one who understood her lost world and who shared her loss.

They took several turns around the small deck, and by the time Paul returned her to Marie's side, Charity felt better able to face sorting through the few things salvaged from Tournay.

As the women went below, Charity wondered about their destination. Paul had said only that they were bound for Virginia. She remembered her last long conversation with her father and her laughing reference to going north to live among the savages. She felt tears start at the back of her eyes, but with a great effort suppressed them. It wouldn't do to let Maman see her like that.

The cabin shared by the two ladies was larger than Charity's but was filled to capacity by hastily dropped trunks and boxes. Obviously Madame LaRoche had salvaged a great deal of her wardrobe. The girl was glad to note that the possessor of this comparative wealth was not in residence at the moment.

On the narrow bunk nearest the door her mother lay still, propped by an assortment of makeshift pillows. Charity was appalled at her pallor and at the vague look in her sunken, black-rimmed eyes. Sitting on the edge of the bunk, she took a delicate hand in hers.

A slight smile hovered at the edges of Émilie's mouth as she regarded her daughter. "You look very, how shall I say, demure today, Charity. Have you been working at your lessons?"

Charity gulped. "No, Maman. I have been walking on the deck."

"The deck?"

"Yes, on the quarterdeck with Paul."

"With Paul," Émilie repeated.

Charity glanced up at Marie and found the maid regarding her mother sadly. Dear God, she thought, don't tell me Maman does not even realize we are aboard a ship, leaving Saint Dominque. Impulsively she leaned over and kissed her mother's cheek. Summoning up a smile, she said, "Maman, we are on an American merchant ship, going to Virginia. We are safe and in good hands now."

There was a short silence, then Émilie said quite brightly, "Of course we are, dear."

Charity blinked. Perhaps her mother's mind wasn't wandering after all. "Would you like Marie to dress you, so you can come up and enjoy the sun?"

"Dress me? No." A slight frown creased the ivory brow, then quickly faded. "But you could brush my hair."

Surprised at this request, Charity nodded, trying to look eager. She had not brushed her mother's hair since she was a little girl. However, if it would comfort her . . . She took the tortoise shell brush proffered by Marie and moved to stand beside the bed. Then she sighed. "Perhaps you could see if lunch could be served to us here, Marie."

The slave nodded and left the little cabin quietly.

As Charity worked over he mother's raven hair, a tranquil silence descended which she was loath to break. Émilie seemed content to just sit without speaking, and Charity was afraid to say anything that would disturb her.

They ate their lunch in continued silence, and afterward, Charity, not wanting to leave her mother, turned to the little trunk from Tournay. She and Marie removed the few articles of clothing on the top layer, hoping to engage Émilie's interest, but soon her mother's attention wandered and she began to recede into herself once more. It was like the afternoon of her father's accident, Charity thought. And it would take longer for her to recover. She would have to be patient and wait for her mother to return to the real world. Meanwhile, there was their future to attend to.

With shaking hands, Charity sorted through the little trunk. Henri seemed to have simply snatched at things in her father's room, not bothering to sort or discriminate. Here was a small leather box containing her father's best stick pins, there a sheaf of bills yet to be paid for medicines and supplies in the slave quarters. A blue and green enamel box she recognized right away as her mother's jewel box and thanked Marie for saving it. If worse came to worse, they would at least have the few gems it contained to pay their way.

More papers came to light as she dug down through the layers, useless scraps now, inventories and notes on things lost to them all. Even her father's will was here, a document she skimmed with blurred vision, realizing the riches he had bequeathed to his family were either destroyed or in the hands of their former slaves. Hastily she returned the papers to their place. Beside the pile, nestled against the sturdy edge of its leather-bound carrier, she found one thing she was glad to see. A plain wooden box in which her father had kept money in the little safe in his room. Half filled with gold coins, it represented now all the wealth they had in the world. Carefully, she replaced it on top of the papers and closed the trunk.

She'd done it. She'd been through the thing she'd dreaded most this day and she had survived it. The dull ache of agony that seemed to spread from her brain down to her legs was no worse than before, and she resolved she would learn to live with it. Sometime she would have to think more about their future, but for now it was enough to know they were alive and not totally destitute. She must concentrate on trying to help her fragile mother through this most devastating experience, and she must see what else she could learn about the place they seemed to be going.

Her first opportunity came at dinner that evening in the captain's cabin. Madame LaRoche, returning to her cabin in the late afternoon, had informed Charity with tears in her eyes that the refugees were invited to share the captain's board each evening. She had looked sadly at Émilie, who had given her only the vaguest of smiles, and said she knew Marie could bring a tray here to her mother, but she did so hope to see Charity at table. Charity felt quite sure she'd have to share feminine views of last night's horrors with Paul's mother, and she didn't relish the prospect. Madame LaRoche would not have been her choice for a traveling companion, but since she had no option in the matter, she'd have to learn to live with this fact as well.

She needn't have worried though. For as a sailor bowed her through the door of the spacious cabin that evening, she discovered that there were others to distract Madame La-Roche's attention. Besides the gray-haired Captain Winslow, who bowed gallantly over her outstretched hand and offered his condolences briefly with an air of sincerity, there was his first officer, Mr. Hampton, and another man whose back was to the room as he inspected a rack of books behind the captain's desk. Mr. Hampton, an earnest-looking young man, nearly overturned a chair in his rush to greet her and extend his regrets. He couldn't seem to take his eyes off her or let go her hand after their introductions, and Charity was just wondering how to extricate her fingers from his rather clammy grasp when she was saved by the entrance of the LaRoches.

Paul, looking incongruously elegant, was supporting his mother, who looked as though she'd just finished a bout of heartbroken weeping, and Charity felt a rush of sympathy for the woman. Going to her, she took a plump hand in hers and Paul's mother smiled tremulously at her. Gently she steered the older woman toward the table. Then stopped in her tracks. Across the room, gray eyes surveying her lazily, was the man, Adam Crandall. She had time to notice that his shirt, far from being open at the neck, was surmounted by a low cravat and that his dark coat was of a simple but good cut, before introductions were made, and she was forced to acknowledge him formally. She inclined her head only slightly, aware he was enjoying her predicament, hating him for his arrogance, and thinking irrelevantly of the triangle of tanned chest she'd glimpsed that noon. Obviously the man couldn't be a common sailor if he was here in the captain's cabin for dinner. How insufferable of him to have allowed her to think he was, and to taunt her with the promise that they'd meet again later on. He may not be a seaman, she told herself, but his tact was no better than the worst of that breed, and she didn't care *who* he really was.

Adam watched her firm, round chin go up and her stormy eyes slide past him as she led Madame LaRoche to the chair being held by the captain. His breath caught in his throat as he stared at the girl. Her hair, so brilliantly golden in the blazing sun of the deck, now glowed amber in the candlelight, and her lovely face, made pale by her somber clothes and by the dark smudges beneath those huge eyes, looked like alabaster. He remembered her as he'd first seen her, beautiful thick hair wild and tumbled over her shoulders, full breasts nearly exposed by her torn gown. His eyes narrowed at the recollection, and he inhaled deeply. Then he tore his gaze from her face and shrugged. Haughty, aristocratic little bitch was what she was. And even if she wasn't, he'd met her at the wrong time. One could hardly approach a girl who only twenty-four hours before had lost her father and her home and had been molested by a gang of drunken seamen. Heaven knew what else she'd been through, too. He gritted his teeth at the thought, then shoved it rudely aside. A bad throw of the dice that would be, he said to himself, and took his seat beside the older woman at the table.

The food was not exceptional, but better than might have been expected on a ship not equipped for passengers. And the wines were very fine indeed. The table, not meant for so many settings at once, was crowded but elegant with white cloth, handsome china, and gleaming cutlery. Charity discovered her appetite was enormous, and forgot all strictures about young ladies eating dainty portions. She was brought back to a memory of better manners only when Paul inquired in his halting English if Captain Winslow could tell them when they might expect to arrive in Virginia. She lowered her fork and looked up then, meeting a twinkle in Adam Crandall's bright gray eyes across from her. She dropped the utensil and vowed not to eat another mouthful in front of a man boorish enough to show he had noticed her appetite. Taking a sip of wine, she turned ostentatiously to the head of the table.

The captain sat back in his chair, fingering the stem of a handsome goblet. "In a few weeks you will be safe in Norfolk, if we're lucky. This is the start of the hurricane season, as you know, but we will head a bit east and try to outrun any storms that may be pushing from behind."

His deep voice was reassuring, but Charity had a momentary vision of his small ship at the mercy of hurricane winds and she shuddered. "Tell me, Captain, about Norfolk," she said brightly, trying to dispel the image. "I've never visited the United States, and have no idea what to expect."

The captain cleared his throat and looked at Paul. "Norfolk is like any seaport, Miss Ashton. But I believe it's not your final destination."

"Oh?" Charity too turned to her old neighbor.

"No, *petite*. We go up the James River to a plantation where we will throw ourselves on the mercy of my aunt and uncle. You and your maman will, of course, be under my protection and will share in whatever fortune we find there."

Charity's eyes misted and she smiled tremulously at him. She felt a weight was being removed from her shoulders by his words. Now she and Maman and Marie would not face the terrors of an unknown land alone. "You are very kind," she managed to say, and wondered why she had never really liked him before.

"Not at all, Charity. Our fathers agreed long ago that they would take care of each other's families if anything happened." He reached across Mr. Hampton and patted her hand.

Captain Winslow, who had understood Paul's words, was looking pleased for her and she felt emboldened. "Well, Captain, can you tell me more about this Virginia then, since we will perhaps now make it our home?"

Winslow hunched forward. "I would like to tell you about Virginia, Miss Ashton, but the job more rightly belongs to a native of the state. I come from Connecticut, farther north. But Mr. Crandall here can help you."

Charity's smile froze into place as she looked unwillingly across the table. A slow grin tugged at the corners of the wide mouth, and she felt that once more Adam Crandall was enjoying her discomposure. Quickly she turned back to the captain and gave a little laugh which sounded horrifyingly false to her own ears.

"Ah well, Captain, we do have many days yet before our arrival, don't we? I find now that with little sleep last night, I am feeling exhausted. Perhaps another time."

Chapter 6

Although she'd ended dinner abruptly last night simply to
avoid conversation with the strange American she so disliked, Charity discovered she'd been telling more truth than
she'd realized when she stated she was exhausted. Perhaps
it was delayed reaction to all that had happened two nights
ago, but she found that a long sleep had not refreshed her
and that she couldn't get up. Thankfully, she realized she
didn't have to, and so spent the day being ministered to by
Marie and sleeping whenever the need overtook her.

By late afternoon she was able to shake off the terrible
lassitude that had gripped her and dress once more in her
navy gown. Before venturing to the captain's cabin, she
stopped to see Émilie, but found her to be no different from
yesterday; sometimes lucidly in the present, sometimes receded into a private past. She told herself she need only allow
enough time for Maman to recover in her own way and all
would be well.

The days that followed took on a restful pattern for Charity as the brig *Angelique* sailed north under clear skies. She
would eat an early breakfast and then go on deck to get what
exercise she could and to enjoy the sea air. Rarely did she
see Adam Crandall on the quarterdeck, though occasionally
she would spy him standing with the captain deep in talk,
or by the rails in the waist of the ship. Once she even saw
him in the rigging, scrambling with the crew when orders
were shouted for more sail. But he made no attempt to speak

to her or to capture her attention, even though she sometimes felt his eyes on her as she walked with Mr. Hampton or Paul.

Her mind was not on the handsome American these days anyway, because a greater worry was pressing her. On their third day out, Paul, escorting her on her morning promenade, had ventured to ask about the things she and her mother had brought from Tournay. When she explained to him that nearly nothing had been salvaged, he'd turned brooding and dark.

"You mean Henri didn't save your father's strong box?" he'd inquired incredulously.

"He got the cash box from father's room," Charity said with some pain. "But there was little in it, and the safe in father's office was beyond reach. We have enough money to help with our expenses for a while, though," she added hastily, seeing his scowl.

He waved a tense hand. "There will doubtless be few expenses at my uncle's plantation. But you and your mother will have to spend money for suitable clothes."

"We will not need so many now," Charity reminded him gently, wondering what thoughts were behind the dark face.

"True." Paul eyed her simple brown gown with distaste.

Charity looked down, worried that Paul, always so conscious of the latest turn in fashions, would be embarrassed by her appearance in their new home. She tried to turn the subject. "From what you've said you are well situated, at least. You could perhaps buy land in this new country and begin again."

Paul's hawklike profile turned to her as he looked out to sea. "We shall have to see what the savage place is like first."

"Nothing will be the same as on Saint Dominque," Charity said softly. "It will all be new, and we will have to shape our destinies according to new circumstances."

The man's eyes returned to rake over her quickly. "Yes," he agreed slowly. "We will have to begin anew."

Charity had smiled at him then, but she hadn't liked the inflection in his voice. Was he perhaps reconsidering his offer of protection now that he'd discovered she and her mother were in much reduced circumstances? But surely as a gentleman he could not go back on his word to them. It was more likely, she reflected in the days that followed, that he was thinking the possibility of marriage to her was a good deal less attractive now. Well, that was one thought on which she'd love to put his mind at rest if he'd give her a chance.

But of course there had never been a promise from which she could release him, and no word of their former status was ever mentioned.

Her conversation with Paul, and his scowling thoughtfulness thereafter, rankled but Charity pushed it away from the front of her mind in the routine of her days. At midmorning she would go below to spend the hours before lunch tutoring Madame LaRoche in English or sitting with her mother. Captain Winslow had kindly offered her free access to his small library—a strange and diverse collection ranging from the historian Josephus through Shakespeare and even some books on the unlikely subject of agronomy—and sometimes she would read to her mother till the dark, cloudy eyes closed and the raven head turned on the pillows. Then Charity would shut the book and sit watching her mother sleep. It was the one time Émilie Ashton looked as her daughter had always known her, fragile and beautiful and happy. For now when she was awake she either sparkled with brittle gaiety over imaginary pleasures to come, or sat staring vacantly at a point beyond the girl's shoulder. Try as she might, Charity could make no contact with her mother's faraway thoughts, and at times she had to fight back tears of distress and leave the cabin.

On the sixth day of their journey, though, as Charity prepared to go for her afternoon constitutional on deck, her mother's eyes focused on her movement with a look of interest. In her clear, lilting voice, she asked where Charity was going.

Startled, the girl said, "Only on deck for a short breath of air, Maman." With little hope for success she added, "Would you like to join me?"

Émilie sat up straighter and nodded. "I don't know how my legs will work, though. They feel like rubber."

Charity laughed with sheer relief, and realized it was the first time she'd done so since the night of the ball. "Don't worry, Maman, I will support you."

Fearing her mother might change her mind if there was a moment's delay, she and Marie raced to dress her in dark green and to do her hair. When at last Émilie was ready, Charity nearly danced as she and Marie helped her onto the deck. No matter that Émilie had said nothing since she'd begun to dress; she was obviously concentrating on moving steadily with her customary grace. She was smiling. That was enough.

Gaily Charity led her forward. "Isn't it glorious, Maman?"

"I would not perhaps choose quite such a strong word for the lovely but monotonous vista of sea and sky, but it *is* impressive."

The tall figure loomed before them, leaving Charity no option but to stop and acknowledge the remark. Reluctantly she made the necessary introductions, noting with interest that Mr. Crandall was already dressed in one of his simple coats for the evening meal. She was relieved for her mother's sake that he was respectable in his attire, but she thought he took too much on himself when he offered Émilie his arm. Charity turned up her nose at the thought of promenading with him and watched with annoyance as he led Émilie away, bending over her solicitously. Her mother was actually smiling when they returned, and confided to Charity back in the cabin that she liked her new young man very much.

"He is *not* my young man," Charity stated flatly.

"Oh. Then you should exert yourself to make him your slave, *chérie*." Émilie smiled dreamily. "He would be a fair conquest. For all that he has pretty manners and seems to have a keen mind, he is, I think, a man of passions. He will take what he wants, that one."

"That's precisely why I dislike him, Maman."

"You do? That is too bad. If you could tame such a man... You could at least practice with him."

Charity made an extremely unladylike face. "That is practice I don't want."

"Ah... Anyway, you are promised to Paul, I think."

"I was never promised to Paul." Charity's tone was sharp.

"Perhaps not quite. And now there is Mr. Crandall." Her mother's eyes took on the familiar faraway look. "So like my Mark in some ways, but for that dark hair."

The girl wanted no more talk of either Paul or Adam Crandall. "Will you come to the captain's cabin for dinner, Maman?"

Émilie's faraway look remained, but she seemed to weigh the question. "I think not, *chérie*. Marie brings nice trays to me here. Run along and have fun." She moved to the porthole, leaned her forehead against it and stood staring sightlessly at the endlessly rolling waves. Charity felt her dismissal.

She was early, she knew, for the dinner hour, but she thought this a good opportunity to look through the captain's books for something new. The seaman at the door saluted and let her in, looking askance at the heavy volume she carried. She crossed behind the sturdy desk and peered at the three racks of books fastened to the wall, trying to decide if there was anything there her mother might enjoy. She was replacing her own volume and wondering about William Bartram's *Travels* when a deep voice spoke beside her.

"Ah, I wondered who had Josephus. Are you returning it for someone, Miss Ashton?"

Startled, Charity spun, a quick flush of anger blooming on her face. "Do you always sneak up behind people that way?" she asked.

The dark eyebrows before her rose a fraction. "I didn't mean to frighten you. In fact, I made quite a noise coming through the door as I talked with Bailey out there. You were just absorbed." He reached up and replaced two books on the second rack.

Charity stared at the titles, and her own eyebrows went up. "Surely you were not studying *Gentleman Farmer* or Young's *Course of Experimental Agriculture*?"

Adam smiled. "Surely you were not reading Josephus?"

"He happens to be a great historian."

"Yes, he is. And these happen to be great books on agronomy."

"Oh. Are you a farmer then?"

A smile tugged at just one corner of the man's mouth. "Perhaps I will be one day."

Charity turned and walked around the desk from him. She had a feeling he was laughing at her, but she couldn't see why.

"How fascinating," she said, trying to load her voice with sarcasm. She heard a low chuckle behind her. What an infuriating man. She wished someone, anyone else, would come in now.

"I didn't realize that well-bred young ladies read historians for pleasure, Miss Ashton."

Charity glared. "You display your ignorance, Mr. Crandall."

"Yes, Miss, I guess I do," he drawled, looking not at all abashed. He followed her out from behind the desk. "I was glad to see your mother on deck this afternoon. I hope the exercise didn't tire her too much."

Charity's stiff back unbent a bit. "You were kind to offer her your arm. She enjoyed the walk. But it was her first time out of her cabin and she felt it was enough for one day, I think."

"Of course. But tomorrow she may feel stronger. I hope I have the pleasure of offering my arm many more times."

"I'll tell her you said so."

"I would like to offer my arm to her daughter too, but I fear she would claw it."

Charity turned her back again and stared out the stern windows. There was no response, she felt, to that.

"Well, would you, Charity?"

"Mr. Crandall!" The girl looked over her shoulder, about to object to his use of her first name. He was right behind her now and she could feel his warm breath on her neck. "What a ridiculous thing to say," she faltered, feeling trapped against the window.

"Then you would not refuse if I offered?"

She tried to laugh, but bit her lip instead as large hands grasped her shoulders and turned her to face him. She raised her eyes and the grip on her shoulders tightened. She flinched and he dropped his hands instantly.

"I'm sorry," he murmured.

Charity looked up through long lashes. "To answer your question, Mr. Crandall, no, I would not claw you." She held up slender fingers and displayed perfect oval nails. "They are not strong enough or sharp enough to pierce your armor, sir."

A small smile played across the wide mouth. "Then I dare you to take a walk on deck after the meal, Miss Ashton."

Those were challenging words, and Charity's chin came up. She'd show this insufferably arrogant man that she neither feared him nor felt a single missed heartbeat for his charms.

"Although I don't claw, I do occasionally bite, Mr. Crandall. If you are unafraid of taking that chance, I will show you I am unafraid to take your offered arm. Anyway," she added with girlish candor, "I'd like to see the ship and the sea at night."

Adam laughed aloud then and his face looked almost boyishly alight. But whatever he was about to say was forestalled by the entrance of the others. Their conversation was at an end.

When Madame LaRoche finally stood at the end of the dinner and signaled for Charity to follow, the girl saw nothing but a polite mask on Crandall's face as he bid them good night, and she wondered if he'd reconsidered his offer of a walk. She wasn't going to show that *she* remembered, certainly, so she said her farewells with a bland expression and went in Madame's wake.

Bailey led them along the passage to their own cabins and Charity decided to spend several minutes with her mother before retiring. If they had been alone it would have been pleasant, but she soon felt she'd heard enough of Madame's talk this evening and left Émilie to grow drowsy under the soft waterfall of endless words from her cabinmate.

Once out in the passage again, Charity hesitated. She felt a stab of disappointment that Adam Crandall had forgotten or, worse, ignored his invitation. But perhaps she didn't need him. Certainly she knew the way to the quarterdeck by now, and surely no one would be about for just those few moments it would take her to look around. Before she could consider further, she stepped determinedly down the dimly lit passage.

She hadn't gone many yards when a figure loomed from the shadows in front of her. She started and stepped back before she saw it was the tall American.

"I thought you'd be in that cabin all night," he said lightly, grinning down at her.

Charity practically stamped her foot. "You have the most abominable habit of sneaking up on people," she said furiously.

"Shhh, dearheart. So you've told me. But in truth, I was only standing here waiting. It was you who came sneaking along this passage like a thief."

"Oooh!" Charity whirled at his words and started back to her cabin. A hand caught her arm and brought her up short. She tried to jerk away, but the grip was iron hard. She found herself being pulled along the passage.

"Come, come, Miss Ashton. You fire up too easily. I was merely speaking the truth, and well you know it." Crandall's voice held mirth as he dragged her in his wake.

They were at the open door now and Charity knew that short of screaming and bringing the whole ship down on them, there was little she could do. Anyway, this was where she had been heading when the insolent American had intercepted her. So she might as well follow through with it. She stopped struggling and felt his grip loosen.

"You may take your hand off me, Mr. Crandall," she said in a low voice. "I'll not worry anyone who may be watching out there."

"Good girl. Come on then."

They stepped onto the deck and Charity looked around.

Like ghostly garments, the sails billowed above her, their lower reaches illuminated by the ship's dim lights. High overhead an unbelievable myriad of stars danced between the masts like far-off twinkling elves playing hide and seek. Unaided, she crossed the deck and peered beyond the rail. An eerie phosphorescence poured along the ship's wake, and stretching far across black, rolling waves, a silver road of moonlight shimmered, curved, and broke on the moving world. Forgetting all her anger, Charity leaned on the rail and stared into that vast emptiness.

"It's magnificent," she breathed.

"Yes. It was scenes like this that once made me think I wanted to go to sea. But I've learned that life aboard ship is too constraining. You're confined to the limits of these timbers." He looked across the water and was silent for a space.

Charity studied the dim, chiseled profile beside her. She wondered how far this man had traveled, and she wished she could see some of the vistas which were perhaps even now in his mind's eye.

He felt her eyes on him and turned slowly, appraising her. In the near darkness her hair looked like the darkest copper, framing the perfect planes of her face. Her eyes were dark pools above her straight nose and ripe, full mouth. He had to look away and hold his hands very still on the rail. The urge to touch her was nearly overpowering.

"You should wear more color, Charity. That dark blue doesn't become you," he said in a gruff voice.

Charity was startled. She turned and began walking along the rail. "You forget I am in mourning, Mr. Crandall."

He followed her. "No, I do not forget, Charity. But from what I have heard I would venture to guess that your father would want to see you in lovely clothes, not in somber weeds fit for a widow of advanced years."

The girl walked in silence for a bit, then started for the door. As he came alongside her, she looked up at him. "As usual, you are presuming too much, Mr...."

"Call me Adam, Charity. I'd like to hear you say it."

"Mr. Crandall," she finished firmly. "I am not used to being spoken to in the way you always do, and I find it distasteful."

The man suddenly barred her way. "I'm sure you're not used to being spoken to like a mere mortal, dear Miss Ashton, only kowtowed to by servants and simpered at by fops like LaRoche, but..."

"I'll thank you not to mention Paul to me." Charity swerved to pass him, but found her way blocked once more at the door.

"What does that mincing Frenchman know about you, Charity?"

To the girl his voice sounded sneering and his muscular closeness seemed threatening. "Paul knows me a great deal better than you do," she flung at him, "since he's known me all my life. We're practically engaged to be married."

In the blackness beside the door there was a moment's silence. Then violently she was hurled back against the wall and pinned there by a lean, hard body. She tried to twist away, but his hand held her hair and pulled her head back. Brutal lips were on hers, and an arm was around her, holding her hard. She struggled, beating at his shoulder with her free fist. Slowly, his hands released her, running down the length of her arms till they gripped her wrists. She tugged, but she was imprisoned by fingers of steel. Remorselessly her arms were pulled behind her and both hands were grasped by one powerful vise.

She gasped as her arms were drawn back, lifting her breasts harder against his chest. His other hand stroked her throat, then cupped her chin, pulling her mouth up to meet his again. Acutely aware of the muscular chest against her breasts, she tried to pull back further into the wall. She felt his lips brush hers softly and she opened her eyes in surprise. Then searchingly he kissed her, his mouth moving over hers in a way she'd never experienced. His tongue came out and caressed her upper lip. She gasped again, allowing his tongue to explore her teeth before he molded his mouth to hers once more. She closed her eyes and tried to hate his kiss, but small shivers were thrilling down her spine. She remembered the first hint of these feelings when she'd experienced them with Jacques at the *vaudun* ceremony, and fear gripped her.

His hand smoothed her throat and moved slowly downward over the swell of her straining breast. His lips were on her neck now and she heard him say, "Does your Frenchman know how to do this to you, Charity?"

Charity turned her head slowly and felt his ear next to her mouth. She opened her teeth and bit down as hard as she could.

She felt her arms were going to be torn from her shoulders as he jerked convulsively. His other hand circled her throat, forcing her head back further.

"I warned you that I sometimes bite," she hissed, feeling he was going to strangle her.

"Bitch," he choked, and tightened his grip, bringing her nearly to her knees.

They both heard the voices then. The captain was coming along the passage.

Immediately Adam released her. She started to rub her sore wrists, but found she was being shoved rudely behind the open door. Adam leaned his weight on it, pinning her into the black corner. Stunned, she stood still, listening to the men exchange greetings and move out onto the deck. When she was sure Adam had led the captain well away, she pushed out from the door and slipped down into the passage.

There she stopped to straighten her dress and hair. Damn the man anyway! How cool and collected he'd sounded as he'd greeted the captain. No thought in the world but to leave her in her humiliation behind that door. She fumed as she smoothed her sleeves, trying to ignore the small voice of reason that told her Adam had protected her reputation by shoving her into hiding. And so what if he had, she raged inwardly, groping down the dim length of corridor. He had talked abominably, handled her roughly, and taken unbelievable liberties with her. If she were on Saint Dominque, she could have him flogged for what he'd done. How she'd like to see his back striped by the whip, see him broken and humiliated!

She reached her cabin without encountering anyone and found Marie waiting for her. Explaining she'd been on deck for a brief look at the stars, she undressed hastily. Then she climbed into her small bed and curled up on her side, wondering if all men in barbaric Virginia were so forceful and rude. And so obviously practiced in the sexual arts. She summoned up all the hatred she could manage for Adam Crandall and fell asleep seeing a wave of black hair falling across an arched brow above piercing gray eyes, and feeling a strong, hard body pressing her back against a rough wall.

Chapter 7

In spite of her fears, Charity's first view of the low shoreline of Virginia was an exciting moment for her. After all her time at sea she yearned for the feel of solid land underfoot, even an alien and frightening land of strangers. Now that her new home approached, she felt impatient to face whatever was to come.

"Soon we will see what a plantation in this barbaric country is like." Paul's smooth voice joined her at the rail. He spoke in English now, and Charity noticed he was becoming more fluent.

"So you remember your aunt and uncle?" Charity wished to appear eager. The voyage had given them time to come to grips with their losses and to begin to think of the future. She must keep her mind there, and not look back, not repine at what might have been. Saint Dominque and their former life was behind her now. And she must come to some new understanding with Paul. He had turned cool and distant for days after their conversation about her near penniless condition, but he had not said anything specific to show his displeasure, and she had finally decided his reaction had been normal disappointment if in fact he had ever hoped to marry her fortune. Now she wanted only amicable relations between them if they were to survive together in this alien place.

Paul shaded his eyes shoreward and answered slowly. "They visited us once in Saint Dominque, but I was very young and don't really remember them. Maman assures me her sister married a man of great property, though, and that they will take good care of us. However, I would have wished to arrive in grander style than this." In fact, he thought sullenly, I would rather not have to arrive at the bosom of dear Maman's family at all. The sympathetic Captain Winslow had put the germ of an idea in his head. If he could persuade the new government of the United States to try to help him, he would soon have no use for backwoods American planters anyway. He would have to make a journey to this Philadelphia to find out. And once he had LaRoche back, he would see about regaining Tournay. He glanced down at the girl beside him. Yes, perhaps his plans were only being postponed a bit.

Charity noticed his abstraction. "None of us ever thought to travel as refugees," she said softly.

Paul turned toward her awkwardly. His high neck cloth made it difficult to swivel just his head. He straightened and Charity thought his rich but subdued gray coat and snowy linen very elegant, but perhaps a bit too dandy for their surroundings. Still, she understood his desire to appear at his best when they disembarked.

"Refugees is too strong a word, I think. We are relatives who have met with misfortune. But we are hardly penniless and at anyone's mercy." He spoke stiffly.

The girl tried to smile. "That's true." She pretended not to notice his scrutiny of her old blue dress. It was just like him to remind her now of her own refugee circumstances. Swiftly she quelled her anger and looked over the water again. She could make out sandy shore and waving grasses on a low bluff, and her spirits rose despite the swarthy figure beside her. She thought of her mother below and stifled a sigh. Getting Émilie off this ship might help. Although Virginia would certainly not be familiar, it might be an easier place in which to adapt to their new circumstances. With an effort, she held her smile. "I wonder how long it will take us to reach your uncle's house."

Black eyebrows met over the high nose in frowning thought. "We will have to wait in a town called Williamsburg for a few days, I am told, to send a message ahead. This town was the capital of Virginia until a few years ago, but one wonders if it is civilized."

"I don't care so long as it isn't far from the port where we land. I look forward to a bath in fresh water this day." She rubbed her hands in anticipation. It had begun to seem that her skin and hair would always have the slightly sticky feeling that washing in salt water had given them. Her impatience mounted.

But it was hours before their farewells were finally said and the little party was landed. Mr. Hampton saw them across the James River, and took woebegone leave of Charity before explaining that Mr. Crandall was even now hiring a coach to convey them all to Williamsburg.

A short while later Charity came face to face with Adam for the first time in nearly two weeks, and she was furious to discover she was flustered. Deliberately she had made this arrogant man a part of the past she was leaving behind, and had put him as far from her thoughts as possible. In this last she had been aided by a storm at sea during which she discovered she was the only one of the passengers able to continue to take dinner in the captain's cabin. She'd reveled in secret delight at the thought of Adam lying ill somewhere, and had been disappointed to discover that far from being ill, he had chosen to help the crew through the bad weather and had then taken to eating with the seamen. She'd scarcely laid eyes on him after that, and had thought that her memory of him would fade completely with time. Now here she was, blushing like a school girl! But he took no notice of her, addressing only the ladies and explaining he would ride beside them to the town and see to their accommodations.

Probably put us in a room with rats, Charity thought spitefully as she climbed into the crowded coach behind her mother, and hoped he had not seen her flush.

But when at last the weary travelers alighted in the yard of a small inn in the center of Williamsburg, Charity had to be honest and admit that the place didn't look to be overrun by rats. In a low-beamed, cheerful parlor whose walls were hung with lovely blue and white china plates, Adam took his leave of all of them, assuring them they were in good hands and that they would be comfortable here for a few days.

"I have taken the liberty of writing down the names and directions of various shops where I thought you might like to entertain yourselves." Adam handed a piece of paper to Madame LaRoche, but his eyes flicked to Charity's face.

She could not read their expression, but she knew he was thinking of the gayer clothes he'd told her she should wear. He stared at her for a long moment as she stood beside Paul and held her head high. The faintest of smiles played across his shapely mouth as his eyes traveled from her hair to her lips and then down the length of her body, making her feel naked in front of them all. Her lips burned as though his mouth and not his eyes had touched them, and her cool gaze fell. When she dared to look up once more, he had turned away to bow over the ladies' hands, explaining he would take word of their arrival to Wentworth with all possible speed. Then with the smallest of shrugs, he came and stood before Paul, offering him his hand. The two young men eyed each other. Paul, thin and elegant, his dark hair brushed with powder, his ruffled cuffs folded neatly over his hands, tried to look down his high nose at the taller man. Lifting languid fingers to the other, he said, "You've been decent, Crandall, and we are grateful for your services."

"I'm sorry you've had such misfortune, and hope you will like Virginia," Adam returned formally. His eyes flicked to Charity and back. "I wish you luck," he added stiffly.

Then he put his hands behind his back and turned his gray-eyed stare on Charity. Their eyes locked for an instant and a strange light leaped into his. Immediately it was extinguished as his lids drooped. "I wish you happiness, Mistress Ashton," he said in a low voice.

Charity's mouth felt dry as she groped for something to say. Before she could formulate any words he had gone and she could only watch as the door closed behind his broad shoulders. She stared at the white planks of the sturdy door with a queer feeling in the pit of her stomach. I must be starving, she thought, and was grateful when the landlady bustled in to announce their rooms were ready, if the ladies would please follow her.

In the next few days Charity almost managed to push Adam Crandall from her mind as she explored Williamsburg with the LaRoches. They took long strolls down the Duke of Gloucester Street and admired the capitol building at one end, the Wren Building and the small College of William and Mary at the other. She remembered Adam had said one evening that he had attended this school, and she tried not to wonder which of the buildings he had frequented the most. Although it was unlike anything she had known in the Caribbean, Charity found the orderly town with its red brick or white clapboard homes, its well-tended gardens and huge old trees a charming place. She was equally surprised and pleased by the shops where she and Mrs. LaRoche (they had decided to use the English forms of Mr. and Mrs. instead of the French Madame and Monsieur now they were in America) spent long hours choosing materials and trims and contracting to have one or two dresses made posthaste.

Try as they might, they could not persuade Émilie to accompany them on their outings. She preferred, she said, the quiet solitude of her room. Charity worried about her and brought her endless samples of material to choose from, but Émilie insisted she wanted no clothes. Charity gave up in the end, thinking there would be time later for her mother's customary finery. But she found that she was impatient for herself. She couldn't resist pale peach chintz or a deep rose silk, even though she knew she could not have the luscious materials made into dresses yet. Using some of the hoarded money from her father's box, she bought these lengths of cloth and stashed them in the little trunk against the day when she could pull them out again. Firmly, she pushed down the wayward thought that Adam Crandall would approve her choices. For the moment, she too must settle for more of the dark clothing that would be considered appropriate.

At the end of the week when Charity, escorted by Paul, returned from a brief expedition to buy gloves and some ribbons, they found an imposing green coach standing before their inn. A coachman in simple green and beige livery sat on the high box watching them approach.

"Heavens, who do you suppose is staying at our little inn now?" Charity asked, eyeing the handsome equipage.

Paul shrugged, shifting his bruden of small boxes. "A duke, no less."

"A duke would require his crest on the door, you ignoramus."

"Ignoramus?" Paul's tongue stumbled on the word and he frowned.

Charity laughed. "It means you know nothing of the subject."

There was no answering smile and Charity turned with relief as the bustling figure of Mrs. LaRoche came out the front door.

"Ah, there you are. It is too exciting. Hurry and come in. We must all begin packing our few belongings. My dear brother-in-law has sent his coach for us and says we will all be most welcome in his home. Is it not wonderful?"

"Wonderful," Paul agreed heavily, still scowling.

Charity hid a smile.

* * *

Emilie was coerced into joining them this night, for everyone agreed it was a special meal of celebration for all of them on the eve of their departure into a new life. Ordering the best wines the cellars held, Paul offered toasts to their new country, to their host- and hostess-to-be, to the general good fortune that was about to befall them. Charity would have been amused at his elegant phrases if she hadn't thought she detected a note of sarcasm beneath the flowery words. She looked across the table to see if her mother noticed too, and was stricken to see Émilie's pained expression and the faraway look. She knew her mother was thinking of Tournay and of her lost husband, and she wished she had some means of erasing her mother's memories.

Very early the next morning the Wentworth coach rumbled down the Duke of Gloucester Street, past the sleepy college and out the Richmond Road. It was a golden September day with a hint of autumn chill in the air; the sort of day to lift the spirits and excite anticipation. Charity, jammed into the corner by her mother, could not still a welling of optimism as they started out.

Late in the morning they crossed a pretty river with the strange name of Chickahominy, where it flowed into the broader James. From the banks they obtained a view of several stately homes set on high bluffs on the south banks of the James, and Charity wondered if Wentworth looked at all like the very long white house, or a later tall brick one. Through the afternoon she caught rare sightings of other plantation houses too, and she thought them all very handsome, though not built on the scale of the plantations of Saint Dominque.

A gray and pink sunset had long since faded into the somber shades of night when at last the laboring horses drew to a halt before high stone steps set against dark brick walls. Immediately a wide paneled door swung open and lights came toward the coach. Firm hands helped them out and up the stairs to the front hall, where an array of servants and well-dressed people were gathering.

Blinking dazedly in the lights, Charity stood helping Marie support her mother and watched as a short, balding man with a red, jovial face sprang forward to greet them, and an equally short, chestnut-haired woman fell on Mrs. LaRoche, sobbing her name over and over. At last the Wentworths' attention shifted as the round-faced man bounded toward the three lone women, holding out both hands to Émilie. His balding pate, surrounded by a heavy fringe of sandy hair, bobbed up and down.

"Ah, Madame Ashton, forgive us. We are so overjoyed to have Sara's sister and nephew with us. It has been so long since we saw them." He waved both his hands in the air as though shooing away a flock of birds. "And now they have added two more beautiful and charming guests to swell our pleasure." He bowed first over Émilie's languid hand, and then over Charity's. Holding both of them at once, he pulled them forward. "My dear Sara, come and meet our other friends," he called. "They are all that Adam Crandall said they would be."

Charity's head snapped up at the words and her eyes darted around the hall.

"Ah, is Crandall here too, then?" asked Paul suspiciously.

"Alas, no. We could not persuade him to wait for your arrival, I'm afraid. He was mad to push on, saying he hadn't seen his family in so long. If you ask me," Mr. Wentworth chuckled, "that sort of haste's more likely to mean a petticoat at the end of the journey than just a loving family." Then he sobered. "Uh, pardon me, ladies." Coughing behind his hand, he tried to suppress another chuckle.

Charity's smile felt stiff as she curtsied to Mrs. Wentworth. She fought to bring her mind to focus on the words of welcome and to respond warmly to them while being led with the others into a heavily elegant maroon and white parlor where a fire and refreshments awaited them. Don't be a fool, she admonished herself severely. He's just the sort of man to have a woman in every port and one waiting for him at home. As Maman said, he's used to taking what he wants. She smoothed her dress as she sat beside her mother on a tapestry-covered sofa. It's just as well he didn't want me in the end, for he would have met with perhaps his first disappointment. Her teeth clenched as she thought of all the conquests he'd undoubtedly made and wished she'd had the chance to give him a severe set-down. But now he was gone out of her life as quickly as he'd come into it, and she should be grateful for that and forget her desire for revenge.

With an air of finality, she jerked her mind away from the abominable Adam Crandall, looking up in time to see an auburn-haired girl enter the room, followed by a thin, teen-aged boy whose unruly thatch of sandy hair and round, open face proclaimed him a Wentworth. She was sure that these

73

were Paul's cousins, Helen and Timothy, and was pleased with herself when introductions were made and she found she was right.

"Helen, dear, I am told that Charity is seventeen, only two years younger than you," Mrs. Wentworth said. "It will be nice to have a companion so near to your own age, won't it?" she asked somewhat nervously, glancing at her son who was staring openly at the new companion.

Smiling demurely, Helen nodded without undue enthusiasm.

Impulsively, Charity held out her hands to them. "I have never had any brothers or sisters. I will so like staying in a family with young people."

Her clear voice with its slight French accent seemed to intrigue Timothy, and immediately he fell to asking her how she knew English so well, whether everyone on Saint Dominque spoke both English and French, what she thought of the exciting revolution in France. Charity laughingly tried to field the barrage of questions until his scandalized mother interrupted him, reminding him that Miss Ashton had had a long hard journey, was in mourning for her father, and could not help but be wearied by his endless inquisitiveness.

"Oh, but I am not so very tired," Charity smiled at her hostess, "and I think his questions good ones."

"Yes, I'm sure. But I mustn't allow him to plague you, dear. You will have more than enough questions to answer tomorrow when you meet our youngest child, Sally. She is eleven now, and will make herself very trying unless you are firm with her."

Charity assured the woman that she looked forward no end to meeting this last member of her family.

Mrs. Wentworth smiled vaguely, pressed refreshments on the girl, and then moved on like a good hostess to try to draw Émilie from her silent shell. Succeeding only partially in this endeavor, she soon gave up and fluttered off to see that everyone ate to her satisfaction before being shown upstairs.

Charity was surprised to discover how tired she actually was when they were all ushered up the dark-paneled stairs and down spacious corridors to their rooms. She kissed her mother good night outside a handsome Wedgwood blue bedroom where Marie awaited her, and was then led by the housekeeper to the next door down the hall. To her delight, it opened to reveal a small but perfectly proportioned corner room with jonquil yellow walls and green and yellow figured curtains at the tall windows.

A wide-eyed young slave girl, who introduced herself as Sophie, asked if there was anything Miss required now. Charity looked at the simple canopied bed where her nightdress was laid out against the pale yellow coverlet, and could only shake her head in weariness. She thanked the girl for unpacking her two boxes and dismissed her, pushing back a wave of homesickness with speculations about what her life might now become.

PART TWO

Chapter 8

Morning found Charity eager to survey her new home. She was awake and at her windows in the early light, pleased to discover she had a view of the sweep of circular drive at the front of the house and of gently sloping lawns and giant locust trees marching down to a narrow creek at the side. Choosing her new dark brown dress, she donned it quickly and tied her hair back with a matching ribbon. She thought perhaps she should try to pin it up into an older and more demure style, but knew she would waste time and achieve uncertain results.

She slipped from her room, retracing her steps of the evening before and came eventually to the central hall. From there she simply followed her nose toward tantalizing smells. At the door to a large dining room she hesitated. Mr. Wentworth and his son were seated alone at one end of the long polished table.

"I'm sorry, I'm afraid I've intruded," she stammered, glancing longingly at the dish-laden sideboard where she could see covered plates and pitchers in mouth-watering array.

"Not at all," cried Mr. Wentworth, on his feet now. "Tim and I would welcome company. Come in, come in."

Immediately Tim was at her side, urging her to inspect the dishes set out, recommending the fried ham and steaming hominy. So these were the foods giving off the unfamiliar aromas. Charity felt her mouth water as she decided to sample nearly everything. Then she took a seat across from the boy.

"I appear to have been too early this morning," she observed between mouthfuls of fluffy hominy.

"No, you aren't. Tim and I are often alone at breakfast, the ladies preferring to rise later and eat in their rooms."

"I hope you won't be like that, Charity," Tim put in as his father frowned.

"I'm afraid I've always liked rising rather earlier than might be considered fashionable," Charity laughed.

"Splendid. Then we shall count on your company in the future." Mr. Wentworth beamed. "Though I must warn you that you will occasionally be as bored as Tim here. I find I often have to conduct business over my first meal of the day, to get the ball rolling so to speak."

"Oh, I won't be bored, Mr. Wentworth, if you don't mind my eavesdropping. My father and I usually ate together very early and he met with his overseer or other men of business at that time."

"Then you have a strong stomach, my dear."

Tim leaned forward earnestly. "I warn you, you'll hear all about the split fences in the south pasture, the ailments of every field hand, the rising cost..."

"Now, Tim, don't frighten Charity from the table her very first day." Her host sat back and crossed his hands on his ample stomach as a servant brought in a fresh pot of steaming coffee.

"It would be difficult to frighten me, I think. I used to hear all of that and more, you know. And I sometimes got a double dose when I helped Father with his correspondence or his accounts."

"Did you, indeed? What a help you must have been to him. And I'll warrant you didn't go about spraining your wrist at inconvenient times." Mr. Wentworth frowned belligerently into his cup.

Charity put her fork down and thought a moment. "No," she said at last with a twinkle, "I don't believe I ever did that precisely. Though Father said I did other 'bloody inconvenient' things sometimes."

Her host smiled then. "Well, there's very little that is more inconvenient than having one's secretary sprain a wrist just when one is trying to write for information about matters of importance."

"Oh? Well, perhaps I could help you, Mr. Wentworth."

"Oh no, my dear. Wouldn't think of it. My secretary will be right again in a few days, and I can manage meanwhile."

"I should really like to do something useful for you, if you'll let me," she insisted rather breathlessly.

Mr. Wentworth still looked dubious. "I must admit that if you are really willing, I'd be most grateful for some help this morning. For only a little while," he added quickly.

"For as long as you like," the girl assured him and smiled brightly. "Maman tends to sleep late, so she will not be needing me for a while yet."

Mr. Wentworth slapped the arms of his chair. "Splendid," he repeated. "Then follow me, Miss Ashton. Tim, you'd best see if your cousin is up yet. Perhaps you could keep him company through another breakfast."

"I expect I could manage that, Father." Tim waved an airy hand and stood aside to let Charity precede him from the room.

At the door Mr. Wentworth wagged an admonishing finger at his son. "And I don't care what your aunt was telling you last night, you're not to begin Paul's first morning here with requests that he teach you his skill with a sword." He sighed as he watched his son grin and dart off down the hall.

For the next hour Charity sorted through notes and jottings from the master of Wentworth, and wrote letters of inquiry to two companies in Boston. She would have been perfectly content to stay there all morning, but Mr. Wentworth wouldn't hear of it.

"You've taken care of the two pressing matters, and that is all I needed for now. There is a ship in Richmond which goes downriver tomorrow and will be calling at Boston. I had wanted those letters to be on it, and I am very grateful to you for making it possible. But there is nothing else of importance." He glanced at the dark old clock on the mantel behind his desk. "I must be off now, anyway. I promised to take Paul on a tour of the plantation this morning."

Charity replaced her pen in its holder and stood up, hoping he would invite her to join them. But when he didn't, she took her leave and made her way back upstairs.

Finding her mother had just finished breakfast, Charity stayed to watch her dress. Émilie seemed tranquil and accepting this morning, but distant as always. As Marie did her mother's hair, Charity stood by a window and looked out on the serene landscape beyond the drive.

"Were you comfortable last night, Maman?" she asked, her back to the room.

"Very, thank you, *chérie*. And you?"

"Oh yes. I do think this a handsome if rather heavy house, don't you?"

"From what I've seen of it, yes."

"And the Wentworths? What do you think of them, Maman?"

"They seem very nice."

Charity was wondering how to enliven the conversation when a patch of darting blue color caught her eye. She leaned forward and saw a girl with pale yellow hair and a cornflower blue dress jump behind a tree and peer stealthily out at the drive. Charity followed her intent gaze and spotted a little black boy about the girl's own age, creeping along a line of bushes a few yards away. Just as he reached the last clump the girl erupted from behind the tree and ran toward him brandishing a thick stick and screeching horribly. The boy's eyes rolled in fright, then he grinned and darted into the center of the heavy bushes. The girl began to circle, still yowling, and now Charity could see crazy whorls of smudged gray and copper color all over her face.

"What on earth are they doing?" she muttered, fascinated.

"What did you say, Charity?"

Charity turned back to the room. "I think I have just seen the fifth member of the Wentworth family, Maman, and she looks quite like a little savage."

"A savage?" Émilie looked alarmed, and Charity wondered where her sense of humor had gone. Surely it had been obvious she was teasing.

"Yes, quite. She has on a lovely little dress, but her hair is tangled, she has a torn stocking and her face is covered with what looks like painted dirt."

"Tiens!"

Charity's smile broadened. "Come, Maman. Let us go for a stroll outside and see if we can come face to face with the beast."

"You go along, dear. I'm sure the air will do you good."

"And it would do you good," countered her daughter. "You're too pale by half, Maman. Come and walk with me."

"No, *chérie*. I am not up to it yet. Marie has said she would sit with me a while, and I will take a bit of air at this window."

Charity felt like stamping her foot. Though hardly a sportswoman, her mother had never been adverse to getting a little exercise. "You must not simply languish in this room, Maman."

"No. But it was a long journey, *chérie,* and I prefer to rest again." Émilie folded her hands and sat, staring out at gently waving leaves against a brilliant sky.

She has gone away again, Charity thought, watching her. "Very well, Maman," she said aloud, and when her mother didn't answer, she slipped quietly from the room.

Knowing no other entrance to the house, she used the front door and turned to her left toward the sloping lawns she'd seen earlier from her bedroom. There was now no sign of the boy and girl. Crossing at the top of the lawns, she felt a twinge of something like envy for the girl's youth that enabled her to run free with her friend on this glorious morning.

Turning another corner of the house, she set her feet down a smooth path of grass between colorful perennial borders that ran beside a stone terrace. Grassy steps led down from the terrace to a small circular pond surrounded by magnificent roses. High, boxwood hedges made a broken half-circle beyond the pond, and through the opening she glimpsed more paths and flower beds surrounded by tall trees. It was all rather overwhelmingly formal, but had a certain beauty, she thought, and walked to the pond to watch six fat goldfish swim lazily in the shallow water.

A shrill, drawn-out yowl behind her made her jump. She turned slowly to see the girl in the blue dress staring owl-eyed at her from the edge of the box hedge. Unmoving, Charity returned the stare.

The girl advanced a few quick steps and stopped. "Didn't my yell scare you?" she asked, eyeing Charity dubiously.

"It startled me," was her answer. "But your face is even more startling."

"Is it? Then, I must have done a better job than usual." The girl crossed her eyes as though to look down at her own cheeks and nose.

Charity laughed. "If this is your usual face, I would hate to see you do anything unusual. Now let me guess just what it is you're supposed to be."

"You mean you don't know an Indian warrior when you see one?"

"No, I don't. I've never seen one. Have you?"

"Well, not many. But I've heard a lot about them. Tim has

a book that says Indians to the west of here are eight feet tall and have huge horns and..."

"Sally! What on earth do you think you're doing? You'll frighten poor Charity to death." Mrs. Wentworth bounced down the terrace steps toward them, shaking a round forefinger at the young girl. Helen and Mrs. LaRoche followed at a more sedate pace.

"I'm afraid I've disappointed her, Mrs. Wentworth. I didn't know an Indian warrior when I saw one." Charity grinned and the smudged little face before her grinned back.

Mrs. Wentworth put her hand on the ample flesh above her heart. "You will be the death of all of us yet, child. Now go inside and take that filth off you. We will have proper introductions at luncheon."

"But I already know who she is," answered the girl, "and I bet she knows who I am."

"Go!" An imperious finger pointed to the house, and the girl scampered off, grinning.

Charity smiled at Mrs. Wentworth. "I believe I just met your younger daughter."

"Yes, I'm afraid you did. I must apologize for her behavior to you."

"Please don't. I was just thinking that she reminded me of myself at her age."

Three sets of eyebrows rose at this remark and Charity tried to pull her face into more sober lines.

"I doubt your mother had such trouble controlling you, though," Mrs. Wentworth said rather stiffly.

Helen, who had been standing with a cool smile on her face, now looked toward the house. "We really should have employed that dragon of a governess, Mother. At least she would have kept Sally in line."

Mrs. Wentworth shuddered. "That woman scared even me. And Sally hated her on sight. I had hoped that by now she would be old enough to want to emulate your good example, dear."

Helen smiled again, and Charity wondered what went on behind those remote blue eyes and that detached smile. Helen was more than attractive, the girl decided. She was really very lovely, with the sun bouncing off red highlights in her dark, thick hair. Her softly rounded face matched perfectly her softly rounded, almost voluptuous figure, and although Charity was sure she would run to fat one day like her mother, she had to admit that Helen was just the sort of self-contained and poised young woman of obvious physical charms that many found irresistible.

At that moment Helen's look became speculative. "Well, Mother, it seems Charity and I will have to undertake some of the governess's duties this season, then. Someone had best start teaching her a little decorum and some of the social graces. What do you think, Charity?"

Charity smiled into the cool blue eyes. "I'm afraid I am better in the school room than in the parlor," she admitted, "but I'd be happy to help in any way I can. I like Sally."

Perfectly arched brows rose once more. "Marvelous. Then it's settled."

Charity nodded. In one morning she had managed to discover ways of being useful to the Wentworths. It made a great deal of difference to the way she viewed her own position in the household. The nagging worry she'd had for so long about how she and her mother could justify their coming to live with strangers was stilled for the moment.

The next weeks sped by for Charity. The bright Virginia fall marched on into winter before she had time to notice its passing. Her days were filled to capacity and if sometimes she wished she could shrug off the mantle of mourning she was forced to wear, at least she couldn't complain of long periods of boredom.

While Mr. Wentworth's secretary nursed his wrist, Charity helped in the office whenever she could, and she found her time was filled more and more with the care and handling of eleven-year-old Sally. Rapidly she grew to have greater respect for females whose lives were spent in being governesses.

It was apparent from the start that Sally was a bright but undisciplined girl, whose headstrong ways and vivid imagination had succeeded in disencumbering Wentworth of a number of governesses. It was evidently from her brother's tutor, a cadaverous young man named Rupert Breame, that she had learned her sums, some geography, a smattering of history, and the rudiments of Latin. But since Timothy's tutor had been engaged only to teach the young master, Sally's education had been achieved in fits and starts whenever she felt inclined to eavesdrop on a lesson.

Charity decided almost immediately that one reason Sally was often difficult was that she needed to occupy her active mind. So, collecting any of Helen's and Tim's discarded school books she could, she set Sally a course of study, and dealt firmly with her young charge to keep her at it. To Charity's surprise, the girl, after a week of wary testing of her limits, suddenly declared Charity was the greatest and most interesting friend she'd ever had and she was so glad she'd come to live at Wentworth.

Sally's education in the social graces was not so intense. Helen would occasionally take Sally for sedate walks in the gardens, lecturing her sister on the way to move, sit, and talk. At first Charity would accompany them, but finding Helen's constant instruction and superior ways irritating, she soon quit, noting that thereafter the promenades became less frequent. Helen, it seemed, was not so eager to maintain her side of the bargain.

Charity's evenings, once the men left their port and came to the parlor, tended to be more interesting. Often they were enlivened by discussions of plantation difficulties, talk of new lands opening up to settlers and even politics. She listened avidly to Mr. Wentworth's descriptions of debates in the Virginia legislature or of personalities in the federal government in Philadelphia and slowly began to develop an understanding of her new country.

She discovered further that her relationship with Sally benefited her as much as it did the girl. From her charge she learned her way around the great house, its dependencies, and gardens. And it was because of Sally that she finally got to ride again.

It had been a ticklish moment when the subject first came up one noon several weeks after Charity's arrival at Wentworth. Sally had declared a desire to ride with her father to an outlying pasture, and when Mr. Wentworth shook his head, she'd pouted for a minute before brightening.

"You'll come along, I'm sure, Tim. And that will mean Father won't have to watch out for me. And Charity can come too if she wants."

Charity looked up from her plate and held her breath. The thought of riding again was one she'd entertained for days, but she hadn't known how to ask for a mount.

"Sally, you mustn't try to drag Charity in your wake that way," said Helen softly from her seat across the table. Her mother and Mrs. LaRoche nodded agreement.

Sally shrugged. "I thought she might *like* to ride out to the pasture."

"Now, Sally, you must remember that dear Charity is in

mourning and might not feel like gallivanting about the countryside," said Mrs. Wentworth at last.

Charity felt her jaw muscles tighten, but she pulled her mouth into a smile. "I would love to ride, in fact. If that is all right."

"You don't need to humor Sally, you know," said Helen. "Besides, you haven't any clothes, have you," she added in syrupy tones.

Charity bit her lip. She thought longingly of her wardrobe at Tournay. Helen was right. She felt defeated.

"Oh, Helen. You have an old habit Charity could wear." Sally looked brightly at her sister. Helen's fine eyes narrowed, but Sally lifted her chin defiantly. "You had a new one made just this summer, and declared you wouldn't touch the old gray one again."

There was a moment's silence when Charity had to duck her head to hide a smile. Then Tim spoke up. "Come, Helen. Lend Charity the clothes and let her come along this afternoon."

When Paul and Mr. Wentworth added their endorsements, the matter was settled without more words, but Charity had the feeling that the incident had turned Helen into her antagonist, and she couldn't understand why.

Although the gray habit was too big for her, Charity wore it with pleasure. She would have worn anything for the chance to sit a horse once more, to feel the breeze on her face and the power of strong muscles moving smoothly at her command. It had been a glorious long ride, and Tim and Paul had exerted themselves to be charming escorts. Charity hated to admit to herself that it would have been even more fun without Helen along always to interrupt and ask Charity to please keep an eye on Sally. But it seemed a small price to pay for her freedom in the open air.

After that day there had been many more rides around the acres of Wentworth plantation. At those times she couldn't think about the past, or even the present, and the future would surely somehow take care of itself. Though in more sober moments she wondered just how it would manage to take care of itself to any degree of satisfaction.

Her life was now very circumscribed. Cut off from the rich, gay life of Saint Dominque, Charity had been thrown into mourning in a strange country surrounded by strangers. Social decisions were now made for her by her hostess and Mrs. LaRoche since her mother refused to participate in everyday life here. It was not considered proper, for instance, for her to accompany the others to formal parties they attended. As the weeks passed, she found she was thrown more and more into her own company, or into Sally's since Helen and Paul were often engaged elsewhere. And even Tim, who occasionally had time to take her riding or offer challenges to games of cards or chess, was bound by convention and by what his mother thought proper.

Paul, after discovering that many refugees from Saint Dominque had gone to Philadelphia, took himself off in mid-November, telling Charity he had hopes, when in the company of others like himself, of persuading the government to help the dispossessed men to regain their lands. Charity didn't see what the young government could do, but she wished him Godspeed and tried to keep her own hopes in check. She wished only that she too were a man and could go with him. Though she found she did not miss his brooding presence here at Wentworth, and was amused to see Helen visibly annoyed at the loss of her ready-made escort.

Charity's first real outing from Wentworth, in fact, came soon after Paul's departure, when all the ladies were taken into the town of Richmond, only a few miles away, to do some shopping. Charity felt like a child let out of the schoolroom as she strolled the streets, admiring the impressive capitol building and hearing of the people who lived in the handsome houses. With more of the money from the little trunk, she searched the shops for Christmas season gifts and felt very daring when, after selecting fans and gloves in one fashionable shop, she ordered a riding habit made for herself. It was to be a rich chocolate brown edged with black piping, and she felt sure no one could complain that she was being forward with her wardrobe. The ordering of the habit made her feel better than she had for days, and she returned to Wentworth with renewed spirits.

Perhaps it was because she had been away from the house for a full day, seeing new sights and faces, that Charity felt something like a sense of shock when she went in to say good night to Émilie that evening. Her mother was already in bed, a heavy wrap around her shoulders against the chill night air. And suddenly to Charity she looked smaller and more frail against the white pillows. The smile that was turned to her seemed wan and as the girl described her day, she noted the blue patches beneath Émilie's lovely eyes, the hollowness of her cheeks, the lack of luster in the raven hair, even the prominent blue veins on the backs of the slender, expressive hands. It was all she could do to keep her voice steady and her smile broad until her mother's eyes closed with fatigue. Rising gently, Charity stared down at the thin, pale figure under the bedclothes.

Nodding to Marie, she walked over to one of the windows and gazed out at bright moonlight etching deep silhouettes across the front lawns. Behind her she heard the maid arranging the bedclothes and blowing out the small bedside lamp.

Then Marie padded softly up to the girl and put a hand on her arm. "What is it, Mademoiselle?"

Charity looked at the woman who had been maid, nurse, confidante, and close friend to her mother for so many years. "Mother looks too pale," she said at last. "I should insist on her walking in the gardens more often. And I'm sure she's eating almost nothing off those trays she has up here each meal."

"She does not *want* to walk in the gardens, or to eat the food, or to talk to people, Mademoiselle."

"But Marie, how will we ever make her strong again if she will not do anything?"

"She does not want to be strong, *chérie.*"

"What are you saying?" Charity snatched the firm dark hand on her arm and squeezed it tightly. "What do you mean?"

Marie shrugged and looked out into the night. "There is nothing for her here. It is all back at Tournay."

"But you said yourself there was nothing back there for any of us," Charity reminded her.

"Yes. And it is true; there is nothing left there but memories. That is all your mother wants, though, her memories."

"Memories aren't very nourishing," Charity snapped.

"Perhaps to the soul."

The girl looked across the dim room to the big bed, and felt a chill foreboding she'd felt once before, in the picture gallery at Tournay the night of her father's accident. Only she hadn't recognized the feeling then. Now she knew, and she was determined that this time she would fight it.

Chapter 9

When Charity Ashton put up a fight, the world was aware of it, and no one at Wentworth, in the next weeks, had any doubts that Charity was fighting for her mother's life. At her insistence, doctors were called in, remedies tested, special menus prepared. On sunny days Émilie was wrapped warmly and carried to the terrace, there to watch any activities Charity could muster. For endless days and nights the girl hardly left her mother's side. She read to her, gossiped about the servants, reminisced when it seemed appropriate and planned for the future when she thought she had an ear. But it was all to no avail. In the end, Émilie Ashton, in her own quiet, fragile manner, had her own way. Five nights before Christmas she died, a faint smile and her husband's name on her lips.

When her father had died, Charity had had no time for thought; she'd had to fight for their very lives. And she'd had to take care of her mother. But now she felt bereft in a way she'd never before thought possible. She'd lost her fight, and now in four short months she had gone from being a carefree girl living in lavish security to being an orphan in an alien land. Desolation overwhelmed her.

The Wentworths were kind, of course. Mr. Wentworth took on all arrangements and insisted that she must always consider his house her home. Sunk in the well of her own grief she acceded dumbly to any suggestion and allowed herself to be waited on and whispered over endlessly. Only to the one other person who had truly loved her mother, did she openly show her despair. And Marie, dry eyed but suddenly older, did her best to aid the daughter of her beloved Émilie. Slowly and gently she brought Charity out of her shell of despair, pointing out that the girl must begin to live for herself and must stand on her own feet.

Bleakly, Charity recognized the need to be less of a burden on this household that had taken her in, and after a few weeks she insisted on returning to the schoolroom with Sally and to any other occupation where she might be useful. Over the long winter months, a pattern began to emerge to her life, and although the dim recesses of her mind told her to beware for the future, she felt too desolate to really care. She went quietly about the house, taking on duties to keep herself occupied, eating half her meals in her room, becoming thin and withdrawn. Even the advent of spring did not work its magic. She viewed the budding crocuses and then the spreading magnolias through apathetic eyes. Her lovely new riding habit hung in the wardrobe unused, and she never looked at the yards of beautiful bright material she'd bought in a spirit of adventure in Williamsburg.

Paul's return in March did nothing to pick up her spirits, for he was morose and sullen after his months in the north, saying that help would not come from the ignorant and single-minded men who were running this country. He was sunk in thought, snappish and autocratic, and even Helen did not seek out his company after the first days. The only lift Charity received from his presence was his announcement in April that he would return to the city to pursue other interests with new friends. She felt no curiosity about what these new pursuits might be, and only looked forward to his departure. When he left she forgot to wish him well.

As spring drew on to summer, Sally, who had been docile and studious all winter, began to rebel. She wanted to be out doing things, and she complained that no one else ever had time for her. It was more for Sally's sake than her own that Charity began to take long walks again, and even consented to ride occasionally. Sally would apprise her, as they walked together, of the comings and goings of family and friends, but Charity felt only the smallest spark of interest in their activities.

She felt no interest at all in the evening gossip of the ladies, who never seemed to tire of worrying about fashions in frippery and about who wore what to which event. As a result of her never listening, people became used to talking in front of her as though she weren't there, and Charity hardly noticed. On the hot summer evenings, she would listen to the ceaseless drone of the cicadas, or watch foolish moths burn their wings batting at the tall candles in the drawing room, and wonder dully what might become of her. But the question never took on much force, and no one else ever mentioned her future.

It wasn't until a warm day in late September that Charity even noticed this omission. She had gone to her room to fetch a writing tablet, and hearing voices and the jingle of bridles outside, she paused at her window to look down on the drive. A group of horses milled near the door, and Charity could make out Helen's royal blue habit in the center of the throng. She remembered now that there was to be a picnic outing today. Looking down on the laughing faces turned up toward the sun, she had a pang of something like regret for her lack of invitation to go along. They all looked so cheerful and eager to be off, just as she had once looked in a lifetime far behind her.

Then suddenly down the drive a figure appeared astride a big gray horse. Something about that approaching form made her lean closer to the panes. The rider, a tall man in a buff-colored coat, was leaning across his horse's neck, but as he straightened and rode on, Charity caught her breath. She could never mistake that toss of the head as he shook dark hair off his brow, or the straight set of the broad shoulders. The twinge of regret at missing the outing disappeared as she realized Adam Crandall was the man the group had awaited. Hastily, she stepped away from the window and closed her ears to the sounds of laughter floating up on the morning air. She wanted no reminders of times past, any more than she wanted to look into the future.

Unhappily, her day was not to be made any easier by her charge. Sally alternately chafed and sulked at the fact she was too young to go along on the exciting party. Patiently Charity explained there would be many more such picnics when the girl was older, but nothing helped till Sally suddenly looked at her in wonderment.

"Why aren't *you* going, Charity? You're old enough," she asked, snapped out of her sulk by the provoking question.

"I was not interested," Charity answered, neglecting to add that she had not been invited. Carefully she straightened some maps on the table before them.

"But why weren't you interested? You never go anywhere. You're losing your looks because you don't eat right or exercise or enjoy yourself."

"Indeed!" Charity's tone was sharp.

Sally looked sideways at her as though appraising the truth of her own words. Then she dimpled. "Anyway, how will you find a husband if you refuse to meet anyone or go anywhere?"

"And who says I'm looking for a husband?" Charity's bile was rising steadily, and although she knew she shouldn't take the girl's bait, she was unable to resist.

Sally looked wide-eyed at that. "Doesn't every girl? Helen's been looking for two years now." She grew thoughtful. "I think there have been a few men who might have come up to scratch, but she and Mama are awfully picky."

"Sally," Charity remonstrated, "you shouldn't discuss your sister's personal affairs." Her words were automatic, for her mind was on what Sally had just said. For the first time in a long time she became aware of her own predicament. An orphaned girl living on someone else's largesse was not in an enviable position. Her sole dowry would be the contents of that little trunk and her few clothes and jewels. Who would now be interested in her?

As though in answer to her question, Sally's voice broke into her thoughts. "If you could get out of those old clothes and begin to look the way you did when you first came here, I'll bet no man around would care whether or not you were rich. You'd even put Helen in the shade, and that would be fun to watch." She practically smacked her lips with relish.

"Sally!" Charity frowned and finished stacking the papers in front of her. "You have gone far from the course in geography we were discussing."

"*You* were discussing," the girl pouted. "I just want to go outside." Suddenly she brightened. "I know. Why don't we go have a picnic of our own? We don't have to stay here just because the others have gone off without us."

Sighing, Charity went to change her clothes and tell Mrs. Wentworth of their plans. She supposed that going out with Sally was the least she could do to make up for the girl's disappointment over the picnic.

When they returned to the house late in the afternoon, she went to her room, intending to request a tray there, but found the brisk ride had made her restless and hungry. She decided she would go down to dinner this night.

Her regret at this decision came the moment she crossed the drawing room's threshold and encountered the surprise on Adam Crandall's face. Her own must have registered shock at seeing him there, and she stopped in her tracks. She saw his eyes narrow as though in disbelief, but she had no time to wonder at his expression, for the men were all on their feet, and Helen was gliding smoothly across the room to pull Adam forward.

"Charity, allow me to present Adam Crandall to you," she began, but Charity nodded coolly.

"Mr. Crandall and I have met."

Helen gave a short peal of rich laughter and glanced coquettishly up at Adam. "Of course you have. How silly of me. You were on the same ship coming out of Saint Dominque."

"A coincidence Miss Ashton would prefer to forget, I'm sure," said Adam, unsmiling.

"Yes, I imagine so. Such a painful journey that must have been." Helen batted sympathetic eyes at Charity, then turned back. "But you know, you never told me why you were in the Caribbean, Adam."

"My uncle asked me to see to some land he'd acquired there. I'm afraid he lost a nice investment."

"You certainly are familiar with far-flung places," put in Mrs. Wentworth, coming up to the three young people. "Helen was telling me earlier that you are newly back from Kentucky. Were you there long?"

"Yes, I was. For much of this past year. Though I went up into the Ohio territories too." His eyes held Charity's own wide ones. "There's a lot of beautiful country beyond the Blue Ridge."

"Yes, I'm sure," Mrs. Wentworth returned absently, looking around to check that everyone was present and accounted for. "We would all like to hear more over dinner. Shall we go in?"

Charity, who had not moved an inch since she'd entered the room, lowered her eyes and stepped aside to wait Tim's arm. She felt Helen sweep past her with Adam and looked down at the old navy blue dress that had seen so much service this past year. She supposed it was too late now to plead a headache and make a dash for her own room.

Although she'd been hungry earlier, Charity found she couldn't eat very much when the food was set in front of her. It would have been difficult to miss the sparkle in Helen's eye this evening (a predatory gleam, Charity decided), or the smooth gallantry of her dinner partner. It was unsettling to be facing Adam Crandall across the table this way, and she could only feel relieved that his attention was wholly taken by either Helen or her father, who wanted to hear about the year in the West.

Charity kept her eyes on her plate for the most part, hearing the deep voice describe the lush Kentucky wilderness and the wild, forest-covered, often swampy country north of there. She heard of the great rivers that crisscrossed the vastness beyond Virginia and of the beautiful game to be had. His enthusiasm for the frontier was evident in every word, and Charity found herself wishing she could see some of these wonders he described so vividly. When asked about the availability of land in the new territories, though, Adam laughed and said he would spare the ladies a discussion of that nature. Charity looked up at that, unable to hide her disappointment that she was not to hear more, and saw him cock one eyebrow at her in an expression she remembered all too well. Hastily she looked away again, and was glad when Mrs. Wentworth rose and she had to follow.

In the drawing room Charity picked up a piece of sewing she'd been meaning to finish for days, and listened with half an ear to the other three discuss the guests who had been on the picnic that day. Her attention wandered until she heard Helen's sultry voice say, "You would not have believed, Mama, how delirious Katharine Wainwright was to see Adam. She positively threw herself at him the whole of luncheon. It nearly spoiled my meal to see her behave so. I believe she's carried a torch for him this entire year. Imagine."

"Isn't she that sweet but mousy girl who lives in Richmond?" asked Mrs. LaRoche, and when her sister nodded, she chuckled. "Surely a dashing young man such as Mr. Crandall is not interested in her." Her small round eyes darted from one to the other of her companions.

"Of course not, *Tante* Hélène. Though he was very nice to her, I have to admit that I was the object of most of his attentions."

Helen's voice was positively unctuous, Charity thought, and she felt sorry for the unfortunate Miss Wainwright.

"Well then, it wasn't Katharine who brought him back to this part of the world," said Mrs. Wentworth comfortably. "Perhaps it was you, Helen."

Charity raised her head just enough to be able to watch Helen's face, and was interested to see that only the barest hint of a flush appeared as the older girl smilingly shook her head. "I'm sure his family was glad to see him, Mama."

"Of course. But they live up near Charlottesville, dear, not around here."

"He has many friends around Richmond too, you know."

"Mmmm...I do wonder, though, just why he dashed off into that frightening country in the first place, don't you?"

"Perhaps he is speculating in land."

"Well, it's not as though his father doesn't own miles and miles of land right here in Virginia."

Charity blinked and stared sightlessly at her sewing. It had never occurred to her that Adam Crandall was anything more than a handsome wanderer who was entertained in the best homes simply because of his dashing good looks. She felt slightly piqued that she had not known he came from a landed family. Though that fact made no difference to his basic character, she reminded herself, and jabbed her needle into the cloth with unaccustomed ferocity.

"Well, Mr. Crandall's return gave a nice excuse for what sounds like a lovely picnic," Mrs. LaRoche was saying. "And I suspect that Charity is now a bit sorry she didn't go along."

Charity nearly looked up at that, gasping at the viciousness that must have prompted Helen to let the women think it was Charity's choice not to go today. She held her hands very still and heard the conversation continue.

"I'm quite sure she has nothing appropriate to wear, dear," Mrs. Wentworth said, as though Charity were up in her bed asleep instead of sitting not three yards away, "and she would have felt awkward among all the gay young people. Although Helen would have been nice to her when Adam could spare her a moment, I expect the others might not have paid her much attention and it could have hurt her feelings."

Schooling her face to be blank of expression, Charity drew a deep breath and looked straight into the hooded gray eyes of Adam Crandall, now standing just inside the hall door. Her own flew wide with horror, and she flushed hotly.

The horrible moment was broken as the other four entered the room and came to find seats by the ladies. Behind them Adam moved at last. With deliberate paces, he crossed to Charity's chair and leaned over her. Charity, who was studying her sewing, jumped when the low voice said, "Once again I find I must offer my condolences to you, Charity. I have only just learned about your mother."

Without looking up all the way Charity nodded. "And once again, I must thank you, Mr. Crandall."

Adam leaned closer. "I came back expecting to see you married, Charity. Was it your latest misfortune that postponed the happy event?"

Charity's eyes flew up to his. "Married?" she gasped. Then suddenly she remembered the last words she'd flung at him aboard the ship and her rash announcement that she and Paul were practically engaged. "N-n-no," she stammered, wondering wildly if she could bolt for the door.

"Don't tell me he was cad enough to cry off? Is that why the Caribbean rose is drooping so?"

"Why, you," Charity sputtered and tried to jump from the chair. But a strong hand on her shoulder held her firmly in place.

"Charity!" The soft voice was little more than a whisper, but it held absolute command. She sat very still. "Look at me."

Reluctantly, she raised her eyes again. She wanted to pin him with daggers, but was afraid she was going to cry instead. Through a mist she saw Helen glance over at them with narrowed eyes.

Then the older girl smiled brightly. "Adam," she called. "You must come and settle a ridiculous argument we are having. Tim is claiming that buffalo have huge horns and flaring nostrils like a dragon. And I say he's been reading too many of those silly books about the West. You're the only one I know who's seen the beasts, so you must come and set Tim straight."

Through the same mist Charity saw Adam's wry smile as he bowed beside her. "But of course I shall," he said in a perfectly normal voice. "I warn you, though, that at times the truth really is stranger than fiction." Then he nodded to Charity. "If you will excuse me, Miss Ashton," and he strolled across the room to take the seat beside Helen.

Charity's temples were pounding. If she stayed here to watch him being entertaining and to fawn over a pretty face without a backward thought for the appalling behavior he'd exhibited, she would begin screaming her rage at him. Slowly and carefully she stood up. Stiffly erect, she walked from the room and up the stairs. By the time she reached her own door she was crying quietly, but had lost track of her reasons why.

From the corner of his eye, Adam watched her go and

silently cursed himself. What a muddle-headed, hot-tempered fool he'd been. He'd come back from Kentucky convinced he'd gotten the beautiful Charity Ashton out of his system. He'd thought she'd be married, or at the very least betrothed by now, and that seeing her again, if he must, would be nothing more than an aesthetic pleasure. And there was always the chance that someday, married or not, he might sample the delights of the body that had haunted him. But the hollow-eyed girl in the dress that was too big for her, who had walked into the drawing room that evening had staggered him, and he'd felt a totally alien sensation come over him. He'd wanted to take her in his arms, to protect her and keep her safe. The feeling had shaken him. That must be why he had behaved so abominably just now.

He was furious with himself for not having guessed that her words about marrying Paul LaRoche had only been a ruse to put him off; he was furious at her for playing that game; he was furious at the fates for decreeing that he would spend a year wandering the western countries trying to forget her and that she would spend that year sinking into misery. He knew he still wanted her, and he knew he'd given her yet another reason to hate him. Why was it that his usual control seemed to shatter in her presence? But blast it all, Charity Ashton *was* just another pretty face and he'd be damned if he would allow *any* woman to haunt him, to interfere in his life.

Suddenly the room was unbearably hot to him, and he realized he had to get out. The quarter of an hour it took to extricate himself was the sheerest torture, and at the end of it he all but flung himself out the door. A mad gallop back to Richmond, the wind on his face, the freedom of movement was all he wanted now.

Charity's headache was still with her two days later when Mr. and Mrs. Wentworth confronted her after luncheon and presented her with a fresh worry. Prodded firmly by his wife, Mr. Wentworth explained to Charity that the economics of this year's crops was forcing him to cut a few expenses. The primary way he was going to do this was by selling some slaves. There was an auction coming up in Richmond to which he planned to send two unmarried field hands and a stableboy. It had come to his attention that an economy they could practice in the house was cutting down on the domestic servants. The most obvious to go, he was afraid, was Marie.

Charity stared from one to the other of them, dumbfounded. "Sell Marie?" she said stupidly.

Mr. Wentworth, seeing the look on her face, twisted his hands and didn't answer. But his wife was made of sterner stuff. "You must see, Charity, that as long as your mother was here, we had every reason to keep her maid. But now...well, you do perfectly nicely with the occasional help of Helen's girl, Sophie."

"But Marie is not for sale," Charity said dully.

"Well, dear, I hardly think you have the final say in the matter."

"No, no. You don't understand. Marie is not really a slave. She...she is part of our family. She was a girl with Maman. Her whole family has always been with us."

Mr. Wentworth cleared his throat. "Yes, we do understand, Charity. That is the way we all feel about many of the slaves, particularly the domestic servants. But in this case..."

Charity's mind raced. "If it is her upkeep that worries you, of course I'll pay for it. I should have thought of that before."

"My dear, you would have a hard time maintaining her for very long."

"Then I'll pay while we try to find her a more suitable position."

"It is more than mere money," Mrs. Wentworth took up the argument again. "She makes some of the other servants nervous. She's different, you know, doesn't quite speak their language. And they fear she knows voodoo."

"Speak their language?" Charity almost laughed. "She speaks two African dialects, French, the Creole of Saint Dominque, and English. As for the voodoo, Marie is a Catholic."

Mrs. Wentworth's jaw set. She had obviously not been prepared for an argument from the girl. "Nonetheless, she makes some of them nervous," she repeated. "It is easier for all of us if she goes to auction."

Charity stood up. Forcing her hands to her sides to stop their trembling, she faced her hosts. In a low voice she said, "You both have been kind to us this past year, and I have tried to do your bidding and make myself useful and not any more of a burden than I must necessarily be." Mr. Wentworth opened his mouth to protest, but she went on. "I have never wanted to go against you in anything, but I find that now I must. If you insist on labeling Marie a slave and on selling her, then I am forced to remind you that she belongs to *me*." The shock on Mrs. Wentworth's face was apparent, but Charity ignored it. "I can only beg you to try to find her useful employment elsewhere."

"And where would we 'find employment,' as you say, for a foreign slave?"

Charity felt hot tears collecting behind her eyes. She'd grown up with slavery. She knew the facts of the slaves' existence. But perhaps because of her own indebted position now, she was appalled at the thought of buying and selling a human being, especially one she had always considered a part of her family. She put her hands together and looked at Mr. Wentworth as steadily as she could. "I have to repeat that Marie belongs to me. And I feel the decision about where she is to go belongs to her."

Mrs. Wentworth leaned forward, her eyes narrowed. "Are you saying you would set her free? You would be mad to do so when you might have the money from her sale to add to any dowry you could have."

"I want no money from anyone's sale," the girl answered firmly. "And I should be grateful for guidance in the procedure of giving Marie her freedom."

Mr. Wentworth's broad face split into a smile. But his wife still looked askance. "I do think this is carrying the talk of Mr. Jefferson and his followers a bit too far."

Charity smiled across the woman's head at her host. She'd certainly heard of Thomas Jefferson's views on slavery, even though she knew the Secretary of State to be a large slave holder himself. At the moment, though, she cared for no one else's views. She knew only what she must do, and she knew Mr. Wentworth stood ready to help her.

That very evening, when Marie brought hot compresses for her aching forehead, Charity told the woman as gently as she could of the decision that had been forced on her. Marie showed no surprise at the announcement, but she straightened from the bedside and crossed the room to the shadows by a window.

"I am amazed they allowed me to stay this long," she said at last. "I do not mind leaving this place, but I do not like to leave you, *ma petite.* Things have gone badly for you this year, and I do not see how you will get away from a life that is not what you should have."

Charity sat up and hugged her knees. "I will get away, Marie," she said softly, but with conviction. "I see now that the only way I can change my life is to find a man who will take me away from here and make me mistress of my own house. It will take some time, but I will get away."

"Ah, my poor child. You are at their mercy now. You have no dowry, and you are surrounded by those who do not love you. That Helen, she is jealous of you and will not allow you to encourage any man worthy of you."

Charity shrugged. "She should be glad instead if I find a husband and leave Wentworth."

"Not if that husband is one she wants herself," answered Marie darkly.

"I doubt that we have the same taste in men." Charity smiled then. "But come, Marie, it is *your* future that we must talk about now. You will be a free woman. Where will you go?"

"I would like to remain somewhere nearby. In case you ever need me."

"Oh, Marie, don't think I haven't thought of that first. But I am assured I could find you nothing but menial work here. No, you must go where there is more opportunity. Would you consider returning to Saint Dominque?"

Marie actually smiled at that. "*Non, petite.* I will not go back there. But perhaps to another place of French people. I have heard about a city called New Orleans."

"Yes, I've heard of it too. It is under the Spanish now, but it is a French colony, really. And it is a port city, with much going on. Would you like to go there?"

It was Marie's turn to shrug. "If I must leave you..."

Charity turned her head, blinking back the tears that always seemed to be ready to spring from her eyes these days. "I think it is a good decision, Marie. Mr. Wentworth and I will get you passage on a ship. And don't worry. You shall have some money to tide you over until you can find work."

A strong, dark hand came out and covered Charity's own trembling one. The two women looked long at each other.

Chapter 10

Parting from Marie had been yet another cruel blow for Charity, and she could take small comfort from the fact that she'd done the best she could by her. She had sent her mother's maid off with papers declaring her a free woman and with most of the remaining money in the little trunk. But now she was completely alone, and she'd wept bitterly the morning of Marie's departure.

But thinking of Marie's own stern resolves for her, Charity had dried her eyes even as she'd watched the swaying figure on the seat of the small wagon fade from sight. She was coming perilously close to being a homeless spinster dependent on the Wentworths' charity, and she must think just how she could re-establish herself as an independent young member of the household.

Standing in the center of her little yellow room, Charity clenched her hands in thought. It was ten months now since her mother had died, and she felt suddenly that she had mourned long enough. Her first act would be to come out of the somber clothing she'd worn for so long.

Going through her mother's things that very afternoon, she selected a simple lavender dress for her trial run. Taking some material from the length of the full skirt, she created a ruffle at the bottom to give necessary length, and wished Marie could be here to help and give approval. Brushing aside the thought. she redid the bodice to give her the fullness she needed. When, in a few days, she completed that dress to her satisfaction, she started on one of aqua lawn she'd always admired. Both dresses were demure enough, she felt, with high necks and long sleeves and lovely flowing skirts. Trying them on in front of her mirror, she felt prettier than she had in a year, though she could see now how thin she'd become and how pale. If she was going to start trying to find a man, she'd have to do something about that.

Her next move in what she considered a deliberate campaign was to resume riding with Sally. Within days the exercise and fresh air had begun to return a bloom to her cheeks, and she found she was eating more as well. She took all of her meals with the family now, and discovered that this departure caused no comment. In fact, nothing had changed. The women continued to confine themselves to their usual requests for her to fetch this from their rooms or to see to that for Sally. As always, she continued to help Mrs. Wentworth with notes and household accounts, helped Mrs. LaRoche with needlework, which her poor eyesight sometimes made difficult, and listened quietly while all of them talked. Only now she listened, noticed, and assessed possibilities.

Once Adam Crandall had come to the house, but as soon as Charity had heard his deep voice in the hall, she'd slipped from the parlor and gone upstairs. From her window she later saw him walking with Helen down near the creek, and was amused to see Sally stalking them like one of her Indian warriors from behind bushes and trees.

The next day, as she'd sat with Sally in the sparkling morning light by the fish pond, trying to teach her the finer points of drawing a vista in perspective, she'd had trouble holding the girl's attention. Finally she gave up and, putting down her own piece of charcoal, she said, "You might as well tell me what's on your mind now, so you can stop daydreaming and finish that line of trees."

Sally grinned at her and tossed pale curls over her shoulder. "I wasn't really daydreaming. I was thinking."

"Oh, dear," said Charity in mock horror.

"If you must know," Sally turned on the bench, "I was thinking that Helen seems to have a new beau. This summer I would have bet on Joseph Hadley to win her, but now I don't think so."

"Joseph Hadley?"

"Oh Charity, don't you ever pay any attention to anything? You've seen him. The very sensible young man who has beautiful brown curls and a handsome square face. I thought he was just right for Helen, really, since he's very rich and very high-

102

minded. But now that Adam Crandall has come back, I don't see how Joseph can compete." The girl sighed. "I'd rather hoped that Adam would stay out West until Helen was safely married." Her eyes suddenly sparkled. "Then one day he would ride home, having made his fortune in great adventures, and I would be all grown up and all those girls who'd always been after him would have gone away, and he couldn't help but notice me."

Charity's mouth fell open. "You don't even know Mr. Crandall."

"I do too. We've known all the Crandalls forever. He's a great horseman. His family breed some of the best horses in Virginia. One of his own mares has won several races." She stopped, kicked at a twig on the ground, then went on, "Everyone says if he would just settle down and go into law and politics, he could one day be one of Mr. Jefferson's successors. I'm sure that's a very grand thing to be, but I don't think he'd be as much *fun* then, do you?"

"Fun?" Charity echoed.

"Yes. And he's so awfully handsome. I can see how Helen might like him. She'll probably get him too. She usually does get her own way." Sally sighed again and looked off across the gardens.

Charity followed her gaze through bright chrysanthemums and lovely fall color as she pondered this youthful view of Adam Crandall. She was sorely tempted to tell Sally what Adam was really like; that he was a rude, arrogant man who would be very apt to trample her ideal vision of him into the ground given half a chance, and that Helen was more than welcome to him as they probably deserved each other. Instead she said, "Why don't you set your sights on someone a bit closer to your own age? One of Tim's friends, perhaps. I shouldn't wonder if Adam Crandall is practically old enough to be your father."

"No, really? How old do you think he is?"

Charity shrugged. "He's probably twenty-seven or twenty-eight."

"Oooh. That old! Well, mother once said older men are more experienced."

Charity smiled at that, knowing perfectly well Sally didn't have a clue what her mother really meant. She bent again over her own sketch pad, and soon the younger girl followed suit. She wished she could stop thinking about Adam Crandall.

Several days later, Paul returned from Philadelphia looking rather like a cat cleaning his whiskers, Charity thought. Wearing what he assured them all was the very latest fashion in embroidered waistcoats, he regaled them over lunch with tales of evenings spent in taverns with the first men of the land or in the drawing rooms with the first ladies. Charity, sitting quietly unobtrusive, noticed he said nothing about the colony of people from Saint Dominque reputed to be living in the capital. He seemed absorbed with his new friends, especially some general he'd had the fortune to meet.

"General Wilkinson is newly made commander of a Fort Washington on the Ohio River. He's from Kentucky now, and knows the fortunes to be made there," Paul explained loudly over the cheese tarts and green salad. "He'll be second in command of the army going West soon, and when he is done with his campaign, the British as well as the Indians will be out of the Ohio country. There are fortunes to be made in all that rich wilderness, he says. And there is the Southwest where the Spaniards sit on the fabulous trade of the Mississippi River. Wilkinson's already controlled most American trade allowed with the Spanish-held city of New Orleans. He'll let friends help him out there, too, now that he's back in command of a legion. I've half a mind to go and see for myself."

His air of vast knowledge and smug self-importance was irritating, but Charity listened, wondering if Adam Crandall planned to make his fortune along with this General Wilkinson.

The afternoon would have been spent hearing more of Paul's adventures during a long walk, but happily Helen's Joseph Hadley, his mother, and two sisters came to call and to stay for tea. Charity and Sally had been on their way upstairs to get walking shoes when Sally spied the coach, cast aside the afternoon walk, and darted off to put on more presentable clothes. For once, Charity followed her example. Better a long afternoon in the parlor than out walking with Paul. Besides, she wished to see for herself this paragon of a young man who would be so suitable for Helen. Donning the lavender dress, she felt suddenly shy and girlish. In all her time at Wentworth, she had worn only clothes proper for mourning. Never had she deliberately dressed and done her hair to meet someone. She descended the stairs twenty minutes later on trembling legs and thought no one had even noticed her departure from her usual attire until Paul, coming across the room to her, took her arm and steered her deftly to a corner chair.

"You look charming today, Charity," he said as he seated her, appreciation lighting his swarthy features, his black eyes traveling down her dress. "Are you coming out of mourning now?"

She nodded rather tentatively. "I couldn't go on wearing those old clothes forever," she said, fearing she sounded arch.

"I'm so very glad. I went away fearing you would never emerge from your shell."

"Emerge from my shell?"

"My dear Charity, the last time I was here you scarcely even heard me if I addressed you."

"Surely I was not as bad as all that."

"Worse," he said, lifting dramatic eyes to the ceiling. Then he returned them to her face. "I wanted so much to comfort you, but you were always so unapproachable."

"I didn't mean to be that."

"And now, Charity?" Paul bent closer and his eyes took on more warmth.

Charity smiled, trying not to be repelled by his look. "I think we will become obvious in another moment." She stood up. "We'd better join the others."

The Hadleys proved to be a lively and interesting family, and Charity was more and more pleased with herself for deciding to come downstairs this afternoon. She thought the worthy Joseph a charming, if too serious, young man, and wondered why Helen held him off. However, when Joseph, looking admiringly at Charity, attempted to engage her in conversation, Helen noticed and made sure the young man's attention did not wander from her again.

After that day, Charity examined herself a bit more closely. Aware that her eyes were clearer, her skin healthier and her figure fuller, she began to take more pains with herself, spending time brushing her hair and even having Sophie experiment with new hairstyles. But for all her physical efforts, the pattern of her life remained depressingly monotonous.

Her first chance to effect a change in that pattern came when Mrs. Hadley appeared one afternoon in November and announced she was planning a party and included Charity in the invitation. The girl was so busy plotting how she would come up with a suitable dress for the occasion she nearly missed hearing Mrs. Wentworth begin her automatic rejection of the invitation on Charity's behalf. As the woman spoke of her period of mourning, Charity's head jerked up and her eyes began to snap. Not again was she going to be excluded from a chance of entertainment.

"What Mrs. Wentworth means," she cut in smoothly, smiling at Mrs. Hadley and not daring to look at the others, "is that I have been in mourning for so long I hardly have anything suitable to wear."

Mrs. Hadley smiled back. "I'm sure something can be conjured, my dear. We do not stand on great ceremony, you know. And we have far more need of a pretty new face at our gathering than we do a fancy new gown."

Charity bowed her head, blushing. "You are too kind, Mrs. Hadley. Of course I would love to come." She thought she detected a small gasp from across the room, but didn't look up. She wasn't going to let anyone intimidate her. And now there was no way they could prevent her attending her first dinner outside Wentworth Hall.

Ten days later, on the evening that Charity stepped from the Wentworth carriage and followed the others up the wide steps at Hadley, she knew she had been right. The brightly lit hall, the liveried servants, the sound of many voices in the drawing room all brought a reminiscent glow to her cheeks. Once more she was glad she had been able to make up a dress that would embarrass no one this evening. Knowing there was no time to go to Richmond and order up clothes, she had at last opened the trunk and brought out the peach-colored material she'd bought in Williamsburg long ago. Now her endless hours of listening to gossip and talk of fashions paid off too, as she created a dress she thought would be in style this season. Whether it was or not, she knew its scooped neck, puffed sleeves with tight wrists, long bodice, and gathered skirts were just right for her. The only touch that had been needed was her mother's single strand of softly glowing pearls at her neck.

It was a large gathering that the Wentworth party joined a few moments later. Charity felt a small thrill of anticipation as she scanned the room from behind the other ladies. There seemed to be a number of young men here, and she wondered how many of them were already spoken for. Appraisingly she eyed a tall, thin-faced man in a rich brown coat whose air of intelligence attracted her, and smiled at herself for looking over the room as though she were judging horse flesh. Then suddenly the man's companion turned to see the newcomers and she started as she met Adam Crandall's piercing eyes. Forced now to greet the two young men by the mantel, she kept her eyes fastened on Adam's immaculately folded neckcloth, thinking irrelevantly of the curling chest hair it concealed, and nodded her head curtly. Only when she was turned to his friend did she look up and smile in acknowledgment of her introduction.

"Mr. Harrison," she said, extending her hand and turning as far as she could from Adam.

The young man's long face split into a boyish grin. "Miss Ashton," he returned, bowing. "I had heard that Wentworth Hall was hiding a lovely new flower, but no one told me it was a blossom of such perfection."

Charity blushed, not knowing how to respond to such an extravagant compliment, but William Harrison, keeping hold of her hand, covered her confusion by leading her away and chatting lightly about activities expected this season in Richmond. She was very pleased when she discovered she was to be his dinner partner and he escorted her to the long, gleaming table where crystal and silver were set for twenty-four.

Thanks to the attention of her escort on one side and of Joseph Hadley on the other, Charity had the first really good time she'd had in well over a year. The delicious and abundant food, the sparkling conversation, and the elegant company transported her far from the dreariness of her present life, and put a new color in her cheeks. When Bill Harrison, brushing long fingers through the high shock of dark hair above his forehead, told her he was down from Philadelphia on just a short visit, and looking at her meaningfully, added it was a great pity, she felt half drunk on the heady wine of appreciation.

"I'll hate to leave Virginia more than ever," Harrison declared gallantly, "but there's a war to be fought in the West, and I'm off to join General Wayne after the new year."

Charity's eyes widened. "A war?"

"Well, a campaign, really. Against the Indians. Surely you heard about General Arthur St. Clair's terrible defeat a year ago in the Ohio country."

Charity shook her head.

"A massacre it was. The Indian confederation, under Chief Little Turtle, destroyed our western army in one dawn attack. The settlers are in a terrified uproar, and Congress has appointed Mad Anthony Wayne to head up another army and finish this business once and for all. Wayne's drilling his troops in Pittsburgh right now, and we hope to march on the Indians next summer."

Charity had heard of Pittsburgh, a rough frontier settlement somewhere beyond the reaches of the civilized world of the East. But looking at the light in Bill Harrison's eyes, she forbore to say anything, asking him instead about his role in the coming campaign. In so doing she earned his undying admiration and friendship, for he was eager for a willing ear.

107

The ladies' conversation in the parlor after dinner was very dull fare after all she'd heard about the war hero, Anthony Wayne, and about the wild country of the Ohio. Charity found it hard to sit still and smile at the inane chatter. Her ears were straining for the sound of masculine feet at the door and gruff voices talking of more interesting things. But when the men did join them she was disappointed to discover they had laid aside their masculine subjects in deference to the ladies. Helen, flanked by Adam Crandall and another young man, showed annoyance when Bill Harrison and Joseph Hadley sought Charity out again. Some subtle manoeuvering brought both young men to her side very shortly. In the past, Charity would have been wryly amused at Helen's tactics. But tonight she'd been having fun, and she found her annoyance growing.

Her temper wasn't improved when Adam detached himself from Helen's circle and came to her side. Offering his hand, he said jovially, "Charity, there's someone here you haven't yet met, and I'm sure you'll both be charmed." Giving her no time to reply, he lifted her from her chair, then said in an undertone, "I feel sure you will find his conversation more stimulating than that of these hens." His eyes twinkled, and in spite of herself, Charity gave him a grateful look.

Across the room a small knot of men had gathered around a tall, angular figure lounging in a deep armchair. Charity noted with relief that Mrs. Hadley was also in the group and was nodding a welcome as the two approached. Talk stopped as Adam led Charity across the deep carpet, and the lounging man pulled himself to his feet.

"Mr. Jefferson, allow me to present Miss Charity Ashton. Charity, this is our Secretary of State, Mr. Thomas Jefferson."

Charity's eyes flew wide as the tall man bowed his head over her hand. "Mr. Jefferson, I have so admired all I've heard about you here in Virginia," she said rather breathlessly. "It is an honor to meet you."

"The honor is mine, Miss Ashton," Jefferson returned, looking at her with an appreciative twinkle in his eye. "I perceive you are not a native of this great state. Come, sit here with us and tell me which French colony has had the misfortune to lose you."

The girl flushed as he seated her beside Mrs. Hadley and she realized all eyes were upon her. But Jefferson left her no time to be embarrassed. Resuming his casual position across from her, he led her immediately into talk of Saint Dominque and the slave uprising, and from there to the French Revolution. Soon they were in a lively discussion of the philosophic principles behind revolution and reform. It was a heady and stimulating experience, and she couldn't remember a time when she had enjoyed herself so much.

At one point a young man whose name she hadn't caught waxed lyrical over the victories of the American army in the War for Independence and expounded on the benefits of freedom that were produced. When he finally paused for breath, Jefferson gave him a wry smile. "You sound much too cheerful about war, Jenkins. There's nothing wonderful about it, and it should never be entered into lightly. You young men can't remember what it was really like."

"And they contemplate the next war with such enthusiasm," Charity exclaimed, then flushed as Mr. Jefferson turned to her with an inquiring arch to his eyebrow. "Mr. Harrison has been telling me of General Wayne's coming expedition," she explained hastily.

"Ah. William Henry Harrison is bound to make a name for himself out in the wilderness. But it won't be fun." Jefferson smiled. "That will be a messy campaign, if the defeat of two of our generals in the Ohio country tells us anything."

"We shouldn't even have to risk another defeat," put in Adam. "If the British would give up the towns, like Detroit, and the trading posts as they bound themselves to do by treaty, the Indians wouldn't have the British encouragement and supplies to continue their warfare."

"The British will be made to abandon their posts ... in time, Crandall." Jefferson shrugged. "But the settlers need protection from the marauding Indians now." He stopped and glanced up as Mrs. Hadley stirred, then rose from her seat.

Clasping her hands as the men stood, she reminded them all regretfully of her duties as hostess. "We mustn't monopolize Mr. Jefferson, you know," she smiled. "Others will want the benefit of his invigorating wit, too." And rising, she led the famous man down the room.

The group soon broke up and Charity suddenly found herself alone, looking up at Adam's dark gray eyes.

"You've looked positively blooming tonight, Miss Ashton," he said with a slight bow and took the chair nearest her.

Smiling, Charity dropped her eyes. "It has been a lovely evening," she murmured. Then looked at him. "I've so enjoyed meeting Mr. Jefferson. Thank you for that."

"I knew you would. And you needn't thank me. He would

have insisted on meeting the prettiest girl in the room sooner or later."

"Your flattery is outrageous, Mr. Crandall."

"Not at all. And, Charity, I do approve of that dress." His eyes lingered for just a moment on the low neckline.

She stiffened, but he took no notice. Smiling at her, he went on. "You know, I've never seen you in anything but dark clothes, and I had only suspected what a dress with color might do for you."

Charity sighed. "As usual, Mr. Crandall, you are going beyond the bounds of propriety to talk to me of my clothing."

At that Adam laughed outright. "Don't you know by now that I'm seldom inside the bounds of propriety, Charity? For that matter, you're a bit beyond the bounds yourself, wearing that dress when your year of mourning has still two weeks to go."

Charity sputtered. "Why, you ..."

Still laughing, Adam caught her hand. "Come, come, Charity. You should live up to your name for a change. We should be in charity with one another on such a nice evening, and should celebrate your coming out of mourning."

The girl tugged her hand away, but made no move to rise. Adam sat back and contemplated her still form. "There, you see. It isn't so hard. You haven't gone off in a pet, so I assume I'm being given another chance."

Charity looked up from beneath thick lashes as a small smile tugged at the corners of her full lips. "You really are the most outrageous man."

"Of course I am. That's why you have stayed here and not returned to the perfect manners of those dull good ladies and the, for the most part, equally boring but well-mannered men."

"There's nothing boring about Mr. Jefferson. Or Mr. Harrison, for that matter."

"True." Adam leaned toward her now, and fastened his eyes on her face. "But they don't share our memories of a sea voyage."

Charity's eyes flew open. She knew perfectly well just what part of that sea voyage he was referring to, and she stopped herself from slapping him only just in time.

Watching her struggle for control, Adam laughed once more. "I'm right, aren't I, Charity? You remember just as I do. It's too bad I'm not the marrying kind, and have no desire to woo you for a year."

"You are abominable," Charity hissed and stood up, trembling with anger.

Adam, on his feet too, laughed again. Taking hold of her wrist, he held her beside him. "I won't woo you because I won't wait a year for you, Charity."

Practically spitting with rage, Charity jerked her hand away. "A lifetime, Mr. Crandall. You will wait a lifetime. And I would count it my good fortune if I were never to see you again."

"But you will see me again, dear. And you won't go off in a huff from me now. You don't want to embarrass our hostess or give reason for gossip."

His words brought the girl's head up. Carefully she averted her face from the rest of the room. "I hate you," she said with a tight smile.

"That's better. And now give me your arm and I shall lead you decorously down the room."

Turning on wooden feet, Charity moved at his side. Once before, Adam Crandall had taken advantage of her. How much more vulnerable she was now, alone, living on the Wentworths' charity. She must be very careful not to let men think she was easy prey. Straightening her shoulders, she forced a smile on her stiff lips as they approached the others. No one must know of the turmoil and anger inside her.

Chapter 11

The Christmas season came and went with no more sign of Adam Crandall, and Charity wondered if he was making ready to go off to the Ohio country again. She was sorry to see William Harrison leave in the new year. He had been a source of support at the parties she now attended, where she'd known no one but Helen. And Helen was not about to go out of her way to help Charity socially.

Remembering her first party at the Hadleys', Charity was careful always to act with the utmost propriety. If she was to find a husband to set her free from her bondage at Wentworth, she must have no hint of gossip connected with her name. Never mind that constant propriety became boring in the extreme.

Perhaps it was because she was being so careful that she began to view Paul LaRoche with some alarm. She would have had to be dim-witted not to realize that the man was paying her rather marked attention.

One evening at a large informal gathering where a fiddler made everyone dance to the point of overheating, Paul, who had very haughtily cut out her former partner, took Charity's arm and led her to the hall to cool off. Escape from the heat was a welcome thought, but Charity would not have gone if she hadn't spied Adam Crandall walking in their direction. Once outside the room, Paul took her arm and steered her toward the library. As they passed behind the tall staircase, he turned to her.

"Do you remember that evening in Saint Dominque, Charity? The evening of our small ball?"

Charity's eyes clouded with memories.

"No, not all that happened after, *ma belle,* but the ball itself. Never had you looked so beautiful, so desirable. You were just becoming a woman. In a few months, all the Plaine du Nord would have been at your feet."

Charity made a small sound, demurring. She groped for a way to break into Paul's train of thought.

"I could hardly take my eyes off you then, Charity. And now, in the months since I returned you've grown to be like that beautiful girl again. Only you are more beautiful than ever, more..."

Light footsteps sounded in the hall behind them. Charity drew back as Helen rounded the corner. The girl was alone and Charity wondered if she had left the party just to ferret out clandestine meetings.

"Well!" Helen's eyes were slits.

Paul turned at the voice and his thin face lit in an unctuous smile. She looked coolly at him and then stared at Charity. In a positively sugary tone she said, "Sneaking off under the stairs is a servant's trick in the United States, Charity. Perhaps you didn't know that where you come from."

Charity returned Helen's stare, her eyes kindling at the spiteful words. The relief she had felt at the interruption of Paul's words disappeared in a wave of dislike. "Where I come from young ladies do not interrupt private conversations. But perhaps you don't know that in the United States." Moving smoothly to Paul's side she took his arm. "Paul and I were reminiscing about old times at home." She dimpled up at him. "Weren't we, Paul?"

Paul was apparently at a loss for words and Charity saw he would be of no help. So she turned him deftly and steered him back down the hall, leaning toward him in what she hoped looked like a confidential manner.

It was highly satisfactory to leave Helen in stupefied fury behind her. But she wished her escort were nearly anyone but Paul. She could take no pleasure in leading *him* away from Helen.

And the next day he seemed to be back in Helen's good graces, though Charity was not to be forgiven so easily. Helen spoke to her only when absolutely necessary, a punishment Charity welcomed.

It wouldn't be long before the coolness between the girls was noticed, and Charity was sure quiet speculation was going on. She wondered only what Helen would do next. Her answer was not long in coming.

She and Sally were walking near the house through the late winter wood one dreary morning when Sally suddenly wrinkled her nose and looked sideways at her companion. "Mama says I mustn't repeat things I hear. She also says I mustn't ask personal questions all the time."

"Very good advice," approved Charity, knowing Sally was about to ignore both strictures. She wondered what the subject would be.

"But *you* don't mind if I ask you things, do you?" Seeing Charity's smile, Sally giggled. "Is it true that you were very wild and wicked when you were younger?" She was amazed to see her beautiful friend's blue-green eyes spark with anger before the lashes were lowered and a smile curved the full mouth.

"Whoever said such a thing?"

Sally felt vaguely that she shouldn't tell. "*Tante* Hélène," she answered reluctantly.

"Ah..." Charity shrugged. "Mrs. LaRoche did not approve, perhaps, of my riding horses in boys' clothing when I was

113

young. Or of the fact my father took me everywhere and taught me the business of our estates."

"Did you *really* ride in boys' clothes? Oh, how I should like that."

Charity grinned at her charge. "Yes, sometimes, and it was much more fun than wearing the riding habits I must now don. I suppose that does make me very wild and wicked."

"No, I don't think that is why you were supposed to be wicked. *Tante* says you made friends with the slaves, and were seen often with your overseer's son. I think perhaps she was warning Mama of my playing with Benjamin, Cook's son."

Charity's mind was whirling as she answered absently. "Yes, perhaps that was her reason for saying such things about me."

Sally nodded and they returned to the house in silence.

Not for a moment did Charity think Mrs. LaRoche's motives for gossip were only to protect Sally, but she wondered what they really were as she climbed the stairs to change her clothes for the noon meal. Standing before her mirror she tugged at the bow behind her head and stared at her reflection. She was aware that neighbors had considered her a bit wild on Saint Dominque. Her father had allowed her such freedom, and had insisted she had every right to any education she wanted. Learning business was not considered proper for a young lady of her station—but it could hardly be called wicked. Then she remembered Mrs. LaRoche's words about being seen with Jacques.

She pulled the ribbon off with a snap as her eyes kindled. That mean-minded woman was implying that her behavior had been improper. But never, until that *vaudun* ceremony in the hills, had there been an improper gesture between Jacques and herself. What was the woman's game? She removed her heavy dress and stood still in her shift. Her full breasts swelled against the thin material, and she remembered Paul's eyes resting on them too often recently. Paul. Of course. Mrs. LaRoche was worried that Paul might be enamored of the poor orphan girl, and might not make an advantageous marriage. A sardonic chuckle escaped her. How paper-brained the woman was to think anyone with half a mind would fall in love with her foppish, self-important son. She wondered now what else was being said about her and tossed her head defiantly as she slipped into the demure aqua lawn gown.

Her curiosity was to be satisfied, at least in part, that very afternoon when Sally sought her out in the library where she'd thought to escape in a romantic novel.

Plunking herself down in a tall wing chair opposite her friend, Sally waited till Charity looked up. "I'm bored," she announced.

"Then find a good book to read." Charity waved toward the dark shelves around the walls.

"I don't feel like reading," Sally pouted. Then she brightened. "Tell me why you and Helen aren't speaking."

"Whatever gave you the idea we weren't speaking?"

"Oh, I've noticed. And anyway, I heard Mama and Helen talking yesterday."

"Oh?" Charity pretended interest in her book.

"Well, I didn't hear much. But Helen seemed to be pretty angry with you. And Mama said they must find a suitable man and marry you off. Mama seemed to think that even Mr. Breame might do."

"Mr. Breame!" Charity was startled out of her pretense at reading.

Sally giggled. "Imagine! But he's said to have come from a perfectly respectable, if poor, family in Richmond."

Charity thought of the shy and unctuous little tutor who appeared five mornings a week to teach Tim, and she would have laughed if she hadn't been so appalled. She managed to keep her voice light, though, as she said, "I should hope I might do a bit better than Mr. Breame."

"Oh, much better. I don't think he'd be much fun to marry." Then the girl smiled slyly. "Maybe *that's* why Helen's mad at you. You could do so much better. You're going to parties now, and I'll bet the men are swarming around you, and she's jealous."

"Sally. What a ridiculous way to talk."

"But I'm sure it's true. I've seen Paul looking at you. And even Joseph Hadley and Jim."

"Sally! You're imagining things."

"No, I'm not. And if *I've* seen them, Helen has. Yes, I'm sure that's it. And I'm sure she'd like to see you married to that stuffy Mr. Breame and safely out of the way. Though perhaps," the girl added thoughtfully, "they'd let you marry someone nicer."

Let me marry someone nicer indeed, Charity thought, and thumped her book on the table beside her.

Sally seemed not to have noticed Charity's scowl. "I think

Adam Crandall would be much more fun and much nicer for you."

"Who?" Charity's composure threatened to break completely.

"Well, you pointed out that he's too old for *me*. He's so magnificent, though," she added dreamily. "And you're very beautiful." Her innocent eyes appraised Charity. "He's never interested in anyone who isn't beautiful, I hear. You'd make the handsomest couple in the county. Don't you think you could like him?"

Charity choked. "No," she said shortly. The room seemed stifling to her of a sudden. Quickly she stood up. "I'm going for a walk."

"Oh, good." Sally bounced up as Charity swept from the room. "Let's go see father's new horse," she called.

With narrowed eyes, Charity appraised the group at dinner. Had Mrs. Turner or Mrs. Hadley been exposed yet to Mrs. LaRoche's gossip? She would not put it past Helen to make sure it had reached their ears. But surely Mrs. Hadley at least would see it for the idle gossip it was, and would not enjoin her son to avoid the Wentworths' guest. She looked across the table at the subject of her thoughts and found warm brown eyes resting on her face. She lowered her own and wondered about Joseph Hadley.

Helen, while keeping Joseph on the string, was certainly casting her eyes over the field these past months. And Joseph, who at first had exhibited signs of jealousy, seemed now to have accepted the situation. Tonight, for instance, Helen was practically whispering in Adam Crandall's ear and Joseph paid no attention. It was too bad Joseph was so very serious, Charity reflected, but perhaps if she knew him better...

Continuing her speculation, Charity looked up at the table at Paul. She had been amused, even while repelled, to see that although he danced attendance on Helen and her friends, he could hardly keep his eyes off Charity. It must annoy Helen no end. My, how hard I've become, she thought, and ended her ruminations as the next course arrived and she realized she'd neglected old Mr. Turner at her side.

After dinner, when the men joined them in the parlor, Charity exerted herself to be agreeable to Joseph. They talked of horses and of the spring planting and even of books, but after half an hour Charity realized it might take more than a few chats to find the humor in the man. Pompous was too harsh a word for him, but she did wonder if he ever unbent. So it was with something like relief that she saw Helen and Adam bear down upon them.

"More reminiscences about old times on the tropical isle?" Helen asked as she came up to the chairs where Charity and Joseph sat apart.

Charity smiled sweetly. "Mr. Hadley and I were discussing his library. I gather he has some priceless volumes." Her big eyes turned admiringly to Joseph, who beamed. She knew how little Helen cared for priceless volumes.

"Oh." Helen sighed dramatically. "I thought perhaps you were explaining the caste system in Saint Dominque and telling of your friendship with the mulattoes. I'm sure Adam and I would have been fascinated."

Charity threw a quick glance at Joseph, whose face was registering shock at Helen's words. Spiteful witch, she thought, but kept her smile in place. Sea green eyes widened in innocence. "Oh, I'm learning that so much is different in Virginia," she purred. "And I do hope Mr. Hadley will continue to instruct me in the ways of his people." A dazzling smile was turned on the nonplussed Mr. Hadley.

Feeling himself sinking into the pools of her eyes, Joseph began to stammer. "M-m-most happy to instruct you any time, Miss Ashton." Then he blushed crimson.

Charity turned back to Helen. Smiling radiantly, she looked into blazing eyes above her. "Isn't that nice of him?" She saw Helen's hand tighten convulsively on Adam's arm and smiled even more broadly. Adam's eyes were hooded, but a muscle at the corner of his mouth was twitching.

"I'm sure you'll spare Mr. Hadley the necessity of beginning your education now," Helen snapped. Still clutching Adam's arm, she held out a round, white hand. "Come, Mr. Hadley. I'm convinced you will prefer to hear Katharine Wainwright sing for us."

Joseph looked acutely uncomfortable as he glanced from one lovely girl to the other. He stood up. "I'm sure Miss Ashton..."

Adam moved then. Gently disengaging his arm, he held up a hand. "No need to worry about Miss Ashton, Hadley. I'll see she has company while you listen to the singing."

Charity enjoyed watching Helen turn nearly scarlet at his defection. But there was nothing the furious girl could do now but take Joseph's proffered arm and march stiffly away with him.

Heavens, Charity thought as she watched them go, I'm not only becoming hard, I'm becoming positively catty.

"Bravo, Charity."

She'd forgotten Adam, and his soft voice made her jump. She started to dimple, then thought better of it.

Adam sat down in Joseph's abandoned chair. "The Caribbean rose has gotten her thorns back, I see."

"What a very odd thing to say." Charity let her eyes rove past him in an insulting manner. Paul was down the room, pretending to listen to Miss Wainwright sing, but his eyes met hers.

"And what is your fertile little brain working on now?" Adam was amused as he followed her gaze. "Surely nothing to do with your dandified countryman."

Charity looked slowly at the tall man sitting so near her, and tried to keep from comparing him to the others in the room. "I can't imagine what you mean," she said and fluttered her lashes.

"Oh, come, Charity. You needn't practice your coquettish airs on me. Besides, they don't become you."

Charity's eyes flew open. "*Will* you stop telling me what becomes me?"

Adam chuckled. "That's more my Charity."

"I am *not* your Charity." She practically jumped from her chair.

"Yes, do let's go for a stroll." Adam was up before she could move, and his firm grip guided her toward the nearest door. "You don't want to add to your reputation by hitting me in front of everyone down there."

As they passed through the door, Charity tugged her arm free. "What do you mean, 'add to my reputation'?"

Adam smiled down on her and caught her wrist. "Surely you're aware the good ladies of this house are not enamored of your charms." He was steering her down the hall now, rushing her past the open door of the game room.

She tried to pull away, but his hold was tight. Deftly he pushed her into the library and quietly closed the door. He released her then and she moved away quickly, crossing to the fireplace where a small fire flickered brightly and two tall candles burned on the flanking tables.

Adam watched her go with narrowed eyes. Even from behind she was beautiful. Those masses of amber-colored waves rippling down her slender back toward that tiny, supple waist...A wave of desire threatened to overtake him but he fought it down. He wasn't going to lose control with her again. "Do you know how long I've waited to finally get you alone?"

Before the fire, Charity turned. "You were about to explain about my adding to my reputation," she said in a cold voice.

Adam frowned, then waved a languid hand. "The ladies will gossip, my girl."

"Oh, will they?" He moved toward her and she backed a step. "Since I appear to be the subject of that gossip, and since you are rude enough to refer to it, you will now be so good as to tell me what the ladies are saying."

"If I give you that information, what will you give me in return?" He was close enough now for Charity to see the gray eyes were dancing.

"What an insufferable man you are."

"You repeat yourself, my dear."

"Only for lack of a stronger vocabulary."

Adam laughed aloud. "Charity, you're wonderful. Very well then, I will tell you that they are hinting of wild doings in your past. Something, I believe, about an overseer's son."

Charity's eyes closed in angry frustration. This was Helen's work, she felt sure. Mrs. LaRoche was ambitious, even calculating, and had certainly given the fuel for the gossip fires. But only Helen was malicious enough to be sure that everyone heard anything bad to be reported.

So, thought Adam, the tales must be true. Our Caribbean beauty becomes more interesting by the moment. He reached out and grasped a slender hand.

Charity drew back, but her hand remained trapped. Willing herself not to tremble, she looked up at him with bright eyes. "Evidently you enjoy the gossip of idle women."

"Mine was an unwilling ear. But I confess I do enjoy any information I can get about you."

"The feeling is not reciprocated," Charity snapped, and tugged again at her hand. "The only information about you that I would enjoy receiving would be that you were leaving for the West."

"Alas. I do not plan to travel at all, yet."

"Yet? Then there is something that would change your mind and make you leave for distant lands?"

Adam caught her other hand. "Yes, Charity, there is."

"Then may I wish you Godspeed in finding it so that you won't linger in Virginia longer."

Adam threw back his head and laughed. "If you weren't so well-bred, I'd swear you were a fishwife."

"I neither know nor care about your breeding, sir," Charity lied, "but you certainly have the manners of the common sailor I once thought you were."

"So you did." Adam pulled her a step toward him. "That does bring back memories, Miss Ashton."

Charity tore her eyes from his and sought to quench her body's recollection of his embrace. He pulled her hands up to his chest and she tried to push him away. "Adam, please." Even through his waistcoat she could feel the hard muscles of his chest against her fingers. There was so much power there and she felt suddenly helpless.

He was very still. "Do you know that's the first time you've ever said my name, Charity?"

She shook her head and tried once more to free her hands.

"Charity, look at me." His deep voice held command again. She felt her strength draining from her as though he were truly a magnet. Slowly she lifted her head.

As his mouth covered hers, the shock went through her entire body. Slowly, insistently, he kissed her, still holding her hands. Her fingers began to curl against his chest and her legs trembled. She thought she'd suffocate if he didn't release her. The grip tightened on her fingers, and then his lips were in her hair. She drew a shuddering breath as he kissed her temple.

"Charity, why don't you come with me?"

His voice was husky and Charity thought she'd mistaken the words. She turned her head to look at him, but his mouth came down on hers again. The months of anger, grief, and loneliness began to slip away as her lips responded. When at last he raised his head, Adam's eyes were clouded. She put up her hands to touch the strong planes of his face. She felt as though she were in a trance and she abandoned herself to it.

"Come with me," he repeated, his voice under control again.

"Come with you where?" she whispered.

He kissed her again and then let her go. This was more like it. With a sweep of his arm he indicated the spaces beyond the long windows. "West. To the Ohio country, to Kentucky, perhaps to Natchez and New Orleans." Her eyes glittered and he went on quickly. "Do you remember last fall when I first came to Wentworth and talked about the western country?" She nodded. "I saw how you looked then. You'd like to see it, wouldn't you?" She nodded again, speech beyond her. Adam moved to the fire and looked down. "There's nothing for you here." Then he glanced at her, a smile tugging the corners of his mobile mouth. She watched in fascination, drinking in his features, remembering his gentleness. "Unless of course you've lost your heart to one of the worthy young men here."

She smiled glowingly then.

Adam spread his hands. "You're unique, Charity. You're one of the most beautiful women I've ever seen, and you have more courage than most men. We could have adventures together, you and I."

Charity found her voice at last. "Are you asking me to marry you, Adam Crandall?" She was surprised at the pounding of her heart. She'd thought to make a marriage of convenience, one that would set her free of this house, but one that would also be uncomplicated by the question of love. But now she found the magnetic attraction of this man something beyond her powers and wondered if love was a word for what she felt at this moment. She watched, breathless, as one black brow went up and a furrow appeared in the broad forehead.

"I would always see you were cared for, Charity."

For the space of a heartbeat there was total silence in the room. "Always..." Charity's knees felt weak and she grasped the back of a wing chair. "What does that mean?" she asked in a strangled voice.

"It means just what I said." Adam was impatient. Surely this fiery girl who'd learned about men from her mulatto friend and heaven knew who else on her tropical island, understood. But her pale face registered total incomprehension. A kernel of doubt imbedded itself in his mind, but he pushed it away. Damn, he should not have let her go just now. She'd been trembling in his arms. If he could kiss her again...He shrugged. "If we ever get tired of each other, I won't abandon you, if that's what worries you. I'll see you're well situated somewhere."

Charity's eyes were so enormous they seemed to swallow her face. "You're asking me to be your mistress?" Her voice rose a notch and nearly broke.

"Perhaps you'd prefer another word."

Charity shivered. Her body had turned to ice, and now her voice did the same. "No, that word does very well. You are a low, despicable..."

"Come, come, Charity." Adam moved toward her. "I told you I wasn't the marrying kind. But I will take care of you.

You needn't fear for the future. And think of the good times..."

"Good times!" Charity spat. "Don't touch me." Her voice was very low and very commanding. Adam stopped, surprised. "I feel as though reptiles have been crawling on me where you touched me. You are the vilest..."

"Excuse *us!*"

Charity whirled in her place and nearly broke into hysterical laughter. It was so fitting that Helen would come into the room just now. But she managed to hang on to her dignity as she saw Joseph Hadley at the girl's elbow.

Helen's eyes were narrowed, appraising the situation. Obviously this was no lovers' tryst. She relaxed and prepared to enjoy the discomposure of her rival.

But neither Charity nor Adam said anything. As the silence lengthened, Joseph cleared his throat. "Ah, we were coming to search for cards. Sorry to interrupt." He looked unhappily at Charity.

"Not at all, Mr. Hadley." Charity's voice was steady and melodious. No one, least of all Adam Crandall, was going to see her soul-searing embarrassment.

Helen advanced into the room then. "Well, we'll find those cards, and then we hope to organize some games of whist." She looked invitingly at Adam.

Charity lifted her head higher. Compelling her legs to move gracefully, she went to Joseph's side and smiled up at him. "That sounds like a wonderful idea," she said and smiled more broadly when a look of gratitude sprang into the young man's eyes.

Chapter 12

Sitting at the card table with Joseph, Katharine, and Paul, Charity laughed and chattered gaily, pleased to see both men hanging on her every word. She played her cards swiftly and well, clapping when she was victorious and congratulating the others when she was not.

"Oh, Mr. Hadley, that was a brilliant move," she flattered. "I can see I will need lessons to keep up with you."

The man leaned across the table earnestly. "Please call me Joseph, Miss Ashton."

"Why, thank you...Joseph." She dimpled at him reflecting that the memory of finding her in the library alone with Adam must be already dimming. "And you must call me Charity."

They smiled benignly on each other, ignoring the scowl on Paul's face and the pink in Katharine's cheeks. Never, Charity was thinking, never will I let that awful man see what he did to me. Never will I let any of them see anything. And no one will ever make a fool of me again.

Her rage sustained her through the evening, even allowing her to nod graciously at Adam Crandall as he took his leave. She reveled in the perplexed look in his eyes, and kept her own opaquely blank.

Not until she was in her room did she allow the great knot in her stomach to uncoil. But the flood of tears was over almost as soon as it began. With hard eyes she stood at her window, watching the last carriage disappear down the curving drive.

"They will not beat me," she said softly. "Not those old cats, not Helen, not that awful man with his low proposal. I will get away from them somehow, even if I have to run away." A picture of her father flashed through her mind. She must truly be his daughter, determined to take on a new world and the wrath of the people in it to get what she wanted. But he had known that all he wanted was Émilie Tournay. If only she could be sure of just what she wanted.

As spring drew on, Charity watched with satisfaction the growing astonishment of the ladies of the household. Never again, she had vowed, and she intended to keep that vow.

Taking care to dress fashionably at all times, and keeping her smile intact, she drew slowly and carefully away from her former life of subservience and apathy. Though she continued with Sally's studies, went on riding with both younger Wentworths, and helped the master of the house on the rare occasions he asked, to the ladies she was polite but more distant. Fewer evenings were spent in their company and with greater difficulty did they find her when they wanted her to run an errand.

Methodically, she set about making herself agreeable to everyone she met. Grimly aware now of the gossip that was spread about her, she determined to counteract it, and began to cross off those who obviously were swayed by it. She had decided that she had until summer's end to play this game. If she hadn't snared a man by then, she would somehow strike out on her own. Not another winter would she spend in this house.

Attempts to combine Sally's lessons with Tim's and thus throw Charity together with Mr. Breame were met with firm, if smiling, resistance. She was definitely hunting bigger game. Rarely did she allow herself to think of her humiliation at the hands of Adam Crandall. And if the memory of strong arms around her and of a safe feeling returned she would push it away with the thought that there were other men who would hold her, other arms in which to feel safe.

She faced Adam coolly when she had to, but observed only the most basic rules of civilized behavior with him. The continued perplexity in his eyes gave her grim satisfaction, but soon that look became too bright, and she thought often his breath was too heavy with brandy. She made sure their meetings were the briefest possible despite the fact that he seemed to be at Wentworth more than ever.

It was not long before this last fact was remarked on by the youngest member of the household. She and Sally were riding one May morning, and Charity was about to exclaim over the heavy-blossomed trees on the road when the girl tossed her head and sighed. "I do wish you liked Adam." A shrug was her only answer and she went on pensively. "Helen is practically crowing over her success with him, you know. She seems to think she'll have the famous Adam Crandall in her snare by summer."

Charity smiled enigmatically, wishing Helen well of the man. She thought they deserved each other.

"He comes all the time, and he sits with Helen when she works it so he has no choice, but I've seen his eyes follow you, Charity." She turned her head. Charity heard the steady clop of hooves behind them at the same moment. "In fact," went on Sally brightly, "I see him following in person."

Adam reached them just as Charity was turning her horse on the verge of the road. "Ah, ladies." His smile was lazy. "I felt I couldn't let you go off unescorted on this fine morning. No telling who this good weather might bring out on the roads."

"But we ride alone all the time," said Sally, grinning in her pleasure at having him act the gallant.

"We have no need of an escort, thank you, Mr. Crandall. We were just returning." Charity guided her horse past his.

"But we just came out," sputtered Sally.

Charity drew rein and looked over her shoulder at the two. "I'm sorry, dear, but I find my head is simply splitting. Perhaps Mr. Crandall will be so good as to keep you company if you will ride nearer the house."

Adam had a funny quirk to his mouth as he bowed to Sally. "My pleasure, Miss Wentworth. It is too bad we will not have the company of your lovely friend, but we'll contrive to make do, won't we?"

Sally, flushed with absolute pleasure, barely remembered to hope that Charity's headache would go away soon. Then she and Adam turned once again to trot off down the road. Charity heaved a sigh and went back to the stables. She'd have liked an invigorating ride today, but now there was nothing for it but to go upstairs for an hour until her supposed headache and Adam Crandall had both disappeared.

* * *

Joseph Hadley was probably the best prospect she had at the moment, Charity thought, though James Henshaw and one or two others might be promising. She sat very still as Sophie did her hair, and ticked off names in her head. A warm breeze ruffled the chintz curtains and the late sunlight bounced on the window ledge. Charity watched the dancing light and began to review her wardrobe.

"There, Miss Charity. Now don't that look fine?"

Charity held up a hand mirror and surveyed the soft mass of hair artfully piled on top of her head. Loose golden coils hung down her back and stray waves of yellow escaped before her ears. She smiled up at Sophie. "Well done. Thank you." She tapped a finger on the mirror. "I think the deep rose dress tonight, Sophie."

"Oh, yes." The girl clapped. "You ain't never worn that one, Miss Charity."

Charity thought of her pleasure when she bought the silk material in Williamsburg so long ago. Knowing that she really had Adam's approval in mind when she bought it, Charity had been slow to make it up. And then had let it hang untouched after the vile man had shown he was worthy of nothing but her deepest contempt. But tonight at the Hadleys', there would be such a large assemblage, she wanted to look her very best.

When she descended the stairs a few minutes later she received instant confirmation of her hopes. Paul's eyes gleamed as he looked at her and he threw one hand over his heart, bowing dramatically. Ignoring his offered arm, she smiled at him and went on to the parlor where the others waited. She had avoided being alone with Paul these past weeks, not wanting any more of his imaginative memories. And she had been amused to see his mother relax as the great threat of Charity's lure seemed to abate. The girl wished Mrs. LaRoche knew that she too hoped for his marriage, for his leering black eyes were disquieting and unappealing.

Helen's expression when she entered the room helped to bolster Charity's confidence. This evening the voluptuous girl wore royal blue, which was very becoming, but perhaps a bit bright for her full figure.

As Helen's eyes scanned the flowing rose silk, dipping low to reveal the tops of swelling breasts, narrowing to the small waist and swirling softly around long legs, she could not conceal the flash of envy and dislike that appeared. With a petulant look, she turned away and focused on Paul. "Why, don't you look handsome tonight, cousin."

Paul bowed and Charity wondered that he didn't split his tight silk breeches. She eyed his carefully arranged hair and the intricate folds of his neck cloth thinking he might pass these vanities off in Saint Dominque, but in this young, less formal country they looked very close to ridiculous. Her own taste was simple, preferring the perfection of line and form and color to the use of embellishment. Through her mind flashed the image of elegantly simple attire on a perfect male form. With a light sigh she pushed the picture away. Adam Crandall may be one of the best-looking men she'd ever seen, but his character was as black and twisted as the lowest villain. She thought instead of Joseph's somber, expensive clothes and his brown curling hair.

Hadley House looked as lovely as Charity had ever seen it. Spring blossoms graced every room and their heavenly scent filled the air. All was beautifully arranged, every need anticipated, every desire for a beautiful evening fulfilled. The rooms were aglow with the color of elegant clothing and jewels. Laughter surrounded the whole and gaiety was in the air.

Charity drew a deep breath as she relinquished her wrap to an immaculate servant and followed her party to the door of the main parlor.

Immediately Mrs. Hadley was beside them, kissing her friends and admiring Helen's good looks this evening. As they pased through the door their hostess smiled at Charity.

"You will make us all half sick with envy tonight, Charity. You will have to take pity on the other girls and unhand some of the gentlemen to do their duty by them. Ah...I see my son has already spied your entrance. Will he reach your side before James, who seems about to knock over the furniture to get here?" She dimpled merrily, tapped Charity's arm and turned to greet new arrivals.

"Charity, I thought you'd..."

"Charity, how good..."

She twinkled at the two young men charging down upon her, and held a hand out to each. Her arms were captured by both and she was led down the room laughing and talking to them by turn. They were nearly to the table where servants guarded crystal bowls of punch when a pair of steel gray eyes caught hers.

"Ah, Crandall," Joseph was saying before she could turn

him aside. "Glad you're here. Several girls just came in and we shall need all the men we can muster to do our duty tonight." He patted Charity's hand in a rather fatherly way as he looked up at the tall figure before them.

Adam inclined his head at the group, but somehow his eyes never left Charity. She stared at a point past his shoulder as his gaze seemed to burn down her throat and over her breasts. She wished that just for this moment she could tug the neckline up and hide the deep cleavage where she knew a telltale blush was beginning to appear.

"I'm sure Mr. Crandall has seen Helen come in and is eager to do his duty in that direction," she said, meeting the gray eyes and seeing the full lips twitch. "We don't want to detain him."

Her host seemed happy at the suggestion. "Just so," he agreed. "Perhaps you could take her a glass, Crandall."

With a lift of his eyebrow at Charity, Adam murmured, "Honored, I'm sure," and turned away to procure the drink.

Charity drew a deep breath and looked at her companions brightly. "Now, which one of you gentlemen is going to give a thought to *my* poor parched throat?" And she laughed as they both sprang to the table.

As the evening progressd, Charity was reminded of her last ball on Saint Dominique. Here again were the blazing candles, the open doors letting in sweet-scented night air, more partners than she could dance with. Nostalgia was lost in the realization that she actually liked this strange new land and its people. They were not as bound by old world, stiff convention of manners and they spoke their minds more freely. One was as apt to hear a stinging appraisal of the young government's policies while one danced as a prettily worded compliment. And it seemed that when attention was truly paid to one here, it was paid in all seriousness. This much she had known for months, so she viewed Joseph's almost constant attendance on her as a very hopeful sign. But she mustn't let him monopolize her. She must let him worry and wonder a little, perhaps become a bit jealous. Jealousy was more likely to bring him to declare himself than anything else, she thought, and smiled to herself as she realized those were her mother's reflections. Accordingly, she accepted the arm of Burke Canfield before Joseph could reach her, and smiled reluctantly over her shoulder at him as she moved off to join the forming set.

"Oh, dear, I'm so sorry, Miss Ashton." Mr. Canfield stopped

short. "I'm afraid I've been very clumsy and stepped on your gown."

"I'm sure it was nothing. I hardly felt it, sir." She looked down.

"But I have torn the hem. I do apologize."

He looked so flustered and unhappy, Charity gave him her widest smile and saw him color. "It is nothing a needle and thread won't fix in a moment." She looked around and found Joseph hard on her heels.

"I see you've had a mishap, Charity. I'm convinced you would like to go and have it repaired. Allow me to show you the way."

Charity felt a momentary exasperation with all the fuss, but she nodded to Joseph and looked up at the embarrassed Mr. Canfield. "Perhaps another dance, then."

He flushed with pleasure and stammered that he would await that moment. Then Charity allowed herself to be led from the room.

The wide hall was deserted for the moment, and Joseph led her to the foot of the stairs with directions on how to find the bedroom where servants waited to help the young ladies.

As Charity put her foot on the first step, Joseph looked around the hall. "Charity." His voice was unusually deep, and his hand on her arm felt cold.

"Yes?" She turned back to see his brown eyes rise hastily from her waist and then bosom.

His honest face colored, but he kept his eyes steady. "Charity, you must know that I have come to hold you in the highest regard," he began.

Charity spread her hands. "I must know that indeed, for you have been so kind as to save me from the embarrassment of watching my skirt fall in tatters to the dance floor." His color deepened at her exaggeration, and she went on quickly. "It won't take me a moment to have this fixed, and then I hope to dance all night." With that she lifted her skirts and sped up the stairs, thankful that someone below was calling Joseph back to his duties as host. She felt, suddenly, she couldn't face him in the deserted hall again.

As a maid stitched her hem, Charity wondered at her change in heart. Hadn't she been scheming to have Joseph say just what he had begun back there at the foot of the stairs? Why was she suddenly reluctant to hear him speak? He was the nicest of men, a very eligible bachelor. As once before tonight, she remembered Émilie's words, that there were many worthy and eligible young men to be had. And she heard her own response that she'd rather have something *more*. But those had been the words of a foolish romantic young girl, pampered and secure and unaware that life could be anything but what she thought it was at that moment. She knew better now. You had to take what you could from life, create your own security. Take what you could...Émilie's face swam before her. "He will take what he wants, that one."

Impatiently, Charity smoothed her hair as the woman at her feet finished the hem and sat back. "Thank you," the girl said and walked firmly to the door. There would be no more romantic imaginings. She knew what he wanted out of life and she meant to see she got it. Perhaps Joseph had managed to come back to wait for her. This time she would hear him out. And *his* proposal, if he made it, would be an honest one.

Her eyes kindling and her head high, Charity descended the stairs. But Joseph was not at the bottom waiting. As she went down, Charity wondered how she might make another opportunity for him to speak. The figure which appeared, to lounge against the newel post, surprised her. For a fraction of a second she wondered if she could turn and run up the stairs. But she wouldn't show him that she even noticed his presence.

Adam, brandy snifter in hand, watched her descend with a now familiar ache. The conceited witch. Did she think she could ignore him forever? Did she really mean to *marry* Joseph Hadley? He was tired of her game, by God. But it wouldn't do to shout at her. Just get that beautiful back up and the claws out. He was still baffled by her resistance to him. In his experience, women were eager to bed him to get something they wanted, and surely Charity wanted to be rid of Wentworth. Staring at the willowy form in the color of the deepest blush, he felt his heart thud harder. Perhaps this chase was worthy of even more of his attention for the prize would be almost unimaginably rich.

"I was sent to be sure the damsel was no longer in distress," he said lazily as he unbent from the newel post and looked up at her.

Charity's magnificent eyes flashed. "The damsel was *never* in distress, Mr. Crandall, so you have wasted a dance." She meant to pass him by, but he moved to block her way. Their eyes were nearly level, though she stood above him.

"Pity," he drawled. "I specialize in rescuing damsels in distress."

"Well, St. George, you've missed your mark." She stood very straight and looked down at the glass in his hands, smelling the heady fumes.

"Does the sight of a gentleman working his way into his cups upset you, Miss? Surely you've seen the sight before."

"It does not upset me, Mr. Crandall. In fact, if you were to fall flat on your face right here, I would only be thankful the brandy had done its work."

His grin flashed. "If you were dull-witted I would not find you so beautiful, Charity."

"And if you had any wits at all..."

"Charity, let us stop dueling." His eyes were opaque, but his mouth was set.

"I have no wish to even talk with you, sir." Charity sidestepped quickly and practically jumped the last stair. He reached for her, but she pranced away and fled through the drawing room door, nearly colliding with Paul. Behind her she heard a low chuckle.

"Do not go so fast, Charity." Paul held out his too smooth hands to her. "It is practically the first time we have seen each other this evening."

"And practically the first time we have seen Mr. Crandall." Helen and her mother stood only feet away, and Helen's eyes were fastened like a predatory animal on Adam, now emerging from the hall shadows. In an arch tone she went on. "I know men enjoy having a glass together sometimes, to get away from the terrible crush. So I suppose I must forgive you your inattention."

With a lift of one eyebrow, Adam inclined his head. "You can imagine my relief."

Charity choked as her wide eyes met a flicker from his. Then she turned quickly away and allowed Paul to lead her into the room. She felt flushed from her encounter with Adam, and dancing only added to her inner heat. After a few minutes she begged off, saying she would prefer to sit for a bit. Paul led her from the floor toward one of the tall doors onto the terrace.

"A walk in the fresh air will revive you better, *ma belle*."

Charity hesitated, but then she saw another couple ahead of them. She would much prefer to walk outdoors, and that couple promised some chaperonage. Charity nodded and stepped into the soft air.

There were torches on the balustrade, throwing soft pools of light across marble, grass, and bushes. Wide steps beckoned to the garden walks and tree-lined vistas of cool grass. But Charity resisted her impulse to run down those stairs. She would like nothing more than to throw off her shoes and feel the lush coolness beneath her feet. Instead, she turned and strolled decorously in the wake of the other couple, letting Paul trail behind. The gentle breeze played about her naked shoulders and through her heavy hair, refreshing her instantly.

At the end of the terrace, more stairs led to side gardens. She looked at them longingly, but turned away as the other couple reversed its direction and started back.

Suddenly Paul was beside her, a hard grip was on her arm and she was practically hurled down those stairs. In the shadows below she regained her balance, but before she could draw breath, arms were around her, pulling her past the dark corner of the house. She twisted away. "Paul, for heaven's sake," she hissed, not wanting the couple on the terrace to hear and look back. .

Sinewy hands grabbed at her shoulders and pulled her around to face him. With a moan Paul buried his face in her neck.

She pushed at him and was surprised to find she was held fast. Her shoulders hurt where he gripped them, and she could feel her right sleeve slipping down her arm. "Stop this," she hissed again and pushed harder.

"Charity, you will not avoid me longer. I have burned for you." Paul's voice was muffled, hoarse.

She stood very still, hoping he would relax his grip and she could break away. But he only held her tighter. His wet mouth was searching for hers, and she twisted her head, filled with revulsion.

Her sleeve tore as he jerked her back and threw his arms around her. She staggered and fell against the trunk of a cedar tree. The rough bark scratched her back and tore at her dress as she struggled in his frenzied embrace. He had flung himself against her and she could feel his hardness pressing her thigh. Filled with loathing, she fought him, wondering if the sounds of their struggle would reach the terrace, afraid to cry out. His mouth was devouring her throat, searching lower as he gripped her hair, pulling her head back. At last one hand was free and she scratched at his face. His grip only tightened.

"You will not deny me. I can not wait longer," he growled.

Charity clawed at him again. Then suddenly his weight

was gone and she staggered upright. A huge form had gripped Paul from behind, spinning him in place. There was a resounding smack as a fist connected with Paul's jawbone. Then the Frenchman was lying still at her feet.

Chapter 13

"Are you all right?"

A wary eye on the prone figure in the grass, Charity stepped around him and faced the tall form of her deliverer. "Yes." Even in the dark, she could see his teeth flash in a grin. She put up her hand and tried to pull her right sleeve back in place, but it was torn in back and wouldn't stay on her shoulder.

"Don't try to fix it," Adam said softly. "Rather puts me in mind of the first time I saw you. Seems you're always getting yourself molested by men, Charity."

"Once again I must thank you," she said between clenched teeth, wishing she could get the sleeve back in place to hold up her bodice.

Adam was still grinning. "Of course, this time I may have mistaken the situation."

"Mistaken! You think I'd willingly let that...that *lizard* touch me?"

Adam laughed.

"Hush," Charity admonished. "Someone will hear us. I must get back."

"By all means. Let us return. The bark in your hair and the tears in your gown will hardly be noticed."

Charity's hands flew to her hair to discover the artful masses had come loose. She looked down at her dress and moaned.

"I think we will not return to the terrace just yet." He took her arm and moved her further into the shadows away from the walk. She could smell brandy on his breath, but he couldn't be very drunk if he could flatten Paul with one blow.

She went with him unwillingly, all the time wondering how she could get back upstairs to the repairing room and trying to concoct a story for the servants there.

When they were well away from the house, Adam stopped. As though reading her mind, he chuckled. "I, too, have not yet hit on a plausible reason for your condition."

They were under the trees at the edge of a narrow sloping lawn now, and he let her go. Their eyes, accustomed to the dark, sought each other out. "Tell me how severe the damage is," she said and turned in place so he could inspect her.

He lifted her hair to peer at her back and she flinched at his touch. "I am only trying to do your bidding, my dear." He let her hair trail through his fingers and stood back. "Sewing is not among my many accomplishments," he said at last, "but I suspect it will take more than a few stitches to put the back of your dress in order again. But perhaps I'm wrong. As for your hair..." He shrugged.

Charity was already pulling pins out of the disheveled pile on her head. "Adam," she said, *"you* could put my hair back. I'll tell you how. And we can leave more of it down to try to cover the tears at the back. The skirt is all right, isn't it?"

Adam grinned. "Yes, the skirt is all right. But how you expect me to..."

"Here are the pins. You must try. Heaven knows who else saw me leave the room with Paul. We've been gone too long already. Joseph will wonder..."

"Ah yes, the estimable Joseph. We mustn't keep him waiting to make his proposal." But he made no move to take the pins.

Charity's eyes flashed. "At least his will be a proposal of marriage," she snapped.

"Oh yes. How honorable...and how tedious for you."

Charity stamped her slippered foot. "Do stop talking, you boorish lout." Then she clenched her fists and switched tactics. Putting honey in her voice she said, "Please, Adam, will you *try?*"

Still grinning, Adam took the pins. "It means so much to you, Charity, to have the kindly and boring Mr. Hadley offer you marriage?"

"How else am I to get away from that awful..." Charity bit off her words and suppressed a giggle as she felt his hands clumsily twisting her hair. She tried to help him as he fumbled with the pins, and finally she lost control. Shaking with silent laughter, she pulled away. "You're hopeless. Let me try."

Adam crossed his arms. "Do you know, I've never seen you laugh before?"

"There has never been any reason to laugh in your presence," she replied, ducking her head and working at pinning a stray tendril. She would get some of the hair in place only to find a lock falling on the other side. She struggled another minute, then dropped her hands with a sigh. Her bright hair tumbled down over her shoulders.

Adam had stood still for so long, she looked up at him, afraid he'd gone to sleep in an alcoholic stupor. But hooded eyes watched her steadily.

"Whatever am I to do?" she wailed.

Adam shook his head slowly as he surveyed their surroundings. Then still with his arms crossed comfortably, he looked back at her. "Well, Charity, it seems you have two options." His grin flashed.

Charity tossed her head. "I'm glad to hear that."

"You can either walk back into that house now after an absence of thirty minutes, your dress in tatters, your hair in disarray, smudges no doubt on your face and brazen your way through the ordeal, hoping your precious Joseph will still have you after this night's work...or..."

Charity looked around wildly. "You know I can't do that. You know what it would do to the last shreds of my reputation."

"Or..." he repeated firmly, "you can come with me."

"Come with you where? How would I ever explain my absence?"

Adam waved an arm in a gesture she'd seen once before. "Away," he said simply.

Charity stepped back with a gasp. "You're mad. What's worse, you're drunk!"

"Of course I'm drunk, you little vixen. D'you think I'd have followed you like a hound when you left the room with your Frenchman, or nearly killed him when I saw him mauling you, or tried to put up your bloody hair, or...or any of this if I were sober? As for mad...undoubtedly."

"You're disgusting," she said, and put all the hauteur she could into her voice. "It is apparent that I have only one alternative, and I shall take it." Then in a smaller voice she added, "If I use the front door there's a chance no one but the servants will see me." With that she turned and began to thread her way among the trees.

"And by now Paul is recovered and furious. Joseph is searching for you. A room full of ladies is wondering at your departure. Paul will prove ungallant about your *tête à tête*. Helen will make the most of it." The soft voice ticked off points as it followed her.

At the edge of the grass she hesitated, then gritting her teeth, she stepped forward.

An arm shot out and stopped her. "No, my girl, you're not going back in there. If you can't imagine what your life would become, I can. A spinster at Wentworth is not what you were born to be."

She turned furiously. "Let go of me."

In answer, his other hand came out and stroked her arm, sliding up to her neck and face. "I think not, lassie."

"You drunken fool, let go."

He laughed aloud, and to Charity's ears his laughter had an unholy ring. "We're off on an adventure," he crowed, and began to drag her back through the trees.

She tried to kick him. She tried to bite him. She tried to twist away. All to no avail. It was like being carried before a whirlwind. Her breath was coming in ragged gasps when they reached the rear of the stables, and she all but collapsed when Adam stopped. Swiftly he pulled her to the ground. She clawed feebly at him, but he pinned her arms and bent over her. "Quiet, spitfire. I will get my horse, and then we're away."

She choked and tried to shake her head, but he was already gone. Unsteadily, she got to her feet. "Oh Lord, he's kidnapping me," she moaned. She leaned on the stable wall, fighting for breath and coherent thought. Obviously, she couldn't stay here. He'd be back soon. She looked around, wondering where she could hide. From inside the stables she could hear voices and the stamp of a horse's hoof. At the corner of the building was a fence. Pastures stretched beyond.

Thinking only that she must hide from this frighteningly powerful man, she groped down the wall. When she reached the fence, she caught her skirt in her teeth and started over it. So intent was she, she didn't hear the horse come up behind her.

"So much easier to mount from a fence," Adam's voice was filled with mirth as an arm came out and yanked her off her high perch and across his saddle. Automatically, she snatched at the horse's mane and pulled herself upright, thinking dully that the man must be the devil himself to saddle his horse that fast.

The deep voice in her ear brought her back to her senses. "Now, if all the stories be true, you will find it more comfortable to throw the other leg over Gabriel's neck."

She kicked out, trying to unseat them both, but a vise held her in place.

"Gabriel is quite capable of carrying you, dangling on one side, but I assure you it will not be comfortable." He turned the horse then and made to move off.

"No." She tugged frantically on the horse's neck and righted herself again. Then, as he leaned back, she fought her left leg free of her skirts and pulled herself astride the front of his saddle.

"A bit cozy, but we'll manage." Adam chuckled and set his horse to a brisk walk.

Powerful muscles beneath her and behind her kept Charity rigidly silent as they rounded the corner of the fence and headed for deep woods beyond. She was truly finished now, she thought. There was no returning to the Hadleys' beautiful house. There was no hope of ever marrying a respectable young man who would give her a place of her own in Virginia's tidewater aristocracy. There was no going back to Wentworth, to the memories of her dying mother, the lost Marie, the endless fetching, the sidelong looks, the lecherous advances of Paul. She felt her heart lighten as they entered the trees and Gabriel picked his way between branches to a dim forest track. On the road before her lay the ruins of all her past life, but she was not yet nineteen. She would start again. She would escape this lunatic who held her so she could hardly breathe, and she would make her own way.

The uncomfortable ride was interminable. Once she'd tried to ask where they were going, but Adam's deep chuckle so enraged her she didn't ask again. On cart tracks and across fields they skirted farms and great houses. A brilliant moon lit their way, and horse and master seemed to know every stump, rock, and turning in the landscape. Once Charity saw what looked to be the outskirts of a large town, but she was too weary to even wonder which place they passed.

At last Gabriel was slowed to a walk and Charity's dulled eyes picked out a small cabin in a long clearing. She looked around and saw fenced pastures and dense woods beyond. She twisted in the saddle. "What is this place?"

"An old settler's cabin. Belongs to a friend of mine. He uses it when he wants to get away—hunt, fish on his own. Also works on his horses from here." And Adam said no more till they'd stopped at the door and he'd handed her down.

Inside, the cabin was spare and masculine. By the light of the fire Adam made, Charity could see four bunks ranged along one wall, blankets neatly folded at their feet. Behind the plank table at the opposite end of the room halters, tethers, and ropes hung on pegs and branding irons stood in a corner. Before the great stone hearth a huge bear skin offered a luxurious touch. Utensils and pots hung neatly on nails beside the chimney.

Charity shivered and drew nearer the fire. The night air had grown cooler. Adam was already going out the door to see to his horse. He hadn't said a word. She went and got one of the blankets and, wrapping it around her shoulders, returned to the firelight. He was back in brief minutes and went instantly to a box in the corner, from which he extracted a flask. Taking a long drink, he looked at her at last.

"Good rum," he commented. "Comes from your part of the world."

Charity stared at him, wide-eyed.

"Like a drink? Help take off the chill."

She shook her head, her huge eyes still staring. This cabin was something she'd never imagined. Somehow she'd thought he would take her to a roadside inn where she could demand her own room; or perhaps to the house of one of his low friends where there would be chaperonage of some sort. The realization of how completely alone they were made her legs tremble. But she mustn't show she was afraid. Perhaps he had no intention of... of anything, but if she could show him his attentions would be unwelcome, then certainly he would not try to touch her. She drew the blanket closer and eyed him with what she hoped looked like disdain. He was walking toward her now and she was painfully aware that there was nowhere to run.

"Warmer?" He stopped in the circle of firelight.

She nodded.

He stood with legs apart and took another pull at the flask. "Good," he said, and reaching behind him, he put the flask on the table. He took a step forward.

Charity found her voice. "Don't come near me."

"Don't? Oh come, Miss Ashton. You were willing to sell your soul for the strong arms of the honorable Joseph Hadley tonight. And you were willing to step out the door with the mincing 'almost fiancé' from the old country. But you aren't willing to share a fire with a man who has risked life and limb for you in these past hours?" He removed his coat and waistcoat with deliberate ease.

"You're drunk," she snapped. He was unbuttoning his shirt.

"Once more you repeat yourself, Miss Ashton." He moved closer and with one swift movement her blanket was whisked from her shoulders.

Adam caught his breath as firelight played across her.

Seeing his look, she backed a step. "You...you are no gentleman, sir, to bring me to this place."

"Are you trying to appeal to my better nature? Useless, I'm afraid. I haven't one at the moment." A quick movement and Charity felt the torn sleeve of her dress give way in a powerful hand. She looked around wildly for a knife, a pot, anything with which to fend him off, but already her bodice was tearing and the heavy lining of the rose silk was giving way. She tried to slap him, but her hand was stopped in mid-air. His breath was hot on her neck and she arched backwards to avoid it. With a loud rip the bodice gave way, suddenly exposing her creamy breasts to his searching mouth. She tugged at his hair with her free hand as his lips found one straining nipple and she felt a flame shoot down through her body.

His hands pinioned hers behind her and he lifted his head. She thought her back would break with the strain and she felt her eyes grow hot with tears of rage and pain. She bit him as he kissed her, but he only chuckled as one hand reached down and scooped her legs out from under her.

She fell on the bearskin, sobbing, and tried to roll away. But his powerful body lay on top of her and she couldn't move. Her arms were still behind her back, pinned by their combined weight, and her legs were held under one strong thigh.

"Please," she choked. "Please don't."

But he seemed deaf, as he tore at her dress, ripping the side seam down to her waist. His shirt was open and she

139

could feel the curling hair on his powerful chest against her breasts. Still sobbing, she turned her head from his kiss and felt him bite her ear.

"That was for your rude treatment aboard ship," he explained huskily as she gasped in pain. "But all the rest is just for the two of us, alone at last."

"You're a beast." She tried to shout, but her mouth was dry and her throat nearly closed.

"A beast like all men, Charity. But one who wants you more than any of the others did."

The waist of her dress gave way and the skirts were tugged aside. She kicked out, but met only his leg, spreading hers apart as he kicked off his pants. Then suddenly his body was hard on hers. She moaned and tried to twist again. His hands were caressing her breasts, her side, her hips and she felt her skin was being set on fire. Then he was touching her between her legs and she cried out. "Nooo..."

Wrenching one arm free she beat at his back and clawed his side, till suddenly she felt him enter her and a bright pain dissolved all else. As he thrust into her again she clenched her teeth to keep from crying. The pain began to subside, and a strange feeling started to take its place. But suddenly he stopped with a shudder and it was all over.

Slowly he lifted himself off her and pulled her against him. She lay still, hot tears scalding her cheeks.

"Charity," he said softly. "I didn't hurt you, did I?"

She lay immobile, not wanting to admit to either pain or pleasure.

Adam got up and retrieved her fallen blanket. The firelight flickered over her smooth curves and he stood looking down at her, watching her try to pull the remnants of her dress over her naked limbs. Flecks of blood showed on the silk where it had lain beneath her, and he drew in his breath sharply as he saw them.

She closed her eyes to avoid his scrutiny and felt him pull the blanket gently over her. He knelt beside her on the rug, one hand smoothing tangled hair from her forehead. "Charity, I didn't know, didn't think... I needed you so much. And I didn't think I was the first."

Her eyes flew wide for an instant. But she didn't meet his gaze. She stared at the beamed ceiling for a long moment, then closed them again, trying to shut out all thought.

After a minute she sensed Adam get up. He moved around the room for a space, then she felt him lie down next to her. Pulling her stiff body to him, he cradled her till, exhausted, she fell asleep.

PART THREE

Chapter 14

Early sunlight slanting through the narrow windows woke
Charity. She stretched her legs and was aware of the dull
ache between them. Coarse wool scratched her skin and her
body felt bruised but oddly relaxed. Her eyes flew open as
the sensations brought her to full consciousness. Beside her
the thick bearskin rug lay empty and she had a flash of hope
that she was waking from a dream.

The door opened then and her brief hopes were dashed.
Clad only in his breeches, Adam entered the room softly.
When he saw she was awake he stopped. It was too late to
feign sleep, but she pulled the blanket up to her mouth and
watched him with wary and frightened eyes. His black hair
was wet, the familiar stray wave plastered to his forehead,
and tiny rivulets of water made bright streaks on his bronzed
skin and in the curling hair of his chest and stomach.

Their eyes locked in the silence and Charity felt a blush
covering her whole body. Glad the blanket hid it from his
view, she waited tensely for his first move.

Adam put down the bucket he carried and ran a hand
through his jet hair. "No, Charity, I'm not going to leap on
you with slavering fangs." His voice was tired. Then he gave
her a small rueful smile. "Your charms, as powerful as they
are, are not equal to a splitting head, an empty stomach, and
the prospect of a hard ride ahead of me."

Charity felt her blush deepen, but didn't know if it was

from embarrassment or anger. "Serves you right for drinking so much," she said from under the blanket. "Ride where?"

Pulling his shirt off a peg by the door, Adam shrugged into it and leaned back against the wall. "To Richmond, to see how we may improve our lot. Though we won't quite starve this morning. There's some beef jerky and some corn meal. Don't suppose you'd know how to cook up something with the meal?" He began to do up his buttons.

Charity shook her head.

"No, I was afraid not. Well, I could make an Indian mush, but without some honey or maple syrup, I doubt you'd find it appetizing. Beef jerky it is, then."

"What is beef jerky?"

Adam grinned as he worked on his left cuff. "Dried beef. A bit chewy, but sustaining."

Charity grimaced and wished she could sit up, but the abominable man was still doing up his shirt and looking at her. The silence dragged on, and finally Charity's patience gave out. "Do turn around so I can get up."

Adam's eyes danced, but at last he bowed mockingly and moved away to the corner box. As he rummaged for the beef, Charity tucked the blanket under her chin and pulled it around behind her. Awkwardly she gained her feet. Clutching the blanket before and behind, she crossed the bearskin to the table. Adam was grinning from a chair across from her as she sat down. She reached for the hunk of dried meat he offered, then clutched at the blanket again as it began to slip down her chest. She felt his eyes on her and wished she could cover her bare shoulders.

Still grinning, Adam showed her how to bite off a mouthful of meat and chew it till it was soft enough to swallow. She nearly spit out her first taste, but she was ravenous, so she chewed doggedly. Soon she found she could tolerate another bite. It was better to sit working over this meat like a cow over a cud, she reflected, than it was to have to think what was to become of her now. What if she saw someone she knew in Richmond?

"Well." Adam thumped the table and stood up. "I hate to break off such a scintillating conversation, but I suppose I must be going."

Charity's sea green eyes flew to his face. "Going?" She swallowed a half-chewed mouthful. "You mean to leave me here alone?"

145

Adam looked down at her blanket. "You'd make a pretty picture walking around in that."

"My...my gown."

"Alas, dearheart, your dress would no longer conceal your true beauty."

Charity followed the indication of his hand and her face crumpled as she saw the shredded silk on the rug.

"You'll be perfectly safe, Charity."

"But what are you going to do?" She had thought never to see the day she actually dreaded his leaving.

"Get us some food," he said shortly. "And some clothes." Then he eyed her wrapped figure. "Though perhaps I'll forget the clothes."

She stood up then and tilted her chin in the air, daring him to make fun of her sorry state.

"You're as lovely this morning as you were by candle-light," he said and moved toward her.

She stepped back and nearly collided with the wall. Flinging out a hand she snatched an iron skillet off its hook. The blanket came loose, but she disregarded it. She held his eyes and brandished the skillet.

Adam threw up an arm in mock dismay. "Please. Have a thought for my poor head."

She lowered her arm a fraction, but her eyes continued to smolder and he became serious. "I said I would not touch you this morning, Charity." Then he turned and was gone.

Not until she heard Gabriel's soft hoofbeats fading down the track did she return the skillet to its peg. She tiptoed to the door and peered around the clearing but nothing moved anywere. The morning sun was warmly soothing and she brought the bucket outside to the door sill. With another look around, she shed her blanket and set about bathing as best she could. The cold water washed away traces of blood and passion spent, and she felt nearly refreshed when she was done. Now to her gown.

But it was apparent as she picked up the wrinkled silk that the dress was beyond hope. It was split nearly all the way down the right side and the waist was half torn away. She felt hot tears starting and pushed them back with the heels of her hands. Crying would do her less than no good. She began to search the cabin.

An hour later, Charity gave a crow of triumph and surveyed her handiwork. Thin leather strips bound the torn seams together again and the ragged sleeve was nearly back

146

in place. The large holes she'd had to make to force the leather
through might tear the material further, but she hoped the
lining would hold. Tossing her torn petticoat aside, she
slipped the gown over her head and did up what buttons she
could reach. Her stitches held.

A comb for horses was washed twice and then used to
smooth her tangled hair. When she was done she discovered
she felt much better. Aches were gone from stiff limbs and
from her loins. She wanted to walk. Taking another piece of
beef from the box, she returned to the sunshine and began
to explore her strange environment.

For several hours she roamed across a little creek, through
the woods and around pastures, absorbing the fresh air and
healing sun. Once she spied a group of horses on a far meadow
and thought briefly of trying to catch one and ride away. But
becoming a horse thief was no way to escape her predicament.
If only she knew where she was! She might even walk to
Richmond. She'd lost all sense of direction last night, but
they couldn't have come so very far. She followed Gabriel's
hoofprints down the track for over a mile, but found no dwellings or even signs of a road. Her feet began to hurt in the
thin slippers and she retraced her steps through the sun-
dappled woods feeling desperate and lonely. When she
reached the little cabin she was so exhausted she flung herself down on one of the bunks and was asleep instantly.

The bang of the door against the wall woke her with a
start. She jumped from her bed with a thudding heart and
backed toward deep shadows. The open door showed dusk
was descending, and the thought of what it might be bringing
made her hand go to her throat. Then a big form filled the
doorway and she choked.

"Charity?" Adam stood still, holding paper-wrapped packages, and strained to see into the darkened room. As his eyes
grew accustomed to the dim light, he spied her still form half
crouched in the corner. Relief overwhelmed him, but then
concern took its place. Quickly he threw the packages on the
table. "Charity, what's the matter? Are you all right?"

Slowly the girl removed the hand from her neck. "I ... I
was asleep. You startled me." She wasn't going to admit she'd
been frightened half out of her wits.

"You mean you thought a band of marauders had come
to your door. I'm sorry I 'startled' you. Let me light the fire
and some candles. Then I'll show you what I brought." He

stopped, staring at her. "How on earth did you contrive to get that gown back on?"

Charity gave a shaky laugh. "Leather for fixing tack," she said.

Adam's tired face split into a grin. "Very ingenious." You had to give the girl credit. Nothing could keep her down for long.

Curiosity brought Charity forward. "What did you bring?"

"All in good time. Did you have a nice day?"

Charity glared at him. "If being a prisoner in the middle of nowhere can be called nice, it was lovely, thank you."

"Hardly a prisoner." Adam undid some string. "But solitude is good for the soul, they say."

"You were gone such a long time." Her voice was small and she hated herself for it.

Adam held out two candles to her. "Did you miss me?" His eyes caressed her.

"Not for a moment," she snapped and snatched the candles.

He chuckled. "Ah well, I'm back now, and shall see what I can do to make your heart grow fonder."

Avoiding his eyes, Charity moved away and went in search of holders.

Soon a fire was kindled and the candles added bright spots of light on the table. Adam got some water from the little creek and put it in a kettle, then unwrapped a parcel of vegetables and meat. Using a new hunting knife, he cleaned and chopped the food into the kettle. Charity sat with her chin in her hands and watched him. How skillfully his long fingers worked. Her gaze traveled up one powerful arm to his head. The candlelight highlighted the hollows beneath his cheek bones and threw his hard jaw into relief. She moved a bit and studied his chiseled profile, softened by the unruly lock of black hair that curled over his brow. It was such a strong face. And so beautiful that that profile might have come from some ancient coin. Her heart skipped a beat as his eyes lifted to meet hers and she reminded herself sternly that his was a willful, self-indulgent face, a dangerous face for unwary females, perhaps for those who crossed him too. She looked away and he resumed his job till presently he lifted the kettle and swung it onto the iron hook over the fire.

"There. A stew fit for kings. Now I must see to Gabriel, but then we will unwrap the other things."

The girl felt restless after her long sleep. She got up and

searched out a large wooden spoon to stir the stew. Then she followed Adam outside. She found him tethering Gabriel in the clearing and walked over to watch as he rubbed the horse down with a rag. Then she turned and matched his long strides back to the cabin.

"You're pacing like a tiger," he remarked as he held the door.

"A caged tiger."

There was the familiar lift of an eyebrow. "Don't tell me you never left the cabin all day."

"I walked for hours," she began, then stopped.

He smiled. "That's what I imagined. In fact, I was half prepared to spend tonight searching the woods and trails for you."

"If I had found a road I would have had too great a head-start."

"The thought did cross my mind, but I felt sure it would go hard with you without any clothes." He looked at her leather-held dress. "I don't think you would have enjoyed explaining to anyone the very peculiar aspect of your gown."

Charity bit her lip.

"But come, let me show you what I brought you."

Her curiosity up once more, she put aside her argument and went with him to the table. Deftly he undid the biggest of his bundles.

"I fear the fit will not be perfect, but Polly is very nearly your size."

"Polly?"

"Friend of mine." His laughing eyes met hers as he pulled a dress from the wrappings.

Charity stared. "Adam Crandall! That...that thing is positively indecent."

"Yes, isn't it?" he agreed. "But I assure you Polly has worn it to good effect, and you will look utterly fetching in it." He shook it out and held it up.

Charity gazed at the tiny puffed sleeves, the laces crisscrossing the front and the wide green skirt and flushed. "It doesn't have any neckline."

Adam roared with laughter. "Yes it does. This bit of frill does wonders. And as Polly says, 'If you have something to show off, why not show it off?'"

"Just who is this Polly?" Charity was actually laughing.

"She's a serving wench at a tavern owned by a friend of

mine. I assure you all the men approve of the way she dresses."

"A serving girl?" Charity still stared at the garment. "More likely a..."

"Whore? No. Though I admit she likes men."

"She must indeed to flaunt herself in that." Her eyes narrowed. "And she *gave* you this?"

"Of course not. I paid her rather handsomely. But I did realize you were unlikely to go out in public in it. So I found something a bit more demure." With that he pulled out a plain blue calico gown with tight sleeves and a high neck.

Charity giggled. "Your Polly is a woman of many parts."

"Actually, this belongs to another girl. And I fear she's larger than you."

"Oh?" Charity felt oddly piqued at the thought of these women who were willing to give Adam the clothes off their backs. She wondered what else they'd given him, then quickly suppressed the thought. Adam was grinning at her, and she had the odd feeling he was reading her mind. The thought made her cross.

"How very nice of them to sell their clothes to you. And I suppose you explained just who they were for and why she needed them?"

Adam went on grinning. "Wild horses couldn't drag the story from me, dearheart."

Charity's cheeks flamed as she saw the gray eyes sweep over her. She pointed at the dresses on the table. "Is that what took you all day?"

"Well, no." Adam turned back and went on unwrapping. "I had to make lists for my friend who was a great help in getting us provisions and such. And in sending messages."

"Messages?"

"Yes. You see, sweeting," and he unfolded two soft blankets, "our names were very nearly linked in scandal today." He threw the blankets over a chair and, balling up the paper, tossed it into the fire. "By the way, there are other things here Polly assured me you'd want."

"Thanks," Charity said absently. "What do you mean scandal?"

"If you remember, Miss Ashton, you were at a ball last night..."

Charity made a little gesture with her hand. "Someone saw us go off on your horse?"

"No, thank God. But of course there's been a great hue

150

and cry out for you. I had to spend a deal of time trying to call off the hunt."

The girl stared at him dully and sat down. "What on earth did you do?"

Adam sat too. His eyes were alight with laughter as he continued. "When I heard half the county was looking for you, I went to Wentworth, of course."

"You *what?*" The sheer audacity of the man took her breath away.

"Went to Wentworth," he repeated, spreading his hands. "I felt I had to offer my services in the search. They were most grateful to me. Happily, while I was there, trying to be consoling, a message arrived from you."

Charity's laugh was tinged with hysteria brewed from the tensions and fears of the past twenty-four hours. "What did I say?" she choked.

The man eyed her appreciatively. "You were very brief and to the point. You said you had been unable to endure the attentions of Paul LaRoche, had knocked him out, had then realized you could no longer face your confined life with the Wentworths, had stolen my horse, and were safe in Richmond."

Charity's gasp made him smile more broadly. "I naturally corroborated that my horse had been stolen practically beneath my eyes, had given chase thinking you couldn't handle Gabriel, had gone so far I'd decided to continue the walk to Richmond in hopes my horse would show up." He tapped his knee and went on with a chuckle. "Further, you said the horse could be found at Nicholson's stable and you would be most grateful if your few personal effects could be sent to Knight's Inn (a most respectable place), where they will be collected by a friend. You ended that you were sorry if you'd caused any worry or pain and hoped they would not bother to look for you."

Her shoulders shaking, Charity bowed her head in her hands. At last she looked up. "Of all the ridiculous stories," she gurgled.

"Admittedly. But it was the best I could do on such short notice. Over luncheon I commiserated with them on having harbored such an ungrateful, unfeeling, and certainly unladylike creature."

"Did you indeed? You cad."

"I did. And I even went so far as to hint that you were much better gone from the bosom of their fine family. I do think the ladies, at least, were rather inclined to agree. But of course, there was still the question of saving you from yourself, and certainly from a Fate Worse Than Death."

Charity's smile froze at that, but he seemed not to notice. "I ended the visit saying that I would be there to meet your trunk at Knight's and would try to follow this friend of yours and discover your whereabouts. Though it was my belief you were wily and will do your utmost to elude capture. You are probably heading north to find others from Saint Dominque in Philadelphia. And for all the flaws in the tale, I think they wish Philadelphia well of you."

The girl sat in silence, her brain numbed by all he'd said. But one thought came through. "I see you, at least, have come out of all this smelling like a rose."

Adam shrugged. "But of course. If I'd disappeared along with you we'd have been hunted to the very doors of my home. I thought you'd appreciate my leaving Paul with a blackened name among women, though. Already he's preparing to leave Wentworth again, hinting that high friends beckon him north. Personally, I think he took my bait and will look for you in Philadelphia."

Before she could consider, Charity asked, "And Joseph?"

Adam's face became serious and his eyes searched hers. But he saw only piqued curiosity. "I gather Helen has made him see that you were using him to your own ends. I suspect his vanity has suffered," he said slowly.

Charity stared at him sightlessly and he wondered if she had cared for Joseph after all. The thought made him angry and he stood up, not wanting to hear if it were true.

The girl shook her head in disbelief. She was beginning to realize just what he had done. Deftly, he had burned all her bridges. She could just hear the endless speculation in the drawing room, and Helen's insinuation that there had to have been a man behind it all. Even Sally, in her romantic state, would believe that. Well, better to have the girl think there was a good romantic reason for her friend to leave without a word to her. But she wondered about Joseph. Surely he wouldn't really be taken in by Helen's crude game. If, after he'd gotten over the first shock, he could still believe her in some way innocent...Her cheeks burned once more. After last night she could hardly pass herself off as innocent again. But if she could make him see she had been taken by force, had been held captive...But how was she to ever get the opportunity?

Adam was putting more wood on the fire and stirring the pot. "Be a while yet," he remarked and straightened. His momentary anger was forgotten as he gazed across at the still form and felt desire beginning to burn in his veins. Guilt had ridden with him all day, and the awareness that he had badly misjudged the girl. He realized he had wanted to misjudge her, had been glad to think there were other men before him. It had made it so much easier to give in to his insane impulse to carry her off last night. But he had never wanted to hurt her. He would try to be gentle now.

Lightly, he crossed to her and grasped her hands, pulling her to her feet.

Charity faced him trembling. Not again, she thought, and tugged her hands from his grasp.

His eyes were dark and burning. "I want you," he said simply.

Chapter 15

Charity shrank away from those eyes. "I may have already lost my virtue," she stated as calmly as she could, "but I don't intend to submit to further humiliation." He didn't try to touch her and her chin came up as courage grew.

"It wouldn't hurt again," he said softly.

Her lip quivered, but she kept her face averted. Her eyes had spotted the huge fire poker beside the hearth. Inchingly she moved across to the fire, stopping to check on the stew. Then with her hands behind her she turned slowly to face him again. Her fingers closed around the poker and she held it in the folds of her skirt. Forgotten was the laughter of a few moments ago. If he tries to touch me, I'll kill him, she thought. She watched Adam carefully, her fingers curling and uncurling around the twisted iron handle.

The man was still, enjoying the sight of her so straight and proud in the fire glow. Her ragged dress only just covered her full breasts and without the petticoat, the soft silk outlined her curving hips and slender legs. He drew in his breath and quietly removed his coat. What was she thinking right now? Was she afraid? He wanted to show her what making love could be like. His blood pounding in his ears, he went toward her.

Charity waited until he was two strides away. Then she raised the poker. "Don't come any closer," she said steadily.

Adam stopped in surprise. His loins ached with his need of her. And here she was, brandishing that great silly poker at him. "Don't be ridiculous, girl," he smiled. "Think what you'd be missing if you brained me now." He took another step, still smiling confidently.

She sprang like a cat, the heavy poker slicing through the air at his head. Adam jerked sideways and flung up his arm to catch her wrist. The poker glanced off his shoulder and thudded to the bearskin at his feet. The realization that she had tried to kill him made him half blind with rage. He hardly noticed the pain in his shoulder as he twisted her wrist cruelly and dragged her arm down. Charity choked with frustration and clawed at him, trying to free her arm.

He grabbed her shoulders and shook her till her eyes rolled. "Don't you ever pull a fool trick like that again," he ground between clenched teeth.

Charity kicked at him and yelped as her toe connected with hard bone. He spun her like a rag doll, and an iron arm wrapped around her. She tried to reach behind her head to scratch his face, but he ducked and the arm tightened. She felt her breath being squeezed out of her and desperately she brought her foot down on his instep as hard as she could. She heard him grunt, but the arm didn't slacken its grip. With his free hand he was slowly undoing the buttons at the back of her gown. Wild with fright now, she twisted and kicked and pounded at his arm until she was exhausted.

As her struggles grew weaker, she heard his voice, hard with anger. "I could break your ribs, you little hellcat. But then you would be of less use than you already are. Make up your mind that you have no choices. I am not your gentlemanly Joseph to be intimidated into leaving your precious body alone. I am not your mincing Paul to be scorned and teased by turns."

He paused and the grip on her ribcage grew even tighter. She gasped and tore at his arm to no avail. "You are stuck here with me." Each syllable came out like a separate word, each word containing the hard bite of rage. "I will have you whenever I please, and I am quite capable of knocking you senseless to get my way."

Then suddenly the arm was gone. Charity gulped for air and tried to still the trembling that threatened to collapse her legs. She was sure that if she now showed she was half insane with fear he would strike her in earnest.

Grasping her shoulders, he spun her around and shook her again. "Did you hear me?" he snarled.

Charity, her eyes closed against threatening tears, nodded once.

"Good." Adam stepped back, releasing her. She staggered, and the gown, undone all the way down, began to slip from her shoulders. She snatched at it.

"Let it go." His voice was like a whiplash.

She jerked her hand away and shivered as she felt the neckline slip further. At last she dared to open her eyes and found he was seated, pulling off his boots. The iron poker lay across his lap. Dully, she wondered if he meant to use it on her.

Adam kicked off his second boot and sat back, his hands playing idly over the length of iron. He watched her narrowly, and his voice when he spoke was soft and icy.

"If you plan to keep that lovely skin of yours in one piece, if you plan on even having any food after your long fast, you will now do as I say."

Charity's eyes flicked involuntarily to the bubbling stew.

He chuckled mirthlessly. "Take off the dress." He watched the turquoise eyes grow huge. "I won't repeat it."

With mechanical movements, her gaze never leaving his powerful hands, she obeyed. In moments she stood naked before him, the rose silk in a pile at her feet.

Adam expelled his breath with a whistle. Her eyes were closed against his scrutiny and even from here he could see the thick lashes curling against her scarlet cheeks. Her full lip was caught in her teeth, and her chin trembled. He felt his fury dissolving as his eyes roved over her lovely body. Firm round breasts were deliciously pink tipped. Her satiny

155

skin flowed down over her slender waist, flat stomach, curving hips, and long shapely legs. In the firelight she glowed with creamy perfection, and the softly curling triangle of hair at the base of her abdomen glinted palely.

His limbs felt thick with longing as the rush of anger left his body. Slowly he removed his own clothes.

Charity heard his movements and opened her eyes.

"You have the most magnificent body," he said in a level voice. "It would drive any normal man to the edge of madness."

Charity felt the hot color rising clear to the roots of her hair. She watched with horror as his breeches fell to the floor and Adam stepped over them. Unwillingly, she stared at his beautiful body, moving with catlike grace toward her. But her eyes only skimmed up his long legs to his chest. Fear of his manhood kept her gaze pinned to the curling hair near his throat.

His hand came out and cupped her chin, tilting her head up. "You needn't be so afraid," he whispered. "I can give you as much pleasure as you can give me, if you'll try to relax and enjoy it."

His hand caressed her throat and she wondered if he meant to strangle her into relaxation. She fought down the urge to pull at that hand and stood perfectly still. His lips touched hers soft as breath as his hands stroked her throat and moved down to her breasts and sides. She flinched, waiting for the impact of his body on hers. But the hands went on exploring, caressing her breasts, till his fingers found the pink nipples and she felt them grow hard at his touch. A tremor went through her.

He felt her tremble and took her hands. "Come," he said, and pulled her down to the rug.

Stretching out beside her, Adam rolled her onto her side. She felt his chest hair tickle her taut breasts as his hand ran over her backside and down her leg. Then he was pressing her to him and she felt a hot hardness against her thigh. He pushed her shoulders down and leaned over her kissing her deeply.

She lay on her back, afraid to resist him and unwilling to admit she was sinking into a haze of peculiar sensations. His fingers caressed the inside of her thighs and moved upward to touch her more intimately. She whimpered then, and tried to close her legs against him.

"No, little one, don't fight it. Let me make you want me."

156

He was kissing her again, his tongue exploring her mouth as his fingers explored her below. Hot flames seemed to engulf her and she lacked the will to resist as he spread her legs and lowered himself onto her. His hand probed deeply and she whimpered again.

"You want me, Charity," he whispered. "You want me as much as I want you."

She tried to shake her head as he covered her mouth again. Then suddenly he entered her and she was surprised to feel no pain. Her hips moved to meet him and, beyond thought, her arms went around him and held him to her.

Slowly at first, but soon with mounting fervor she felt the tension build inside her. Then a tidal wave overwhelmed her and crested with a throbbing ache in her loins. She cried out and felt him ride her wave with a long deep thrust. Burying his face in her hair he held her very tight and still.

Charity lay wondering at her vast contentment. Only minutes ago she'd been deathly afraid of this man, and now . . . The fire crackled and motes of light danced across the ceiling. She felt Adam stir beside her.

"You must be famished, my sweet." His lips brushed her cheek and she nodded dreamily. He left her side and she watched him move around the cabin collecting wooden bowls and spoons, taking the kettle from the fire. He met her eyes once, smiling, and she marveled at his unselfconsciousness, as though having a woman stare at his perfectly muscled body was the most natural thing in the world. She wondered how many women had admired him this way, and her eyes narrowed. Or how many women he had broken to his command. She squirmed at the thought and sat up, crossing her arms over her breasts.

Adam was pulling on his breeches, and glancing over his shoulder at her, grinned. "Here," he said and tossed her Polly's indecent dress. "Put that on if you'll be more comfortable clothed."

She snatched at the flimsy garment wondering if you could call this "clothed," and slipped it over her head. When she stood up, she saw the skirt reached only inches below her knees, and was reminded of the shift she had worn in Saint Dominque so long ago. Try as she might, she could not get the little sleeves to go higher than the curve of her shoulders, nor the frill on the bodice to lift more than an inch over the tip of her breasts. She sighed in exasperation and found Adam was laughing at her softly.

"Let me help." His deft fingers pulled the laces tight beneath her bosom, making her breasts swell even more alarmingly. The tip of one finger traced the neckline as he kissed her lightly and tugged the sleeves down off her shoulders. Then he stepped back and surveyed her. She blushed at the thought of all that exposed flesh, and at the slow smile that spread across his face.

"Polly would scratch your eyes out if she could see you in her dress. I never knew it could be so devastatingly fetching." He held out his hand. "Come, Miss Ashton, a feast awaits you."

Never, thought Charity, had she tasted food so good. In her hunger she forgot to be embarrassed by her garb, or even by the intimacy they had shared only a short while ago.

Adam watched her eat with amusement. "How can you stay so slender with an appetite like a woodsman?"

"No gentleman notices a lady's appetite," she replied, reaching for another spoonful from the kettle.

"And no lady has an appetite like yours."

She grinned and went right on eating.

Afterwards they took the bowls down to the little creek where a half moon gave them enough light to wash them and to refill the bucket.

In the cabin Adam put things away and tossed more wood on the fire. "It'll burn for some time now. Shall we go for a walk?"

Charity nodded eagerly. The open door beckoned to dewy grass and she realized that here at last she could do what she'd longed to do last night (was it really only last night?) at the ball. A few steps from the door she broke into a run. She heard Adam hoot with surprise, and she laughed. Arms outstretched, she sped down the clearing until strong arms snatched her from behind and pulled her down at the edge of the woods. Laughing and breathless they rolled over and over in the grass till Adam released her and she sat up to hug her knees.

Adam lay back and tugged absently at the grass. Watching her, he bit down on a coarse blade and thought, by God, if you had to go and get yourself embroiled in a crazy mess, you picked quite a girl to do it with.

There had been other scrapes, other impulsive madnesses, but never had he abducted anyone and very nearly become a hunted man in the bargain. And never had rape been one of his accomplishments. He shook his head. It didn't do any good to swear off brandy now, he reflected. Anyway, he wasn't convinced that brandy had been the root of his madness last night. There was something about this girl that had haunted him since the night he had dragged her from the fighting sailors in Cap Français. And it wasn't only her glorious body.

Memory of that body made him stir and he sat up. "You could have broken your neck, running around like that."

She smiled lazily. "Not really. Anyway, you didn't have to follow."

She sounded so like a little girl he laughed. "Where did you learn to run around barefoot, you little hoyden?"

"At home," she said simply.

Suddenly Adam wanted to know about this strange, wild girl he'd always sensed was beneath the frosty exterior she'd chosen to wear with him most of the time. "Tell me about home."

She looked quickly at him, but his still form in the moonlight showed it was no idle question. She hugged her knees tighter, swallowing hard. When she began to talk, she knew the dam was loosening. And soon it was all pouring out; from her great-grandfather who'd first come to Saint Dominque to her mother and father and their life at Tournay, through her own childhood and up to that fateful evening when nearly everything had been taken from her in a few nightmare hours. She was crying by the time she'd done, and wishing fervently she hadn't been such a fool as to bring it all out from the deep hiding places of her mind.

Adam had sat without moving through the whole of it, his rage at the LaRoches and the Wentworths growing as he formed a picture of the loving, loyal, endearingly headstrong young girl Charity had been. He knew already to what she had nearly been reduced this past year. When he saw the tears glistening on her cheeks, he felt the same unfamiliar urge he'd felt once before—to hold her and protect her.

When he reached for her, Charity stiffened in automatic reflex, but he pulled her to her feet and held her, smoothing her hair. "Charity." His voice was very low. "Dear girl."

Her head on his chest, her cheek pressed to the curling hair, she cried with relief and abandon. Strong arms protected her and she found the storm passing more quickly than she could have hoped. At last she raised her head and with a hiccough announced she was fine now.

Adam kissed her forehead and let her go. Then hand in hand they walked back to the creek where Charity washed away her tears, knowing they were now gone forever. New ones might come, but the tears for home were over.

Drying her face on the hem of her dress, she smiled tremulously. "I'm sorry."

He took her face in his hands. "No, I'm sorry."

"Thank you," she said, then gently pulled his fingers away. "I'll race you to the cabin."

With a guffaw, Adam snatched her hand. "Not on your life. I have better things to do with your limbs than to spend the rest of the night bandaging them."

Once back in the cabin, Charity felt a rush of shyness. Never before, except to her father, had she opened her soul to a man. She was suddenly very vulnerable and afraid.

But Adam seemed unaware of her mood as he poked up the fire and spread out the soft blankets he'd brought. When he looked up she was standing where he'd left her. The flickering light played over her tumbled hair and down across her naked shoulders and rounded breasts. Her slender arms were drawn in front of her, her hands clasped. Instinctively he knew she was retreating from him, and he reached out to stop her as he realized he wanted her once more.

"Come, Charity." He touched her hands, her face, her hair. Her eyes were opaque, and he hesitated. Then he reached for the laces at her waist, knowing only one way to bring her back to him now. He loosened them, then pulled at the frill above. One rosy-tipped breast spilled out of the tiny bodice, and he leaned over to kiss it as he pulled harder.

His lips and tongue played on her nipples till they grew hard with desire and Charity felt her knees buckling with longing. She put her hands in his thick hair and held his head to her, feeling the ache growing between her legs. Her mind strayed to the night of the *vaudun* ceremony in the foothills of home. Perhaps this is what it is to be possessed, she thought, and closed her eyes.

Lifting the full skirts of her dress, Adam grasped her naked hips and pulled her down on top of him on the blanket-piled rug. Expertly, he tugged the dress up over her head and slid out of his own breeches. She lay over him, touching his face, feeling the firm length of his body beneath hers and welcoming the hot hardness of his manhood against her legs. Spreading her thighs, she let him move her hips till he could thrust into her. She gasped as he went deep inside her and burying her head in his neck she lost herself in a world of tumultuous excitement.

The embers of the fire glowed softly when the two spent themselves at last and lay tangled and breathless before it. A cool night breeze stirred one flame, which sputtered and died slowly. Adam pulled the edges of the blankets over them. Charity curled tight against his side, and he lay breathing the fragrance of her thick hair. Smiling, they slept.

Chapter 16

Charity stirred when she felt the warmth of Adam's body leave her, but slept on until the sun was climbing over the trees. When she woke, she stretched sensually and looked around the cabin, listening for the sound of footsteps. The place had been picked up; her dresses hung on a peg, fresh water stood by the door, packages were piled on the box in the corner, and food sat out on the table. But there was no sign of Adam. Even his boots were gone. Charity sat up with a jerk. Forgetting to wrap herself up, she kicked off the blanket and got to her feet. Quickly, she opened the door and peered outside. The clearing was deserted. With a crash she slammed the door and stamped her foot in vexation. The villain had gone off and left her.

She splashed water over herself and combed her hair, thinking of names she'd like to call him. Then she jerked the blue calico dress from its peg and pulled it on over new underthings from the package. The very fact that it was too big through the waist and hips and too long in the arms gave her satisfaction as she plucked the buttons through their loop fasteners. Then she stalked to the table to see what food he'd left her.

Black smudges across the table top caught her eye and she bent closer to see. Using pieces of coals from last night's fire, Adam had scrawled messy words on the planks.

"Had to go. Back soon as can. Is food. A."

Wiping off the hasty message, Charity pretended she had never doubted his return, but she felt strangely better now, and looked at the hard biscuits and jar of peach preserves with more interest.

Sitting outside on a crude little bench, she munched her breakfast and let the morning sun warm her. She had discovered the new knife Adam had left, and its presence added now to her sense of security. But by the time she was done, she had worked up her anger again. She had hoped to go to Richmond with him this morning, and she did not look forward to another day of waiting to see what was happening with nothing to occupy her. How dare he just go off without a word to her, leaving her to fend for herself in this deserted place? Even worse, what if the owner decided he needed to get away from home today? *That* possibility didn't bear thinking on. In fact, most of her predicament didn't bear thinking on.

Briskly she busied herself with tidying up. She found that Polly had sent her not only a comb, brush, hairpins, and ribbon, but a small hand mirror as well. She wondered again who this Polly was to Adam, and held up the mirror. It seemed to her that not only did her cheeks have unusually high color, but that her eyes were brighter and her lips more voluptuously soft. Was this the way you looked when you had given yourself to a man? Did whores have perpetually doe-like eyes and overripe mouths? She shuddered, feeling irritable and ashamed. She had been abandoned here by a man of degenerate character who came back at his convenience only to use her again for his base desires. She was appalled by her own lapse into sin last night, and determined to set about correcting the situation. Clumsily, she pinned her hair into a large knot at the base of her neck, hoping it gave her an unflatteringly respectable air. He couldn't keep her in this cabin forever, and when he tired of her and returned her to civilization, what was to become of her? He had said once he would never abandon her. Perhaps he would give her some money and she could make her way to Philadelphia, to the colony of people from Saint Dominque. If Paul were there, that would be unfortunate, but she should be able to avoid him.

By the time Gabriel's hoofbeats sounded in the clearing in midafternoon, Charity had worked on her plan till she thought she had a plausible story for the French emigrants. It remained only to get away from her captor. If she showed him she no longer desired his embrace, a man of his fiery temperament should tire of her quickly and let her go.

Accordingly it was a picture of a prudish young miss who stood in the doorway to greet the returning rake. Though her composure suffered at the sight of the second horse behind him, and nearly cracked when he guffawed as he dismounted.

"Even an ill-fitting dress can't hide all your charms, my girl." He strode toward her. "What did you do to your hair?"

Self-consciously she put up a hand to her ragged bun. "Merely an attempt to look respectable for a change," she said in her primmest voice, trying to meet his eyes.

Adam stopped. "Why, may I ask, this sudden desire for respectability?"

She colored, but kept her chin high. "I hardly think an explanation is necessary."

He cocked his head and, folding his arms, he inspected her more closely. "If we weren't in a hurry, I would say an explanation was definitely necessary. I have a distinct preference for the dress you wore last night." He watched her color mount and grinned. "But whatever the reason for your sudden urge, it happens to coincide with my plans."

She stepped back automatically. "P-plans?"

"What an infuriating girl you are. You can hardly pretend shyness with me after last night. You know you enjoyed all of it as much as I did."

"You are a cad to throw that up at me," she flared. "Apparently it would never occur to you that although a woman might submit to your base desires, she might also regret it later."

"When she responds to my 'base desires' the way you did—no, the thought would not occur to me."

"Then I regret to inform you I am not like your other women," she flung at him.

His eyes narrowed, but then he shrugged. "Whatever your crazy reasons for this masquerade are, they'll have to wait. We must be going."

"Going? Going where?" Illogically, Charity suddenly felt deflated by the thought that her appearance had already made him weary of her. "Are you taking me off to see that I am 'well situated,' as you once so delicately put it?"

Adam's brows rose in surprise. "That particular thought hadn't yet crossed my mind. Though I gather you wished it had. And perhaps it should," he added wickedly and watched the pulse in her neck jump. "At the moment, however, I plan only on getting us away from here before we're discovered."

"And you are exposed for the libertine and abductor you are!"

"Indeed." The corner of his mouth twitched. "And before you are branded a fallen woman in the eyes of the local worthies."

"Oh!" Charity's mouth clamped shut.

Adam said no more, but went about erasing the signs of their occupancy. When the last bundles were strapped to the horses, he shut the cabin door and pulled her over to the second horse. "Like it or not, Miss Ashton," he said lightly, "you're off to adventure with this libertine and abductor. Hike up those skirts. You'll have to ride astride." He lifted her onto the horse. "Besides, I shall enjoy the sight of your well-turned ankles."

She glared at him, but picked up the reins obediently and turned her horse to follow him.

At the edge of the clearing Adam pulled up and looked back. "I'd hoped for one more night alone here," he said, and his grin flashed. "But perhaps another time."

She glared again, but found herself looking over her shoulder as they trotted into the trees.

Adam offered neither explanation for their hasty departure nor information on their destination. He's trying to make me beg, Charity thought, and was determined not to ask. They rode in frosty silence for several miles till Adam, spotting some horsemen on the road ahead of them, took them into the woods and seemed to ride in slow circles.

"We've crossed this stream before," Charity said at last. "Was your great plan to get hopelessly lost in the forest?"

Adam's infuriating grin was back in place. "I wondered if you'd ever notice. And since I know you yearn to be lost with me forever, I hate to disappoint you and say we've been marking time." One long hand indicated the lowering sun. "I'd rather not enter Richmond until dusk."

"Richmond! You've gone quite mad."

"I can only hope others will feel as you do, my sweet, and

will not dream of your being right there where your trunk
was delivered this morning and later fetched and carried off."

"So they did send it."

"They did. And Mr. Wentworth was in tow, to see it was
safe and to find out any news I might have. I was able to
assure him I would do my best to discover you and keep you
safe, and he was most relieved. He left some money for you.
He's come to the realization that his wife and daughter would
not have you darken their door again, but he seems to have
had a genuine fondness for you. I think he hopes I'm right,
and that you are going to Philadelphia to find old friends."

Charity let out her breath. "Then they won't be searching
for me any more."

"That is my hope. But I won't take any chances until you
are well away. What if your dear Joseph has had second
thoughts, and has concluded he can't live without you after
all?"

Charity reflected bitterly that Joseph was far too respectable to come to that romantic decision. No, Helen would have
him now, and she could only hope the girl would treat him
decently. She said nothing, though, and watched Adam's face
set into hard lines. Soon he started them on their way again.

The evening was nicely advanced when they rode into
Richmond, and they passed few people in the short blocks to
Knight's. In the rear of the stableyard Adam made her dis-
mount and wait in the shadows while he gave the horses into
the care of a groom. Wryly Charity wondered if she was
doomed to skulk behind stables for the rest of her life. But
Adam was back in a moment and, guiding her firmly through
a rear door of the sprawling building, he whisked her up
servants' stairs to a small, neat room with a rag rug and
lavender floral curtains. She halted as she spied the large
brass bedstead.

Adam followed her gaze. He put down her trunk, then
with a gesture of impatience he pulled her inside the room
and shut the door. Brusquely he lit a second candle and pulled
out some boxes already piled under the bed. These he stacked
beside the trunk. His gaze flicked across the room again. "I'll
leave you to your fearful ruminations," he said harshly,
"while I see about some food."

Then he was gone, and Charity could only stare at the
whitewashed planks of the door.

Half an hour later, after she had explored the contents of
the trunks and boxes and found she now had two night-

dresses, her riding habit, and five gowns, there came a knock at the door.

"Come in," she called, still shaking out the old glazed chintz that had come with her from Saint Dominque.

The latch lifted cautiously, and a saucy face topped with suspiciously red hair peeked around the corner. "I've brought you dinner, ma'am." The door was pushed open and in came a buxom girl bearing a tray.

Charity eyed the plunging neckline on the girl's dress, her petite stature and her wide inquisitive gaze, and she felt sure she knew who this was. With an expert flick of her foot, the girl kicked the door shut and advanced with the tray.

"Over there will be fine, thank you," Charity indicated the table by the window.

"Mr. Crandall said to tell you he hoped you enjoyed your rep—" her tongue stumbled, "the food."

"How kind of Mr. Crandall."

The girl set the tray down and bounced back to the door. "My name's Polly." She gave Charity and the dress she still held an audacious look. "If you require anything more."

Charity nodded. "Thank you, Polly."

"Though I don't suppose you will. Mr. Crandall thinks of everything. He even ordered some of Mr. Knight's *best* wine for you."

"So thoughtful," Charity murmured, not moving.

"Well, I'll be off then." Polly batted big eyes in her direction and disappeared.

The girl took a long breath. It seemed that Polly did not know who she was. She wondered what wild tale Adam had told downstairs to account for her presence and lifted the cloth on the tray to inspect the food. She sniffed mouth-watering aromas and realized there was just one glass and one plate. So Adam had chosen to remain in the common room, probably for appearance's sake.

She discovered she was famished and made short work of the delicious mutton, corn, and vegetables, all the while sipping the excellent wine so thoughtfully provided. Several times she looked up when she heard a footfall in the passage outside, but no one stopped at her door, and she finished her meal in peace.

"So Mr. Crandall thinks of everything, does he?" she said softly as she put down her glass at last. Far from feeling grateful, Charity found her anger mounting. Evidently the man was an old hand at seeing to the needs and desires of women. Well, she had no intention of standing second...or fifth...or tenth in line for the pleasure of his favors. She flounced from the chair and returned to sorting her clothes with vengeful interest.

A little while later Polly reappeared for the tray. "I hope you enjoyed your meal," the girl said.

"It was delicious, thank you. You may tell Mr. Crandall that was indeed a good wine," Charity answered and watched coolly as Polly threw the cloth over the empty dishes and picked up her burden.

The girl shrugged. "Yes, ma'am. If he'll hear me."

"What do you mean?"

"Well, they're all..."

"Drinking?"

Polly giggled. "I guess all that serious talk they did over dinner made their throats mighty dry. They're singing and carrying on now."

"Singing, too?"

"Yes, ma'am. All manner of songs Mrs. Knight says aren't fit for a young girl's ears." She giggled again. "But I don't mind. They're fun when they're..." She seemed to recollect herself then, and began to back out of the room.

Charity thanked her again, and went to close the door after her. So, Adam was drunk. She wished there were a lock on the door. She'd already learned how unpredictable he could be in his cups, and she wished there were somewhere to hide. But perhaps he'd be too drunk to...With little hope of that, she disrobed tensely and put on a nightdress. Then climbing between the coarse sheets, she steeled herself to wait. Now she could hear the distant sounds of revelry from the front of the building, and she wondered how long they could continue. Would he be brutal when he came up? Surely not...after last night. But he was angry and disgusted with her, she knew. And he was drunk! If only this mattress would open up and let her disappear into it!

The bed felt so good after two nights in the cabin, she found herself dozing off. But every lifted voice or footstep outside brought her awake with a fearful jerk. At long last, though, silence descended and she slept peacefully.

A knock on the door brought her upright at dawn, and she looked around wildly to see she was alone. "Who is it?" she called in a faltering voice.

The door opened in answer and Adam strode purposefully into the room. He surveyed the unpacked trunk and then her cringing form in the center of the bed. "Polly will be up with breakfast in a few minutes. You have half an hour to get everything packed."

"Wh-where are we going?"

"Toward Charlottesville. Half an hour." And he was gone.

Charity jumped from the bed. To Charlottesville! Her knowledge of Virginia geography was scant, but she felt vaguely that it was a place north and perhaps west of here. Charlottesville! That's where his family lived. What was he thinking of? But if Charlottesville were north, it would put her that bit closer to Philadelphia, she reasoned. Surely after last night's avoidance of her, he meant to be rid of his burden now. She scurried to stuff everything back into the trunk and boxes and to eat a hasty breakfast. Then reflecting that they must be going by carriage or wagon because of the trunk, she dressed in the vine embroidered chintz with frantic speed. Never for a moment did she doubt he would drag her downstairs in her nightdress if she weren't ready on time.

A few minutes later she was seated beside him in a small farm wagon, and they were clattering out of the yard, Gabriel tied on behind. The sun was just tinting clapboard walls a rosy pink when they passed the last dwelling of town and headed for the open road. Whipping up the team, Adam drove in grim silence and Charity, deciding that his head hurt again this morning, kept her own counsel. Though after nearly an hour, as they passed two slaves leading a mule, she dared to peek over at him and found the lines around his mouth were finally relaxing.

Shortly, he turned the rig off the main road and, at the same relentless pace, drove past small farms and wooded tracts. When the horses showed signs of tiring, Adam pulled into one of the farms. With a story about having lost their way, he got directions, procured food for the two of them and water and rest for the animals. But it was not long before they were on their way again.

The afternoon was a glorious one, and Charity felt her spirits lift with each mile that was put between them and Richmond. Adam, intent on keeping the horses on the narrow way, said little, but he no longer looked so forbidding, and occasionally they exchanged views on the sights they passed. When at last the late afternoon sun began to dip behind the largest trees, he turned off the wooded track and took them to the grassy banks of a clear stream where a massive willow dipped pale branches into the running water. Entranced,

Charity jumped from the seat and walked under the leafy bower. Clapping her hands, she turned back to find Adam watching her as he began to unharness the horses.

Her eyes, made more green by the color of her dress, showed her surprise. "Do we stop here for long?"

"For long enough," he answered. "You might get the hamper from the floor and see what good Mrs. Knight has provided in the way of nourishment."

Charity sped to do his bidding and carried the heavy basket to the base of the willow tree. Then she went to help him with the horses. It was Adam's turn to look surprised as she untied Gabriel and began to walk him up and down the banks to cool him off before leading him to the stream to drink.

"Mind your gown," he called, following her. But already she was twitching her skirts aside as Gabriel splashed into the stream and ducked his head.

Laughing, Charity backed up the bank and came to stand beside him. They watched that the horses didn't drink too much. She stood so close Adam could smell the perfume of her hair.

"You're much too distracting, my girl," he said, and moved toward the stream. "Go and unpack that thing."

She stuck her tongue out at him and he laughed. To his own amazement, he returned the gesture and watched her flounce away to spread a blanket under the tree. As he tethered the horses, he shook his head. Never had he met a girl like this. She could fire him to fury or passion so quickly it made his head spin. And just when he would brace himself for another of her tongue-lashings, she would delight him utterly in some completely unexpected way.

Still shaking his head musingly, he joined her a few minutes later, and watched as she spread tempting food out for him. Munching cold chicken, bread, and cheese, they sat in companionable silence, watching the eddies of water around leafy fingers. Thrushes trilled an evening song and a toad hopped up the bank to inspect the intruders. Nearby the tearing of grass as the horses ate was the only other sound in their peaceful world.

The light was the softest haze when at last they'd finished and began to clean up. Charity hated the thought of leaving this idyllic spot, and gathered things for the hamper with reluctance. But when she'd done packing, she found Adam was sprawled on the blanket in his shirtsleeves, watching. His coat was hung neatly over a branch and she looked from it to him inquiringly.

169

A lazy smile spread across his face. "There are more branches for your clothes."

Her face grew hot as she looked down at her gown. "But we're out in the open here," she said in a small voice.

Adam's eyes twinkled as he sat up. Throwing out his arms, he looked in every direction. "There's not another soul around, save the horses. And they don't mind a bit, I promise you."

Her face crimson now, Charity avoided his eyes. There was nowhere for her to run from him; she was at his mercy once more. Slowly she raised a quaking hand to her neck and closed her eyes.

"Here, let me." Adam's voice was at her ear and his hands were working on the tiny buttons. As his lips brushed her neck, Charity felt a tingling through her limbs and realized she wouldn't run now if she could. Her body was going to betray her again with this man, and she couldn't fight it.

Her dress and chemise came away from her shoulders and in their place Adam's warm mouth covered her rosy skin. As in a dream she let him pull everything off her and stepped out of the billowing skirts. Carefully Adam hung her clothes over a branch next to his. Then he undid his own linen shirt while his eyes traveled hungrily over her still form. When he pulled off his breeches she tried to turn away, but found she couldn't take her eyes from his magnificent bronzed body. The broad shoulders rippled and flexed with taut muscles as he moved, and when he straightened again she gazed at the tight line of his flat stomach and lean hips and at the supple power of his long legs. She knew her eyes were bright with yearning, and she was powerless to close them, to stop what was happening to her.

Strong hands caught her waist and then she was against him, her arms twined around his sturdy neck as she drank in his scent and the feel of him. One arm under her legs, he lifted her and stood cradling her. She let her head fall back, exposing her creamy throat to his hot mouth, and she moaned softly.

Gently he laid her on the blanket and took her slowly, playing her body like a finely tuned instrument. Drowning in waves of desire, Charity moved to meet his rhythm, torn between wanting to prolong the communion and wanting to reach the crest of her wave. Sensing her need, Adam toyed with her until she moaned and called his name. He groaned then and soon her frustrating ache gave way to a flood of ecstatic pleasure as Adam groaned again, shuddered, and lay still at last. In the dim dusk they lay staring at each other in wonder.

In the morning light Adam propped himself on one elbow and looked regretfully at her. One hand caressed the curve of her hip as she opened her eyes. "I wish there were time," he said and kissed her temple.

She stretched, stifling a yawn. "Are all men so insatiable?" she asked, curling up against him again.

"They are if you are the object of their passions," he answered and slapped her hip lightly. "Twice in one night is not near enough, my siren."

She ducked her head under one arm, remembering the twinkling stars through the willow branches when she woke to find Adam, hard against her once more, nuzzling the sensitive places in her neck. She'd responded with an ardor she'd not thought possible and afterward she'd felt as though she'd sleep for days.

But now he was tugging her to her feet, and she saw that for all his talk of no time, desire was beginning to creep into his eyes once more. She pulled away and jumped for her clothes, lithe limbs flashing as she grabbed the garments and danced away toward the stream.

Resisting the urge to follow her, Adam watched her firm round buttocks prance upstream and wondered how he would get through the next several days without seeing her this way. Knowing cold water would help to still the throbbing in his veins, he went to give the horses a drink and to dunk himself in the stream.

Jolting back to the cart track, they took regretful leave of their night's lodgings. "How far is it to Charlottesville?" Charity asked, as she hung onto the seat and tried to keep her voice matter-of-fact.

Adam grinned at her and she realized with a pang he was happy to be going home again. "Tonight we'll be near. And you will have a soft bed once more."

Charity, who had never slept on the ground in her life, was amazed to discover she now felt she would gladly give up a year of feather beds to stay here one more night. But reality was intruding and she felt a lump in her throat. "Oh," she said in a strangled voice.

He looked at her sharply. "What's the matter? I should think that idea would appeal mightily. Though I am sorry I won't be able to join you. Propriety, and all that."

"When was the last time you worried about propriety?" she demanded.

Adam laughed. "When it last suited my purpose," he answered and refused to say more.

Chapter 17

They passed into a country of softly rolling hills in the afternoon and Charity found herself comparing the landscape favorably to the flat reaches of the Tidewater area behind them. She still wondered what their destination was to be and surveyed an approaching inn with an appraising eye. But the wagon rumbled past it without a pause. For nearly an hour they'd been traveling on the main road, and Charity began to worry that he was taking her into the town after all, when once more Adam turned down a side road that took them into trees. Charity was flagging as much as the horses after the hours of suspense, but she sat up straight when they passed between brick gates and went sedately up a tree-lined avenue toward a handsome Georgian house flanked by low wings and outbuildings. She was appalled when Adam waved to a groom running to meet them, and wondered anew if he'd taken all leave of his senses. Obviously this place was familiar to him. How did he dare bring an unchaperoned girl to its door? She wished she could snatch the reins and turn them around.

It was already too late though. Adam was tugging her down and the front door was opening. Charity caught her breath as, in a whirl of lavender skirts, a tall, black-haired girl ran down the steps and flung herself into Adam's arms.

"Where on earth did you come from?" the girl cried, hugging him and laughing. Then she turned large eyes the color of her dress on his companion. Holding out both hands to clasp Charity's, she eyed Adam with a twinkle. "You scoundrel. Where have you been hiding her?"

"In Richmond," he laughed and Charity colored to her hair.

"So this is what took you away so much these past months." The girl grinned and Charity felt her own mouth curving in response, though her heart felt like it was lodged in her stomach.

"May I present Miss Charity Ashton, my dear." Adam grasped Charity's elbow and grinned wickedly at her as she sucked in her breath. "Charity, this is my sister, Abigail Babcock."

Appalled, Charity stared at the girl, who stared back. Of course, it was obvious, now that she knew. The same chiseled features and wide sensuous mouth, the same black, waving hair, arched brows, and thick lashes. Only the color of the eyes was different. That and the feminine softness to the determined chin. Under any other conditions, she thought, she would like this girl instantly. The circumstances were so appallingly awkward, however, she could think of nothing to say.

Abigail seemed to take no notice of Charity's stiff smile and frozen grasp on her hands. Tugging her up the stairs she was all bubbling laughter. "I have no doubt you've abducted her from some dastardly villain and have brought her here for safe keeping." Ignoring Charity's gasp, she led them through the hall to a blue and white morning room.

Adam's laugh sounded boomingly masculine in the delicate room. "In fact, that's precisely what I've done, sister dear."

"How famous." Abigail clapped. "And how romantic! But come and tell me all about it." She pulled Charity, whose legs had turned to wood, down beside her on a velvet-covered window seat.

Charity looked wildly at Adam and saw him give her a slow wink. Pinker than ever, she sat rigidly waiting to hear what sort of fantastic story he would now concoct for his sister. But she was totally unprepared for his choice when he made it.

Pacing up and down the small room, Adam ran a hand through his thick hair. "You remember, Abby, when I returned from Saint Dominque and told you of the slave rebellion and the devastation to the plantations."

His sister nodded and he stopped pacing. "I also told you of the French refugees aboard our ship coming home, and of one girl in particular."

Charity saw Abigail nod again, her eyes bright with interest, and turned away. What had Adam told her then?

Jamming his hands deep into his pockets, Adam went on with a rush. "Well, Charity is that girl. She went to live at Wentworth where they were fairly beastly to her. Her mother died there and her only personal servant was sent away."

Charity's head came up. How had he known about Marie? She felt violet eyes rest on her sympathetically and tried to smile.

"You remember Helen Wentworth."

"Indeed I do." Abigail spoke for the first time.

"Well, she behaved in characteristic fashion, in league with the older women, and practically reduced Charity to the role of a servant. You can imagine her jealousy at having anyone who looked like *that* in her house."

The one who looked like *that* stared at him with mouth agape. "B-but I thought you liked Helen," she blurted.

Adam hooted as his sister watched them both with lively curiosity. "*Liked* her! She's a... Never mind what she is. We all know. And the reason you thought I liked the witch was that whenever I came to see you, you would disappear and leave me in her clutches."

Charity dimpled at that and enjoyed the idea of Adam discomposed.

Abigail's brother took another turn around the room, and stopped to lower his brows at her. "And then you went and caught Joseph Hadley in your snare."

Charity stared at him indignantly as Abigail patted her hand and said, "Good for you." She felt she would burst into hysterical laughter in a moment, but held her breath. How on earth did he plan to explain everything else?

Now Adam rounded on his sister. "Good for her? Would you wish her married to that pompous, unsmiling, self-righteous prig?"

"No, of course not, dear," answered his sister soothingly, "if you didn't want her to marry him."

Charity put her hands to her face at that. She felt she was

sitting in a madhouse and didn't know if she could listen to much more without going quite mad herself.

"Well, I didn't. But I couldn't think how to stop it. And all the time an oily compatriot of hers named LaRoche was lying in wait for her, living right there at Wentworth when he wasn't gallivanting off to Philadelphia. I didn't know which was the one she should worry about most, or what action I should take."

Charity giggled then and dropped her hands. "And so you took to drink to solve my problems," she gurgled, afraid she really had slipped over the edge at last.

There was a tense silence as Adam and Charity stared at one another.

"Well, *did* you drink a great deal?" asked Abigail in a prosaic tone.

"Of course I drank too much," Adam thundered and spun on his heel to resume his walk. "Wouldn't you?" he threw over his shoulder as he rounded on a corner and started back.

"I expect so," sighed his sister, "under those conditions. But how did you contrive to get her away?"

"I *contrived* by getting so mad..."

"In your cups," prompted Abigail.

"...in my cups, that when I found LaRoche manhandling her outside a ball we attended at Hadley House, I knocked him down and carried her away."

"Carried her away," Abigail echoed faintly. "But you don't just carry someone off into the night from the middle of a ball."

"I did," he said firmly and looked mutinously at them both.

It was the last straw for Charity. She sank into the corner pillows and wept with laughter as Abigail patted at her distractedly.

"Now see what you've done, Adam," she scolded. "You've sent the poor thing into hysterics reminding her."

Charity tried to raise her head. "No, no. It isn't that." She caught a gleam in Adam's eyes as he watched her and choked on more laughter. "If you could see yourselves...this ...this whole conversation." She made a helpless gesture as she covered her mouth.

Adam was grinning as he threw himself down on a damask-covered chair and they heard it creak under his assault.

His sister frowned at him. "You both sound as though you left your wits back at Hadley House. Are you saying that the two of you galloped off on Gabriel, thumbing your noses at the offensive Frenchman?"

Adam glanced at Charity, who was still fighting for control. "Not quite," he said shortly. "She did not come willingly."

"Oh dear." Abigail resumed her distracted patting of Charity's arm. "So you forced her to leave, and have had her locked in a closet since then. Or did you come straight from the ball?" She eyed Charity's neat day dress dubiously.

"You read too many romances, Abby." Adam was on his feet again. "But yes, I had her hidden for two days."

"I've never read a romance that could equal this," his sister said with some asperity. "Have you at least *fed* her?"

Charity choked again, but Adam ignored her. "It was not my intention to torture her, dear sister."

"Only to abduct her from her new home! And what of the Wentworths? And of Joseph?"

A black eyebrow rose in wry amusement. "You may imagine Helen's relief at finding her rival gone. And as for the rest, they hope that I am correct in surmising that Charity has run away to Philadelphia to find friends from Saint Dominque. The hunt, I hope, has been called off."

"I see." Abigail tapped one foot thoughtfully on the parquet floor. "And I see further that you have engineered this entire escapade, leaving Miss Ashton no say in the matter."

"Not until now." Adam's face was serious, and Charity looked at him wonderingly.

Abigail glanced at each in turn, then stood up, peering at the gilt clock on the mantel. "I also see it is getting late and Charles will be wondering where I am. Not to mention the children." Holding out a hand to Charity, she said, "Come, Miss Ashton, I will show you to your room, for I feel sure you would like a chance to freshen up before dinner." She tucked Charity's hand neatly under her arm and turned to her brother. "Your room is the red one, as always. And would you tell Thomas we will be four for dinner and to please send the trunk I saw in your wagon up to the green room?" Pulling Charity from the window, she continued in the same breath. "I do hope he managed to buy you plenty of clothes, my dear."

"N-no," Charity faltered. "That trunk is my own."

Abigail's eyes turned skyward. "I will *not* ask how that was managed. For right now we will have to go and see your sheets are aired."

"You're so awfully kind, Mrs. Babcock," Charity began.

"Nonsense. And please call me Abby. All my friends do."

Adam leaned over at that and pecked her lightly on the cheek. "Dear Abby," he said and went out the door.

She smiled mistily at his back as she led Charity from the room.

By the time dinner was over, Charity felt quite at home despite her circumstances. It was such a relief to have the Babcocks know the truth (without any details of the past few days) and not to have to play a part with them. Charles Babcock, a portly, blond man some years older than Abigail, had proved the soul of tact, and had never let Charity feel she was anything but a most welcome guest. Charity formulated the theory that Charles, who gave the air of languid indulgence and vague understanding, was in fact a very capable gentleman who was very much in love with his vivacious young wife, and who had long since grown used to the eccentricities of her family and friends. Although sympathetic to Charity's history of trials and tribulations, he never questioned her sudden appearance in his home, seeming to assume it was perfectly natural for Adam to bring her here for asylum.

During dinner, Adam and his sister had kept up a light, bantering conversation while Charles had set himself the task of putting their guest at ease. But occasionally Charity had heard snatches of talk about the other Crandalls or gossip about old acquaintances, and she wished she could attend more closely. Their words would tell her more about Adam, and Abigail seemed just the sort of sister she would have liked for herself and she wanted to know her better.

When the last covers were removed, the lady of the house drew Charity from the room, saying she knew the gentlemen would want to talk horses in peace, but that they mustn't linger more than half an hour. Smiling, they promised, although Adam's eyes were serious when he watched them leave.

Across the wide central hall Abby threw open double doors to the library. "So much cozier for small groups," she explained and went and sat in one of the leather-covered chairs by the fireplace.

Charity's eyes sparkled. What delightful informality, and what a wonderful room. Her eyes traveled over high white bookcases filled with well-thumbed volumes, walls hung with prints, and a big mahogany desk in one corner piled high with papers and books. Quite the sort of library she would create, she thought, masculine and comfortable. Smaller than her father's at Tournay, but in much the same spirit. Then she recollected herself. "Forgive me for staring," she said to the seated figure. "It's just that this is such a marvelous room."

"Isn't it though," Abby agreed. "We spend a great deal of time here. Charles likes to sit among his horses when he's not outside with them." She waved at the sketches and prints around the walls. "But come sit down."

Charity took the proffered chair. "Did you decorate the room to be like your own library at home?" She was suddenly very curious about the Crandalls.

Abby laughed. "No, no. Father's library is a great massive thing with ladders around the walls and dusty corners full of dark books. It's driven Mama wild for years, but it's his sanctuary and he won't let her touch it. Happily, Charles lets me share his." She paused and looked around. "No, I wish Alan and his wife well of Bentwood."

"Alan?"

"Our elder brother." She held up a hand. "And don't think all of us haven't suffered from our parents' quaint notion that all our names should start with 'A'." Then she smiled. "Adam has never mentioned him?"

Charity squirmed. "Not directly."

"Well, I shouldn't wonder. Alan's a bit stuffy. Always concerned with what's proper." She bit her lip as Charity flushed. Then violet eyes danced in the candlelight as she eyed her guest. "Do you know much about horses?"

"Some." Charity was startled at the change of subject.

"Then no wonder you and Charles are already dealing famously together."

"But we hardly spoke of horses."

"Ah, he can always tell...He'll have you out inspecting his racers at dawn if you let him. You'll have to be firm."

"I should love to see his racers."

Abby sighed. "Then you're the first Adam..." She stopped abruptly. "Tell me how long you plan to stay with us."

"I...I don't know. I don't want to impose."

"You couldn't impose," her hostess said firmly. "We love having company. One never knows about Adam, but I do hope you'll plan to stay just as long as you can."

Charity smiled gratefully then, and they fell to talking

about many things. It was all so unlike the evenings she'd endured at Wentworth for so long, Charity thought, listening to Abby tell of an awful gaffe she'd made with a milliner in Charlottesville and laughing delightedly at the vivid picture she described.

When at length the men appeared, the conversation remained spritely and general, and although Charity felt Adam's eyes on her often, he never alluded to their past association or made any effort to speak to her alone. She in turn watched him often, realizing how little she knew of this man beyond the profound intimacy they had shared.

At the end of the evening they parted company from the gentlemen at the top of the stairs and Abby walked Charity firmly to her room, fussing over the covers and checking to see that all was in order for her. Charity got the strong impression that she was being thoroughly chaperoned, and thought ruefully that Abby must know a great deal about Adam's reputation with women.

She spent some time tossing in the soft bed, listening to the sounds of the house settling down for the night, and trying not to admit she missed Adam's strong arms. She was as bemused as ever by his actions this day, and wondered for the hundredth time why he had brought her here. Though he could hardly take her to his own home and present her to his parents, he needn't have inflicted his latest paramour on his sister and brother-in-law this way. But perhaps they really didn't suspect her true relationship with him. Abby's watchful eye indicated that she was concerned for Charity's virtue, and perhaps that was precisely what Adam had wanted her to be. But why? One didn't bring one's new mistress to one's sister's house to be guarded and put in a separate room, she thought bitterly, and tossed some more till she gave it all up to sleep.

With a feeling of *déjà vu*, she discovered the next morning that Adam had already departed. The only difference was that she was not to be thrown on her own devices in a woodland cabin. In fact, she soon found that she was to be given no moment for her own thoughts, what with Abby, her husband, and the two little tow-headed moppets who were their children. An inspection of the stables and a walk through a meadow with the little boys took up the morning. And after lunch Abby and a maid helped her sort through her wardrobe and get her clothes in order.

It was late in the afternoon when masculine voices from the hall made Abby jump up from the chair she'd flung herself into and look at the lengthening shadows out the window.

"Goodness. Adam is back. I do hope all went well at Bentwood."

"Adam went home today?"

"Why yes. It's only a few miles. He always does when he comes here. In fact, he prefers to stay with us and just visit our parents. He says Alan is always reading him lectures on his irresponsible existence. Though what Alan expects him to do when the home farm is already in perfectly capable hands and Adam has no family of his own to look after, I'm sure I don't know." She looked appraisingly at Charity. Then cocked her head as more voices came to them through the open door. "Ah, he seems to have brought Simpson with him," she said enigmatically. "I shall have to go and see the servants don't get into an uproar at his arrival."

Charity looked her bewilderment, and Abby laughed. "Simpson is Adam's valet, though heaven knows why since the man has never been trained to service. And the last time he came here he frightened the servants half to death with descriptions of the savages he'd seen in the West."

Charity remained bewildered, but she flew to change for dinner, her only thought being that Adam was back.

The evening was a repetition of her first in this house, delightful and invigorating, and always impersonal, as though everyone were deliberately avoiding any reference to Adam's behavior bringing an unknown girl to stay for an indefinite period. Charity learned only that he had had a full day at home, had conducted considerable business, and had decided to bring his valet back with him. The only time her plight was mentioned was when they all rose to retire and Adam said he was sending Simpson back to Richmond to return the wagon he'd hired.

"Oh, Charles will send someone with it," Abby exclaimed, looking to her husband.

Adam held up a hand. "No, I want Simpson to go. He'll know how to listen and find out if everyone has truly called off the hunt for Charity."

Abby looked as though she were going to say more, but her husband coughed and took her arm. "I'm sure Adam knows just what he's doing, m'dear. Shall we?" and he propelled her firmly to the door.

Abby planted her feet. "But Charity will want a candle, and I want to be sure all is well in her room," she said a little wildly.

Charity and Adam both hid smiles as Charles glanced back, then taking his wife's arm again, he continued walking. "Of course you do," he said mildly. "Let us get that candle for her now."

Abby looked rebellious for a brief moment, then she gave in with what grace she could muster. "There should be some right on the hall chest, dear. I'll just go and get one."

Nodding, Charles followed her, pulling the doors to as he went.

Adam's chuckle was long and low. "She'll be back in a flash. For some reason she seems to fear I have designs on you."

"Do you?" Charity asked with gleaming eyes.

"Don't ask," he said touching her face, "or I might have to show you, and I'm trying to behave myself for the moment."

Charity dimpled. "It must be a dreadful strain."

"Assuredly. But speaking of strains...you've been grand. I know it wasn't easy for you to be brought here this way."

"No indeed. But I'm sorry I behaved rather wildly yesterday when you were telling Abby how I happened to be with you."

Adam chuckled again. "I had a bad moment until I realized you were *laughing*. I nearly came out with the whole story then, just to see what you would do."

"Beast."

"So you've told me. But you can't run through the litany of my faults now. Abby awaits you. You have been superior. Will you just trust me now?"

"I never have trusted you, and I was quite right," Charity laughed.

Adam's answering smile was lopsided. "You had no choice then."

"Do I now?"

Adam hesitated, and in that fraction of a second, Abby appeared in the door. Her relief at finding them only talking was obvious, and Charity had to duck her head to hide her smile as she accepted the candle. All the way upstairs she wondered what Adam had meant.

Chapter 18

Breakfast was brought to her room the next morning by the two little boys. Charity was so overwhelmed by this childish gesture of hospitality, she lifted them onto the bed to share it with her, and then spent nearly an hour hearing about their ponies and telling of her own home in a distant land.

When they ran out with the dishes, she jumped up and dressed hurriedly. Tying back her hair with a broad aqua ribbon to match her dress, she noticed the sparkle in her eyes and realized she hadn't dressed with this sort of eagerness in a very long time. She remembered the advice she had given herself about taking from life what you could. When she had told herself that, she had decided she must try to take Joseph Hadley. But that was before she'd been with Adam. She threw her arms wide. "You must still take what you can," she told herself gleefully. "But how wonderful to be taking happiness where you find it, instead of second best where you must."

Buoyantly she went down the stairs in search of Abby. But when she found each room empty, she decided to walk in the gardens and breathe in the sweet scent of freedom in the warm, early June air. She passed through the doors at the end of the hall and turned toward the luxurious cutting gardens behind the smoke house. As she rounded the corner of the building, though, she saw the entrance to a maze. Delighted, she turned into it. The boxwood had not had the many years' growth needed to make it both thick and very tall, but it was high enough that she couldn't quite make out where the center might be. She wandered down a grassy path to one dead end, tried to retrace her steps, took a wrong turn and soon was happily lost in the twisting paths. If she stood very straight, she knew she'd be able to see where the plants blocked avenues, but she decided she'd rather guess the way. However, after ten more minutes, she realized she was on the outer walks again, no closer to her objective, and sank down on one of the little stone benches that were dotted through the maze. Kicking off her shoes, she wriggled her toes in the soft grass and leaned back against the thick foliage.

Adam's voice only feet away made her sit upright. Was he entering the maze? Should she call or sit still and let him try to find her?

Then Abby's tinkling laugh followed. "Oh Adam, I'm not such a ninny-hammer as to think you don't have designs on the girl."

Charity held her breath. Where were the voices coming from?

She heard Adam chuckle softly then. "Of course I have designs on her, Abby. Dastardly ones. Why else would I have snatched her away?"

"Is she rich?" his sister asked suspiciously.

"Not any more."

Charity looked around wildly. If she stood up, wherever they were, they'd see her above the hedge. She wondered if she could crawl away down the path. But the thought of their coming on her on her hands and knees was too hilariously appalling. Perhaps if she sat still they would move on.

"Then I don't understand," Abby said. "She's beautiful and well born and obviously has a mind of her own. If you wanted to marry her why couldn't you court her in proper fashion at Wentworth?"

Charity heard the snip of scissors and realized with the sense of panic she must be sitting beside the cutting garden. The two seemed so close now she was afraid to even reach for her shoes for fear they'd hear the rustle of her skirts. Cheeks flaming, she sat still and listened, knowing with a bitter sense of foreboding that those who eavesdrop rarely hear well of themselves.

"I tried," Adam was saying. "But you remember we did not meet in proper formal fashion, and nearly all our en-

183

counters since then have gone awry. She always hated me and avoided me."

"Hated you! If the look in that girl's eyes is hate, I will eat every flower in this basket."

Adam guffawed as Charity gasped and put her hands to her face. "Abby, you don't know. Perhaps she doesn't hate me so much now," and his tone was soft, "but she would as soon have scratched my eyes out as have me speak to her for most of the past twenty-two months."

"But why? There's never been a girl yet who didn't fall into your arms at the first opportunity." Her tone became suspicious again. "What did you do to her to make her react that way?"

There was a long pause and Charity wished the stone bench would open and swallow her whole.

Then Adam's voice resumed, and she could hear laughter in it. "I made thoroughly improper advances."

"Well, that's nothing new," his sister said shortly. "But she's the first I've heard of who didn't jump at the chance. Good for Charity." Her tone changed as she went on reflectively. "Perhaps that's why you have gone to these lengths to secure her. She's a new experience for you, isn't she?"

"She is definitely a new experience for me," Adam said with emphasis.

Abby's laugh floated over the boxwood hedge again. "You know Priscilla will be wild with jealousy, and poor Laura will go into a final decline after these two years of waiting. You'll have to break the news gently."

"I don't intend to break any news to anyone, dear sister. Priscilla has undoubtedly already taken someone else to her bed in these months I've been away, and Laura is not as delicate as you seem to think. Anyway, I never gave her the slightest reason to hope I would offer her marriage."

Charity's lungs were bursting with held breath and she expelled it in a whoosh.

"Well, I must say, it will be nice not to have to worry any more about an enraged husband shooting you. Anyway, I approve heartily of Charity, and think it's about time someone got you to settle down."

"Settle down?" Adam's voice receded, as though he'd backed away. "Wait a minute, Abby. I brought her here because I didn't know where else to take her. I couldn't just keep her hidden forever. And now..."

Abby's voice held exasperation as she followed him, cutting in. "So you lost your senses in one impulsive gesture, and now hope that by coming here everything will somehow sort itself out. You are finding, perhaps, that this time you got more than you bargained for?"

Adam's laugh was distant. "*That* I assuredly did. And..."

His sister's irate voice followed him again. "Well, you can't treat this girl so cavalierly. You'll have to...Adam, come back here."

Their voices were too distant for Charity to make out the words now, but she couldn't have stood any more anyway. Torn between the urge to pick up her bench and hurl it through the hedge and the desire to throw herself on the ground in a fit of tears, she sat still, clasping her hands as tightly as she could and trying to think. But presently she put on her shoes very slowly, smoothed her skirts, and, after making sure she was quite alone again, walked steadily down the path. Using every cheating trick she could, she discovered her way and left the maze.

The loveliness of the morning had disappeared for her, and she wanted only to be alone. How dare they talk about her as though she were an object to be pitied, a toy for Adam to play with till he grew bored, a girl to be protected in her languishing condition by Abby. She went up the stairs with deliberate tread and entered her room. There she threw herself down on a green and white chaise, her pleasure in this spring-fresh room gone, her eyes stormy. Obviously, she could not admit she'd heard their conversation, but she could show them she was not a shrinking violet unable to hold up her head in the face of a wind. She nursed her anger for a while, then, remembering she was to go riding with Charles and the little boys before lunch, she changed to her brown riding habit and stalked back down the stairs.

With a great effort of will, she behaved normally all day, though she avoided Adam's eyes whenever he looked at her. Through the afternoon she thought up and rejected one wild scheme after another, and dressed for dinner with her mind still in turmoil. When she came downstairs, she found Adam waiting for her in the hall. He walked toward her and as she reached the last steps his long fingers covered hers on the banister.

She felt her heart skip a beat at his touch. Looking at his tall immaculate figure in close-fitting dark breeches, bottle-green jacket covering broad shoulders, buff-colored simple waistcoat, and snowy neckcloth, she found it hard to reconcile

185

the image with the furious, half-dressed man with burning eyes and iron arms who had frightened her into submission. She began to wonder if she'd imagined it. She tossed her head. It didn't matter if she had imagined it. She was not his toy.

Adam noticed her look, but chose to ignore it. There were any number of reasons he could think of for that mutinous expression. God knows he'd put her in a hell of a position. There were a lot of things he'd better say to her, he supposed, explain her options. But not right here.

"Peaches and cream you are this evening," he said. "Definitely good enough to eat."

Charity lowered her lashes, more to shut out his face than from embarrassment, and pulled her fingers from his.

"Come, Charity, our chaperone will track us soon enough. Let us take a very proper walk until she does."

Pretending she hadn't seen his offered arm, Charity picked up her skirts and descended the last stairs, following him to the front door. Adam did not make another attempt to touch her as they walked sedately under spreading branches along the drive. Hands clasped behind his back, he slowed his long strides to hers and made light conversation about the horses and the ride she'd had that morning. If he realized that her answers were less enthusiastic than usual he gave no sign. They were nearly out of sight of the house and Adam was at last reaching for her, when the bushes beyond the drive erupted with squeals and whoops. Abby's two small children, faces smeared with mud, came charging around a tree right at them.

"Damn the little brats," Adam muttered, dropping his hands and turning to face the howling attack.

Charity smotherd a giggle as Adam caught a wriggling form in each arm. "You young men are far from your natural territory for this hour." He slung one boy on each hip and looked at them sternly.

"But Indians like to attack at dusk," said the eldest stoutly, his little legs pumping the air as Adam started back up the drive.

"No, they prefer dawn. And the wouldn't bother to attack empty-handed strangers when their own dinners were waiting for them."

"Have you ever been attacked at dawn?" The younger squirmed in his uncle's arms the better to see his face.

"Only once. And I'll tell you all about it another time.

186

Right now Ullah and your mother are looking for you, and if you don't get that warpaint off quickly there'll be nothing but rice pudding for hungry warriors' stomachs."

Charity, following the trio up the drive, felt her heart contract as the boys shrieked and sped for the rear of the house when Adam released them. What a cheerful and happy home this was. How she longed to stay here. But she'd already put aside the thought of asking to be the boys' governess. Not only would the Babcocks not consider such a proposal, but she couldn't stay here and see Adam come and go, beyond her reach.

She sat through the evening with a sinking feeling in her stomach. In just two days' time she'd come to care for these people, and the thought of leaving made her sick. But leave she must, somehow, sometime. She tried not to think about it now, deciding that inspiration would come.

The following afternoon, as they all sat over a cold luncheon in the cool dining room, Abby suggested they go for a ride. Shortly thereafter Charity, dressed and waiting by the front door where grooms were to bring the horses, saw brother and sister come down the stairs together. Abby, still in her sprigged muslin gown, gave Charity a sad look.

"I find I have the most dreadful headache, dears, I couldn't manage a ride now after all. But you mustn't let me spoil your time. Go ahead and I shall lie down and be perfectly fit by supper." She put a dramatic hand to her head, then dropped it. "But do take James with you," she said hastily, "so you won't get lost."

Charity, expressing sorrow at her friend's indisposition, eyed her dubiously. Abby looked no more struck with the migraine than she had on the first day she'd seen her.

Adam was laughing outright. "Do go lie down, little sister. We will contrive to overcome our sorrow at missing your company. And James won't be necessary."

"Yes, he will," flashed Abby, forgetting to languish in agony.

Adam just laughed again, and taking Charity's arm, he whisked her through the door to the waiting horses. As they trotted away from the house, leaving behind the groom intended as escort, Charity wondered at Abby's sudden headache. What would make the girl, after all her watchfulness, throw her together with Adam this way? She was as unpredictable and impulsive as her brother. Charity sneaked a sidelong look at Adam's profile and suddenly she thought she

187

knew just why Abby had played her charade. She hoped that Charity, left alone to entice him, might be able to lure him into matrimony after all. Apparently Abby didn't know her brother so very well. The whole idea would have been laughable if it hadn't unsettled her stomach in a nasty way.

Her companion seemed not to notice her brooding as he guided the horses at a faster pace across a pasture, whistling as he rode. At the far side he dismounted and led the animals through a gate onto a rutted track. Charity looked back at the pasture they'd left and at the last view of the sprawling barns, then cantered up the track through a meadow to where it wound among pale saplings in a young wood.

Beside the gurgling water of a small brook, Adam dismounted once more. Charity gripped her reins more tightly as he came to stand at her stirrup. Her heart lurched as she looked at his upturned face, the boyish lock of stray black hair curling down the center of his forehead. It was a face she might have loved, she thought, and turned her head away.

"Am I going to have to drag you from the horse like a sack of grain?" he asked, grinning up at her.

She looked back quickly. He'd do it too, and probably leave her to explain away the tears in her habit. Swiftly she kicked her foot free of the stirrup and tried to slide off before he could catch her. But his hands circled her waist as she touched the ground, and he was pulling her to him. If he kissed her she was lost. She put her hands on his chest, resisting his tug, and his smile faded.

"What the devil's the matter now? There's no one following, I assure you." His lips brushed her hair. "I'll go mad if I have to wait any longer for you." Already his hands were moving up her sides, stroking her breasts, reaching for the top button of her habit.

She felt her legs turning to water and pushed against him again. "Let me go," she said in a strangled voice.

His arms released her so fast she staggered, then stood trembling as he bent to peer into her face. "What the hell has Abby been saying to you?" he demanded.

His voice was still husky with desire, but an undercurrent of anger was welling. Frustration and annoyance mingled with the indecision he'd been feeling all day. Seeing Charity at his sister's house, elegant, poised, and controlled, but warm and laughing, had made him wonder what it might be like to have a home like Abby's, a home of his own. He'd listened more than idly to Charles's talk of the Davis land that was coming under the auctioneer's gavel in a few months, and had surprised himself. He wasn't sure he liked this new drift to his thoughts, had wanted to cut them off, to lose himself in Charity's beautiful and willing body. He'd been struggling with the enormity of what he'd done to her, and had thought of several alternative answers to the problem. But none of them satisfied him, and he wanted a respite from thought. He was more than put out by her newest attack of coyness.

Charity clutched the stirrup leathers to hold herself up as she watched hints of his inner thoughts play across his face. "It's no good, Adam."

"What's no good? Our lovemaking?" he rasped.

"No, no," she faltered. Then, taking a deep breath, she went on. "Abby has said nothing to me about you, or about us. But surely you see this situation cannot go on. I can't just stay on as your sister's guest forever."

Adam's feet were spread, his hands dug deep in his pockets as he shrugged. "Is that what is bothering you? Well, let me set your mind at rest."

"You can't," she wailed. Then dragging in another breath, she looked squarely at him, watching his eyes darken. "You can't reassure me about anything. I am not your plaything, Mr. Crandall. I will not go on being dragged about in your wake, used at your convenience, wondering where it will end, where it will be that you tire of your game and cast me adrift."

His eyes grew darker till they were almost black, the color of mounting fury. The chit wouldn't even listen to him. To hell with her. His hands in his pockets clenched into fists as he stared at her. Then slowly he withdrew them and crossing his arms, he lifted one corner of his mouth into a sneer. "But you have been my 'plaything,' sweetheart. There's no denying that. And you haven't many choices at the moment."

Charity's own eyes were the color of a turbulent sea now. "I have sufficient choices if you'll give me the money Mr. Wentworth left for me."

"It would not take you very far."

"Far enough," she snapped.

His voice was lazy now, but his expression hadn't changed. "And if I refuse?"

"You wouldn't!"

"I might well, my dear. And then where is your sanctimonious air going to carry you?"

"You vicious swine," she stormed, all her French blood rising to choke her with anger. How dare this arrogant man think he could toy with her this way? "Two can play your game. I'll tell your sister precisely how you've used me." As soon as she'd said it she regretted the hasty and, she knew, empty threat.

But it was too late. The sneer on Adam's mouth had traveled up to his eyes. "Are you trying to blackmail me into marrying you, you harridan?"

Charity hit him then. With all the strength she had, she slapped him. She'd never slapped anyone in her life, and had always scorned girls who resorted to this display of temper, knowing no gentleman would raise a hand in return. But Adam had already shown he was no gentleman, had provoked her to this feeling often, and her only regret now was that she hadn't had the iron poker from the cabin fireplace in her hand when she connected. Sparing only a glimpse for his furious face, she spun and flung herself onto her horse. Too stiff with pain and fury to even wipe the tears from her face, she pulled her animal's head around and rode back into the trees.

Unable to bear the thought of the questions and fussings that would result if she asked for dinner in her room, Charity steeled herself to face everyone downstairs. She washed her face and pinched her cheeks to bring back the color now completely drained by her despair. Then she dressed carefully and slowly, waiting until the last possible minute to descend to the dining room.

She needn't have gone to such elaborate trouble, though, for there was no sign of Adam at the dinner table.

Abby, watching her rather closely, explained that Adam had sent word he was going to Bentwood for dinner and would perhaps return very late.

Charity did her best to receive this news with only mild interest, and to keep up her end of the conversation during the meal. But after dinner, when she pleaded exhaustion as an excuse to go to her room, Abby followed her. The girl tried to assure her hostess she was really nothing more than tired, but Abby was not to be put off.

Closing the door to the room firmly and lighting candles above the mantelpiece, Abby moved purposefully until she came to stand before the chaise where Charity sat. "Some-

190

thing happened this afternoon," she said in a voice full of foreboding. "Did you and Adam quarrel?"

Charity shook her head, not trusting her voice, but she tried to smile.

Abby gestured impatiently and threw herself into a chair opposite. "I knew it," she said darkly. "I should never have sent you off alone like that."

"You can hardly blame yourself," Charity began, then bit her lip.

"So," Abby pounced. "You did quarrel." She stood up again and paced before the fireplace. So much like Adam, Charity thought, watching as Abby stopped and turned to her. "You mustn't let him frighten you, you know," the woman said, clasping her hands. "He's always had an awful temper if he's crossed, but it never lasts. When he cares about someone... well, he cares a great deal, and that can bring out both the best and the worst in him." She stopped, coloring, knowing she'd said far too much and presumed far too much.

Charity was staring at the candles, willing herself not to cry.

"Oh, my dear, what is it?" Abby came and sank down before her. "I do know him better than anyone, and I promise his bark's a great deal worse than his bite. He's obviously upset you. But he's probably regretting it all right now, and will ride back all repentant."

Charity smiled mirthlessly at that. "I don't think so."

Abby clasped her hands again. "He has done something awful, hasn't he? Did he...did he behave improperly?"

Charity had to turn her head. How delicately Abby was trying to put things. She didn't know if she was going to laugh or cry. But suddenly she saw the way out of the whole awful business. Turning back, she nodded slowly.

"Oh dear. And it upset you."

Charity nodded again. She hated to take advantage of Abby's warm and trusting nature, but she couldn't ever tell her the truth.

Abby's fist hit the floor. "Damn," she said and Charity jumped at the unexpected oath. "You're not like any of the others. He told me himself you'd resisted his advances. I thought that might be just what he needed. But now he's gone and made a muddle of everything." She looked up. "I'm right, aren't I, that he not only behaved lecherously, but compounded it by losing his odious temper?"

191

"You seem to have heard all this before." Charity's stomach churned at the thought.

"No. I just know Adam. And I've seen the way he looks at you. Why do you think I've been dogging your footsteps? But I thought today that perhaps I was wrong..."

"I have to leave," Charity said quietly, and found her admiration for Abby growing when the girl didn't try to argue or make excuses. "I have to leave," she repeated, "but I have very little money. Mr. Wentworth left some with your brother, but I'm afraid to ask him for it."

Abby waved this aside. "Money is not the problem. Where will you go?"

"To Philadelphia."

Abby looked thoughtful for a long time. "Yes," she said at last. "That would be good. And I will write you letters of introduction." So Adam will know where you are, she thought.

"No, no. I wouldn't impose on anyone any more. I plan to find others from Saint Dominque. Perhaps I could stay with one of them. And then I will discover a way to support myself."

"Support yourself? But what could you do?"

Charity had thought about all this far too long to hesitate with her answer. "I could be a governess."

"A governess! *No* governess looks like you, Charity, and no woman in her right mind would hire you."

"They would if I had references. And if I looked very prim and proper."

"If you wore an old sack cloth and screwed all that red gold hair into a knot, you would still be far too beautiful for most women to allow near their husbands and sons," Abby said frankly.

Charity flushed at the compliment, but went on doggedly. "I was practically a governess at Wentworth, so I've had some experience." Then she brightened. "And you could write me a recommendation."

Abby stared at her. "Yes," she said slowly. "I suppose I could. When do you plan to leave?"

"Tomorrow."

"Oh, you can't leave so soon. You have arrangements to make. In fact, you should write ahead..."

"How could I find a position if I'm not there to hear of one?"

"Well...But you have to tell Adam."

"No, I don't. I never want to see him again," Charity said vehemently. Then she remembered to whom she was speaking. "I'm sorry."

"Don't be. It is I who should say I'm sorry. We will all hate to see you go."

Charity held out her hands impulsively, feeling tears welling. They looked long at one another.

"Very well. You shall leave tomorrow. And I shall send you off in style."

They spent the next half hour planning Charity's departure, then Abby kissed the girl lightly and left her, saying she would need a good night's rest, since roadside inns had notoriously lumpy beds.

Charity sank into the soft pillows in a daze. She'd done it. She'd found a way out, a way to escape from her torment at the hands of Adam Crandall, and she wished fervently that once away from here she might never lay eyes on him again. She closed her eyes and a bronzed face with black, waving hair swam before her. She lay still, wondering if her memory of skilled hands and a sensuous mouth on her body were all a dream. It must be, since she was certain that she now hated that handsome face with a loathing she'd never before experienced.

Chapter 19

"You will send back word that you're all right, and then write to let us know where you are?" Abby asked anxiously, clinging to the door of her small traveling coach and clasping Charity's hand.

"Of course I will," Charity answered and squeezed the nervous fingers. "You've been so wonderfully kind—all of you." She looked past Abby to where Charles stood on the front steps, still frowning.

He'd argued with her till he could say no more, and had watched the preparations for Charity's departure with a constant shake of his head. But now as he saw her look to him, he summoned a smile and came to take her other hand.

"I still feel you're very ill-advised to go off this way. Not only will we miss you a great deal, but I predict Adam will be ready to lynch us when he returns and discovers we've let you talk us into this mad scheme." He sighed, and his practiced eye went over the horses, the coachman, the carriage wheels, the maid sitting quietly in a corner. "But only you can know what is best, I suppose. Now take good care of Miss Charity, Ginny. See she's comfortable through the trip."

He stepped back then and, pulling his wife to him, he closed the door. Charity watched them from the window as the coach rumbled away from the steps and tried to wave with enthusiasm. It wouldn't do to cry now. This was another road closed to her and she must put her mind on the future.

Her one fear this morning had been that Adam would

suddenly appear. Though she felt quite certain he would applaud her decision to leave, she hadn't wanted to face him. Now if they could just get away before he returned. She peered anxiously out both windows, half expecting to see him ride up from behind some bush, demanding to know what was going on in that frightening way of his. But the countryside remained empty around them and soon the coach had turned onto a main road, heading north. They were not to enter Charlottesville, Charity had learned with relief, but go directly north and east toward Baltimore. She tried to be happy at the opportunity to see more of this new country, but she found her thoughts straying back to the Babcocks and the warm hospitality she had left behind. Sternly she shut her mind to times past. It seemed that everywhere she went her presence caused trouble and she must always be saying good-by. But no longer. She would stand on her own two feet now, as she should have from the first. Annoyed with herself for not feeling the sense of elation she should at this prospect, she turned to Ginny and suggested they see what was in the lunch hamper on the floor.

In the late afternoon it began to rain and Charity, sinking back into the tufted seat, felt the weather all too accurately reflected her mood. She could only hope it wouldn't become a downpour and mire the coach in mud on the deserted road. The rain let up toward evening, but once the coach did hit a low place in the road and stuck briefly. She and Ginny had climbed out to help the horses pull it free, and before they resumed their seats, the coachman had come to them saying he didn't want to chance the road in the gathering dark.

"We can't make any town tonight anyhow, Miss, and there's a small inn not so far ahead. It would be wisest to stop there."

Charity eyed his dripping form and thought of her own wet feet and mud-spattered cloak. She nodded, and climbed wearily back inside. The rain had brought a cool wind, and the thought of a fire and a bed, however lumpy, was welcome.

The inn proved to be a weather-worn clapboard house whose ancient sign had long since been obliterated by the elements. The main room had a bright fire against the evening damp, though, and the proprietor was almost pathetically eager to please. Charity gathered he got few customers here, and wondered if a bed could be made ready. She was assured that all would be in order, and she sank down on a settle by the hearth to await her dinner. Ginny disappeared up narrow stairs to see to the rooms.

When the door opened, letting in a draft of damp air, Charity jumped. Two large forms stood on the threshold, and her heart pounded as she drew as far away on the narrow settle as she could. Then her frightened eyes saw it was two strangers coming in from the wet night, and she felt foolish for her reaction. But the proprietor had noticed.

Wringing his hands in solicitous manner, he came over to her. "I've lighted ye a fire in the little parlor, Miss. Ye'll be more comfortable there, with no one to bother ye. The wife will bring dinner presently."

Charity smiled her gratitude and followed him into a small musty room where a popping little fire fought an unsuccessful battle against the clammy air. Drawing her cloak close, Charity sat in one of the high wooden chairs by the central table and wondered how long she'd have to wait for food. Staring at small tongues of flame licking at damp logs, she shivered. She was *glad* it had been strangers who had come into the inn, she told herself forcefully. Besides, Adam was as pleased to be rid of her as she was to be gone. What had started as a drunken game for him had turned into a large headache, and to have his problems solved so neatly would likely restore his humor for the first time in twenty-four hours. She wondered forlornly if he had even returned to find her gone. Perhaps he had been so angry he had stayed away altogether. But surely he would not just leave his sister with her new houseguest. Eventually he'd have to go back and discover the good news. She hunched in her chair and began to wish she were dead.

When supper finally arrived, she was still staring sightlessly into the fire and barely noticed as a thin woman set out bowls and plates on the dusty table before her. The proprietress left and Charity turned to her meal without enthusiasm, soon giving it up. She supposed she should thank the woman anyway and go upstairs, but it seemed too much effort to move just yet.

Loud voices beyond the door made her lift her head. Evidently, the strangers had started an argument. She'd as well wait till they settled it and left before venturing out through the main room again. Her elbows on the table, she sank her chin in her hands and looked at the congealing fat swimming on top of unappetizing soup.

The loud voices drew nearer till with a crash the parlor

door slammed back on the wall and Charity dropped her hands in annoyance. She turned to ask the meaning of this interruption and met Adam's blazing eyes. Behind him the proprietor was wringing his hands and whining in a high, thin voice. Mud spattered Adam's boots and clothes, and his hair was black with wet. He looked like Lucifer himself as he whirled on the little man, who threw up his hands and scuttled away. With an oath Adam slammed the door after him and turned.

In one quick movement Charity slid from her chair, putting the table between them. His face was dark with rage and his eyes still glared with an unholy light. She wondered, trembling, at her own flash of desire to run to him. But that had been before she'd seen him clearly.

"What devil's game do you play?" thundered Adam, taking a long, menacing stride forward.

Her hands flew up imploringly and she swayed.

He lunged then, brushing the table aside as though it were made of matchsticks. It went over with a crash and the dishes clattered to the floor. Then she was in his arms and he was saying her name over and over. She clung to him sobbing and laughing, not caring that his wet coat was ruining her dress. Only when they heard the door open again did they look up and draw apart. The scared face of the proprietor eyed the overturned table, the smashed dishes, and the tall man looking at him wrathfully, and ducking his head, bobbed back out of the room.

Adam held her at arm's length and shook her lightly. His still smoldering eyes searched her face. "You haven't answered me, you little fool."

Charity smiled tremulously at him. "I thought you would want me out of your life. And I hoped I could regain some self-respect by making my own way."

"As a governess? You haven't half the brain I thought you had." The hard line of his mouth had softened, but fire was still in his eyes. "And what about *my* self-respect if I let you go off to sell yourself as another man's servant, or perhaps to find Paul LaRoche in the capital? No, Charity, you belong to me and I don't let my possessions run off helter-skelter about the countryside."

Charity was too relieved to feel anger at his words. He had come after her. That was all that mattered. "H-how did you find me?"

Adam let go her arms, then grasping her hand he led her

to a chair by the fire where he planted her firmly on his lap. She clasped her hands behind his neck and leaned back to watch his face.

"Abby told me where you'd probably be when I finally gave her a chance. She'd run out to meet me with the news you were gone, and I fear I very nearly strangled my own sister when I heard it."

Charity dimpled. "And she told me your bark was worse than your bite."

Adam grinned ruefully. "She knows me too well. Except where you're concerned. You try my patience a great deal more than any female has a right to do, and I find I'm in a fury half the time."

"Oh Adam, I'm sorry." Charity put her head down on his neck and felt him stroke her hair.

"You should tell Abby that, for getting her to agree to this paper-brained scheme, and for nearly getting herself murdered for her trouble. It was as well Charles arrived in time to make me listen to them, or I've no idea what I might have done. But I got the oddest impression that Abby had really planned the whole thing."

Charity looked up. "Is that why she agreed so easily to my borrowing her coach and servants? She planned to send you off after me and stop me before I'd gone far."

"She could only *hope* I would come after you. I don't think she bargained for my temper this time." He kissed her quickly. "Don't you ever pull a fool stunt like this again. I do not plan to spend any more time defending my life against you or chasing you about the country."

"Never," Charity whispered, clinging to him. Gone were her resolves to stand on her own feet alone, gone was her desire to act respectable in the eyes of the world, gone was all consciousness but that of being in Adam's arms.

She felt is arms grow tighter around her. Then suddenly he let her go and stood her on her feet. "We can't hold our good host at bay forever. You go upstairs. I will deal with him now."

Charity touched his damp sleeve tentatively. She had a horrible fear that if she let him out of her sight she'd never see him again. "And then?"

He cupped her chin as his eyes caressed her face. "And then, my sweet, I expect a reward for my exertions."

Her eyelashes curled on her cheek as she tried to hide her relief. So he would stay with her, and soon she would feel his arms again. She skipped away from him and heard his chuckle as she ran for the stairs.

Ginny had unpacked her night things and was waiting for her in the little low-ceilinged room. Charity undressed quickly and sat impatiently while Ginny brushed her hair and hung out her clothes. Then donning her nightdress, she yawned elaborately and dismissed the girl to go and get some dinner and to discover her own sleeping quarters.

Jumping for the bed, Charity snuggled under the covers and turned to watch the door. She held her breath, listening for the heavy tread of boots on the old floors, but all was silent. She waited without moving as minutes dragged by, and slowly her heart began to slow its happy pounding. A small bubble of fear started to grow in her stomach. He wasn't coming to her after all. He had decided propriety was demanded by this inn, and he was going to leave her alone tonight. She flung herself onto her back, wishing she could feel nothing. And then the door opened. Charity turned her head and felt all her insides melt at the sight of him.

His eyes took in her still form beneath the covers, lingering on her tawny hair spread out on the pillow, copper highlights glowing in the flickering light of the bedside candle. Large turquoise eyes gleamed above full parted lips. He shrugged out of his clothes, never moving his gaze, and coming to the bed, he stripped back the covers. With a frown he leaned over and jerked up the thin cambric of her gown. "I want see you," he said gruffly, and pulled the material over her head.

Charity lay quietly, drinking in the sight of him, a beautiful bronzed animal who would devour her at will. Her arms were imprisoned above her head by the sleeves of her nightgown, and he held them that way as his eyes roved slowly over her sleek body. Her skin grew taut under his scrutiny.

"You are an utterly magnificent creature," he said and ran one finger lightly down her exposed underarm.

Her skin quivered at his touch as delicious little darts of fire ran through her. Then his mouth was on hers, his tongue exploring sweet depths as his hand was stroking her smooth skin. She arched her back, moaning as his hand and then his mouth found sensitive areas of her neck, her breasts, her thighs. His tongue strayed around one nipple and she whimpered. She felt molten lava pouring through her as his fingers probed her most secret places. Tugging her arms free of the

199

binding sleeves, she reached for him, touching his chest and his sides, pulling him down to her. As he lowered himself she could feel his hard thighs over her, the wild pounding of his heart against her breast, his hot breath on her neck. He grasped her hand and pulled her head back until her body arched higher. Then opening her legs she met his thrust with a gasp.

The candle on the table had guttered and drowned in its own tallow when at last they lay spent and smiling among the churned covers. In the soft moonlight that now entered the chamber Adam brushed a golden curl from her temple and, propping himself on one elbow, studied her shadowed features.

"I have not played fair with you this night," he said, his voice still thick from their passion. "For now that I've found you and made you mine again, I must leave you."

Charity, who had been watching the line of his throat where it flowed out to broad shoulders, pulled away abruptly. Her eyes flew up to search his dark face. "What do you mean?" He nuzzled her neck, but she pushed at him. "Where are you going?" she demanded.

"To the West, Charity. I have to go. But I will see you back to Abby's before I leave."

"*Why* must you go west again?"

"There's an army moving down the Ohio now. It's been sent to defeat the Indians in the Ohio country once and for all. Perhaps this time it will succeed where others failed. But it won't get far if General Wayne isn't allowed a free hand to wage his campaign without the constant interference of Congress and without constant trouble from his second in command, James Wilkinson."

Charity recognized Wilkinson's name as the general Paul had met and befriended in Philadelphia last year. "But what has all this to do with you?"

"There are those who are not sure Wayne is still capable of a full command. The President thinks he is, or he wouldn't have sent him, but he has to listen to his advisors. I'm being sent, unofficially, to observe the army once it reaches Fort Washington and to see if Wayne can maintain control. Letters were waiting for me when I reached home a few days ago. I thought you'd be safe at Abby's and I returned my answer. So I must go." His fingers traced the line of her collarbone and he felt the soft mound of her breast press harder into his chest. And we can forget the alternatives I've been worrying about, he thought. I want you waiting for me when I return.

Charity considered arguing, but knew it was useless. There was no turning a man back from a course he had set himself if he thought it was his duty to pursue it. She knew she should be pleased that he wanted her to wait in his sister's home, but she couldn't find the pleasure in it, knowing he might be gone for months. Besides, how would he explain her presence in Abby's house? Despair gripped her as she clung to him, hoping that somehow in the morning light the need for him to go would dissolve like the shadows of the night they now shared.

Over a late breakfast, however, Charity realized that his decision wasn't going to disappear with the bright sun. They talked of other things, but his words about the army in the Ohio country hung in the air between them. She wanted to ask why he had come to get her if he'd known he was leaving, but she knew he would only say that he wouldn't have his "possesions" leaving him without his permission. She remembered he had seemed angry at the thought of her being a governess, but he had also seemed angry at the thought she might meet Paul again. He had always disliked Paul, but he must know she would as soon see herself dead as to go to that man for assistance. None of it made any sense to her, but an idea began to take shape in her mind.

Adam, who had been watching her as he ate, narrowed his eyes. "What are you thinking about, vixen? Your face says clearly that your feverish little brain is up to no good. If you mean to dash from the inn and make off to Philadelphia, I warn you I'll turn you over my knee."

Charity pouted at him, but her eyes were wide with innocence. "I was thinking that Ginny may be vastly disappointed at not getting to see a real city," she lied, wondering how she would tell her real thoughts.

Adam finished the slab of ham on his plate and sat back, still eyeing her narrowly. "Are you vastly disappointed too, Charity?"

"I'm sure Philadelphia is an impressive city."

"Sufficiently impressive to make you want to leave for it again as soon as I am gone?"

Charity nearly jumped. She had been going to ask him if she could come to the West with him, but she'd been sure he would refuse. Her problem had been how to make him see he couldn't leave her with the Babcocks. Now he was giving her a clue on how to proceed. She lowered her eyes demurely. "Why, what a thing to suggest."

"I warned you not to try any more of your fool notions." He stopped abruptly, staring at her. She kept her eyes down, afraid to meet his now.

The tension that was growing in the little parlor was suddenly broken as the two heard the proprietor greet someone outside the open door. The sound of the second man's voice brought Adam to his feet.

"Simpson," he bellowed, "what the devil..."

A wiry figure of medium height, dressed in fringed buckskin shirt and brown leggins, appeared in the opening. "Mornin', Cap'n." He stopped when he saw Charity at the table and a slow grin spread across his blunt features.

Adam grabbed his arm. "Get in here, you old reprobate." He dragged the smaller man forward.

"Charity, this is Jedediah Simpson, whom my family insist on calling my valet. He is, in fact, nearly useless in the wardrobe and downright dangerous with a set of hair scissors." He paused and eyeing the leathery face, he stroked his chin. "Through with a razor he excels. He is also a jack of many trades, and has on more than one occasion shown that I shouldn't try to live without him."

Charity, who had been annoyed at the interruption of her grand scheme, found herself grinning back at Adam's valet as the man ducked his head at her.

"Furthermore," Adam continued, smiling broadly, "he has never learned proper respect for his betters, and so will never rise to the head of the table in the servants' hall."

Jedediah Simpson raised his eyes to the ceiling. "Whatever you say, Cap'n."

"Captain?" Charity looked bemused.

Adam sat down again and flung one booted leg up to a chair opposite. "Jed persists in calling me 'captain' for no reason other than we were once at sea together. I have never been captain of a vessel larger than a canoe."

The other shook himself and the fringes of his shirt danced. "Never mind that you're better'n the whole shipload put together." He turned to Charity. "If'n it hadn't been for him, I'd still be on that godforsaken tub, and long since dead, too." He seemed to think this explained everything and fell to staring at his boots.

Adam laughed. "I might as well explain that Jed was

unwary enough to be in an alcoholic stupor in New York when a ship I was on put into port there. We'd lost some crew in a storm and our captain, who was in a hurry, wasn't in a mood to observe niceties about hiring new men. Jed and two others were simply brought aboard to help fill the gaps. For the other two, this was little more than a chance to go adventuring. For Jed this was unmitigated disaster because being on a body of water larger than a still beaver pond made him violently, unbelievably ill."

"The death of me it would have been," Jed muttered at his toes.

"What's more, he couldn't stop being ill, and our good captain took it upon himself to 'discipline' Jed back to health. He came very close to killing him with his discipline. So, in a fit of unguarded impulse, I took Jed with me when next we put ashore, and I've been saddled with him ever since."

Charity was familiar with his unguarded impulses, and wondered when he would talk about being "saddled" with her. She looked again at Jed and saw that, far from taking any offense at Adam's words, the man was grinning hugely.

"I got your message when I reached Babcock's yesterday evening, and when I heard how it was you went haring off in a wet night," he nodded a graying forelock at Charity, "I went back to Bentwood and came on this mornin'. I've brung your horses and gear."

"My what?" Adam's boot hit the floor with a thud.

"Horses and gear," Jed repeated, his brown eyes holding the hint of a twinkle.

Charity, who had never heard a conversation like this between master and servant, watched owl-eyed as the two men stared at one another. Then the corner of Adam's mouth twitched and his open hand came down on the table with a smack that made the dishes jump. "Why, you wily old goat, that's it."

Jed's face remained impassive, but his eyes flicked to Charity, and she had the odd feeling that in that glance she had been judged in some way. Resting his gaze on Adam once more, he shrugged. "Thought you might be needin' them," he said. Then he turned and left the room.

Adam started after him and his laugh rang out. But at the door he spun and came back to stand in front of Charity. She sat very straight and held her breath as gray eyes caressed her until she felt naked before him. She didn't know why, but she sensed this was an important moment and she returned his look without blushing.

Taking her shoulders, Adam pulled her to her feet. "I'm going west," he said evenly, "and if I send you back to Abby will you stay there?"

Charity knew if he demanded it, she'd promise him anything. But she had learned something about this impetuous, strong-willed man in the past week. So, looking at him squarely, she asked, "How long will you be gone?"

"Perhaps months."

"And perhaps forever?"

"I'll come back."

"How am I to know that? I am not going to live on your sister's largesse forever."

"Promise you'll stay."

Summoning up anger she was far from feeling, Charity glared at him. "I will promise you nothing, Adam Crandall, that you haven't promised me."

"If I promise to return?"

She shrugged. "A foolish thing for a man to promise when he may have no say in the matter."

His grip on her shoulders tightened and she fought to hide her welling hope. "Then I shall have to make sure I do have some say in matters—at least between us."

"You cannot hold me when you are gone," she flung at him.

"Then you will have to come along, won't you?" His voice was hard and Charity flinched obligingly under the authority of it. But she had no more words to throw at him. He'd said what she wanted to hear.

Chapter 20

There was never a time, thought Charity, not even on Saint Dominque, when she had been as carefree and contented as she had been these last two weeks. Tomorrow, though, they would reach the Ohio River where Adam planned to find passage on a flatboat for all of them, and he had warned her that comfort would be at a minimum. Not that they had traveled in high style so far, she thought, and laughed aloud with the memory of this trip.

Adam, in front of her, turned at the sound, raising an eyebrow. "What makes you smile so, Mistress Ashton, after another long day's ride?" His own face was alight, and Charity's heart lifted even higher to see it. He'd been alternately pensive and worried through much of their travels, and she knew he had more than once regretted his latest madness at bringing her.

She pushed her horse closer to his and leaned forward. "I cannot help but think of the real bed you have promised for tonight."

"Wanton," he grinned. He tilted his head the better to see her exposed calf and ankle. "But I confess I've thought of little else since sunup."

Charity heaved a sigh of happiness. After the past eight nights on the ground, any bed would seem good now, but one she could share with Adam would be blissful beyond words. Anyway, she longed for a cessation of the constant watchfulness, the wary waiting for a twig to snap, an arrow to thud beside them. Several times they had not even made campfires, so sure were Adam and Jed that others were too near. And for nights she had had to lie on the ground between the two men, vividly aware of Adam's nearness, unable to do more than press close against him.

She tugged on her skirts now, wishing there were some way a lady could ride astride a horse and still look decent. She yearned for Adam's old shirt and Jed's extra breeches she'd been wearing. They were so much more comfortable than this ballooning calico dress. But she had agreed with Adam that she must try to look more the part of a long-suffering female when they reached Point Pleasant, and so she'd donned this outfit for their last day's ride. Too bad a side saddle was one of the few things Jed had not provided for their trip. He seemed to have thought of nearly everything else, as overloaded saddle bags and the heavily burdened packhorse attested.

Adam, who had checked everything carefully that morning back at the inn above Charlottesville, had praised Jed's resourcefulness. He'd dispatched Ginny and the coach back to Abby with a letter of explanation and within an hour he'd started his little caravan west. Charity never knew what was in that letter, and she shuddered to think, but she'd been too happy at the prospect of leaving with Adam to wonder overmuch, or even to question his decisions on what she would be allowed to take. Her little trunk had returned to Abby along with its papers, the few jewels, and most of her clothing. She'd given it scarcely a thought as she'd mounted a shaggy little mare and turned her to follow Adam's own gelding up the road. Gabriel had been sent back along with the coach, for Adam had said he would not chance losing his best horse on this trek.

She looked behind her now and saw Jed, his narrowed brown eyes searching the woods on either side with his accustomed vigilance, and once again she was glad he rode in back of her. It made her feel less exposed to the unknown dangers that might lurk in these virgin forests.

As the shadows lengthened in the towering wood, and dark shapes seemed to move among the trees, the trio passed a narrow clearing where small children tumbled over each other before a new log cabin. A few miles farther on they came to the outskirts of a small settlement. At the door of a rude little inn Adam drew rein and lifted Charity from her saddle. Beyond the next buildings she could see steep banks falling away to the gray water of the Ohio.

The innkeeper, a burly man with a cast in one eye, looked up when the three entered the room. In one corner squatted an impassive Indian, black eyes staring unconcernedly at the newcomers. He was the first Indian Charity had ever seen, and she gazed in wonder at the fact he was simply a swarthy man with straggly black hair, dressed in the same sort of buckskin shirt and leggins Jed now wore. He looked unkempt and unsavory, but hardly the horned monster of Sally's dreams back in Virginia. She might have smiled at this, but the three men at the table were gaping at her in leering appreciation, and she felt Adam's muscles tense beside her. Though his voice was even, almost jovial as he bespoke two rooms.

Rubbing his big hands together, the owner came forward. "'Tis in luck you are, lad. Party pulled out just this morning."

Adam took Charity's hand casually in his. "My wife and I have had a long trip, friend. Your best chamber would serve us well."

Charity's fingers jerked at his words, but she kept her face still, even when the burly man winked. She was glad when she could ascend the stairs and remove herself from common view. The room they were shown was bare and unlovely, but it provided privacy and shelter, all she could ask for now. When the keeper had left, she tore thankfully at the pins in the awkward knot of hair at her neck and shook her head.

"Now why would you do a thing like that to me, when you know I can't stay just yet?" Adam's voice was deep and very low behind her.

She shook her head again, turning to face him. "Then you will hurry about your business," she answered rather breathlessly.

Adam's eyes held hers for a moment, and she saw the fire kindling in the gray depths before he spun and left. She busied herself with sorting the packs, and then, when Jed brought water, with washing herself and many of their things. She had never had to wash anything in all her life, and she felt obscurely pleased when she surveyed chair and bedpost neatly draped with dripping garments.

At length Adam reappeared with another candle and some hot food. Kicking the door to behind him, he looked around the room with a lopsided grin. But he said nothing about her labors and she felt oddly piqued. Setting the tray down on the wash stand, he lifted the covers.

"I'm sorry to confine you to this room, but the downstairs of a frontier inn is no place for a lady after dark."

"Is the 'wife' of a Kentucky settler a lady then?"

Adam shrugged. "Some are. Come, I'm ravenous and this food looks very nearly as good to me as you do."

They ate with gusto, and when the food was gone, Adam left the tray outside in the hall.

"What of Jed?" Charity asked as he closed the flimsy door firmly and turned into the room.

"Jed is downstairs in his element, learning, I hope, what traffic is passing here, and how we may obtain passage to Cincinnati. But I will not talk about Jed now, nor of the river, nor of Kentucky, nor of anything else." He advanced purposefully toward her.

Her face alight with mischief, Charity darted to the far side of the bed. "I have never known where you are taking me. I want to hear about this Cincinnati."

"No, you don't. You want to hear what I have to say about your loveliness."

She brushed heavy hair back off one shoulder. "Compliments to quell my fears?"

"You don't fear me, Charity?" He'd stopped, and uncertainty crossed his face.

She caught her lip in pearly teeth. "I had not meant you. Though there have been times when I feared you, yes."

Brushing strong fingers through his thick hair, Adam looked down at the bed between them. "I am hotheaded, Charity, and your months of coldness drove me half mad. I knew you were afraid of no one after all you'd gone through, and I wanted to bend you to my will. More than that, I just *wanted* you." His eyes lifted to hers again, and she saw a strange light she could not read. "I had thought to win you, but instead I've carried you off again, this time into dangers and uncertainties."

"I wish to be nowhere else," she said in a voice so low it was almost a whisper.

He reached for her then, and the two tumbled onto the hard mattress. He held her close, kissing her cheeks, her eyes, her throat, and at last her mouth. A tenderness welled between them that had never surfaced before, and Charity held his face in her hands returning his kisses softly. They lay whispering of their desire till his hands began to move over her in a familiar way. They shed their clothes then, and stared at each other with a new wonder.

His hands burned with a radiant warmth where they touched her, and as she felt her passion rise, she began to explore his body as she never had before. Tentatively, her fingers traced the line of his neck and traveled down over the curling mat of his chest. With careful deliberation she counted each rib and firm muscle of his stomach, then her arms went around him and she stroked down his back, feeling the muscles ripple and tighten at her touch. His hard buttocks contracted as she ran her hands over them and felt downward over long hard thighs. When she turned her hands to move back up the inside of his legs, he shivered and lay very still till she encountered the burning hardness of his manhood. He groaned then, and she echoed his sound with a low moan. Her temples pulsed against his palms as their mouths came together and their bodies fused in one swift movement, trying to extinguish their aching need.

It was no great disappointment to Charity to learn from Jed the next day that no boat had turned into the settlement in twenty-four hours, and that they might have to wait for days to find passage on a craft large enough to take them and their horses aboard.

"Them keelboats are swifter, what with the sail an' all," Adam's man explained. "But we need a good flatboat that's in need of more hands to help. Somethin'll come along eventually."

Charity sat on the river bank watching him whittle a willow whistle for a boy he'd met near the inn and staring out over the morning water before her. Across the river a low line of hills marched away to the western sky and bright puffs of clouds floated lazily above. She flung herself onto her back, picking out patterns in the quiet clouds and listening to the soft *zlit zlit* of Jed's knife.

"Hmmm...Here comes somethin' now."

Charity sat up again and looked upstream. She shaded her eyes against the dancing sun glare on water, but could see nothing. Dropping her hands, she waited. Jed's eyes seemed to be able to pick out a honey bee on a tree a hundred yards away, so there was no use in staring until whatever he saw came within mortal vision. Instead she fell to studying her leathery companion.

Adam had told the truth when he'd said Jed had never earned proper respect for his betters, but then those two did not have a master-servant relationship. They were more like friends, or an uncle with a headstrong but favorite nephew, she thought. Over the past weeks Charity had learned respect for the capable older man. He was keen and nothing seemed to surprise or upset him. She'd learned that he came from New York State and supposed it was the famous Yankee resourcefulness that made him so able in any situation. Whatever the reason, she knew Adam was glad of his presence, and it had made her feel doubly protected on their journey.

"Jed, why did you never go home again after you got off that ship?" Charity hugged her knees, looking at the back of his shaggy head.

Jed stopped peering upriver and plucked a tall blade of grass. Sticking it in the side of his mouth, he thought for a moment. "Never seen Virginia before. An' it seemed to me, once't I got my legs under me again, that Adam might need me."

"Oh?" Charity thought of all Abby had said of Adam's footloose and irresponsible existence. Though there was nothing irresponsible about this trip he was taking, she supposed it might qualify for footloose. "Yes," she said slowly, "I imagine he's needed you a number of times."

The piece of grass in Jed's mouth twitched. "Seldom seen a lad so bent on gettin' inta scrapes and such."

The girl flushed, wondering if Jed was already figuring a way to get Adam out of this latest "scrape" with her.

"He'd do the darndest things sometimes, and occasionally I got to pick up the pieces." He eyed Charity laconically. "Like the time he was hell-bent on self-destruction after Priscilla Faulkner married another man. Threw hisself on an unbroke stallion, he did, and took a terrible thrashin' afore we could rope the beast and bring 'im down."

Charity flinched and looked away. For a man who seldom spoke, Jed was doing a lot of talking this morning, and she wondered why he would tell her a thing like that. Was he trying to warn her not to play Adam false? Was he trying to tell her not to hope for much, that she was merely the latest in a succession of women? She clenched her fist, thinking of the faithless Priscilla and who knew how many others. Had Adam taken the same pleasure in them that he claimed to take in her? Had he used the same words, the identical caresses? The thought of other hands on his lean, hard body made her eyes burn.

"I'm not Priscilla Faulkner," she said between gritted teeth.

Jed, who had been watching the approach of another keelboat, looked back at her. "Nooo..." he said slowly, "no, you're not." His eyes flicked up then, and Charity turned to see Adam standing only feet away. His face was a mask, but his eyes looked hard and she knew he'd heard this last. Her own eyes, glinting the gray-green color of the river, held his steadily. After a long moment Adam's jaw relaxed and he came to sit by them.

"I sold the packhorse," he said conversationally, though his voice was tight.

"Well now, that'll make lighter travelin'." Jed's head was toward the river once more. "'Cept we'll need to dump some of the other stuff now. Can't shoulder all that horse carried."

"Most of it we can manage. I sold the extra blanket and the big kettle. We'll divide the rest."

"So all's we need now is a boat. Seen only two pirogues an' a keelboat this mornin'. An' some o' them bitty Indian bark affairs."

Adam grinned for the first time. "Looking forward to being on the river again?"

Jed shot him a baleful glare. "I survived it last time, Cap'n. I'll survive it again, I reckon."

Absently, Adam began fingering gold-lighted hair on Charity's shoulder. "Yes, you will, old friend. It's not like the sea." His hand moved to stroke her head, and Charity sat very still.

Jed's face was sour. "Near 'nough," he said shortly.

Charity smiled at that and felt Adam's hand pause on her neck. His eyes were on her now, but she stared straight ahead, thinking of his hands on other hair.

"No, not Priscilla," he said very softly.

She swiveled then, one hand raised, but her arm was caught and the hand on her neck tightened to pull her to him. Then his mouth was on hers, sucking her breath from her body. Horribly conscious of Jed watching impassively, she didn't try to fight him, but she refused to return his kiss. Her cheeks were burning by the time he released her, chuckling softly. She scrambled up, and with incoherent words about mending clothing, she stumbled away up the bank.

For the next six days they scoured the landing places for a boat to carry them, but any craft that put in to the settlement was either too overloaded already or too small to accommodate them. Adam was impatient at the delay, but Charity was unworried. Nothing further had been said about their scene on the riverbank, and she began to wonder if she'd imagined all of it. Adam's lovemaking was as ardent and as careful as ever, and after her first attempt to resist her own desire, she'd realized that even if her mind screamed rage at him, her body was going to betray her to his touch. So she'd put aside her hurt and her anger as fruitless emotions in the face of his powerful attraction. To her surprise, she discovered that the magnetism that held her to him in bed was almost constant now. Just watching him across a room, or exploring with him along the riverbank made her glow with delight. They spent hours in awe-filled discovery of each other, and she felt, as she came to know him, that she understood him less each day. It might take years to find all of him, she thought happily, and moved in a haze of contentment, loath to have anything intrude on the intimacy they shared.

Inevitably the time came, though, when Jed, discovering them deep in conversation by a shallow stream near the river, announced he'd found their transport. Charity was reluctant to hear about the end to their idyll, but Adam jumped up, demanding to know what sort of boat Jed had seen.

"Flatboat headin' to Louisville area eventually. Go right past Fort Washington that way. Seems the best chance."

Adam agreed heartily, though he decried the need to take the slowest craft on the river to his destination. Hurrying Charity back to the inn, he bade her start packing, while he and Jed went to talk to the men on the flatboat.

That evening Charity learned that the craft belonged to a man from eastern Pennsylvania who had arrived in Pittsburgh just before General Wayne had set out from there for the Ohio country. The army had taken all available wood for their transportation, and the man, one John Bowman, had gone overland to Wheeling to get his supplies. He and another man, together with their families, had set out at the beginning of May only to find they were carrying a fever on board which took Mrs. Bowman's life just a week down the river. The other man, fearing for his family, had put in at Marietta, leaving John, his son, and his daughter to carry on alone. It had been a bad trip from Marietta with only the three of them to handle the boat, and they were grateful for the chance to pick up more help.

"A situation made to order," Adam said, rubbing his hands. "The man's determined to get to Kentucky. He has a deed to land there, and thinks to get a share of the riches promised. I warned him half the deeds presented in that state now turn out to be worthless, that the speculators are ruthless. But he's sure his is all legal and waiting for him. So we leave tomorrow."

Charity, trying to disentangle all the information and strange place names, looked at him wide-eyed. "Are titles and deeds really found worthless when these people arrive after traveling all that way?"

"Many are. Surveys are haphazard at best, and more often than not, a man finds he's bought land that sits on someone else's property. If his survey is taken after the first owner has recorded his deed, he's out of luck."

"But who would sell him such worthless title?"

"Ruthless speculators. Our General Wilkinson could name them. They're all hand in glove out here."

"But I thought you'd been speculating in Kentucky land." Charity's brow creased, wondering at this new aspect of Adam Crandall.

His finger traced the furrow on her forehead. "Not I, sweetheart. I bought some land near the capital of Frankfort last year. Signed, sealed, and delivered. But I'll not rob the ignorant, land-greedy folks back East for a quick profit. If I sell any of my land, the deed will be there to show I own it, and I'll charge a fair price, not the ten times its worth that the speculators are asking."

Charity's clouded eyes cleared to brilliant turquoise. "Will we see this land of yours, then?"

"Perhaps. But right now we're for Cincinnati." His hand moved down the side of her face and onto her shoulder. Then he reached for her hungrily and she came to him eagerly, wanting him more than ever now that she knew they were leaving their private room after tonight.

John Bowman proved to be a stocky, determined-looking man with thinning hair, solemn brown eyes, a strong jaw, and a firm set to his mouth. But for all his forbidding appearance, Charity liked him at the outset, for he had an honest air about him that was reassuring. When it came to his children, however, she decided she'd better reserve judgment. The son, Rourke, was a strapping young man whose heavy thatch of auburn hair, brooding eyes, and wide, down-

213

turned mouth gave him a rather sullen look. And the daughter, Molly, she feared she would dislike, for the second the carrot-haired girl laid golden eyes on Adam, she began to pose and swish around invitingly. Immediately Charity wished she weren't dressed as Adam had commanded, in the old blue calico, her hair pulled tight into a spinsterish knot behind her neck. She had taken in the dress to fit her better, but at best it could not be called really flattering. She eyed the girl's homespun shirt, open to her deep cleavage, and wished she could hang a burlap sack over her.

As she and Adam crossed the crude gangplank onto the narrow bowdeck of the boat, she hung back. Grasping Adam's arm she hissed, "I'll be sorry I agreed to come on this journey if I have to watch that creature mooning over you for the next two weeks."

Adam's grin was broad. "I was just thinking it was too bad I've already told Mr. Bowman we're man and wife. But what do you mean 'agreed to come'? I thought I'd left you no choice back in Virginia." He eyed her narrowly. "Or did I?"

Charity fluttered her lashes in a parody of Molly's coy look, but Adam gripped her arm. "You little she-wolf. You played me like a trout that morning at the inn, feigning a desire to be off for Philadelphia as soon as my back was turned." He was still smiling, but Charity thought better of grinning back.

"I never said I would do such a feather-brained thing. It was you who assumed it."

"You're a dangerous woman, Charity. I shall have to give Molly fair warning of you. But I shall also have to give *you* fair warning of her brother. Despite our efforts to have you look matronly, the lout looked at you as though he'd eat you for breakfast."

Charity shivered. "Ugh."

Adam laughed then. "See you maintain those feelings on the matter." He slapped her bottom lightly, and she jumped. "Let's have a look at our new quarters."

The Bowmans led them across the deck, then, skirting barrels and crates and a small stone hearth, turned into the waist of the boat. Here a cabin had been built across the whole fifteen-foot width of the craft, its sides rising vertically from the waterline. A narrow passage down the center showed them two tiny compartments on each side, and a storage area at the rear where a plow, chains, tools, harnesses, quilts, a bed, and a chest of drawers shared space

214

with sacks of oats, corn, onions, dried apples, and hams. Beyond this area another door led under a covered space where a coop of chickens, a pen of grunting hogs, two cows, and two horses made their home. Another narrow deck was reached from there.

Charity leaned against the flat stern of the floating home and watched as the men climbed a ladder to the roof of the cabin area, which also served as a main deck. From there, two immensely long sweeps angled out to the water, and at the rear of the cabin roof the huge steering oar plunged past her shoulder to the river below.

"Them sweeps is heavy things, 'specially at the end of a long day," Molly commented, coming to stand beside Charity and shielding her eyes the better to see the men above. "But Mr. Crandall looks like he could handle one with half an arm."

Charity said nothing and the girl went on. "Sure will be good to have some company around here again. Ever since Ma died, Pa's been sunk in gloom. And Rourke's no good company at the best of times."

Charity looked at the pert little face then. The girl couldn't be more than seventeen, and she found herself sympathizing with her. "I was sorry to hear about your mother's death. That was a hard blow for all of you, I'm sure."

A cloud crossed the girl's face, then was gone. "She did poorly the whole trip. Wasn't happy 'bout comin' in the first place. Saved herself a lot of trouble not finishing it. But I aim to. I cain't wait to see the Kentucky country. There're *real* men livin' out there."

Thinkng there wasn't much she could say to that, Charity turned to watch Jed shifting the gangplank to the stern. Soon he had the horses aboard and in their cramped quarters. Within minutes they were pushing off from shore and Charity could feel the great sluggish craft settle in the water beneath her feet and swing ponderously as the current caught it. Mr. Bowman threw his weight to the steering oar as Rourke and Adam laid hands on the sweeps and began trudging up and down the cabin deck with them, dipping the great oars in and out of the river in long monotonous strokes, trying to help steer the boat down the central current.

Charity, watching the shoreline slide by with agonizing slowness, wondered if this was to be their rate of speed throughout. Adam had said it would be ten to fourteen days to Cincinnati, depending on how cautious Mr. Bowman was with his boat and on how often they had to pull into shore for provisions or game. Her heart sank at the thought of two weeks in this drifting confinement. But, as she looked up again and Adam, stamping back along the roof with the sweep, caught her eye and winked, she knew once more she wouldn't be anywhere else.

Chapter 21

For the next four days, Charity watched the quiet world of the river flow past. Jed, who had recovered quickly from his first day's illness, took long turns on the sweeps, leaving Adam time to be with Charity. They spent hours on the bow deck, watching debris-strewn shores of islands and heavily forested hills slip by as Adam explained that many of the sandy bars and weed-choked bits of river land were drowned in times of flood.

"There are ledges and bars around some of the islands too that are dangerous to riverboats if they don't know of them," he said one lazy sunset as they leaned over the wooden hull. He pointed to a small ripple of water off their port side. "And there are other hazards. That swirl there shows a sawyer about to surface. It's a tree whose roots or branches are stuck in the river mud, leaving the other end to bob slowly to the surface. If we're lucky we ride over them, pushing them down again. But planters are more dangerous."

"Planters?" Charity laughed, loving her few minutes alone with Adam. Rarely were they allowed private conversation in this close living. Molly seemed always to be with them wherever they went, her great yellow eyes following Adam.

He threw a casual arm over her shoulder and she snuggled against him. "Planters are trees caught immovably in the river bed. They stand upright against the current, and if you hit one at any speed at all, it's like taking a sledge to your bottom timbers."

Charity shuddered and leaned forward to stare down into the dark waters. "Are there a lot of those?"

"Not here in the main channel." Molly's flippant voice came from beside them. "When are you going to let us tie up for the night? These sandy islands sure look good after two days of not stretchin' my legs." She looked invitingly up at Adam's tall form.

Charity sighed as he turned to the girl. "The light's still good enough. As long as your father agrees, I'd like to make each day count." It had not escaped his notice, any more than it had Charity's, that Molly now tucked her shirt tighter into her skirt, making her big, firm breasts push noticeably at the thin muslin. Her buttons seemed to be falling off too, he thought, for the shirt was open halfway to her waist. Her glowing eyes met his and her lips parted as her tongue flicked out, moistening them. A tempting sight, thought Adam, and even at her age, she was certainly no virgin. Once he would have found it hard to resist such availability. But he had become aware these past weeks that Charity had ruined his appreciation of other women. The sight of this girl with her cowlike eyes resting speculatively below his belt was vaguely irritating. He wondered how he might discourage her. Perhaps she didn't believe he and Charity were really married. His arm tightened on Charity's shoulders, and she left off watching Molly to look up at him inquiringly. "Come, wife," he said with emphasis, "let us have a look at what you and Molly will serve us this day."

Charity went with him to the little stone hearth, thinking it was a kindness on his part to include her name as a preparer of their meals. In fact, Molly, always with reluctance and a good deal of complaining, or Jed did most of the cooking. But she was learning...

Dusk was settling now and the light was leaving the river, but still they drifted on. Charity was beginning to feel nervous about the hazards Adam had described when a call came from the cabin roof.

"Boats ahead, Crandall," shouted Mr. Bowman. "Waving us into the shore of that long island."

Adam stiffened. "What kind of boats?" he asked, already moving for the ladder.

"Keelboat and two flatboats."

Jed's face appeared above them. "No ambush there, Cap'n. Reckon they've stopped to have a party."

Adam halted at the bottom rung. He shrugged. "Light's going anyway. What do you think, Bowman?"

"Oh, let's stop," squealed Molly from behind him.

"As good a place as any," her father called, already shifting the steering oar.

A lanky, wild-haired man was atop the nearest flatboat now, gesturing them to a berth alongside. "Jine a party," he bellowed across the water. "If'n ya' got a fiddler aboard he's welcome, an' if'n ya' got women they're welcome most of all." He grinned hugely. "Bring yore own likker an' come along." Then he waved and disappeared.

Charity found she was nearly as impatient as Molly to get done with dinner and go down the shore to the fire whose glow could already be seen above the boat roofs and tree tops. It would be good to move freely on dry land again.

They cleaned up in a hurry and then Charity went into their tiny cabin to put on the dress Adam had gotten her in the Blue Ridge mountains, a yellow calico with a frilled neck. Laughingly he'd presented it to her saying this was her new party dress for the wilderness. It was light and easy to carry, and was meant to replace her own more luxurious gowns now back at Abby's home. To Charity's surprise, its fit was nearly perfect, and she liked the light feeling she had when, with only her chemise and one petticoat underneath, she slid bare feet into light slippers and was ready.

She wished she had a decent mirror as she peered into the small glass stuck on the wall and tied back the sides of her thick hair with a yellow ribbon. The rest she left down to shimmer in coppery waves over her shoulders and back. She pinched her cheeks quickly and smiled at herself. That ridiculous little wanton on deck had made her feel she had to compete for Adam's attention. And knowing him, he was enjoying the situation hugely. She bit her lip. Surely he wouldn't look seriously at the brazen creature? She thought of the overripe body displayed more boldly every day for Adam's appreciation and tugged at the square neckline of her dress. Short of cutting the material though, she could do no more than give a tantalizing glimpse of the tops of her own swelling breasts. It would have to do, she thought, and flounced out to the deck, annoyed that she'd sink to Molly's own game.

When they approached the fire, and Charity glimpsed the groups seated nearby, she was less sorry that her dress was rather demure. The wild-haired man who'd first hailed them was sitting amidst a half dozen other roughly dressed strangers, and all their eyes swiveled to stare at the two girls who walked toward them. With a clap the first man was on his feet. "Welcome," he bellowed, and shaggy heads nodded. Immediately they were surrounded by men and women, and Adam was answering questions about where they were from and where they were going. The women soon swept Charity aside to ask about news of upriver, but she noticed Molly evaded them and was next seen flirting with two tall men in fringed shirts and high moccasins.

A fiddler was tuning up, and Charity saw Jed take up another instrument and begin playing along. There was no end to the man's talents. Molly and two other girls were already on the trampled grass with partners of their choice.

When the women realized Charity could tell them little news they didn't already know, they left off questioning and she was free to eavesdrop on the circle of men where Adam and Mr. Bowman sat.

"Well, we like to run our own affairs," one heavy-featured man was saying, "We don't like bein' taxed or run by a furrin gov'ment. We went West thinkin' to do better than we could back home, and we've cleared the land and fought off the savages without any help from yore precious Congress. If it wants to help us any, it can lick the Injuns once and fer all an' get the blasted British outa' the Northwest."

"That's just what the government is trying to do," replied Adam quietly. "Wayne's out here to make the territories safer for all of you."

Another man leaned forward. "Like St. Clair done? Hmph," he snorted. "Wayne reached Fort Washington end of April, but we ain't heard of no battles yet."

"The government is still trying to make peace. Wayne's out here in case we fail."

"Peace!" The first man spat toward the fire. "Won't be no peace till the savages are all dead or pushed out past the great Mississippi. We'll make our own peace in Kentucky. The gov'ment don't give a hang about us."

"You're wrong." Adam's voice was clear, riding over the mumbled assents. "Your state's been a part of the union for only a year now. Give the government a chance to help."

"Yeah. Well what're they gonna do about the Spaniards who've closed the Mississippi to us? We got crops to move down that river, but those slippery varmints claim they own it. How're we gonna' get our rights if'n we stay tied to the East? Spain'll open the river if we go independent."

"The East and the West need each other." Adam's voice rose. "If you try to secede, you'll be swallowed whole by the Spaniards."

A chorus of voices took up the argument. "Wilkinson took goods to New Orleans without hindrance. If he can, others can too. Specially now that he's back in Cincinnati with the army."

Adam shook his head, but his reply was cut short by Molly who pranced up at that moment and snatched him to his feet. "A fiddler's playin' over there for us to dance. You can't sit here jawin' all night."

Adam grinned and left with the girl to catcalls and lewd suggestions from the seated men.

Charity clenched her teeth as she watched them join the others, but she was given no time to develop the slow burn that had started in her mind, because Rourke was beside her, gripping her arm and nodding. She would have liked to jerk away, but could think of no good excuse, so ignoring his wolfish grin and burning eyes, she went into the circle. The steps of the reel that followed were familiar to her and she found herself enjoying the dance despite her partner, and despite the snide, sidelong glances from Molly's triumphant eyes. No further brooding was allowed her either, for one of the rangy Kentuckians claimed her the second the music stopped, and she was whirled away into the next formation.

After the third dance she pleaded to stop for a minute, and a nice young man from the keelboat, who partnered her, took her back to the fire to get her a drink of water. Her eyes roved over the gathering, looking automatically for Adam. But he was nowhere to be found. Nor was Molly in evidence. Her heart's pounding threatened to suffocate her and she closed her eyes.

"Are you all right, Miss?" Her partner was back, holding her water and peering at her anxiously.

She forced a smile to her lips. "Only tired," she said and thanked him for the drink. Just then she spied Adam. Standing at the fringes of the thick trees, he was bending over a carrot-colored head. Had they just emerged from the concealing darkness of the forest? Charity's hand shook as she held the tin cup. The rage and pain that choked her was beyond anything she'd ever felt, she thought, and dimly she realized that the symptoms had been there before, in the days when she saw Adam laughing and talking with Helen. But this was so much worse. She wanted to fly at them both and scratch their eyes from their heads, to bloody that insolent little face that had watched Adam with longing these four days. But she was powerless to do anything. She had no real claim on Adam.

Squaring her shoulders, she handed the cup back to the worried-looking man before her. "That was good," she said, forcing her voice to be light. "Now I'm sure I could dance all night."

He grinned with relief. "Well, come on then."

The next hour was a whirl of agony for Charity, but she laughed and danced as though there were nothing in all the world she would rather do. Adroitly she avoided the leering Rourke, and when Adam approached her once, she spun away saying her hand had been claimed and smiling at his annoyed look.

Back in their own tiny cabin at last, Charity could not avoid Adam any longer, but she set about undressing in the dark with brisk efficiency, and turned away when he touched her.

"Have all those men turned your head tonight, Charity?" His voice was soft, for the walls were thin.

"I hardly think you need *my* favors this night," she hissed over her shoulder and climbed under the blankets of their narrow bunk.

Adam lay down next to her, but her body was cold and rigid to his touch. She heard him chuckle softly and turned her head to stare at him.

"Something is eating at you, sweetheart, and I have a strong suspicion I know what it is."

Charity glared venomously into the darkness of his face. "Perhaps you would prefer the freedom of the deck tonight. Do not feel constrained to stay with me."

Even in the blackness she could see his teeth flash in a grin. "Why, Charity, I do believe you're jealous."

"Of that little trollop? Never."

"You disappoint me. I had hoped you might defend me from Molly's blandishments."

"You hardly seemed to want defending tonight."

"Then you didn't watch carefully enough. If you had, you would have seen my desperation."

Charity turned away from him. He's laughing at me, she thought, and stared stonily at the rough plank wall in front of her. Adam's hands moved over her body, but she held herself very still and soon his caresses stopped and he was breathing evenly beside her.

In the early afternoon of their seventh day, they passed the settlement of Limestone, Kentucky. Only three more days to Cincinnati, Adam said. They were making good time. An hour or so later, they pulled into shore to try for fresh game. Adam handed Charity an old rifle and bade her guard the boat well while they were gone. He'd spent time in Point Pleasant teaching her how to shoot, and although she was no marksman, she knew how to handle the gun now, and could be trusted to hit her mark if it were not too far.

Molly, eyeing the rifle in Charity's hands, went into the cabin, and remained there. It was the first smart thing the girl had done, Charity thought. She had tried not to hate Molly these past two and a half days, and she thought she'd conquered her dislike. But she'd rather not be tested on her resolve. Adam had laughingly assured her that nothing at all had happened back on that island, pointing out that the girl had disappeared for three dances with one of the Kentuckians. She had wanted to believe him, but feared anyone that open in her desires of a man was apt to get her way. She'd kept her peace, though, and the matter had dropped.

She climbed to the roof of the cabin, hoping Molly would have the sense to stay out of her sight, and fell to dreaming of Cincinnati and of having Adam to herself again. The afternoon droned on to the barely audible rhythm of the river, and she tried to keep from thinking of the fresh worry that had entered her mind that morning. She'd grown up ministering to slaves, and had learned the facts of life at an early age. So she had no illusions about where babies came from, and she was beginning to wonder what might happen with Adam. She counted back mentally and frowned. Her last monthly flow had been as they set out for the West. So she should be due any day now. She thought of the nights of love shared these past weeks. What if she didn't get her flow? The idea of becoming pregnant in this wilderness was frightening.

Better not to think about it unless she had to. But that was easier said than done, and when the men returned in the dying light, she was still brooding over possibilities.

She'd been so lost in thought, she'd failed to notice the scudding clouds coming out of the southwest, and was surprised when Adam ordered her off the deck. "We're going to try to make a few miles before the storm breaks," he said roughly. "Go help Molly and Jed clean the deer we brought."

Silently Charity climbed down to do his bidding.

They ate their dinner in the gathering darkness with the men atop the cabin eating at their posts. But the preliminary grumbles of thunder were drawing nearer, and at last they began to look for a likely spot to land. Adam vetoed one suggestion on the Kentucky shore as too exposed to possible Indian attack. They swung past and suddenly there was a sharp crack and the world was filled with a dazzling light. Huge raindrops pelted them as those below moved things into the cabin and made sure the animals were secured. Charity stood at the bow opening and watched the slanting rain jump on gunmetal water as the lumbering craft steered toward a low island on the northern shore. The bottom scraped on sand and Adam was shouting to Rourke through the downpour to secure them if he could. She saw the young man leap onto the sand and run for a downed tree as a shaft of lightning jumped across the river and the thunder rolled among the hills. She backed away from the door and went inside to get out dry clothes for Adam.

He came in minutes later, to find her standing at the small window. He stripped off his soaking garments by the flickering light of their one candle. Then draping a blanket over his shoulders he came to stand behind her. Outside, lightning shivered the inky darkness and the thunder boomed overhead. She turned to him and lifted soft lips to his. The blanket fell away as Adam crushed her to him, lifting her off her feet. She clung to him and he carried her to the bunk. His body was cold and wet from the drenching, but she warmed him with her legs and arms as they made love with an abandon they'd not known on this boat. Tonight the storm would drown any sounds, and they took full advantage of its cover.

Rain still drummed on the roof when they drew apart at last. Adam got up to fetch the thin blanket, and when he returned he saw Charity's eyes were fastened to the flickering candle, but her mind seemed far away.

"You're very pensive," he said, sitting on the edge of the bunk and smoothing hair off her ivory forehead.

Her eyes remained on the candle, but she sighed. "What if we have a baby?" she asked, and her voice was flat.

Adam's hand paused in her hair. "Do you have reason to believe we will?"

She shook her head slowly. "Not yet."

There was a long silence. Then Adam unfolded from her side and moved around the cabin, picking up discarded clothing, hanging up his wet pants and shirt.

Charity sat up. Her eyes followed him now. "You have spread your seed so far and wide that the thought of another bastard does not concern you?"

His movements ceased. Slowly he stood straight and faced her. "I have not yet made a mistake in that way."

"And how, pray tell, have you managed that?"

A slow grin tugged the corners of his mouth. Placing his hands on his hips, he cocked his head. "I inquire as to the status of the lady first."

Charity considered this with wide eyes. "You never inquired of me."

"No. But then the deed was done. I know you had your flow in the mountains. A relief to all. Since then I have not been foolhardy. And you are due in just days now."

An anguished fury choked her. The man presumed to know more about her body than she knew herself. He was so sure of his own judgment, his own power. "And if you're wrong? What then? What would you do with your first bastard?"

Adam stepped forward and squatted so his face was on a level with hers. His eyes ran over her lightly, then came to rest on her trembling mouth. His grin was broad now, and there was a gleam in his eye she couldn't read. "Are you trying to frighten me into marriage again, sweetheart?"

She flung herself sideways, and snatching at the thin blanket he'd tossed on the bed, she wrapped herself in it. Her face was frenzied as she stood above him. "I would consider marriage to Rourke before I would consent to marrying you," she spat.

He threw up an arm in mock despair. "You wound me sorely, Charity." Then he too stood up. "But I doubt Rourke would give proper care to you and the babe."

"Oh!" Charity searched for something she could throw at him. Before she could move, her shoulders were caught and she was pulled around to face him again.

.   "You are in a passion for nothing, Charity. Your jealousy of that sly minx in the next cabin has overridden your sense. It will be weeks yet before you know if you do indeed carry my child." His fingers tightened. "And if you do, then I shall have to marry you, shan't I? In fact..."

"I wouldn't have you," she railed at him. "Not if you were the last man." The thought of his proposing marriage only under those conditions galled her to the limit.

Adam started to say something but thought better of it. She was in a proper pet now, and there was little sense in continuing. She'd feel better once they were off this blasted boat, and the fright about a baby was over. Anyway, he thought ruefully, you didn't propose to a girl who'd just finished saying she'd rather marry a sullen ox of a man than you. He shrugged and dropped his hands. There was time yet. And the end would be the same. There was not another girl alive who would take this journey with him and complain about nothing save this one silly fear of another girl. More and more he'd realized he couldn't go on dragging her about without marrying her, but he had resisted the further realization that this thought actually pleased him. He shrugged again. When they reached Cincinnati and Wayne's army...

Charity spun away from him, tears glistening on her cheeks, and threw herself on the bunk, her face to the wall. Soon the familiar warmth of his hard body was next to hers, but he made no move to take her in his arms. She squirmed as far away as the narrow space allowed, and listened to the splatter of rain on the wide planks overhead.

She awoke to the same sound in a gray dawn. Her anger had dissolved, and she felt foolish for her outburst last night. Why did she always get so angry with him, when in fact she loved him beyond anything she'd ever known? She blinked and sat up very carefully. Adam lay on his side, one arm cradling his dark head, and she felt tears spring to her eyes as she watched his handsome face. He looked so boyish and even vulnerable right now. She realized this was the first time she'd admitted to herself that she loved him, and the thought overwhelmed her. But once admitted, she knew it had been so for a long time, perhaps even as far back as their sea voyage together. And Adam wanted her. Perhaps he didn't love her as she did him. But he wanted her. What *did* marriage matter now? Smiling to herself she crept over his still form and reached for her chemise. Then she frowned.

What if he'd finally wearied of her after last night? Well then, she'd have to make sure he wanted her again.

Smiling again, she tugged the chemise over her head. She felt the floor sway and planted her feet to don petticoat and dress. She felt the floor sway once more. Tugging her skirts down she crossed to the window as this time the boat lurched. Her gasp woke Adam. He was on his feet before she could turn around.

"We've come loose," she cried, but he was already in his breeches.

Snatching up his shirt, he lunged for the door. "Stay here and out of the way," he said, and crashed into the narrow passage, shouting for the others.

Charity went to the door. Already Jed was running down the passage after Adam, and Mr. Bowman, his shirt only half buttoned, was flinging open his panel. Charity gripped the doorframe as the boat lurched again. There was a dull thud and the unmistakable sound of wood grinding on wood. She heard feet pounding overhead, and Rourke raced out the back entrance to the after deck. The boat swayed and there was more grinding.

Clinging to the walls, she moved down the passage to Molly's compartment and pushed the door open. The girl was sitting on her bunk, and her curving smile changed to a scowl when she saw Charity. Just whom had she expected, Charity wondered as she glimpsed naked breasts and a white thigh before the girl snatched bedclothes around her.

"We've come loose," Charity said, averting her eyes. The noise of the storm, of the animals behind them and the men overhead drowned out her words. She raised her voice, pointing to Molly's clothes. "Get dressed. We've hit something."

The girl went on scowling at her, but made no move. "Quickly," Charity shouted and closed the door again.

Once in the passage she tried to return to her own room, but the boat was tilting and had begun a slow turn that nearly made her lose her footing. She wondered if there was any damage, and suddenly the thought of being shut inside the cabin was more frightening than the elements outside. She stumbled back toward the animals, thinking to try to calm the squealing and mooing coming from the covered deck. The floor beneath her feet seemed to heave and she staggered. There was a crash as the plow in the storage area fell over into the planks of the cabin. Her hands outspread against the walls on either side, she yelled for Molly to follow her.

She saw red hair appear down the hallway and was relieved the girl had shown some sense.

The animals were in a frenzy of panic now, and Charity, gripping the ropes on the heads of two horses, tried to calm them. Beyond, she could see angry water swirling off the stern. The low profile of their island was receding behind, and the boat seemed to be swinging broadside to the current. She grasped the ladder as the wind lashed rain into her face and she saw the ghostly arms of massive tree roots brush sickeningly along the cabin sides. At the same instant the steering oar caught the upturned roots and the huge pole swung, cracking. There was a shout, and a figure hurtled over the side.

Charity ignored Molly's scream behind her. Snatching the rope halter over the ears of the nearest horse, she untied it from its wall ring with shaking fingers. There wasn't much rope, but it was better than nothing. Flinging herself against the stern, she saw Rourke's head bobbing at the base of the tangled roots a few feet away.

"Good girl." Jed was beside her, snatching the rope from her hands. Leaning far out, he flung it hard, shouting. Charity clung to his middle to keep him from falling, and saw Rourke's thrashing arm catch the halter as it splashed on the water.

Another scream made Charity's head come up. They were within feet of the shore now, the boat banging into debris every few yards. From a thicket before them a hideously painted face rose up. At the same instant a rifle report could be heard above the storm. Rourke's head snapped back out of the water, then lifeless fingers let go the rope.

Too stunned to move, Charity stared at the swirl of water where Rourke had been. But already Jed was pushing her back as another rifle shot was heard and wood splintered before them. She glimpsed Molly running down the passage toward the bow, and saw with horror that the girl ran ankle deep in water. Jed pushed her again, and from the corner of the deck she could see Adam and Mr. Bowman moving along the roof. They'd taken the sweeps from their sockets and were trying to use them as poles to push away from the shore.

Jed bellowed at her then. She saw he was cutting loose the animals, and she nodded, frantic fingers working on the latch of the hogs' pen. She saw Jed dart down the passage. The boat was lumbering now, tilting precariously as the current began to carry it back to midstream, and the animals were staggering and thrashing. She backed away to the stern to avoid being trampled and looked up once more. A volley of shots rang out. The girl's terrified eyes watched Mr. Bowman's body arch backward, a ragged hole in the center of his chest. His giant sweep, caught in the river, thrashed like a wounded snake, catching Adam in the side. He tried to jump clear as the boat swirled slowly and his own sweep tugged at his arms. But he was off balance, and in a tangle of huge poles, he lost his footing. Charity screamed as she saw him claw for the edge of the cabin roof. Another shot and one hand stiffened upward. Then he was gone.

Choking on a new scream, Charity flung herself to the listing starboard side. Wildly she sought the rope used for Rourke. Her fingers closed on it just as something crashed into her, knocking her back to the cabin wall. Adam's horse, eyes rolling in fright, heaved against her, trying to keep his footing. Desperation gave her strength. Bringing up her knee sharply into his belly, she pushed with her hands and felt him lurch away from her. Sobbing and calling Adam's name, she clawed past the horse's neck, only to find Jed blocking her path. For a split second they stood, knee deep in water on the careening deck, echoing each other's horror.

Then Jed was shouting at her. "Get hold that horse, girl." Roughly he made her clasp the halter rope on the animal's head. "No sign of Adam. Molly's dead in the bow. Git on that nag's back."

Numb with shock, Charity just stared at him. Gray water cascading over the stern and the ping of a bullet ricocheting off a metal barrel hoop went unnoticed. Jed spun her savagely and heaved her like a sack onto the stamping horse's back. Instinctively she threw her leg across his rump and crouched low. But her eyes were sightless and she was moaning.

The deck slipped further under the horse's skidding hooves, and with that, the frantic animal lunged over the sinking side into the raging current.

PART FOUR

Chapter 22

Powerful shoulders moved beneath her slipping knees and without thought Charity wound her fingers in the sodden mane and clung to her horse's neck. A bullet zipped into the water behind her, making her sink further down in the roiling torrent. She glanced back and saw several figures on the bank. The Indians were waving their spent rifles and holding clenched fists in the air as the remains of the flatboat wallowed deep in the water against the far shore. A horse was swimming near it and debris choked the river around it. Her tear-filled eyes searched the wreckage, but saw no dark head swimming for shore. Despite her horse's fight against the current, she was being swept downstream faster than the boat, and she couldn't keep it in sight.

"Hang on, girl." Jed's stentorian voice came to her through a fog of paralyzing grief. She looked over her shoulder and saw him low in the river astride another horse. His usually swarthy face was ashen, but his dark eyes bored into hers. "We'll make it. Hang on."

She couldn't even nod to him, but primitive instinct kept her atop her surging mount. She wondered, finally, as her brain began to work again, if she could turn her horse across the current to the Kentucky shore. But a long look at the wide, gray water convinced her he couldn't make it.

Just as she thought she'd be in the nightmare world of the river forever and was becoming aware that she didn't care, her horse lurched and stumbled. She flung her arms around his neck and he slipped, went down, then staggered up again. Water tugged at her skirts and she sputtered and coughed, but suddenly she was clear and the horse was splashing and lunging toward a rocky ledge. He reached the dry land, shook himself and stopped, his legs trembling. Charity nearly slid from his back, but once more Jed's voice came to her.

"Stay on!"

She didn't look around, but waited, hearing the other horse's heavy blowing as he splashed out some yards upstream. In moments Jed was beside her, and now she could see a blood-soaked sleeve on his left side. Her head came up then.

"You're hurt."

"Nothin'. We can't stay here. Them Injuns aren't goin' to miss a chance at a couple o' horses and two good scalps. They've gone back for their own horses already, if'n I don't miss my guess."

"I can't go."

"Oh, yes, you can. But I don't aim to argue you into it." He reached for the dangling halter rope and gave her horse's head a smart jerk. Slowly at first the beast moved forward, but Jed tugged and shouted abuse at both animals till they entered the woods at a smart trot.

Their flight was a tearing, crashing progress through the wind-whipped trees. Branches raked at her hair and her clothes, lashing her face and limbs painfully. But mindlessly Charity gripped her rangy mount, her bareback riding long ago now coming to her aid, and soon Jed stopped turning to see if she was still astride and put his attention on their direction.

After what seemed like hours, they came to a boulder-strewn stream and Jed led them along it until a sandy bottom allowed the horses to enter the water and follow the stream up through the forest. Another hour and Jed turned them to the western bank and headed into the trees once more.

The rest of that day became a blur of aching fear and agony for Charity. The man before her was merciless, whipping the horses onward when they would have stumbled and fallen where they walked. But at long, long last he seemed to think pursuit was unlikely and he allowed them to stop by yet another stream.

That night they could do little but shackle the horses with the halter ropes and burrow into nests of half-dry leaves to seek oblivion from the horrors behind them. Their only food was berries, but neither had a craving for anything more.

The next day was little different as they rode in grim silence through the wilderness. Late in the afternoon they spied a clearing with newly chopped trees standing in ragged stumps around a narrow cabin. Not much farther on they came to another.

"Where are we?" Charity finally asked in a lifeless voice.

"Cincinnati, I hope." The first hint of a grin pulled at the corners of Jed's mouth. His color was nearly back today, and his arm, now wrapped in a length of cloth from Charity's petticoat, seemed to pain him less.

The sun had appeared that morning, but to Charity the world still seemed as dark as on the night of the storm. The sight of warm dwellings and the thought of safety only made the ache inside her grow. What did safety matter if Adam was floating amongst the wreckage of the flatboat back on the river? The image haunted her, and with it she carried the knowledge that her last words to him had been words of anger. Had he died hating her? With a strangled cry, she let the tears pour down her face once more, and paid no attention to the path they took.

Uncaring, she saw the walls of a fort draw near, passed through heavy gates and sat, unmindful of words and activity around her. Jed was talking to a man in uniform, but she didn't try to understand what was being said. The man spoke to her but she shook her head, not caring to listen. A rose-hued sky deepened to purple and gray, but she didn't notice.

Till suddenly a voice nearby said, "Miss Ashton!"

She looked down, and was startled back to reality when she saw William Harrison's face turned up to her. She had not seen him since a party at Wentworth last winter, and she barely recognized him now in his ensign's uniform, his dark hair lightened with powder, his thin face tanned by the sun.

Reaching down, she extended one hand. "Mr. Harrison."

He clasped it in a warm grip. "Simpson just told me what has happened. A terrible ordeal for you. Can you wait while I get my horse? The fort is no place for you to be. They'll be shutting the gates soon, so I'll take you to an inn."

She shook her head. "We have no money."

He waved away her words. "Simpson and I have discussed it. Just a moment." He went off at a brisk walk, and Charity, watching his ramrod military gait, felt vaguely better.

The three rode in silence into the town, and Harrison led

them to a two-story wood frame structure. Jed took the horses while their guide steered Charity inside.

The landlord looked askance at Charity's tattered condition, but the young officer at her side seemed to calm his disquiet. A room was bespoken and dinner ordered. Then her old friend drew Charity aside.

"I am on duty with General Wayne, and must return to camp. But you will be comfortable here."

Charity smiled tremulously. "I can't thank you enough. And I haven't even asked how you have been."

An almost boyish grin split his long face. "It has been a long spring, but we are settled now, and General Wayne awaits orders to begin his campaign. This time we will make the frontier safe for settlers." He stopped, looking into her clouded sea green eyes. "But what do you do out here? Simpson did not tell me that much."

"We were coming to Cincinnati." She didn't know if she should say that Adam had been sent by the government, stumbled on his name anyway.

Harrison coughed. "How fortunate for Cincinnati," he said gallantly, filling the pause adroitly. "And now we must see you are properly cared for while we find out just what happened." He coughed again, uncomfortable.

She knew her desolate face told him a great deal, but he could know only a part of the story. She didn't know what to say.

Squaring his shoulders, the young man took one of her limp hands again. "Simpson said he was certain only of the fate of two of the people on your boat. Adam and the other man might have escaped."

Charity's head snapped up. For a second hope kindled, then slowly it died again. Shaking her head, she swallowed hard. "Mr. Bowman was shot on the cabin roof. I don't know if that bullet killed him, but I don't see how he could have saved himself from pitching over the side. And Adam...he was knocked off the roof, and when he tried to hold on...he was shot." She finished with a gulp.

"Did you see him go into the river?"

"No. I tried to reach the side, to help him. But the animals..." She shrugged helplessly and closed her eyes against fresh tears.

"Do not lose hope yet, Miss Ashton." His voice was low. Then it became firmer. "Adam is an old friend of mine. If there's anything to be learned about his fate, I will learn it.

Simpson will scour the town tomorrow, perhaps even go upriver. Meanwhile," and his tone became more hearty, "we must see to situating you in better circumstances. There is a Judge Symmes here, an old friend. His daughter is about your age. I feel sure they would be eager to help if I explain to them what has happened. I would go to them now, but I am already late. Tomorrow we shall see."

"You're so kind, Mr. Harrison."

Smiling, he demurred and said his farewells. But before he could turn to go, he raised an eyebrow. "By the way, you may be pleased to know there is another friend of yours here in Cincinnati. A Paul LaRoche."

"Paul!" Charity's eyes flew wide. "He...he is not such a great friend of mine."

"No? Oh. Well, he is not such a great friend of mine either. He seems to be thick as thieves with General Wilkinson and his men. And they none of them care for those of us who are loyal to General Wayne. But that is not important. I mentioned him because I have seen him here in this inn twice this past week, and thought perhaps you would be glad of another friendly face."

"You are kind to think of it." Charity's eyes were already darting about the hall, looking for a sign of Paul. She wished she could go straight upstairs. What appalling luck that he would be in the West right now. Though knowing that General Wilkinson was here at Fort Washington, she should have expected something like it. Paul had said more than once that Wilkinson was the man through whom he would make his fortune.

Harrison's eyes followed hers. "You needn't see him, I suppose, if you remain in your room. And I hope that tomorrow night will find you in new quarters. Meanwhile, let me caution you about walking out too freely unless Simpson is with you. The town is full of rough rivermen. And the American Legion is camped just outside of town. Many of the soldiers are something less than gentlemen. I would not have you subjected to any unpleasantness."

Charity nodded and thanked him again. She wondered what she was to do about her ruined dress, but decided tomorrow would be soon enough to worry. She bade him goodby then and fled to her assigned chamber.

The food might have been cooked shoes for all that Charity noticed, and the fine bed went unappreciated, though she was amazed to discover in the morning that she had slept soundly. Bill Harrison's words about the possibility of Adam's survival had taken on the nature of a dream. She hated to face the morning light and the likelihood that the dream had no place in reality. On the other hand she had to find out.

Jed appeared with breakfast for her as the sounds of the waking town began to come to the room from the streets below. He had eaten early and had already begun to ask news of upriver.

"No one here knows anythin'," he said, standing over Charity as she ate. "Only party I overheard last night was a group headin' to New Orleans tomorrow. An' they've been here over a week, so they're no help. Boats may be puttin' in today who've passed the spot. Couldn't've gotten here much sooner."

Chewing thoughtfully on a biscuit, Charity waved Jed into a chair opposite. "Mr. Harrison said he'd get us out of this inn if he could. Perhaps tonight. But how will we pay for the time we have spent?"

"I had some coins on me when we went swimmin'. An' Mr. Harrison gave me more. We could stay a month if'n we had to. An' I aim to stay as long as it takes." His voice trailed off.

"You can't do everything. I want to help."

"This town's full of soldiers and rivermen. You can't traipse around."

"Maybe I can." A glint appeared in her eyes, and Jed cocked his head warily. "If I dress like a man."

The other snorted. "Even in my old breeches you didn't look like no man I ever saw. You can put that silly scheme outa your head."

Charity pouted. "If you think I'm going to sit in this room while you're out there, while Adam may be...Well, I won't. I want to come along. If I wore a loose shirt. And a hat." She tapped her fingers on her cheek.

Jed got up and began backing away. "No, you can't have my clothes. Anyway, Adam'd snatch me bald-headed if he knew I let you follow me to the places I've gotta go."

"Well, he won't know. You have money. I am in rags now anyway, and need new clothes. Get me some men's clothes."

"You wouldn't pass for a boy, let alone a man."

"Yes, I will. *Please*, Jed."

They argued till Jed began to lose his temper. Then Charity resorted to tears and he was undone. Backing further away and twisting his old felt hat in his hands he caved in and fled the uncomfortable scene.

235

An hour later he was back, and with an air of injured resignation he dropped a bundle of clothes on the bed. Then he left without a word and she heard him stamp off downstairs to await her.

Pulling off her clothes, Charity stood before the mirror. It was quite true that her curves would be hard to hide, but perhaps...She tore another length of material from her petticoat and wrapped it twice around her breasts, tying it tight. Then she pulled on the breeches and the homespun shirt. Tugging the pants down her hips and letting the shirt blouse out, she managed to conceal her slim waist and most of the bulge of her chest. A loose vest helped the line. But her hair was a problem. There was too much of it to hide in the shapeless hat Jed had brought. And it was too long to club at her neck. With only a hint of regret, she picked up the knife from her breakfast tray and began to hack.

Minutes later she nodded with satisfaction. Her hair, now only a little below her shoulders, could be managed. She took the twine from the clothing bundle and tied the shortened mass in back, pulling it tight. Then she jammed the hat down on her head and looked in the mirror once more. It seemed to her that the transformation was nearly complete. Heavy socks and some doeskin moccasins finished her costume. She felt better already. Any activity would be better than sitting, wondering.

Slowly she worked her way down the stairs. It wouldn't do to have the landlord see her, though she hoped he would fail to recognize the boy now treading quietly into the hall. There was no sign of Jed, and she hesitated to go to the door of the public room. Perhaps he was outside.

The heavy door stood open to the warm summer breezes. She crept to it, blinking as she entered the bright sunlight. Jed stood in the dusty street, talking to three men. "Can't help you fellas. My friend and I, we're bound upriver, not down," she heard him say. She stood quietly, hoping to catch his eye.

"We'll find someone to take Aaron's place before tomorrow, Corbet. Perhaps this man knows of someone else?"

Charity smothered a gasp at the sound of the familiar voice. She turned to dart back into the inn, but already Jed was saying, "Sorry. There's my friend now. Gotta' be off." His voice held relief and Charity could hardly run from him now.

Slowly she turned again, and caught a glimpse of Paul as

he and the other two watched Jed retreat. They all looked at her, but in that brief moment she saw no sign of recognition on Paul's face. Her blood pounding in her temples, she moved to meet Jed and saunter casually up the street with him.

"Characters lost a boat hand in a knife fight last night. He's laid up for a bit," Jed remarked when they were out of earshot. "That's the group goin' to New Orleans, and they don't really need another man on board, but they've got papers for fourteen men, so they're willin' to take someone on in his place. Wouldn't get me on their dirty boat. If'n they got papers already, they know someone close to the Spanish, I'm thinkin', an' I want no part of the Spanish."

Charity said nothing. She was absorbed in putting as much distance as possible between them and Paul LaRoche. And she was concentrating on trying to walk like a boy.

Jed steered her around a corner. Eyeing her speculatively, he rubbed his chin. "What in almighty'd you do ta' yore hair?"

"Cut it," she said stoutly.

He nodded, then shook his head. "Well, it pret' nearly does it. But I wouldn't want you for *my* son. A pretty boy like you could get into a heap o' trouble on his own."

Charity flushed, then scowled at him. "Where do we go first?"

"River." Jed jerked a thumb behind him and sighed. "Might as well try it."

Along the river they found a vast array of boats and rough men, but could discover no craft that had come in in the past day. Charity's ears burned at the language she heard, but she clenched her jaw and followed Jed doggedly, closing the worst of the talk out of her mind.

Discouraged, the two made their way back to the inn after noon. "You don't want to push that fool disguise too far. I'll get lunch for you in that room," Jed said firmly at the door.

Charity nodded agreement. She couldn't take the chance of having Paul see her again. Thank goodness he'd be gone in the morning.

Upstairs they ate in morose silence. But when they were done, Jed flung down his napkin and got up with a jerk. "I'm off to the river. If I don't learn somethin' by tonight, I'm headin' back upstream in the mornin'."

"And I'm going with you."

"Oh no, you're not. I aim to cross to Kentucky and scour the river and the settlements. T'ain't safe out in the woods, and I'm not takin' you in them again. Mr. Harrison said he'd

237

see to you, so you just do as he says an' I'll get back with word."

"I'm not sitting here at some stuffy house, making inane conversation with a feather-headed girl while I wonder where you are and when you'll return." Charity stamped a moccasined foot and glared at him.

But Jed seemed unperturbed. "That jaunt to the river was enough for me. I seen how some o' them men looked at you. I could get myself kilt just bein' next to you." He glared back at her. "You're safe here, just where Adam'd want you. You stay put now. Mr. Harrison'll be in touch." Charity shook her finger at him, but he was already out the door. "See ya later," he flung over his shoulder and his feet thudded quickly down the hall.

The girl paced like a caged lion after he left. Her westerly room became stiflingly hot, and she threw open windows, leaning out to get more air. Once, in the street below, she saw Paul with his companions, and drew back quickly when his eyes seemed to flick to the upper story.

By sundown she was half crazed with the heat and the waiting. No word had yet come from Bill Harrison, and, of course, Jed was still gone. The town should be going to dinner now, and the streets should be emptier than at other hours. She would chance going out. Perhaps she could walk up and down at the side of the building. She had to have air.

Donning vest and cap once more, she slipped silently down the main stairs. Her foot touched the bottom step as, from her right, she heard voices approaching. Too late to retreat upward. She'd have to keep going and try to look confident. A group of men stood in a doorway next to her, but she didn't look at them. With what she hoped was a firm tread, she walked out the front door and turned left.

She had guessed aright; the street was nearly deserted. She looked for the slouching figure of Jed, but saw only a frock-coated man receding a block down. Perhaps if she just went to the street she and Jed had taken to the river this morning... Tugging her hat down over her eyes, she set out.

Dusk was descending slowly, and an occasional flicker of light showed in windows she passed. Beside the long, blank wall of a warehouse several blocks away, Charity paused. There was no one before her on the street. But she could hear footsteps following her. Probably some rivermen returning to their boats, she told herself firmly, and walked on. At the next turning she would head back toward the inn. The footsteps were closer now, and she began to quicken her pace.

A strong hand gripped her arm and, as she whirled, rummy breath bathed her face.

"You headin' anywhere in particular, me lad?" A broad face pushed up to hers and small black eyes peered under her hat brim.

Her voice gruff with fear, Charity turned her head. "Meetin' a friend."

"Well now, we'd like to be yore friends." Another voice, almost wheedling, came from her other side.

Charity jerked back from the grip on her sleeve, but the hand tightened. Now her other arm was caught too. "Boy all alone at this hour could get hisself in trouble. Better you come with us. Can use some help anyway."

Her feet nearly lifted from the ground as the two burly figures propelled her forward.

"Let me go," she hissed.

The men just chuckled and pulled her onward. Wildly she looked around for help. There was no one in sight, and a scream would alert anyone who heard it to the fact that she wasn't a boy. Her fear grew as she thought of the possibilities if these drunken creatures discovered her true sex. Her only hope was that Jed would come along.

She was still struggling when they started over the lip of the bank and her horrified gaze fell on a large keelboat directly below her. She twisted, trying to sit down, and her feet skittered in the sandy soil. Roughly she was hauled upright again. She went limp and the men nearly toppled as her weight hung suddenly dead in their arms. But the man with the black eyes just chuckled. Belching loudly, he jerked her up. Like a sack of grain, she was tossed over one massive shoulder and taken on board the boat.

Another tall man met them on the bow deck. "What's this, boys?"

"Last of the crew reportin', Cap'n." The man with the wheedling voice snickered.

"But that's a boy," the tall man said contemptuously.

"Yeah. But we was told he'd like the adventure. He don't seem too keen right now, but the bosses say he's the one. So we brung 'im."

Charity drew herself up, facing the captain. Clearing her throat, she pitched her voice as low as she could. "It's a mistake, Captain. They have the wrong person."

The captain peered at her again, then looked at her captors. The flat-faced man with the awful breath shrugged. "We was told to follow this un, and bring 'im aboard. Pointed out to us right at the inn, he was."

The captain frowned. "From the looks of him, he'll jump for the nearest shore at the first chance, but if you were told to bring him, that's that. Lock him in the small storeroom tonight so we can prove he's the right one when they come aboard."

Charity started to protest further, but a hand came up and cuffed her across the face. Her head swam and tears of fear and fury sprang to her eyes as a gravel voice said, "You don't backtalk captains, boy."

Her life had become a series of nightmares, Charity thought as she huddled amidst sacks of meal in the stygian gloom of the boat's storeroom. But surely Jed and even Bill Harrison were looking for her by now. Jed would make the captain see it was all a mistake, and those horrid men would have to look again for the luckless boy someone wanted aboard this keelboat. She tried to take heart at the thought and sat up straighter.

Voices not far from her ear came through the thick planking. "Nope," someone shouted. "No one like that." Another voice very far away, said something else. Then the man near at hand called, "Sure will." And there was silence but for the tramp of feet across the deck.

Charity sank back. Surely that had not been in answer to a question about a fair-haired boy wandering near the boats? Why would the men keep her locked away if Jed had inquired? She folded her hands carefully and sat very still. The next voices she heard like that, she'd yell and pound on the walls. If anyone else was out there she'd make sure he knew there was a prisoner aboard this boat.

But the hours crept by, and there was no more to be heard on deck. Fitfully she dozed and a bronzed face with a shock of nearly black hair falling toward one bright gray eye swam before her. With a strangled cry she started up, only to find she was surrounded by heavy shapes barely discerned in the gloom of her hole. Then she would doze again to repeat the process.

The sliver of dim light that crept beneath the door finally bespoke day approaching, and Charity, each limb aching, stretched and stood, glad to have the shadows begin to recede. Soon, she hoped, she would be brought out and could plead her case to whoever these "bosses" were. She tramped back and forth trying to awaken stiff muscles. And at last there were voices and heavy feet outside. The door opened and she threw up a hand to shield her eyes from the sudden light. Squinting toward the opening, she saw three men crowd the doorway. She made out the captain first as he stepped inside to the shadows.

"Yes, that's the right boy," Paul LaRoche's smooth voice said.

Chapter 23

Charity reeled where she stood, her hand still up to her eyes. Before she could recover, the door had slammed again, the heavy bar had dropped and the men were moving away. She stumbled forward and fell on the door, pounding and calling wordlessly. When the footsteps continued to fade down the planking outside, she yelled Paul's name, but there was no answer. She heard feet pound overhead, and from the bow reaches of the long vessel came shouts and the clank of oars. She felt the boat sway beneath her feet. Dear God, they were leaving!

With renewed frenzy, she attacked the door, but the sturdy, upright planks gave back her blows with a hollow sound. At last, exhausted, she fell back, too frightened for tears.

The boat rocked with the current, seemed to swing and then settled. She could just hear the gentle swish of water along the hull. Fighting for control over her panic, Charity sat down. The next time Paul came to that door, she would tell him who she was and demand to be let off. It was all a horrible mistake. She would explain and somehow she would make her way back upstream to Cincinnati.

But the man who opened the door an hour later was not Paul. She flew at him, trying to bypass him at the entrance, but a brawny arm flung her back. Sausage and bread were tossed at her feet, and a canteen of water. Then the door slammed with a final sound, and she was left to brood over her meager fare.

With every passing hour her heart sank further. This boat was not like the flatboat she had traveled on. It was shallow and swift. And the mast she'd seen would hold a large sail. If they could use that and some rowers, they would cover much greater distances than any flatboat could in a day. How many miles had they already come? If she got the chance, could she jump and swim for it? Questions beat at her foundering brain, and wild schemes flew through her head. But she knew if she was meant to be locked away in this hold, here she would stay. For there was no way out. She shrank from considering why she was here, and from looking back. Slowly and methodically she chewed her food and emptied her mind. Grimly she set herself to wait.

For two days she sat in dazed and bewildered determination. Each time the door opened, she rushed for it. Each time she was thrown back with a grunt and more food was flung at her feet.

On the gray afternoon of their third day on the river, as Charity finished the last of this morning's pork rind and hard bread, she heard feet outside on the plank walk. This time she didn't bother to rise when the door opened slowly, but blinked, adapting her eyes to the glare in her prison. Instead of throwing scraps at her, her jailor now stood with massive arms crossed on his barrel chest and squinted into the gloom.

"Git up," he growled.

Slowly Charity obeyed, fear making her legs nearly rubber. "Wh-where are you taking me?"

For answer, the big man jerked his head toward the outdoors. Against the light she couldn't make out his features, couldn't read his expression. Falteringly she moved toward him and stood in the doorway.

"Ever been on a keelboat?" the man asked.

Charity shook her head, astonished at his conversational tone.

242

"Then go easy. Planks are narrow on the walks." And he trod ahead of her toward the bow.

Hugging the walls of the main cabin, Charity followed him the length of the craft till he stepped down onto the bow deck. Here, eight men sat at oars, pulling rhythmically beneath a roofed structure. Behind them, off the small, open deck rose a ladder to the cabin roof. It was toward this the big man led her. With stiff fingers Charity climbed up and looked toward the mast set just forward of amidships. Near it stood the captain with Paul and the older man named Corbet she'd seen outside the inn in Cincinnati.

Her steps flagged, and she tugged the hat farther down over her brow. Suddenly she wasn't sure she wanted Paul to know who she was, not with these others standing around. She was three days from Cincinnati on a boat with a dozen rough rivermen. A girl alone would be at their mercy and Paul could hardly defend her against all of them. She looked off to the banks, unwilling to face him squarely. The banks still stood in occasional cliffs or rocky masses, but one had the odd feeling that the country was somehow opening out into great empty wilderness. There was not a hint anywhere of human habitation.

"Here he is, Cap'n." The big man brought her toward the waiting group.

"Fine, Baker. You keep an eye on him. We can use him on the bow, watching for sawyers and ledges, especially on the Mississippi. And he can help you the rest of the time." The captain looked at Charity then. Waving a hand toward the desolate banks, he peered at her with a stern expression. "There's nothin' out there, boy. So don't get notions of jumping for it. Mr. LaRoche said you were to come, or I wouldn't have you here. See you behave yourself."

Charity's eyes were enormous, but her mouth set in a thin line as she listened to him.

"What's your name?" the captain then asked.

"Mark Simpson," she stammered, combining the first names that came into her head. She stole a quick look at Paul and saw him smiling a tight version of the smug cat smile he'd had when he returned from Philadelphia a year ago. She was given no time to wonder at it, though, for the man named Baker was pulling her toward the bow ladder again.

He led her back through a side passage, past tiny cubicles for sleeping and a vast storage area for cargo, to the stern where he set her to cleaning tack for the three horses aboard.

The horses, she learned, were for Paul and two others if they chose to return overland to Kentucky. The rest of the men would haul the keelboat back upriver with new cargo.

Silently she set to work under Baker's direction, and was thankful she'd been given a job she could handle. But Baker's eyes upon her made her nervous.

"You ever done that afore?" the big man asked, putting down the harness he was holding.

She nodded.

"Wouldn't know it, lookin' at them lily white hands o' yours."

Charity bit her lip. After her weeks in the forest and on the flatboat she would have said her hands were ruined, but apparently they weren't as callused as she'd thought. "Got soft floating down the Ohio, I guess," she answered in her gruffest voice, and was relieved when he just shook his head and returned to his own work. Soon she was taken to her new post in the tip of the bow, and was glad to be away from questioning eyes.

For nearly a week Charity sat disconsolately in the bow, watching the swirling river for dangers, or followed Baker around, feeding horses, serving food to the men, cleaning whatever she was told. At night she was locked in the store-room, by day she was worked till she nearly dropped. Baker was not unkind, thinking her a green lad who would learn to love the life of the river as he did, and she stayed silent at all times, giving no hint of the turmoil and despair inside, inviting no questions. After those first days in the storeroom she had given up hope that Jed was following her, or that Bill Harrison had sent someone after the boat. What lay before her she couldn't guess, and was often too tired to care. Adam was dead. What did anything really matter any more?

They passed the Wabash and Cumberland rivers, and at last the mighty Mississippi spread before them, a great sheet of yellow-gray water streaked by the darker current of the Ohio. Charity stared with appalled wonder at this flat waste. On the near shore, dead trees raised skeleton branches in an attitude of despair to match her own. Around them were tangles of logs and masses of floating driftwood. Sawyers and planters showed blackly in the dun-colored water. Away to the west the forest stretched unbroken on the Spanish shore, a strange, rugged country, vast and flat and lonely.

They had made only one stop on the Ohio, and now at last, they were to make another on the western shore of the great river, in a place the men called New Madrid. She knew this to be the first Spanish port of call they would make and actually looked forward to seeing the town, to walking on solid land once more.

But now for the first time Paul approached her. "You're not to go ashore here, Simpson," he said casually when she stood in the bow watching the mouth of a stream approaching. "Baker and Turner will be here to stand watch. You stay too."

Charity hid what disappointment she felt. She wouldn't even turn to look at him, fearing his recognition.

"While we remain, you will stay in the storeroom, out of sight. But I will bring you something from the town."

Charity's eyes flicked sideways. Did he think she'd thank him for his largesse? It was due to his strange desire to bring an unknown boy along that she was on this boat in the first place. And never, in these endless days, had he spoken to her. His behavior was peculiar at best, and loathsome by her lights. Her jaw set in a firm line, she turned and made her way along the planking to the dark storeroom, hoping her ears deceived her when she heard a soft chuckle behind.

Paul did not speak to her again when the men reboarded the boat, but to her surprise she was given, through Baker, a change of clothes. For only the second time in her life, she had to feel gratitude to Paul.

As the days rolled drearily by in increasingly oppressive heat, she wondered dully what game Paul was playing. Occasionally she felt his eyes watching her, and once he took her arm while giving instructions about food to be brought. She had flinched at his touch, but had not allowed her dislike to show on her face. Increasingly she sensed that he was waiting for something, but she couldn't think what. She began to look ahead to their journey's end. What would happen to her when they reached New Orleans?

New Orleans! She sat up straight in her dwindling bed of meal sacks. The city where Marie had gone! The hot night, alive with the dismal croakings of bullfrogs and the maddening drone of mosquito hordes, seemed suddenly less horrible. They were moored below Natchez, and all the men save two had gone ashore to sample the delights of Natchez Under-the-Hill. Charity had heard the ribald jokes and descriptive tales about the fabled place till she thought this must be one of the most sinful areas on earth. She had resisted guffawing offers to take her along and educate her, and was actually glad when Paul had again decreed she was to remain in her hold for the duration of their stay. She'd been pleased to shut herself away from the sight of the massive bluffs rising above the unsavory jumble of wooden shacks and houses along the river front.

The raucous laughter and strains of wild music were distant backdrops to her thoughts now as she hugged her knees and tried to imagine how she would ever find Marie in a strange city.

A sound outside her door brought her to her feet, the image of Marie's familiar face dissolving into tortured imaginings. The bar was lifted, and she scrambled silently behind a barrel, trying to crouch below its lip. The door swung out, and she held her breath. Light entered the gloom and moved toward her. Suddenly she was looking up into Paul's frowning face. The lantern cast black shadows upward across his high nose and dark eyes, making him look satanic in the second before he lowered the light and smiled thinly.

"I came to make sure you were snug in your place of safe-keeping," he said softly.

She stood up slowly and nodded, saying nothing.

His eyes passed down her slender form. "The clothes were a decent fit, I see."

Again she nodded, but she saw no reason to thank him.

"You are better off here than you would be out there with the drunken crew, you know." Paul leaned one immaculate elbow on the edge of her barrel. Even in this heat his stock was well folded, his waistcoat smooth, his coat buttoned.

Still Charity kept silent, though her every nerve tingled with an unknown dread.

"You have learned a great deal from the rivermen, no? But not too much. And as long as you remain on board and out of sight they will not dare to touch you. That privilege is mine alone." He reached out one long-fingered hand, but Charity drew back till her head was against the wall. The hand patted her cheek with a sharp tap. "I assure you my touch is more pleasing than that of the animals aboard this vessel, little one."

Charity swallowed a sharp retort. Would Mark Simpson hit him now, or try to run away? But Paul had already stepped back out of her reach, blocking her path to the door.

"I will go now to slake my thirst on some willing wench. But all the time I shall be dreaming of the delights that await me in New Orleans." The corner of his mouth turned up in a mirthless smile. Then he was out the door and it was slamming fast.

Charity exhaled slowly. Surely Paul did not know her. But his words, couched in ambiguities, were taunting. She crouched behind her barrel again and tried to bring her reeling mind into focus. On her next deep breath, she began to swear, using all the colorful phrases she'd heard these weeks. It made her feel better to react out loud as the truth came home to her. Of course Paul had recognized her. He had known her back in Cincinnati. He had not had a strange boy kidnapped; it had been Charity Ashton he'd been after. She sat down with a thump and put her forehead on her knees. So this was why he had allowed her to continue her ridiculous masquerade. As long as she remained a boy, the crew would leave her alone and he could enjoy the sight of her brought to degrading depths. Perhaps this was his revenge for that night at the Hadleys' ball. He must have a streak of cruelty that defied imagination to do something like this to her. She rubbed her forehead with both hands, feeling dazed. What did he plan next?

Wishing desperately that she had some sort of weapon, she sat in the dark, half expecting him to return. But the long night wore on in the stifling hold and she heard only the reeling steps of the men returning from their carousing. By morning she was as red-eyed as the rest of the crew, only she lacked their aching heads. Still there was no sign of Paul.

The days passed as before, with Charity staring at the moving scenery on the winding river. For a week now, the landscape had changed slowly. Gigantic cypresses, their strange conical "knees" protruding from the water, grew more plentiful. There were forests of water oaks, and trees were seen hung with the peculiar gray beards of Spanish moss. Everywhere shiny magnolias graced the bluffs, and at the mouths of passing streams could be heard the bellows of the alligators that infested the region. Hordes of cranes rose from the water at the approach of the boat, and Charity would have delighted in the sight under any other circumstances. An endless desolation had settled over her with the knowledge that she was completely in Paul's power. He and Corbet gave the orders to the captain and crew, and except in the handling of the boat itself, their word was law here. She had pondered the question of how Paul had gotten into this position of power, and could only conclude it was somehow through this mysterious General Wilkinson. The background hardly mattered though. The fact remained that she had no way of escape. Her monthly flow had come and gone on the upper Mississippi, but the event had held no consolation for her. She'd only felt vaguely sorry she wasn't to have Adam's child, and knew it was a foolish thought.

Near Pointe Coupée, forests gave way to flourishing plantations of sugar cane, rice, cotton, and indigo. The homes of the owners of this rich and fertile region were substantial and spacious. Once Charity saw Paul eyeing the bluffs with a speculative look, and she wondered if he was now thinking of settling here. Certainly this region would remind him more of his home and of the leisured life he'd once led than Virginia could. Though as long as he set her free she didn't care where he went.

They passed Baton Rouge and its small Spanish garrison, then Pacquemine the next day. The river was now seen to be held in bounds by a wide eastern bank which the men called the *levée*. She was told each plantation owner maintained his section of the wall as a barricade against the fierce floods. They were obviously on the final approach to New Orleans.

It was a fiercely hot late afternoon when the keelboat rounded the last length of a big bend and the roofs of New Orleans became visible above the *levée*, the nearly completed towers of a new cathedral dominating the peaked-roof skyline. A barge manned by haughty-looking slaves in brilliant orange livery swept proudly past them. Ahead the *levée* was crowded with boats, including several oceangoing schooners. For a brief moment Charity forgot everything as she watched the colorful scene of ships and men, the *levée* and the fortifications rising behind.

They landed beyond the formidable bulk of the Spanish custom house near which a sentry in red paced slowly back and forth. Charity stood against the cabin wall as the men leaped to make the boat fast. So intently was she watching them that she was unaware of the man at her side until he spoke.

"Come, *chérie*. Our destination is at hand."

A firm grip on her arm propelled her off the boat and up the slope of the *levée* to the broad gravel walk between rows of orange trees. Abruptly Paul stopped, waiting for Corbet and their baggage.

Charity stared at the vivid turmoil of the *levée*. Here a gay young blade in fashionable light clothing cast admiring glances at a demure olive-skinned beauty promenading with a watchful duenna; there a red-turbaned black woman sat over baskets of fruits and vegetables, hawking them in a singsong chant; farther on, a cluster of scarlet-jacketed soldiers laughed and talked excitedly in Spanish. The heavy blue of the sky, the damp heat, and the colorful costumes reminded Charity of Cap Français on Saint Dominque, and she felt a brief bite of homesickness before Paul pulled her forward once more.

Down the *levée* she was led to a large grass-grown square in front of the cathedral. Ahead she could see an open marketplace between the square and the *levée*, but her guide steered her down the slope to skirt the square. They passed the flagpole where the red and yellow banner of Spain fluttered lazily in the mild breeze and she heard Corbet and Paul mutter something about the blasted Spanish. Beyond the cathedral they walked on wooden *banquettes* set inches above the muddy street. The one- and two-story houses with red or brown tiled roofs hugged the *banquettes*, but for the most part they turned blank faces and shuttered doors to this world of the street. Occasionally, through carriage ways, Charity caught sight of side galleries and patios behind the walls, where lush vegetation made inviting shade for the people who dwelled there.

In front of a two-story house with a steep roof, the little party halted, and Paul drew aside to speak with Corbet for several minutes. A mud-spattered sign beside a wide, shuttered door proclaimed that M. Corbet was a shipper. So that must have been his cargo he was bringing down the Mississippi, Charity thought, and stared at the rotund figure with its thatch of graying hair. He looked prosperous if unprepossessing. Corbet left them then, disappearing through a side door into a courtyard with both of the other men and all the bags save one. Charity's heart thudded heavily as Paul returned to her. But he merely took her arm once more, gesturing ahead.

"This way," he said shortly.

A block farther on, they rounded a corner and Paul gave a grunt of disapproval. Before them was a small hotel, its heavily weathered cypress boards gray with age, its dark green shutters closed fast against the midday heat. After the briefest of pauses, Paul led her quickly across the street to the door.

At the entrance Charity finally balked. "What is this place?"

"A way station, merely," Paul shrugged and jerked her forward.

Charity considered screaming, but who in this strange city would come to her aid? The possibility of falling into worse hands than Paul's kept her silent as she was dragged into the shadows of the dim little lobby and Paul went to speak rapidly with the *concierge*. A narrow flight of stairs and a short passage brought them to a comfortable-looking room of soft mauve and white whose two windows looked over a rear gallery to a small courtyard below.

Hovering at the door, Charity stared about her and watched Paul with narrowed eyes. He flung down the valise he carried and carefully closed the door beside her. Looking around thoughtfully then, Paul was still. The very hairs on her arms stood up as she waited tensely in the charged silence.

At last his black eyes came to rest on her face. "You will find this more comfortable than the storeroom, no?"

Charity didn't answer, but watched him warily. Shrugging, he went and pulled back the light coverlet on the big bed. Sitting down, he waved toward a basin of water on a carved stand. "The more civilized niceties will no doubt please you."

"What do you want?" she whispered.

A black brow flew up. "Why, my dear Charity. I want for nothing any more. I have you."

Chapter 24

"You aim to go after her?" Jed sat back on his heels and surveyed the ragged form on the pallet. The dreary little cabin was dank from the rains, and the small, flickering fire did little but cast grotesque shadows across the man lying so still near it. He watched color infuse the pale face below the blood-soaked bandage.

"I still don't understand." Adam lifted himself onto one elbow, his head swimming with the effort. He focused his unbandaged eye on the leathery face and tried to marshal his thoughts. "You say she just disappeared from the inn Harrison took you to. But how, for God's sake?"

Jed spread his hands for the second time. "I told you, I don't get it. I left 'er there in that room, an' when I came back she was just gone. I wasted a deal of time that night and yesterday lookin' for her," he added with a note of bitterness, "or I would've found you earlier."

"But you did find me, old friend, for which I must be eternally grateful. These are kind people, but their ministrations were crude at best."

"Never seen nothin' like it," said the other succinctly. "An' I'm gettin' you the hell outa here tomorrow. No use thinkin' about Charity till we get back to Cincinnati. Now you lie still while I rebandage that head. Then I'm goin' out to try to find some game to repay these poor folk." Pushing Adam gently back on the pallet, he set to work with a closed face. When he was done, he picked up his gun and was gone without another word.

It was very well to say there was no use thinking about Charity, Adam reflected as he stared at the crude beams overhead. But she'd never left his thoughts from the moment he'd flung out of the cabin to run up on deck that morning of the storm. When he'd been swept overboard and the bullet had creased his cheek, he'd been saved from unconsciousness by the cold of the river, and had had just enough strength left to hang onto the trailing bow painter as the boat made a lumbering turn and dipped onto its side. He'd come close to being caught between it and the downed trees on the Kentucky shore, but had let go in time to haul himself free of the grinding crash that followed. His eye nearly closed with blood and his side splitting where the sweep had cracked him, he'd made a slow and painful search of the wreckage, but had found only Molly crumpled in an impossible heap on the bow deck. The animals were all gone; someone had set them free, he saw, and he could only pray Charity had been that someone and had used a horse to swim the river.

The next twenty-four hours were a blur of pain and despair to him. He remembered staggering along the shore till the very sight of that swollen river had made him sick, and he'd left it to stumble inland. It was a miracle the woodsman had found him, lying at the base of a big beech tree, and had somehow gotten him the mile to his crude cabin. The following two days were hazy too. He remembered only tossing on the dirty pallet, caught in the nightmare visions of Charity

251

calling for help, her arms reaching above the flood waters, her chestnut hair swirling on the wash as she sank helplessly below the surface. The vision haunted him even now, for though he'd learned she'd survived the flood, he was overcome with the fear that her new disappearance meant something horrible had happened to her. If only he weren't so light-headed and weak!

The trip to Cincinnati drained most of the strength Adam had regained in the wilderness cabin, and although it infuriated him, he could do little but lie on the soft bed at the inn and direct Jed to find Bill Harrison. His temper wasn't improved any when Jed returned to say that Harrison had been forced to leave Fort Washington in the wake of his commander. Bill had left a long note for Jed, though, and the older man turned it over hesitantly. Swiftly Adam propped himself up and scanned the scrawled writing.

"Paul LaRoche, by God," he bellowed then, a blaze of anger kindling in his one good eye.

"Isn't he the..."

"The bastard who brought Charity to Virginia in the first place. A sly, conniving piece of goods I thought we'd left well behind us."

"And Harrison says he was here at this inn."

"Yes." Adam tapped the piece of paper in his hand. "He tried to find him after you left, but discovered LaRoche had already gone to New Orleans."

"New Orleans! Gawd Almighty! An' she was cool as a cucumber when she walked right past 'im out front."

"She *what?*"

"Walked right past 'im, she did, in that silly garb o' hers, and never let on that she knew 'im. He was one of the men I told you asked me to join their keelboat. Soon's I read that name it rang a bell, and now I remember the Frenchman calling 'im that."

"You said you checked that keelboat, didn't you?"

"Sure, like I checked all of 'em. Went down there that evenin', but the feller on deck said t'weren't no boy aboard. If I'd'a thought anyone on that craft had anything to do with her I'd've argued with the man." Adam lay very still in the lengthening silence, and Jed began to eye him nervously. "You think she's gone to New Orleans, huh?" he asked at last.

Adam's hand raked through his thick hair on the pillow. "Unless she's dead somewhere, I can't see what else could have happened to her." Silence descended once more as his tumultuous thoughts tried to sort themselves out. He couldn't forget the anger with which she'd stated she'd never marry him. But he'd been sure she hadn't meant it. So damned sure of himself! He'd always thought he could read women accurately. Until Charity, that is. She'd confounded him on more than one occasion, and he'd found sometimes her moods were like quicksilver, slipping beyond his comprehension if he didn't stay on his toes.

He tried to concentrate on what he knew. Charity had been tearful and despairing, according to Jed, but then had turned determined and donned those fool boy's clothes to start a search for him. He nearly smiled at the picture that conjured, but remembered the blank wall at the end of that escapade. She'd simply walked out of the inn, apparently, and disappeared into thin air. Paul LaRoche, he felt sure, was the key to the enigma. And the bigger question that now loomed before him was whether or not Charity had gone with the man willingly. He could have sworn she hated LaRoche, but then he had thought she'd hated him for nearly two years, too. What the hell was he to think of her now? She'd run away from him once before; why wouldn't she do it again? Especially if she thought him dead, no threat?

Damn women anyway. Perhaps it was time he stopped chasing around after that girl. Only once before had he made a fool of himself over a woman, and it had resulted in near disaster. Priscilla had bedded him fast enough, he remembered, though she later let him know he was too callow a youth with no prospects, and had married another. He'd thought he was in love then, and been very dramatic in his despair. But he'd gotten over it quickly enough, had even enjoyed her bed on occasion. And never again had he let another woman ensnare him. Not until Charity...He twisted restlessly on the bed and found Jed's calm brown eyes studying him with peculiar intensity. "What's on your mind?" he snapped, still caught in his own churning thoughts.

"I was wonderin' when you'd be strong enough to set out's all."

"I'll be fine by tomorrow. But I've got to head north."

"North?" The laconic expression gave way to surprise.

Adam's mouth curled in a mirthless smile. "You forget I was sent out here to do a job. I have to send back a dispatch before I can indulge myself in personal fancies."

"Oh." Jed nodded, his eyes on the floor. When at last he

raised his head, the twinkle was back in their depths. "Fine. You go on up to that fort Wayne's rebuildin', and you write your report. I'll start nosin' around to find out how we can get safe passage down the Mississippi."

"And what makes you so eager?"

Jed shrugged. "We're both thinkin' that's where Charity's gone. An' the sooner we find her the sooner we can go home. I'm gettin' too old for this harin' around. That stable of yours and my own room back at Bentwood're lookin' better to me all the time."

Adam closed his eyes. He could doubt her all he wanted—and at the moment he was certain that Charity had gone off happily with Paul LaRoche—but he knew he would not rest until he found her and discovered for himself the truth of the matter. Slowly he nodded. "Tomorrow, then, we will go our separate ways for a space."

Dirty and disheveled, Charity faced Paul in the dim New Orleans hotel room and tried to smother her gasp as she realized how right she had been. Paul had known her all along.

The man heard her gulp and smiled slowly. "Surely you are not surprised. Your disguise would have fooled no one who knew you. Though I admit it made everything a great deal simpler."

Her hand fumbled with the door handle, but when she turned it the door remained shut. Paul's grin was diabolical as he held up a dull brass key for her to see. Tapping it thoughtfully against his cheek, he looked her up and down. "I have always meant to have you, of course," he said conversationally, "even if only as my mistress. It pleases me greatly to know my long wait has come to an end." He stood up then and advanced on her.

Speechless, Charity stared at him and thought his eyes feral. She put up a hand as though to ward off his look. "No," she whispered hoarsely.

Her hand was caught in his and she twisted, trying to free it. His other grasped her chin and strong fingers bruised her cheek as he pulled her face forward. "On Saint Dominque you would have been mine a year since. Pity we had to put off our union for so long."

She tried to bite the hard fingers, but with a quick movement the hand was gone and with a rip the buttons of her muslin shirt were snatched from their threads. Paul jerked at the yards of binding cloth beneath, spinning her around with his force. She staggered and clawed at him, raising a long welt on his throat. The reprisal was immediate. A hard smack to the side of her head sent her reeling. Flattened against the wall, she shook her head, trying to clear her fogged vision. Fingers were tugging at her shirt, her trousers. She pushed her hands against the wall and kicked out with her feet, gasping as her moccasined toe bent painfully against his shin.

Paul swore savagely. Then another blow knocked her into the corner. Dazed, she slumped there and felt her hands caught. Something was wrapped around her wrists and pulled tight. Struggling to get her feet beneath her, she jerked back only to find her hands tied securely together. Her head still swam, but she lunged, trying to knock Paul off balance. He sidestepped and tugged the cloth. She was sent sprawling across the side of the bed, and another tug pulled her backward.

Her tears spattered the sheets as she tried to roll. But her arms were held fast above her head. Her heel found the edge of the mattress and she writhed sideways, ignoring the pain in her upraised shoulders. Paul finished tying the knot on the iron bedstead and leaned back. "You always did need breaking, Charity. Tonight you will learn your master."

"Never," she spat, and twisted away from his hand as it reached for her belt. Roughly he tugged it off her, and catching one flailing foot, he slipped a loop around her ankle, buckling the other end to the bottom bedpost. She kicked out with her other foot and caught him a glancing blow on the shoulder.

His teeth bared in a wicked grin, he recovered and stood over her. "We shall see," he sneered, and slowly removed his rumpled jacket.

Charity lay, panting. Her head pounded and her wrists ached where she'd drawn the knot tight in her struggles. Her torn shirt lay open, exposing her breasts, and her pants were pulled nearly off her hips. But shame was not in her thoughts. She looked at Paul with loathing, and vowed aloud that she would never give herself willingly to him.

His sneer still in place, Paul surveyed her twisting form, and continued to undress slowly. "You will change your mind, *chérie*. You see already how powerless you are."

Charity bit down on her trembling lip. The ache in her shoulders increased as she tugged again on her bonds, remembering another time when her arms had been imprisoned above her head, by the sleeves of her nightdress. Tears rolled down her pale cheeks. Adam was gone, and now she was held in the power of the one man she had always sought to avoid. Fate was more than cruel to play her false twice in succession.

Hot hands touched her breasts and her skin crawled. With one finger he traced the long curve of her hip, down her silky thigh. "You are, as I thought, the most exquisite creature." His voice rasped with enflamed desire.

Gritting her teeth, Charity said, "You are, as I feared, the lowest form of all humanity."

His fingers pinched the soft flesh at the inside of her thigh. The pain nearly made her yelp and her bonds dug into her as she struggled once more, closing her eyes against the sight of him. His hands played over her, making her choke on the acid taste in her throat. With a vicious snap her pants were pulled far down her legs. Then Paul was bending over her again.

"How did you reach Cincinnati?" The soft voice was very near her ear.

She held her lip in her teeth and lay very still until a sharp pinch on her nipple made her gasp. "With an old man and his family on a flatboat," she whispered.

"And how did you reach the Ohio?" His mouth circled the other nipple and she felt his teeth begin to close.

"I convinced a family in Charlottesville to let me travel with them and help them cook and care for the livestock," she faltered. "I paid them with the things in my trunk." She was nearly overwhelmed with the desire to tell him about Adam, to threaten him with reprisal, for she felt certain he had no way of knowing Adam was dead. But some canny instinct told her that if Paul knew she'd been Adam's lover, his reaction would be even more brutal.

"Why Cincinnati?"

"It was where the family was going. I didn't care where I went."

Paul nodded, seeming satisfied with her answers, but his eyes gleamed with a new lust, and his mouth moved wetly over her. Suddenly he was astride her, one thigh pinning her free leg. She shrank as far into the mattress as she could and turned her hips, trying to scissor her thighs against him. Her frenzy only made him pinch her and probe her with increasing fervor.

With his knees he spread her legs farther apart and lowered his body over her squirming form. Baring her teeth, she hissed names at him until with a lunge he was inside her. She grew cold with the horror of it, but mercifully Paul's ardor spent itself quickly. After a few panting minutes lying on her breasts, he rolled off her and stood up. She wished she could stop the tears that were drenching her hair, could look at him with the frigid loathing she felt. But as his fingers grasped her face and pulled it up to look at him, she had only great blue-green pools of stinging tears to show him.

His smile was unpleasantly broad. "You are everything I've dreamt of, Charity. And now you are mine." His hand left her face to run down her throat between her breasts, across her belly.

Desperately she shook her head. "Never," she cried.

He laughed then, low and triumphant. "You already are. And nothing is going to remove you from me now. Together we will build an empire."

Charity hugged her ears with her upraised arms, feeling nausea rise in her. She felt his weight leave the bedside. He was moving around the room, dressing. She watched him smooth his coat and tie his cravat at the mirror above the washstand. When he was done he returned to look lingeringly over her once more. Then suddenly her hands were free. Immediately she clutched the torn shirt over herself.

"You needn't do that now. I have, at last, seen your charms. It was worth waiting for. You are more perfect than I'd dared hope. And full of fire." His tongue came out to wet his lips, and Charity cowered back on the bed. Paul shook himself as though to bring his mind back from his desire. "I must leave you, alas. I could not present you at the Corbets' in your deplorable condition, but I am expected there now. I shall have food brought up to you. And tomorrow we shall talk further . . . Meanwhile, let me remind you of all you have already heard from our worthy rivermen. New Orleans is a strange and wicked city outside the walled homes of the Creoles. You would find yourself in a great deal of trouble, even danger, if you were to venture out alone. So I am sending over one of Corbet's own men to guard you tonight. He will see no harm befalls you here. Do not think to evade him, for the consequences could be a great deal worse than you may imagine."

Charity huddled on the bed, staring wordlessly at him.

"Do I make it all quite clear?" His voice was sharp.

Slowly she nodded, wondering if there was anything so very much more wicked in this city than the man standing at the foot of the bed.

Paul unlocked the door, returned the key to his own pocket, and looked at her once more. Pointing to the small satchel he had carried into the room, he said, "There are more appropriate clothes in there. They may not be the latest fashion, or the most perfect fit, but they were the best I could do in New Madrid. However, I flatter myself that even after the weeks away from you, I had a very good memory for your delectable dimensions." He smiled wolfishly and was gone.

Charity sat still for a long time. The sound of a woman singing a lament in the courtyard drifted up to her on the evening air, spilling over the windowsills with the lengthening shadows. More voices overrode the sad song. There was now laughter and chatter and the call of some child searching for his mother. The happy sounds were the ones that woke her from her trance of dejection, and she remembered Paul was sending food up. She mustn't be found like this. Hurriedly she washed herself, thinking she would never again be really clean now. Then she opened the satchel and found Paul had provided her with a pale yellow chintz dress. Its short sleeves, banded round neckline and two-layered skirt were becoming, if not stylish, and she donned the clothes with a sigh, admitting she was glad to be rid of the scratchy, dirty breeches and shirt she'd worn for so long. It was as Paul had said, too, his memory was good, for the dress fit her admirably for one not made to order. She thought of other, more ill-fitting clothes brought to her when she'd nothing to wear. Fresh tears started, and she sat down hard on the edge of the bed. How she would prefer to be in the shapeless blue calico, waiting for Adam's return. Instead she must wear this gift from a man she despised and wait as his prisoner for whatever new tortures he devised.

The food, when it was brought by a sullen boy with ragged hair and dirty clothes, smelled exotic, but Charity found she had no appetite. Leaving her tray outside her door, she undressed again and crawled into the crumpled bed to try to hide, like a wounded animal, in a curled-up ball beneath the sheets.

Daylight brought some relief from the hours of restless turning with tortured thoughts. Adam had been always before her, his dark hair curling over the wide brow, his piercing gray eyes alight with laughter or desire, his wide mouth grinning with pleasure. But through his image swam the hawklike features of Paul LaRoche, thin lips drawn back in a triumphant leer, black eyes burning with satanic delight. It had been a night of diabolical nightmares, and Charity rose from the bed feeling as bruised in her mind and very soul as she did in her body.

Burying her face in the basin of tepid water on the stand, she shook herself like a puppy. It was daylight now, and those dark shadows had to be put behind her. She splashed more water over herself, then, thinking more clearly, she examined her situation.

Paul had said there would be a guard last night. But would he stay through the day? She went to a window and looked out. An ancient black woman was on her hands and knees, scrubbing the flagstones of the patio below. The sound of voices speaking loudly in French told Charity the hotel was up and about in the early light. The city may be just awakening. She had no idea where she would go, but she had to get away. And she had some advantage in this city of Frenchmen; she spoke French.

Carefully she dressed in the yellow chintz, opened the door and peered into the narrow passage. There was no one about. She looked around the mauve room again. Her discarded clothes lay in a heap atop the old brown satchel. There was nothing here she would need or want. Silently she closed the door and stepped along the passage. At the top of the dim stairs she stopped, her heart pounding. The steep steps curved into the hall below, but there seemed to be no one about. On tiptoe she descended. The hall, with its two wrought-iron chairs covered in rust-colored cushions, was deserted. Through a door at the back, the sounds of pots clanking and voices raised in argument bespoke the fact that the only activity in the place was in the kitchen wing. Before her the open door beckoned to bright sunlight on the dusty street.

Her heart beating ever faster, Charity walked through the portal and stood on the wooden *banquette* outside. The morning glare showed her a narrow street of pastel-washed houses, each with its narrow balcony suspended above the street level. The pale yellows, peaches, and limes on the stucco walls reminded her again of Cap Français, as did the dust and the heat already beginning to rise in waves from beneath her feet. Across the street a stooped woman carrying a large basket over one arm shuffled along the *banquette*, muttering softly to herself.

Charity inhaled deeply, feeling the first thrill of freedom in weeks. Over there was the corner she and Paul had rounded to reach this hotel. She set her back to it and began to walk.

She had not advanced two houses when the sound of footsteps on the wooden planks behind her made her catch her breath again. The brisk but heavy tread told her it was a man, and she walked more quickly. The footsteps increased in tempo and a hand caught her elbow. With a horrible feeling that she had lived through all this once before, she turned to look up at Paul's grim face. Her throat closed and she shut her eyes, swaying. The hand held her upright, and as through a mist, she heard his voice, silky and tinged with amusement.

"My instinct told me you would need no more than the five minutes Jean was gone. So I hurried around myself. I would not have you lack company for even a moment, *chérie.*"

His hand under her elbow guided her stumbling footsteps now as he continued to stroll in the direction she'd taken. The mist was still before her eyes, and her feet had heavy weights attached. Leaning heavily on his arm, she walked where he willed her, a feeling of total defeat enveloping her.

She hardly noticed when he turned under a brick arch and seated her at a narrow table beneath the spreading leaves of a giant banana tree. The heady aroma of strong coffee and the sight of a basket of pastries began to revive her, though, as a hollowness in her stomach made itself felt. Woodenly she ate and drank, refusing to look at her tormentor and realizing, even as she finished, that there was still a great hollowness inside her.

Paul watched her over his own steaming cup, and kept silent until she was done. When at last she raised dull eyes to his, he smiled with self-satisfaction. "Did you gratify your curiosity about what this wonderful city looks like, my dear?" Charity did not move and he raised one brow. "No? Well, you will have a better opportunity this morning. Madame Corbet has kindly consented to take you to her dressmaker and wherever else you will need to go to obtain proper clothing. I want you to pay particular attention to your wedding ensemble and make all decisions necessary right away."

At his words, Charity's eyes widened, and he smiled, leaning back negligently and toying with his cup. "Yes, that, I think, should be the first order of business, since we will be wed as soon as we can arrange matters."

"We...we?" Charity stuttered.

"But of course." Paul waved an airy hand. "I could hardly leave you after the intimacies we have shared, *petite*." He grinned wickedly, his bold eyes raking her throat and bosom. "Besides, I have found that there is no other practicable course. The Creole society into which we will move has rather stuffy rules about such things." He paused musingly. "I had thought to set you up as my mistress. There is a whole area here for just that sort of situation, I hear. Pleasant little houses where the concubines of the wealthy live. But I discover that those women, who are reputed to be of a rare beauty, are mulattoes, nearly all. You would not fit well. And besides, I think I cannot trust you on your own. *Voilà*, I have few choices. And now that I have found you again, have made you mine, I have a strange reluctance to allow you out of my sight."

Charity leaned forward then. Her voice very low, almost snarling, she said, "I would rather die than wed you, Paul LaRoche."

His dark eyes narrowed, but the smile remained as Paul put his cup down with great care. "Alas, you have no choice. Alain Corbet is even now setting in motion the necessary arrangements. You will live under his protection until we are husband and wife."

Charity searched through her mind for words. "But you don't want to marry me," she said at last. "I have no fortune, no great estates to bring you any more."

Paul too leaned forward. "In Virginia that was true. But here in New Orleans your ancestry is as good or better than anyone save myself. There are others here from Saint Dominque. Last night I met one who recognized my name. We are with the Corbets. Our social position is assured. As for your money...that would have been nice, true. But we have no real need of it. I have plenty for now, and have already discovered several means to become rich in this colony. Our fortune, as well as our social standing, shall be of the highest."

His face was alight with greed, and Charity shivered. She sought for more arguments, but her brain was too filled with horror at the prospect of being tied to this man for life to marshal logical thoughts. "You cannot make me marry you," she said stubbornly.

Paul stood up. "Come, *chérie*. I have explained matters to you, and now there is much to be done."

Chapter 25

The house of Monsieur Corbet stood pale and withdrawn in the bright morning light, and Charity's leaden feet moved slowly through the arched carriageway to the large courtyard behind. There the nearly forgotten scent of oleander and bougainvillea mingled with more exotic aromas of spices and meats cooking in a kitchen wing to one side. At the rear of the house a gracefully curved set of wooden steps led upward from another stuccoed arch beside a fan-light window. Up these stairs Paul led her, unresisting, to a gallery above and a double door flanked by louvered shutters. The dim room beyond proved to be a high-ceilinged and spacious parlor dotted with handsome rosewood tables, a straight-backed heather green sofa and some strange-looking wood-framed chairs slung with taut amber-colored leather. It was a cool and gracious room, and Charity felt stirrings of curiosity about the house and its occupants. She'd no more than seen the nondescript, middle-aged M. Corbet on the keelboat, and she knew only what the weather-beaten sign outside had told her, that his business was shipping.

Her thoughts were interrupted by the rustle of a petticoat and the entrance of a round-faced woman dressed in pale gray, thin muslin, a ruffle of snowy lace at her throat. Her ample figure made her seem older than she was, for as she advanced into the light, Charity could see from her smooth face and bright, dark eyes that she was not yet thirty, perhaps Abby's age. Charity felt a stab of pain at the memory of being presented unwillingly at another house where she was to be taken in. But under such different circumstances! She eyed the approaching figure warily.

With a flourish, Paul performed introductions, presenting Charity to Madame Estelle Corbet.

The black eyes above a slightly prominent nose regarded Charity with a polite expression that was almost warm. "Allow me to tell you how pleased we are to have you stay with us, Mademoiselle. And how we regret that you had to spend a night in a hotel. But I understand your reluctance to come here straight away." The soft voice was almost girlish, and Charity smiled as best she could.

"It is kind of you, Madame," she returned, wondering what Paul had told her.

He was speaking, cutting short the formalities, and Charity forced herself to focus on his words. "...know you have much to do, as do I. I leave my betrothed in excellent hands, for which we are both most grateful. Your good offices will do wonders to restore her. So until this evening, ladies." And he bowed low over Madame's hand. Then turning to Charity, he grasped her cold palm and lifted it to his lips. She winced, but didn't dare withdraw, as his mouth left a small circle of moisture on her skin.

He walked briskly from the room, leaving Charity and her hostess to stare awkwardly at each other. Madame Corbet smiled then, showing slightly uneven but startlingly white little teeth. "Come," she said, indicating one of the strange chairs, "we will have a bit of refreshment before we start out on our expedition, no? And it will be more comfortable to chat first." She walked gracefully across the room and pulled at a colored cord beside the door.

Charity wondered how to sit in the leather chair that had no arms, but found, once she lowered herself carefully into it, that it was surprisingly comfortable. Arranging her layered skirt, she assumed an air of composure.

Madame perched on the edge of the sofa as a lithe little black girl appeared at the door and received an order for coffee. When the girl had gone on silent feet the woman turned full attention to her guest.

"Alain and your *fiancé* flatter me by requesting that I show you the shops where you might obtain a trousseau. We will be engaged together for many days, I hope, so you must call me Estelle and dispense with formalities."

Charity nodded, forcing another smile. "And you must call me Charity."

Estelle cocked her head to one side. "I do not wish to appear indelicate, Charity, but I have been told something of what you have gone through, and would like to express my regrets."

The girl, reflecting that this proper young matron couldn't have an inkling of all she'd gone through, bowed her head in acknowledgment. What had that villain told these people?

"But we will attempt to make it up to you now you have at last reached our fair city. It is very romantic to be saved by your intended and protected through a perilous journey. Now we will see that you are well provided for, and will meet your wedding day with all that a young lady requires." Charity's mouth set in bitter lines at these words, but the woman seemed not to notice. "You will make a beautiful bride, and the two of you such a handsome couple. So romantic..." she repeated with a small sigh.

Charity's nails dug into the palm of her hand as she fought the urge to spring from her chair and stamp her foot. In a tight voice that seemed to come from deep in her abdomen she said, "You mistake the situation, Madame. I detest Paul LaRoche."

The other's eyes widened in shock for a moment, then eyelashes fluttered as the slave entered the room bearing a silver tray with the coffee. When the girl had departed Estelle Corbet poured thoughtfully. Handing a cup to Charity's stiff fingers, she looked up at last.

"Many of us have felt fear on facing marriage, you know." Her soft voice grew even softer. "But I assure you it goes away. M. LaRoche is a handsome and refined gentleman. And you have the advantage of many of us in that you have known him nearly all your life. He cares a great deal for you, or he would not have gone to such dangerous lengths to secure your safety in the barbarous country north of here. You must think of that, and learn to care for him in return."

Charity's eyes flashed. "I could never care for Paul."

A small plump hand came up, cutting off the rest of her retort. "You will in time. There is every reason to. After all, your father arranged this marriage. You must know he had your best interests at heart. And your *fiancé* says he has loved you for as long as he can remember. Nearly all of us have marriages arranged for us. Few of us have the fortune to wed a man we already know, and one who already cares so much. It takes time, but mutual esteem grows and a good arrangement is arrived at."

Charity stared at the round woman and choked back more words. She could see that Paul had already paved his way with these people, and had their sympathy. Heaven knew what sort of wild story he'd concocted for them, and how was she to challenge it? This silly woman obviously thought her a fearful virgin. If she told the truth they might not even believe her. Paul would undoubtedly maintain she was half crazed from her hardships. Why did men always have control over one's life? She sighed then. She couldn't imagine what Paul's thought processes were, but it was clear that he had trapped her neatly and securely. She had nowhere to turn for help, but somehow she must avoid the permanent prison of marriage to him. For the moment, the best she could do was stall. Accordingly, she nodded once more at Estelle, hoping her expression showed more fear than anger, and saw with disgust that her hostess relaxed visibly at her seeming capitulation.

"Then as soon as you are ready, let us set out," the woman said.

Feeling like a sleepwalker, Charity moved through elegant boutiques, allowing herself to be measured and fussed over, nodding dully at Estelle's choices of rich materials and colors. When the dresses were made she would insist on alterations, forcing the time spent on her wardrobe to lengthen. She confronted the decisions on her wedding ensemble with real distaste, though, rejecting materials and scorning suggestions, until even Estelle became impatient.

"You have seen the finest lace from Spain, the costliest materials from France. Surely there is something in all this that meets with your approval."

Charity eyed the piles of filmy muslins, silks, and laces and shook her head. "I want none of them."

Estelle's eyes began to look hunted. "This is the one decision your betrothed most particularly wants you to make this morning. I was enjoined to be sure materials were selected. Please, Charity."

The girl looked searchingly at the plump woman and raised her shoulders in a shrug. There was little sense in getting Estelle into trouble for her. "Very well," she sighed, and pointed randomly to bolts of cloth. "But I wish to be consulted on every detail of the design."

"Of course," breathed her relieved chaperone. That difficult piece of business behind her, she became almost buoyant. "Let us begin on the design this evening. Now we must consider the smaller things. Gloves next, I think." Taking the girl's arm she whisked her onto the street once more, where her maid waited for them.

Charity was glad of the Creole custom of lying down to rest in the heat of the day. It meant that nothing could be done in the early afternoon hours. Anyway, Charity's head ached with the heat and the strain of being polite while her whole being revolted at her predicament.

She lay on the tall, four-poster bed with its furled mosquito netting at the top, and stared at the network of tiny cracks in the plaster ceiling. Her mind, exhausted by weeks of worry and speculation, felt sluggish. Now, at last, she knew what her fate was to be, and she should be glad she had something concrete to work against. But her emotions could not rise to the occasion. There was a great dead spot in the center of her being, and her mind kept repeating, What does it matter now? Though even as the phrase went round and round, she knew her self-respect, if not her conscious mind, would not let her bow complacently to Paul's plans. In this highly respectable house she should be safe from his physical assaults, and although she didn't know how long the nefarious arrangements for her forced marriage might take, she felt sure she could stall her own preparations for several weeks at least. She sighed heavily, tracing a spider web pattern to the corner of the wall. If she could just buy time, anything might happen, some avenue might open to show her an escape. Where she would go she didn't know, but it didn't matter. Almost any fate was better than life-long physical and mental subservience to the cruelly sly man who would make her his wife.

It had been a week now since Charity had come to live with Estelle and Alain Corbet, and Paul was beginning to eye her more critically again as her sunburn began to fade, her hair to look more lustrous, her hands to appear softer. Estelle's own hairdresser, clucking nervously, had spent an entire afternoon trying to rectify the damage Charity had done to her cropped waves, and the result seemed to gratify everyone but herself. She found the curls and piles and rolls too elaborate for her own taste, but reflected philosophically that she was not the one who had to view the coiffure, and there was no one she desired to impress by her looks. The first of her new gowns had arrived, and Charity donned a dress of blue and white lawn with an apathy she would not have thought possible for so lovely a creation. However, knowing she was dressing for Paul made her view her finery with indifference, even distaste.

She and Estelle had agreed it was as well that the damp heat kept many prominent citizens out of the city on their plantations and in summer cottages at this season, for she was not yet ready to be presented to the punctilious society whose company Paul coveted. She was restless, though, and miserable at the confinement of her life. So, on the hazy, heat-ridden morning that she finally appeared in the courtyard in the blue and white dress and Estelle clapped in approval, suggesting that now Charity might feel like going out a bit, the girl agreed almost eagerly.

"I feel it is time you saw more of our fair city, Charity." Estelle's dark head bobbed enthusiastically, taking in the slender blonde apparition before her, and allowing only the faintest hint of jealousy to enter her eyes. "This morning I was going to walk to the market with Lucy to see if we couldn't get something special to celebrate your being with us. It is only a few streets away," she added hastily.

To Charity, the thought of stretching her legs in any walk was more than welcome. "I will be ready whenever you say, and I don't care how far away it is." The farther the better, in fact, she thought, sipping her coffee. She might as well begin to learn something of the city.

It was with a feeling closer to pleasure than any she'd experienced since the sinking of the flatboat that Charity matched her own impatient strides to the dainty gait of Estelle and the lumbering steps of the fat, turbaned cook, Lucy, as they made their way past the impressive Ursuline convent and turned right toward the Place d'Armes and the market. Soon her nose wrinkled in satisfaction as it was assailed by the scent of rich spices, the sharp smell of fermenting molasses, the odor of ripe fruit, and the penetrating aroma of West Indian rum. Following the others' lead, she walked wide-eyed past trays of sugared confections, stacks of golden bananas and prickly pineapples and bunches of flowers. Here was a hunter from the bayous with wild duck and a great turtle to sell. There a group of blond Germans from upriver with cabbages, beets, strings of bright red peppers. Choctaw Indians in gaudy blankets offered woven baskets, skins, arrows, jewelry made from silver coins. All around them was the noise of a dozen languages shouted, of hens squawking, money clinking, even parrots screaming.

Charity felt exhilarated. She couldn't get enough of this riotous scene of robust life. With a familiar stab of pain she realized her happiness would be complete if she could share this experience with Adam. The colorful tumult matched his exuberance. His gray eyes would dance with amusement and his rich laugh would mingle with hers as they viewed the contrasts and delights of this spot.

Her heart grew heavy with the thought, and her steps slowed. Estelle was now before a section where layers of gray-blue fish were displayed to advantage beside wriggling crawfish and somnolent crabs.

"Do you know our delicacies of the sea, Charity? We will show you how we prepare these wonders."

Charity smiled absently at the woman and wandered down a row of tempting food. She heard Estelle and Lucy begin the process of selection and watched an earringed man with a Levantine look pass by two nuns whose white headdresses nodded as they talked quietly together.

"Mademoiselle!" The word held surprise, eagerness, and recognition all at once. Charity twirled at the sound, her heart skipping a full beat. Dark hands came out to grasp hers, and she gaped at the familiar beaming face of Marie.

Tears sprang to both sets of eyes as Charity fell into the comforting arms of her mother's maid, crying "Oh Marie, is it really you?"

They held each other off then. *"Ma petite!"* The wrinkles at the corners of the eyes grew deeper while concern flowed through the pleasure that lighted the black depths. "How do you come here?"

Charity glanced around. Estelle was still down the row, pointing at eggs wrapped in bundles of Spanish moss. "Marie, I'd given up all hope of ever finding you in this city."

"Eventually one sees everyone in the market, or on the Place." Marie's soothing voice was like balm, and Charity drew a shuddering breath, feeling a first faint irrational ray of hope.

"Oh Marie, I wish I were here under happy circumstances. But I am not. I cannot tell you all of it, only that Paul LaRoche has forced me to come here and holds me against my will."

Marie's eyes widened with shock as she listened to the rush of words. "Paul LaRoche," she breathed, and the lines around her broad mouth deepened. "That is a bad one."

"Yes," agreed Charity with heat. "But I will tell you more later. Quickly, tell me how you have fared." She took the other's arm and steered her behind a group of flower vendors, noting that the woman had gained weight and looked healthier than she had in years.

"I do well, *chérie*. It was hard the first months, but some were kind. There are many free people of color here in New Orleans, and it is not impossible to find work and pay one's own way. I have been assistant to a milliner for nearly a year. And I have married again."

Charity grinned. "Is he better than Louis?" She could just remember the brawling man who had been Marie's first husband. He had died in a fight when Charity was still small.

"So much better, is my Phillipe. He is a carpenter. His wife died; his children are grown but for one son. He was glad to have someone to take care of his home."

"You are happy then?"

"As happy as I could have hoped to be. But you, *petite*, you are not happy, and I want to help."

Charity shook her head. "There is nothing you can do, Marie. But you have helped me a great deal by being here today. I had thought never to see a familiar and friendly face again."

"But how did M. LaRoche do this thing to you?"

"It is too long a story, Marie. Let us just say he kidnapped me. And now he plans to wed me, but I will kill myself first."

"Ah, *chérie*." Marie's voice was nearly a wail as she wrung her hands. But above the cry, Charity had heard her name.

"Hush, Marie, I must go. Tell me the name of your employer. I can perhaps see you there."

"Madame Morel. It is a fashionable establishment."

"Good. I will find a way. *Au revoir*, dear friend." Afraid fresh tears would start, Charity turned away abruptly and ran lightly down the market to the nearly hysterical Estelle.

"I thought we had lost you in the *mêlée*," cried the woman as Charity reached her.

Forcing another of her false smiles, Charity waved at the scene around them. "I wandered, I fear. It is all so colorful."

Estelle's plump hand rested heavily on her bosom. "I am glad you did not go too far. But come. We have your first fitting for your wedding dress to attend to." She took Charity's arm, and reluctantly the girl turned with her after casting one anguished look back to the spot where she'd seen

269

Marie. The woman was not there now, but Charity knew she watched from the crowd.

"There are delays, always delays. Things move at a snail's pace in this city." Paul paced before the long windows, his nervous hands plucking at the thin mustache he was growing. "It could be as much as two more weeks before we can arrange everything."

It was late in the afternoon of the day following Charity's outing to the market. Paul had appeared early this day, and had sent for Charity to join him in the parlor. The courtyard, where she had been, was apparently not private enough. Charity folded her hands in her lap and waited quietly for his anger to spend itself. Only her eyes, which she kept lowered, would have betrayed her distaste. She had come to the conclusion that the way she could fight this man was to appear docile. She needed to be trusted enough to have some freedom, to come and go more easily.

Paul stopped his pacing and came to stand before her. Beads of perspiration were now showing on his brow. He had dismissed the little boy who would have pulled the rope for the huge ceiling fan, and now he was paying for his privacy. "I do not like having to wait for anything. But most of all I do not like having to wait for you."

Charity fluttered her lashes, but did not look up. His words about delays were the sweetest she'd yet heard him utter.

"My dealings are already going well." Paul flung himself into one of the leather chairs. "Be damned to Wilkinson and his petty schemes. I made money on that cargo we brought south, but I have been made to see that my future lies here, not in the dreams of the barbarians in Kentucky. I do not trust wild schemes the Americans have of wresting the Mississippi from the Spanish. And I do not like most of the men I met in that silly country. They are either too complacent, like that Joseph Hadley, or they are hot-headed fools like that Adam Crandall." Charity sat rigidly erect, her blood pounding in her ears at the mention of Adam's name. Paul leaned forward, watching her. "No, New Orleans is much more reminiscent of Saint Dominque. We will take up where we left off, *ma belle*. I have already begun to think about buying a plantation upriver."

Charity shuddered inwardly at the momentary vision of Paul ruling a tiny fiefdom along the Mississippi.

"More important at this instant is a man named de Boré.

He has with him Antoine Morin, who spent years in Saint Dominque. This Morin I have heard of. He is the first here in this colony to be able to assure the planters their sugar cane can be refined into real sugar."

"They have not been making sugar from the cane?" the girl asked, trying to distract herself from her thoughts.

Paul's smile was appreciative. "No. They have not learned the proper technique. They make molasses and a rum drink, *tafia*, but not refined sugar. Now Morin will make it possible, and de Boré is using his plantation to begin. I have convinced him to let me help. This will be the beginning of something very big."

Charity nodded. She could see the possibilities, and her heart sank.

"The plantation I am looking at was run by a stupid-sounding man. He clung to his crop of indigo, though insects are ruining that plant here. He is dead now, and his widow eager to sell. I will plant the place in cane and eventually I will build in this country a greater empire than my father's." His eyes bored into hers. "And you, Charity, will help me to build that empire. You will be the gracious hostess to only the most important men. Your beauty will be legendary. My name will be famous. Our sons will rule this city."

Charity's hands gripped each other and she looked away from the gleaming eyes.

Paul stood up and resumed his pacing. "With all that before us, I should not chafe so at a mere two week delay in my marriage." He came to her and caught her shoulders, forcing her to look up. His swarthy features hardened as his eyes raked her. "But I have tasted what is to be mine, and my appetite is unquenchable. It has been torture to be in this house with you and to have to pretend propriety." He stared down at the milky skin of her throat above the cream-colored dress she wore. "So, tomorrow afternoon we will go to inspect this plantation, and we will see if we may have a few moments alone, eh?" His hand cupped her chin and she struggled to make her eyes limpid under his hot gaze. She mustn't let him see the horror that possessed her.

Chapter 26

The silver-haired woman standing among hat boxes, yards of tulle and stacks of straw bonnets looked happily surprised at the munificence of the order she was being given by the beautiful honey-haired girl with the large blue-green eyes. But it was all rather overwhelming. She would need assistance in just remembering everything.

"If Madame and Mademoiselle will excuse me one moment, I fear I will have to ask my assistant to help us in this large selection." She fluttered her hands, looking from one to the other of her customers, and receiving their nods, she fled through a small beaded archway to the rear of the narrow shop.

Charity hid her smile of satisfaction. It had been an easy thing to insist she needed bonnets in this sunny climate, and to request the names of good milliners. Estelle had wanted to take her to her own woman, but Charity had claimed she once received hats from a place called Morel in Cap Français and she felt sentimental about the name. Far from showing surprise at the girl's sudden interest in her wardrobe, Estelle had been only too pleased to guide her to Madame Morel. It had been inspiration of the moment that had led Charity to swamp Madame with ideas and demands, forcing her to go for her assistant. It was further inspiration to now point out becoming notions to Estelle. By the time Madame Morel reappeared, leading a smiling Marie, Charity was able to engage

her in discussions with Estelle, and so turn to Marie unin-
terrupted.

"You order many hats for your trousseau, Mademoiselle?"
began Marie, drawing Charity aside, and holding up forms
for her inspection.

"Ah, Marie," Charity breathed. "The day draws closer and
I have still not discovered a way out of here. I am watched
every moment by the people at Corbet's. Only in my room
am I alone."

"I have thought so much about you, *petite*." Marie glanced
over her shoulder. "You despise this marriage because of
another, no?"

Charity's eyebrows flew up. "How could you know?"

"I have known your family for three generations...It is
Mr. Crandall, is it not? And where is he, that you are trapped
here like the hunted rabbit?"

Charity's eyes filled. "I ran away with him. We went to
the west. He...he died in an accident on a river. It was after
that that M. LaRoche found me."

Marie shook her head, but showed no surprise at Charity's
words. "I have thought so much..."

"About what, Marie?" Charity's eyes were urgent, but her
fingers held up a length of lace and an ostrich plume with
a languid movement.

"You knew of *vaudun* on Saint Dominque."

Charity nodded. "That would be good, Marie," she said in
a clear voice.

"There are many believers here. There are dances beyond
the ramparts. There is much that goes on the white people
do not know about. I have always been a Catholic, but I have
learned not to take these people too lightly. I know of
one...but that does not matter. Perhaps we may use her,
though, to see that M. Paul loses his taste for the wedding."

Charity nearly laughed. "This very afternoon he takes me
to see a plantation he hopes to buy as our home."

Marie nodded, briskly pulling at a card of trim. "Mademoiselle, you will be satisfied, I am sure. I will bring the first
of the bonnets for your inspection in just three days."

Charity took her cue and hastily selected colors, hearing
the others moving toward her. "Just to see you gives me
heart," she whispered. "But I fear there is little we can do."

With that she moved away, thanking the proprietress and
chatting easily with Estelle about their choices. But through
the short walk back, Charity was silent, thinking of Marie's

words. She knew better than most the power of the *vaudun*. But she knew too that that power was of the earthly kind. It was invested in determined men of strong will who could bend others to their bidding. Claims of sorcery were only to frighten people into acceptance of these men as leaders. She could put no faith in a hope that some priestess could work a magic for her.

The carriage that called for them later in the afternoon was M. Corbet's own equipage. Somewhat to Paul's disgust, both the Corbets had chosen to accompany them on their tour. It was to be a familial afternoon outing, and Charity was, for the first time, truly grateful for their company.

Up the wide street behind the cathedral they went, past the ramparts, the cemeteries, the muddy areas of Congo Square (where, Estelle whispered, the free blacks danced to hideous music), along low marshes where the near-daily rain had left crystalline droplets on the heavy greenery of twisted cypress reflected in shadowy brown bayous. Farther on they jolted over a track lined with oaks and pecans and the occasional spreading umbrella of magnolia. It was a rich but dark and sultry land, and Charity found herself comparing it to the sunny vistas of Virginia. She felt that even on the cleared plantations, her soul would suffer in this country.

Conversation was desultory on the long ride, and they were all relieved when at last they were brought up a narrow avenue lined with moss and ivy-draped trees to the steps of a fading but still imposing structure. Charity stepped daintily from the carriage and tried not to show her dismay at the view of massive cypress walls and high-pitched roof covering a sweeping gallery supported by heavy brick piers and wooden posts.

The tour of the six rooms was brief, with Paul pointing out the solid construction, the handsome proportions, the architectural detail to be seen beneath peeling paint. The rear of the house gave onto another gallery and overlooked a stable, a kitchen, and four slave cottages. The whole was in disrepair, but Charity could see that with work it could be a handsome enough home. If only she did not have to view this as her own possible prison!

The fetid smell of the cottages and kitchen wing kept the ladies out in the open at first, but Alain Corbet wished to see the whole of Paul's prospective investment. So, dutifully they trudged behind the men, in and out of buildings, around the adjoining overgrown gardens and walks. At length the

Corbets chose to reinspect the house and Paul seized his opportunity. "Come, Charity, I am sure you would prefer the open air. Shall we walk a bit more in the gardens?"

Feigning a girlish giggle, Charity spun away from his offered hand. "I am sure it is not proper for me to walk alone with you, even if you are my betrothed," she breathed, starting after Estelle's safe bulk.

But Paul was not to be put off by female whims. The familiar talonlike fingers closed on her arm, dragging at her with a power that had never ceased to surprise her. She gasped a protest, but quickly she was propelled toward the gardens as the Corbets disappeared through the ground floor door.

On the far side of the gigantic oak Paul spun her against the rough bark. Before she could think, he was leaning against her, his mouth bruising her lips, his hands mauling her bodice. Her carefully nurtured façade of coquetry crumbled away at his touch. Spitting with fury, she slapped down his hands and pushed at him. As his weight lifted off her, she spun around the tree trunk, making for the house. But her arm was snatched and she was jerked nearly off her feet.

"Hardly the way for the blushing bride to act," Paul snarled as he twisted her back to face him. "But then your lack of submissiveness will make our married life more exciting."

Looking at his narrow face leering so close to her own, Charity lost control once more. "You're revolting and despicable, a disgrace to your family's name," she ranted, tugging against his grip.

"If we were alone, I would show you who your master is, Miss Ashton. The Tournay pride is out of place now. As my wife, you will obey me in all things." His eyes traveled slowly, insultingly, down her quivering form.

Charity's knees grew weak with his words and horror flooded her as it always did when he spoke of the appalling future he planned for her. But she was no longer the quaking, inexperienced young girl who had left Saint Dominque. She had learned to mask her emotions, to face the fearful events fate kept throwing in her path. She would not give him the satisfaction of seeing her quail before him. Her head high, she stared coldly at that wolfish grin she hated. "You do not intimidate me, Paul LaRoche. You know I have nowhere to run in this alien place. But once married to you my life will

275

be as good as over. I will feel little hesitation in taking it when your attentions become unendurable."

She kept her gaze steady as she watched the light in his eyes turn to a blaze of anger, though her heart felt as though it was beating in her brain. Her head swam as he shook her then, but she kept her footing and her defiant stare.

"You are part of my schemes, Charity," the man growled at last. "I will have to see you do nothing so foolish." Abruptly he let her go and she put out a hand to steady herself against the huge tree. "Besides," and his low voice held a hint of bitterness, "I do not see why you object so. It is not as though I were your first lover."

For the first time, Charity's stare wavered, but she kept her lips firmly shut, trying not to draw the gulping breath she suddenly needed.

"I am not a green boy to be fooled by you, you know." Paul's voice was full of mockery laced with anger. "Who was it, Charity? Your overseer's boy at Tournay? Someone in Virginia? Perhaps several?"

"How dare you." Charity allowed all the outrage she could muster to enter her words.

"How dare *you!*" Paul's voice was almost an animal growl. "You were my betrothed."

"I was never your betrothed. I was there the day your father mentioned your pretensions to my father. No consent was ever given."

"Unfortunately there are no witnesses for your claim."

"And there is nothing signed, no words to back yours."

"Happily, I need nothing...now. I hold the whip hand, you haughty bitch, and the sooner you acknowledge that, the better off you will be. You are no stranger to a man's bed, and you will be no stranger to mine. I warn you I will tie you down each night if I have to, for I intend to have you more often and in more interesting ways than you can imagine."

Charity heard the voices coming toward them then and sought to unclench her hands and still her rapid breathing. The Corbets, at least, should not suspect her full disgust. If they believed her resigned to her fate, their guard might sometime be lowered. If only she had a plan to use that unwary moment when it came!

A party had been planned for this evening. A small gathering here at the Corbets' house meant to be a first introduction for Charity to a few prominent citizens. Enjoined to look her best, Charity considered rebelling. But when Estelle came to repin her gleaming hair in a fashionable style and to select her dress, the girl saw no way out. Finally, dressed in a flowing gown of amber color whose tight waist and low square neck showed off her figure to great advantage, she allowed herself to be led down to the courtyard for the hour before the meal.

The ladies had just settled themselves on the whitewashed wrought iron seats when an unearthly yowl erupted from the *garconière*, the long building at the rear of the property where bachelor and guest quarters stood. The sound was bitten off, and for a moment, the two thought they had imagined it. But there had been a distinct sense of rage and fear in that quick moment. The hair on the back of Charity's neck stood up. She could think of no one but Paul who occupied that building. As she and Estelle stared at each other in frozen wonder, Alain Corbet ran heavily along the courtyard. At that moment Paul pounded down the *garconière* stairs. From where the ladies sat, the voices were muted but distinct.

"LaRoche, what is happening?"

Paul's voice was almost a wheeze as he caught at laboring breath. "There's a *thing*," he gasped. "On my pillow."

"A *thing?*" Alain echoed in disbelief.

"A...a grotesque doll. With pins in it." His voice grew stronger. "Get someone to remove it at once."

"Assuredly."

Charity peered through the thin network of vines that grew up the columns of the *garconière* gallery. Between the broad green leaves she could just make out the ghostly whiteness of Paul's face, twisted in anguish, and the ashen visage of his host as they started up the steps.

Estelle's eyes showed wide rims of white around darting pupils, and the delicate black lace fan she held fluttered nervously in her shaking hand. *"Mon Dieu,"* she breathed, "who would do such a thing?" She looked at Charity's puzzled face and seemed to recollect herself. Stilling the nervous fan, she sat up straighter. "Well, no one was harmed, and Alain will see to it." She looked around vaguely. "Our guests should arrive shortly."

"A *vaudun* doll?" Charity's soft query made the fan flutter once more.

"Perhaps." Estelle's lips closed firmly, as though this was a subject not to be brought into her well-ordered household.

She was pale but composed as she stood up. "Shall we go and see that all is in readiness?"

Charity followed her obediently, but she was thinking of Paul's frenzied reaction to the doll on his bed. It surprised her that such a ruthless man of obvious intelligence could be superstitious. She had heard of *vaudun* dolls before. Some of the slaves at Tournay seemed to set store by the healing powers of chants said over a likeness of a sick person. And once she'd heard that a jealous wife of one of the field hands had tried to frighten a rival with hideously mangled representations of the girl in various stages of undress. But she'd never known if the stories were true, and now wished she could see this object Paul found so terrifying. Her thoughts flew to Marie and her words about the power of the *vaudun* here in New Orleans. How had the woman managed to slip the thing into Paul's room? She could almost laugh at the look on his face, but she feared for Marie. He had been more than frightened. He was furious. She would have to wait to talk to Marie, though, for she had no excuse to see her till the new hats were brought for her inspection.

The color had begun to return to Paul's face by the time the party of twelve sat down to dinner in the sumptuous dining room and were served the first course of gumbo. Charity made the motions of polite behavior toward the guests, but she found she could not take her mind off Paul's reaction to the doll. Could something more be done to frighten him away from the marriage?

For the next two days Charity worried the idea, but could come up with no plausible way to take advantage of her new knowledge of Paul. She was given little time to think anyway, for Estelle was now busily scheming how to launch Charity into society. The summer heat was as fierce as ever, broken nearly every day by quick downpours that did little but further dampen the already heavy air. But families were beginning to return to the city in anticipation of the upcoming season, and the Corbets intended to be among the first guests on the lists of entertainments to come.

"There will be the small theater party tonight," Estelle said on the morning Marie was due to arrive. She counted on plump, shapely fingers as she planned happily for the week ahead. "We are so grateful to those of Saint Dominque who fled to our fair city, for now we have the first professional theatricals we've ever enjoyed here." She nodded at Charity, who smiled absently, then looked again at her upraised fingers. "There is the ball in two nights, also. Your gown will just be ready, and I do think the watered silk was the right choice for you, though it will be warmer than you might wish at this season." She dropped her hands, sighing. "The ball will be your true debut, and Paul is so pleased to have the opportunity to show you off before your wedding. You are lucky to have a man who is so proud of you, you know."

Charity looked at the round, honest face with its overlong nose and wondered what she should say. The sound of a tinkling bell saved her the difficulty of answering, for she spied Marie trudging through the carriage way, carrying three large boxes. The girl jumped up. "Ah, there are the first of the hats, Estelle. Will you forgive me? I would like to have them taken to my room where I can make sure they are quite what I wanted."

The older woman smiled indulgently, still sipping her strong coffee. "I too wish to see how they are, if this Madame Morel is better than my own Celeste. But you go, and I shall come up shortly."

Charity nodded and walked briskly toward the stairs, beckoning to Marie to follow. "Let us see what you have brought, Marie," she called, stilling the urge to dash headlong down the gallery.

Once behind her closed door, she flung the boxes at the bed and caught Marie by the shoulders. "Are you responsible for the *vaudun* doll which was put into M. Paul's room a few days ago?"

The former slave's thin face was alight from within as she looked the girl in the eye. With a soft chuckle, she nodded. "I remember that it was rumored long ago that Monsieur was very afraid of the *vaudun*. He must have had a bad experience with it. And no wonder, the way he treated his personal servants. Also he perhaps blames the *vaudun* for the loss of his plantation. I could only hope his fear remained."

"But Marie, how did you get the thing into his room?"

"Oh, it was not I who did it, *chérie*. Do not ask more. There is no need for you to concern yourself."

"M. Corbet has questioned the slaves. He and Paul are very upset. I would not see someone in trouble because of me."

"They will discover nothing. I am glad to hear that the effort had its desired effect. What we need to do now is somehow connect that doll with you in M. Paul's mind." Marie's straight brows drew together in thought. "Phillipe and I, we

279

have talked of this. He has forbidden me to consult further with the *vaudun*. He is a man, and so sees a more straightforward solution. If M. Paul will not set you free with your position in this city intact, we are prepared to help you escape by less attractive means. We can hide you until we can get you out of the city."

Charity touched the woman's cheek. "You could not do that, you and your Phillipe. M. LaRoche is a vindictive and ruthless man. If he discovered you..." She shuddered.

"*Chérie*, I owe you my freedom. And I have loved you since your birth. I would not leave you to suffer the fate that man plans for you. He would not discover us. No, that is not so much the difficulty as the question of where you would go once you were away."

Charity sat down among the boxes. "I would go to Virginia," she said softly. "To Adam's sister. From there I would have to start again. I don't know how, but I know she would help." Adam's sister. Could she really bear to face her again? Now, after all that had happened? Sometimes, when she allowed herself to think of how she had been truly defiled by Paul, she was almost glad she'd never have to see Adam again, to see the disgust in his eyes. Would his sister be the same? She could never tell Abby all that had happened, but would it show?

Marie crossed to the bed and began undoing the strings on the boxes. "You cannot go overland, it is too dangerous. This means you must go on a ship." She tugged at a knot. "Something can be arranged."

"I have no money, Marie, nothing to call my own any more."

"We shall see," was all the woman would say.

"Paul claims it is only days until all is in order for our wedding." Charity's brief flare of hope threatened to be drowned in renewed bitterness. "I have returned the wedding dress for extensive alterations, but he is impatient with my delays. He will not allow any more alterations."

"A few days? We shall see, *petite*. Now, let us get out the hats, and you will tell me quickly what I have burned to know these past days. Let me pin this pink one on." Her fingers worked deftly as Charity sat still. "How did you leave that plantation of the Wentworths?"

Whispering, fighting tears, Charity quickly told her story. She was describing the awful weeks on the keelboat with Paul and Marie was clucking in horror when they heard a scratching at the door. Swiftly Charity stood up and went to pose before the mirror as she called for Estelle to come in. When the woman entered, it was in time to see her young guest tug a lovely pink confection from her curls and hand it to the waiting milliner's assistant.

"That will do very well with the addition of a very soft white feather at the back, Marie. And the green one must have its ribbons changed. Can you have them back soon?"

"In two days' time, when I bring another I work on. If that is convenient, Mademoiselle."

Charity nodded and drew Estelle over to look at the hats. She avoided Marie's eyes, afraid Estelle might see the warmth with which she must look at her old servant.

The theatrical performance might have been a pleasure, Charity reflected as she sat, sipping from a glass of mild white anisette in the courtyard two afternoons later, if it hadn't been for Paul's use of the opportunity to touch her in the darkened theater. She could still feel the goosebumps on her neck where his fingers had toyed with stray tendrils of hair. He had even been so bold as to put his arm around her and squeeze her breast till she tried to pull away. Her flesh was still bruised where he'd pinched her then. The play had been ruined; she wanted only the safety of her own room away from the sight and touch of the man. She did not look forward to the ball tonight, either. The thought of Paul's arms around her made her feel physically ill, and she wondered if she could plead sickness to escape it. If Estelle would come back, she could begin now to complain about a headache.

She was watching a bee emerging from a hibiscus flower near her skirt, plotting what she would say, when a splutter of rage made her look up. Standing on the gallery of the *garconière* was an ashen-faced Paul, his mouth working with fury as his wild eyes looked down on her. She put her cup on the nearby tray, wondering what she had done to make him look at her that way, and trying to hold herself to meet the attack that seemed to be coming. But she'd hardly looked up again before he was down the gallery stairs, striding toward her. His usually smooth hair was ruffled as though he'd been running his fingers through it. His white shirt was half unbuttoned, giving her an unwanted view of his smooth pale chest, and his long hands were clenched as though ready to strike something.

Unable to stop herself, she shrank back from his blazing eyes. "You," he practically shrieked. "You are a witch." A finger stabbed at the air before her eyes.

She stared helplessly at the finger, unable to comprehend. Slowly the threatening hand withdrew, as Paul fought to master himself. The blaze in his dark eyes was banked, leaving a deadly burning light. "You will pay for this." His voice was strangled, but he had stopped shaking, and his hands slowly unbent.

"For what?" Charity felt a bubble of hysteria rising in her throat. It was a mixture of fear and insane mirth at the vision of Paul so beside himself.

"If you think to frighten me with ragged dolls, I will show you the meaning of real fright."

"Dolls?"

Her very real bewilderment must have gotten through to him, for Paul's eyes flickered uncertainly before settling on her again with a malicious intensity. "There are two dolls on my pillow this time. The golden-haired one wears that dress." He shook a finger at the pale pink material trailing from her knees to the stones of the courtyard. "And the other..." He choked and coughed once. "And the other has a tiny sword in its heart."

"The other is you?" Charity's voice was clear and calm, and she watched Paul's face contort in furious fear with a feeling of disgust. "How could I put a sword in your heart?" She spread her hands as though to show they were empty of weapons.

Paul's chest heaved with suppressed emotion. "In just one more week, Charity...just one more week," he ground out, then spun and ran for the rear door of Alain Corbet's offices.

Charity watched him go and shivered. Marie had said Phillipe had forbidden her to continue with the *vaudun*. Marie was the sort of woman who would respect her husband's wishes. So who had done this thing? Someone with Charity's desire to be rid of Paul in mind, it would seem, but the effect had been the opposite of frightening him off. He would not handle her gently after this day's work. She sought to cut off the thread of fear that began to tangle in her mind. She must remember that she still had Marie. Somehow, before the next week, she would escape this house. Slowly she stood up and moved toward the loggia stairs. Tonight's ball would now be inevitable because Paul's black mood would not allow her to escape it. But the pattern of her future life need not be so inevitable.

In the candle glow that chased the early evening shadows of the big parlor, Charity saw that Paul's suave composure had returned, though a dangerous glint lit his eyes as she entered the room slowly.

The man stood behind one of the Spanish-style chairs, and the knuckles of his hand went white as he viewed the shimmering blue-green vision that came toward him with reluctant grace. The long, thin lines of fine lace over the bodice and down the front of the filmy silk gown accentuated the fullness of her breasts and the tiny measurement of her waist. Paul's tongue felt thick as he remembered the glowing skin that lay beneath the exquisite material, the smooth stomach and curving hips. Another few days, he told himself, and he could possess that cool beauty again. It was all he could do not to smack his lips at the prospect. Those dolls had given him a bad turn, but nothing would deter him from the goal he'd sought for more than two years. If she was playing some horrible game with him, he'd show her her mistake. He would break that perverse will and bend that stubborn mind to his own desires. He watched her hungrily, trying to ignore the look of dislike she flashed before lowering those thick lashes and turning that exquisite profile to his devouring eyes. His mouth hardened. He would like to know who had had the belle of Saint Dominque before him. It was a question that had taunted him ever since that first evening in New Orleans. His loins stirred as he thought of how he'd tied her to the bed. That was a game that would bear repeating. She would then tell him anything he wanted to know. Only a few more days. And a ceremony in the courtyard below would give her to him legally, to do with as he pleased.

The house of Antonio Salva, official in the government of Baron de Carondelet, was just a short way away on the corner of Rue Bourbon. The party from the Corbets', led by two slaves with lanterns, made its way through the dark, muddy streets where the sewage-filled ditches gave off a foul smell everyone tried to ignore. At the ballroom door, the slaves washed the ladies' feet and reshod them in the satin dancing slippers they'd carried. Charity stood still for the ritual cleaning, and peeked through the double doors to the brilliantly lit room. Despite herself she felt a small thrill of anticipation as she saw the splendor within. Rarely had she seen such rich materials, so many fine jewels, such a sumptuous display. The people looked dressed for an evening at the French or Spanish court, she thought, rather than for a provincial ball in this colony halfway around the world from the mother countries. Scarlet uniforms mingled with the soft creams, lavenders, greens of delicate muslins, and the rich, darker shades of silks and even satins, and over all came the babble of several languages and the sound of laughter and girlish giggles.

Her eyes were lustrous with wonder as she allowed Paul to take her arm and lead her into the high-ceilinged room where sconces of gold and candelabra of ornate silver held hundreds of candles and the highly polished floor gave back the shimmer of silk-hung walls.

Paul was quick to notice the change in her look, and he leaned toward her as they followed the Corbets. "Tonight, my beauty, you will meet *le gouverneur* himself, and you will reign supreme as the most beautiful woman here."

Hearing his voice, Charity lost the dimple that had begun to appear in her cheek, but her mouth still curved prettily as she was presented to her hosts and was moved to stand before the Governor General of New Orleans. She got a quick glimpse of a long, aristocratic face below thinning brown hair before she lowered her eyes demurely and made her curtsy.

The governor said something pretty, and she raised her head again to answer, when her eyes spied a tall form just beyond Carondelet's shoulder. Dark hair in the candlelight glinted with a hint of auburn highlights, and a superb black silk coat stretched tight across muscular shoulders. She caught her breath, waiting for the pain of memory to loosen its hold on her throat. And then the figure turned. As a man lost in an endless desert would stare at a green oasis on the horizon, she stared at the chiseled profile.

Chapter 27

The room swam before her eyes and Charity gripped Paul's arm to hold herself upright. Mumbling something incoherent to the frowning Carondelet, she swayed as Paul moved her off.

"What's the matter with you?" His voice hissed in her ear, but the heavy pounding of her own heart drowned his words. She struggled to stand by herself, and her eyes darted wildly to the spot where she had seen that well-remembered face. But there was no sign of the man now. She shook her head. Was her own yearning heart beginning to play tricks on her mind?

Paul's hand on her elbow was growing painful. "The music has begun. You will control yourself. I mean to show everyone here to whom you belong before you are besieged. And you will comport yourself with grace while His Excellency is watching us." Firmly he guided her wooden steps toward the open floor.

Years of careful schooling came automatically to Charity's aid. A lady did not give vent to frenzied emotions in a room full of people; she went through the motions of civilized behavior even if her heart were breaking. Carefully, Charity stepped forward, drawing her face into a polite mask. She could feel many sets of eyes on them. She must not display anything, or draw more attention to herself. To the lilting strains of a minuet she moved as in a dream, but she must have successfully hidden her momentary lapse, for Paul's face relaxed and he smiled benignly, a bit possessively, obviously enjoying the sidelong glances of those around them.

At the end of the dance she was led toward a far table where Paul put a delicate stemmed glass in her hand. Taking a sip of the cool drink, she heard Estelle's breathless voice beside her.

"This is a splendid way to meet everyone, no?"

Charity smiled into the sparkling eyes. She felt her control returning. "It is a very grand affair," she acknowledged.

"Paul is afraid you will be stolen from him, no? All these dashing young men eyeing you as you danced just now will not give him peace this evening." She tapped Paul's arm lightly with a folded fan.

The man glowered in response, and started to say something, but his expression suddenly froze. Charity, following his hardening eyes, blinked in the piercing light of steel-gray eyes above Estelle's head.

Soundlessly, her lips formed the name that was always on the tip of her tongue. The tinkle of thin glass shattering brought the people around her to fast-moving life, but she was unaware that the stemmed goblet was gone from her nerveless fingers. A slave was stooped at her feet, scooping up the pieces, and Paul was exclaiming furiously at the spattering of moisture on his shoes. Estelle moved delicately away to greet a friend. And still she stood, turned to stone by the apparition before her.

Adam's face, wide mouth set in a grim line above flexing jaw muscles, blurred and she put up a hand to rub her eyes. The surge of unbearable elation was giving way to panic. Was her mind really going at last? The sounds in the room came to her now, everything magnified, pounding at her ears. Giggles and calls for drinks, musical notes, and the clink of glasses, Paul's furious voice berating the cowering slave at her feet. She covered her ears and took a staggering step forward. Adam stood where she'd seen him, the familiar stray lock of hair brushed only partly back from the wide brow, a scowl of such ferocity on his face she was forcibly stopped. With a twist in her thudding heart, she saw the still-livid scar that arched across the top of his cheekbone, finishing in an upturn at the end of his black brow. The scar gave a satanically debonair look to the handsome face suddenly grown older, and she ached as she saw it.

His eyes blazed with a fire that scorched her, and his mouth, the sensual lips whose touch she could still feel, began to curl into a hate-filled sneer. "I see your situation, Mistress Ashton, is not the desperate one I had envisioned." The deep voice was low, meant only for her ears.

Dazed, the girl shook her head slowly. Her breath wouldn't come to help control her voice. She felt as though she'd been slapped, but at last she whispered his name. "Adam, Adam. Is it really you?"

"As you can see," he replied, his eyes now hooded. "So inconvenient of me, I am sure."

The sound of his voice made her knees begin to buckle. If Paul hadn't grasped her waist at that moment she would have collapsed at the feet of the tall American who stared so coldly at her.

Adam's mind was black with rage, and with a kind of pain he'd never experienced. He'd thought those weeks of agonizing fear, of dreadful uncertainty and teeth-grinding determination had given him all the pain he could bear. But the sight of the beautiful girl smiling demurely on the arm of Paul LaRoche had nearly doubled him over. His wild ecstasy at the first sight of her, so unexpected in this crowded room, his relief at finding her at all after the crazy search he'd made, had given way instantly to a fearful blow from cruel reality. His hands clenched each other behind his back, threatening to break his fingers with their force. But if he let go, he would lunge for the creamy throat where a fluttering pulse showed under the satin skin. He had known this might be the case. He had feared it all along. But suddenly he thought that if he had found her dead it would not have been as bad.

"Crandall." Paul's strained voice put deep antagonism into the name.

Mockingly Adam bowed and his hard eyes watched Paul's hand tighten on Charity's waist.

The girl's mind was whirling. Adam was alive! He was standing before her! Her brain seemed to be screaming the news to the world, and she knew her weeks of anguish and her love for this man must be written on her face. But he wasn't looking at her face. His cold stare of disgust had left her to concentrate on the man at her side, and she caught her breath with fear. Her every instinct was to tear herself away from Paul, to throw herself into those big safe arms. But he looked so forbidding. She glanced around and her brain shifted to the dangers of the situation. They were standing in a room of Spanish and French officials and influential citizens who were friends of Paul's. Adam was a stranger here, an alien without influence. She mustn't give Paul reason to turn on Adam. She'd never forget Paul's black look that day at the plantation when he'd wanted to know who had had her before him. She knew he would be ruthless if he found out. Somehow she must hide her thoughts. Somehow.

"You stray far from Virginia, Crandall." Paul's eyes had not missed much of Charity's reaction, but they ignored her now. The irritating pieces of the puzzle were fitting into place. Adam Crandall had been Charity's lover; that much seemed clear. But what did the American do here in New Orleans? Had she run away from him, and now he had come to claim her again? Or was it coincidence? His own determination to have her led Paul to believe Crandall still wanted her. And she? Judging by her face, she was more startled than anything, but what else was there? A cold fury settled over his mind. "What brings you here?"

"Unfinished business, LaRoche." Adam's voice, still low, was dangerously smooth.

"It will keep you long?"

"I don't think so." The syllables came out very slowly, and the hollows beneath the wide eyes and the high cheekbones seemed to deepen.

"Pity." Paul's voice was a drawl now. "But if you return to Virginia soon you could perhaps do us a service." Adam's brows rose, and Paul smiled diabolically. "Charity and I would have my mother know of our marriage."

Charity could not stop the hand that flew to her mouth, and she watched Adam's shoulders jerk, but his arms remained behind him. "I am sure you are most deserving of each other," the deep voice said slowly, and still he did not look at her. "You have both developed a penchant for picking up strays, I see." The wide mouth curled into a sneer, and his face was ashen with suppressed emotion.

Charity felt Paul's tension as he returned the look levelly. "You forget yourself, Crandall. You are alone in this room among my friends."

"Are you threatening me, LaRoche?" Adam knew his jealousy and rage were overpowering the last of his will, and he didn't care. The thought of Charity married to this man swept away any restraint he might have had, and his hatred of them both carried him on. "What is your game now, you swine? To help the American secessionists wrest this city

288

from the Spanish and then set up your own dirty business here? Always with th' help of your blushing bride?" His eyes swept over Charity's body insultingly.

Charity put up a hand imploringly, but Adam had finished with her. She tried to turn and found Paul's arm at her waist held her fast. A smile curved on his thin lips as slowly he reached to the table beside him, picked up a goblet of dark wine, and with deliberate ease dashed the contents in Adam's face. "You insult us both, sir," he said in a silky voice.

"Deservedly," Adam returned, his hand brushing away the wine on his cheek, his eyes like obsidian now.

"You will give me satisfaction."

"With pleasure."

Charity moved then. Tugging free of Paul's arm, she stepped between them. "No." Her voice was a strangled cry. She turned to Adam. "You mustn't." He glared at her and swept her aside as though she were a pesky puppy. "Paul," she tried, but he caught her wrist and twisting it cruelly, pulled her to him. She looked around wildly then. They were standing at the far end of the room. A servant behind the table was gaping openmouthed at them, and Alain Corbet stood rooted a few feet away. But most people seemed not to have heard the low exchange.

"My seconds will call..." she heard Paul say, and put her hands to her ears. This couldn't be happening. She wanted to scream, but her fright closed her throat. The governor himself was here. What would he do to Adam if she brought his attention to the argument? She couldn't think, couldn't think.

Paul had her arm again and was pulling her around the table. Ahead of her she saw broad shoulders going through the doors onto the gallery outside. As Paul shoved her into the night air she saw Adam vault the wrought iron railing, hang a moment, then drop noiselessly to the street below. In moments he was lost in the shadows.

The lights from the doors showed her Paul's face as he shoved her back against the building, pinning her shoulders against the rough stucco wall. "So at last the riddle is solved," he grated. "And now you will both pay for it."

Horror kept Charity limp in his hands, but her mind was racing again. "I...I don't know what you mean."

"Ah, but you do, my sweet." Paul's voice was silky once more, and one hand stroked her throat. The solution to his riddle, the argument with Adam seemed to have inflamed him. Caressingly, his hand moved down to her breasts.

"You're wrong." She tried not to shudder at his touch. "You think Adam Crandall and I...that we..." It was easy to summon up hysterical laughter. "You're so wrong," she choked. "That great brute has never been anything to me."

Paul's breath was on her neck now, and she prayed he'd think her shaking was from laughter. "No?" he asked. "Then how do you explain your look when you saw him?" His fingers pinched her breasts, and she flinched. But she thought she'd detected the slightest note of doubt in his voice.

Drawing a deep breath, she forced one hand up to his hair. "Don't do this, Paul. You will make me feel faint."

His body went rigid with surprise at her words. Then she was in his arms. His lips against her breast, he said, "You still haven't answered me, Charity."

"I was stunned," she gasped. "I had heard from Bill Harrison in Cincinnati that Mr. Crandall had died in some sort of accident. I thought I'd seen a ghost." She pushed at his arms, but not too hard. He must think her fearful for her reputation, but weak from his embrace.

He let her go then and peered at her in the dim light. "I had not heard this."

She managed to shrug. "I did not think it worth repeating. But it is difficult to face a ghost." She laughed tremulously again.

"Then why did he look at you so?"

She tried to remember every nuance of Adam's reaction to her. She thought there had been only contempt and dislike there. "He never had any fondness for me, and perhaps he carried a grudge for the sake of the Wentworths, from whom I ran away."

"You claimed to have run away from me, too, *chérie*," Paul reminded her, his voice nasty again.

"Only to soften the blow to them." Charity's heart was in her throat. Would he believe her? There was a long silence, and at last she dared to go on. "So if you are fighting a duel with Adam Crandall because of me, you are fighting him most foolishly."

"Not just for you, Charity. You are used goods, after all." His look was cruel. "There will be much enjoyment for me in that encounter."

Her eyes were stinging with his accurate description of

her, but she made one more try. "Oh, Paul, what if you were hurt?"

"By that American? I think not, my dear. But your concern is touching. Come, show me how much you care."

His mouth searched for hers again and Charity huddled into the wall. He was mocking her. But did he believe her about her relationship with Adam? She didn't dare give up the game yet. Shrinking, but determined, she let him kiss her.

"Only a few short days," Paul murmured huskily, then he kissed her again, his tongue parting her lips.

Gagging on the taste of him and on her fear, Charity jerked back. "Paul, you mustn't," she repeated breathlessly.

"You are shaking, *chérie*. So much fear for what may happen to me the morning after this?" He was sneering openly now, and Charity wished she could claw at his hateful face. But what did it matter if he sneered? She had no pride any more. And if she had, she would still sacrifice it to stop Paul from killing Adam. A new thought came to her. She had heard that gentlemen of New Orleans demanded only "satisfaction" in their duels, a mere show of blood. That was a bad enough picture, but it was not the fearful vision of death she had had.

"Of course I am shaking," she answered. "A duel is a fearful thought. But I will feel better when you assure me that all I have ever heard is true; that as soon as one party is wounded, satisfaction is given." She remembered the rumors that Paul had killed a man in the past, but pushed the memory aside.

His laugh was harsh. "Leave Crandall to nose around New Orleans, to perhaps interfere in my affairs? To see you again? My dear Charity, you are not so great a fool as to believe that. You may consign Mr. Crandall to the lists of the dead where you thought him." The girl closed her eyes, not even noticing his hands on her hair, smoothing it. "And now that we have that point cleared up, and you may stop worrying about me, we shall return to this delightful ball, and show the world what a happy couple we are."

"No." Charity, already stiff with dread, froze at his words. "I couldn't go back in there now."

"But you will, my sweet. And you will smile and dance with me, or I will wring your beautiful neck." Roughly he pulled her from the wall and straightened her skirts. "We

291

have a certain reputation to uphold. I will not have you seen shrinking and fainting over that unfortunate scene."

Charity's gaze was sightless. How could she go in there and face all those people when she could think only of what was to happen to Adam in thirty-six hours' time? But she *must* not let Paul see what his words had done to her. He might yet be unsure of her motives. She had to take that chance. Anything to lessen his hatred of Adam; anything to possibly stop that duel. Adam was alive. He was here. If she thought only of that, she could even smile. She could dance for joy.

As a heat-laden dawn bathed the slumbering city in pearly tones of gray and yellow, Charity viewed the growing light with heavy but clear eyes. Through the protective mosquito netting she watched the shadows on the walls deepen as the louvres of the shutters were thrown into ever more relief. For the hundredth time she thought of the proud, distant face, opaque eyes glinting savagely at her across Estelle's head. She had no memory of the rest of the ball, of the men she'd danced with, of the compliments paid, the shy, coquettish role she'd played. It was all only a backdrop to a dream, an indistinct, sometimes nightmarish dream. In the way of dreams, it didn't make sense. Places and people were juxtaposed in contorted fashion; she and Adam, the central characters, did not belong in New Orleans but in the gently rolling country of central Virginia; they did not belong in a room patchworked with rich materials on strange people but in each other's arms alone in a place that belonged only to them.

She frowned in concentration, twisting one long strand of her growing hair between two fingers. Of course, no place could belong to the two of them alone now. Paul would always be there. She was not Adam's as she had once been. If he knew...Her fingers jerked, hurting her scalp. Paul! The thought that he had even seen her, let alone possessed her, made her writhe. But she couldn't avoid the fact that it was so. No, her dream of finding Adam, of explaining to him she'd never have come willingly to this city with Paul, was a dream only. She must think instead of how to stop that duel.

Over coffee in the courtyard, she tried to find out from Estelle what Alain had said about the incident at the ball, but found the woman reluctant to talk of it. Frustrated, Charity accepted the invitation to accompany Estelle to the market this morning, wanting the walk to refresh her wits.

Automatically she searched the bright crowds for a sign of Marie. The day was young. Perhaps the woman would come to the market before going to the shop. Dawdling over confections she knew she could not eat, she fell behind Estelle and let her gaze rove carefully.

It was the familiar woodsman's costume that caught her eye and made her suck in her breath. Dropping the delicacies she held, she darted past a calico-clad woman and tugged at the fringed sleeve.

Jed's face was a study in warring emotions when he turned at the pressure. But quickly the deep lines in the tanned skin settled into the familiar laconic expression. Wordlessly he surveyed her.

"Jed, oh, Jed. It's really you." Charity's eyes filled, and she put up a gloved hand to brush away the tears. "Is Adam here?"

Strong fingers removed her hand from his sleeve. "Not likely." He started to turn away.

"Jed, listen to me. You must tell Adam something for me."

"For you? Tell 'im somethin' for *you*? Hell no, lady. You git on back to your fancy husband, and you leave Adam alone. You're no better'n the rest of 'em. If Adam survives that duel, I'm gettin' 'im the hell outa this Godforsaken place and back to where I can start puttin' him back together again. It was a bad day that he ever laid eyes on you."

Dazed, Charity shook her head. "Jed, you don't understand." He was already moving away, and she struggled to keep up with him. "Jed, don't let him fight that duel!"

Her words, ringing with authority, stopped the man for a moment. Knowing he'd not give her time to say much, she concentrated on what was vital. "You've got to stop it. Paul's one talent in his life has been with the sword. He'll kill Adam."

"Then yore troubles are over, aren't they?" Jed's face was furious now; the laconic mask had slipped away.

"I once heard Paul killed a man on Martinique, Jed."

"That'll be a nice tale to take to Adam. But I'll tell you somethin' now, lady. I hope he kills that husband of yours! And you can put that in your pipe and smoke it!" Clamping his mouth tight, Jed turned roughly.

Gasping, Charity picked up her skirts and ran after him. She reached for him, but he shook her off and strode away so fast she couldn't keep up. "Jed, he's not my husband. Oh Jed, please stop Adam." Instantly he was swallowed in the

293

crowd. She didn't even know if he'd heard her last words. "Oh Lord," she said aloud. Then slowly she made her way back to the confectioner's trays.

Estelle, thinking Charity distraught over Paul's upcoming duel, was reluctant to have Marie bother her about hats this morning, but Charity brushed aside her words of concern and dragged the milliner's assistant upstairs to the privacy of her chamber.

Marie eyed the girl's wild face as she put the hat boxes on the bed. "The maid told me M. Paul found more dolls in his room. Is this so?"

"Dolls? Oh. Yes, they frightened him half to death. But he thinks I am somehow connected with them."

"How could he think that?"

"It doesn't matter, Marie. That is not important now. Adam is here."

Marie's square chin dropped. Then her shrewd dark eyes crinkled with laughter. "So, he has come at last."

"What do you mean, 'at last'?"

Eloquent shoulders shrugged. "I did not think him dead, is all. I told you I have learned not to take the *vaudun* lightly. It was hinted that he was alive. I could not be sure till now, though. And I am so glad. You will somehow go with him?"

Charity sat down abruptly. "Hardly. He thinks that I came here willingly with Paul. He even thinks I am already married to that despicable man. He hates me. And now Paul is going to kill him in a duel tomorrow morning."

"Mon Dieu." Marie sat down too. "Then we must find him, little one. He must be made to see he's wrong in thinking you are here happily with M. Paul."

"If I could just speak with him," Charity whispered.

"We will find him somehow." Marie used the same efficient tone she used to use when speaking of the proper selection of a gown, and Charity tried to smile.

"I would do nearly anything to call off that duel. But as for his hatred of me...there is so little I can do." Suddenly she saw her last scene with Adam their final evening aboard the flatboat. Her words then had been bitter and caustic. He knew nothing of her waking thoughts of love, her resolve to win him again. He might well think she had hated him then, still hated him. And he was not one to return a woman's scorn with love. Overcome with the enormity of her despairing vision, Charity gave way as she had not done in all the horrible weeks since Paul had had her kidnapped. Throwing herself across the light coverlet, she broke into a storm of weeping that Marie was helpless to stop. Even if she could convince him of her own feelings, if she had the hours it would take to explain everything to him, she could not overcome the fact that Paul had raped her, had defiled what she and Adam had had. The storm went on unchecked till she heard a light knock on her door. Marie jumped from the bed, and Charity gulped, brushing away the still-streaming tears.

"Charity! What is the matter?" Estelle's matronly form moved swiftly toward her, horrified concern written large on her wide face.

"It is nothing," the girl managed to say. "Poor Marie. I am behaving badly over the straw hat."

Marie took her cue. "It is I who made the mistake, Mademoiselle. It will be fixed instantly." Quickly she took up the boxes and departed.

"It is that you are overwrought about Paul," Estelle said soothingly. "But I have heard from Alain that your betrothed is an excellent swordsman. No American can have had the training or experience Paul has had. You must calm yourself and know that tomorrow at this time all will be over."

Charity wanted to fly at the woman, to smack that complacent look off her face. She turned away, and soon Estelle left softly, saying she hoped Charity would feel better by lunch time.

Chapter 28

The house was stifling. Even the courtyard, surrounded by its high wall and galleried wings, was suffocating her. The heat of the day was just beginning, and she felt she'd not be able to draw breath soon. The very sight of her jailors in this elegantly appointed prison made the blood pound in her temples. She gazed at Paul, who sipped daintily from the delicate little gold and white cup, with a look of such venom that he seemed to feel her hate and glanced up. She made no effort to hide her eyes, and their gazes locked. How she hated him. She felt as though a taut wire were snapping in her brain.

Paul saw her furious look turn to rest on blank space above the brick wall, and mentally he pounded his fist. By God, he'd knock that look out of those haughty eyes. He would take care of Crandall in the morning. And then he would turn his attention to this arrogant bitch. She would pay for her attitude, for her stalling tactics, for what he felt sure was the truth of her relationship with that big American. Oh yes, she would pay!

Charity stood up. "I find the heat is becoming oppressive," she said in a clear voice. "I am going to my room." She spoke to Estelle, but her stormy eyes took them all in before she turned with a swish of her skirts and stalked regally to the loggia stairs.

Just a few more days, Paul thought, as he watched her leave, and you will come and go only at my bidding, bitch. He felt a tightness in his groin at the thought.

The realization of her helplessness had brought cold fury to fill the void left by her confrontation with Jed that morning, and Charity paced the confines of her room, suddenly oblivious to the dank heat. Adam and Jed wouldn't listen to her. Her one further attempt to talk to Paul had brought on a biting rebuke and more insulting language. She was as powerless as a rag doll. Had always been so. She'd been powerless to defend her home and her father; powerless to decide her own fate after the loss of Tournay; powerless to stop her mother's dying. She'd even been powerless before the force of Adam's determination to have her. And she'd been nothing more than his newest toy, a puppet. Just as she now was for Paul. He would use her just as Adam had, only he would not even offer the solace of gentleness and a chance to love. He would kill tomorrow, and then he would return to this house in triumph to bring a kind of slow death to her. She stopped. No. She was not powerless to stop her own fate this time. She could do nothing for Adam. She could do nothing about the events past, but she could still affect the events of the future. She started to walk again.

The afternoon was wearing on. She must act quickly, for soon the house would be stirring again. Without a break in her stride, she spun and went to pull the bell rope. She could not slip from this house unseen. So she would go openly.

"Mademoiselle?" Estelle's maid peered timidly around the door.

Charity got up from her dressing table. "Rosalie, you will slip this note under Madame's door. It explains that I must go out. Then you will return to me. We will be at Madame Morel's shop when it reopens." Her tone was brusque, preoccupied, and although the girl's eyes opened wide in surprise, she scurried to do Mademoiselle's bidding.

Trembling with impatience, Charity snatched up hat and gloves. She must look right for her final walk out of this house.

A quarter of an hour later she left Rosalie outside the shop and entered with a lifting heart. What incredible luck. A group of four women were ahead of her, loudly claiming the owner's attention. Silently she slipped to the rear of the shop and passed through the beaded archway.

Marie looked up as the beads slapped against the wall near her work table, and her angular face split into a surprised smile. "I was coming to you with the straw hat this afternoon, *chérie*."

"There is no longer any need, Marie. I am never going back there!" Charity's eyes flashed in a way Marie recognized. It had been a long time since she had seen that look. It had always meant that Charity was daring the world to say anything against her decision.

"Then we must move swiftly. What matter that it is one day earlier than I'd planned?"

"A day early?" Charity's smile was filling the room with light.

Marie returned it. "There is a ship leaving tomorrow morning. We will talk later. Did you come alone?"

"No." Charity frowned. "I must think of a way to rid myself of Madame Corbet's maid. I brought her because I knew it would make this walk look innocent."

Marie thought a moment. Then quickly the two conferred. A few brief moments later Charity slipped back through the shop, still unnoticed by Madame Morel. Once on the street she sauntered nonchalantly past several shops till she came to the one she sought. It was a men's haberdashery, and she bade Rosalie wait while she considered a gift. Again, her luck was amazing. There was only one man tending the shop, and he had a customer. Swiftly she searched for the side door she'd been told about. There it was, behind the displays of neck cloths. Silently she stepped through it into the narrow alley. Allowing only a brief thought for the girl waiting patiently outside the shop, Charity sped down the alley to the street behind. Repeating Marie's directions to herself, she turned right and walked briskly away into the afternoon sun.

Adam stood silently at the base of the massive oak tree and surveyed the dappled earth before him. His shoulders, propped negligently against the rough bark, moved once as he saw a carriage approach. Then he fell to studying the terrain once more. The faint morning light picked out dark glints of red in his black hair and etched his stern features with pale shadows. His eyes, now the color of molten metal, were half closed; he seemed almost sleepy.

Jed Simpson, a deep scowl on his face, looked from the young man to the slowing carriage and tried to remember his instructions. The tight coat and fitted pants were scratchy in the early heat, and he could feel the sweat beginning to trickle down his sides. Fine white lines of worry showed around his set mouth as he strode over the wet grass. Adam looked cool enough now. He could only hope he would remain that way.

The boy had changed much these past weeks, and it wasn't only due to that witch of a girl they'd been chasing. When he'd found Adam in that dirty little settler's cabin, he'd seen something already starting in the depths of those eyes; an awareness at last of his own mortality? a decision of some sort? Jed wasn't sure. The feeling that he was watching Adam grow and change had been heightened, though, in Cincinnati. The boy had taken his responsibilities with General Wayne, whatever they were, very seriously, and had put off going downriver for four days while he carried them out. The old Adam would have gone haring off the very night they'd determined Charity was headed for New Orleans.

The following weeks of worry, depression, back-breaking labor had left their mark, too. The boy, from the moment he'd left Wayne's headquarters, had looked more like the man Jed knew him to be behind the insolent young face he'd chosen to show the world, and that look had deepened with each passing day. But it had all blown apart two nights ago when Adam had come face to face with Charity, dressed fit to kill, living the high life with that Paul LaRoche. The old temper had taken hold then and gotten him into this duel. And after that everything had dissolved in the grandest drinking spree Jed had yet witnessed. But, he had to admit, there was no hint of the wild boy in Adam this morning. He felt glad again that he'd not mentioned seeing Charity in the market yesterday. No sense in risking another bout of drinking just before a duel. It was bad enough that Adam's jealous hatred of this LaRoche fellow might blind him this morning, without a bad head to compound the problem. Lord, let him keep his head, Jed prayed, and squared his bent shoulders to face the two figures stepping out of the carriage.

"Gentlemen," he intoned in his deepest voice and reached out unwillingly to shake hands.

The square-faced, stout man beside Paul LaRoche nodded once and mopped perspiration from his brow. "Shall we, Mr. Simpson?" He drew Jed aside, and the two began the ritual of inspecting the matched weapons in the long box he carried.

Paul, moving almost on tiptoe, walked across the grass between giant trees. He saw the still figure leaning, arms folded, feet crossed, against one oak and for a moment burning blood infused his pale face. If that tall American had anything to do with Charity's disappearance yesterday, he'd

299

find out soon. Once his sword was at that bronzed throat, he would discover the truth, and then he would finish what he had wanted to do for a very long time. He'd weighed the possibilities of reprisals from the authorities if a man were found to have died in a duel this morning, and decided he would risk it. Crandall's blood would have to spill copiously to satisfy him this day. Carefully he turned his thoughts to the duel to come.

"Good reach," he muttered softly, "but too big for fast footwork." His confidence grew with each reflection, and he swung his arms to stretch the muscles.

His adversary watched him beneath lowered lids, willing his body to relax. "Concentration, my boy, is all you need." He could almost hear the softly accented words of the master swordsman in London. "You have the grace, the reach, the stamina. You must *concentrate*." It had all been a game then, the sort of activity young men took up to fill the afternoons while they waited for the next social event to take place. But the little Frenchman on the Rue Bourbon yesterday had claimed that he had not lost the touch he had acquired that year in London. He supposed it was as well that Jed had dragged him off for those hours of practice after hearing somewhere that LaRoche was an accomplished swordsman. Though he didn't see how it signified a great deal. No matter who drew first blood, their futures remained the same; Paul had Charity, and Adam would leave this tropical hellhole as soon as he could discover a boat heading back upriver. Shrugging away his thoughts, Adam followed LaRoche's slender back to the center of the clearing.

The doctor, who had ridden up on a tired horse, had viewed the contestants with distaste, and had withdrawn to a discreet distance. The formalities were dispatched with haste, coats were shed, the thin, tempered blades lifted from the outstretched hands of Alain Corbet, the calls made. Paul, his confidence at a crest, attacked without preamble. There was a flicker of movement and a click as Adam parried, sliding sideways and withdrawing. Paul followed and if Adam hadn't been warned by Jed, he would have been taken by surprise. Paul LaRoche might be an immaculate fop, but his skill with a sword was not to be underestimated.

Smoothly Adam's brain directed, his eyes and feet, shoulders and wrists answered. Calling up all the tricks he'd ever been taught, he settled down to defend himself. He succeeded at the cost of being whipped backward and forward across the clearing. But he was getting a measure of the man.

In the silence of the early day, the slipping and tapping of the blades went on, each man looking for the thinnest opening, the smallest sign. When it came, Adam was no longer surprised. He was at the end of his thrust, his arm rigid, his point nearly level, when Paul caught the blade flat with his own and circled it deftly, forcing the swords to adhere gratingly. Then suddenly Paul gave way, Adam's arm dropped that fraction and Paul plunged forward. Adam felt quick pain high on his side before he countered. Sticky wetness touched his arm and he lowered his blade. So, it was done!

But the thought had not taken full shape before he heard Jed's gasp and saw the bright point coming once more. His body responded to the deadly intent before his brain could register the act. With an animal-like twist, he was free of the threat and locked in a new and deadlier battle. So LaRoche was not going to settle for the shallow laws of courtesy and fair play! So be it. "Swine," he said with a grin and felt his blood pound faster in his veins.

Paul's answering smile was a weasel's grimace. He said nothing, but all the words he could say were in his burning eyes.

Within minutes both men's heads were soaked, their wrists numb with the vibrations of the blows, their breath coming in retching gasps. The shadow of fatigue and blood loss dragged at Adam's arm, but a hard, analytical light was in his eyes. Despite his wound, he was sure he had the greater strength, the greater stamina. He had spent the past weeks in hard, body-tightening work, while this Frenchman had dallied in drawing rooms and sipped coffee and brandy in cafés. But the other drove him hard, his blade swooping in a blurred rhythm.

Adam backed steadily, buying time, aware of the traps of the tree roots he was being pressed toward. He would have to reverse the direction. Suddenly his heel found one hard bump and he stumbled. The skilled blade rushed toward him. Against his training, he dropped like a stone, right arm upthrust, rigid. Whistling air from the singing sword bathed his ear at the same instant his arm nearly buckled under an impact. With widening eyes he saw the slender form of Paul LaRoche sink slowly to the ground, a look of surprised anguish and twisted hate on his face, Adam's sword deep in his chest.

Regret had had no place in Adam's mind when he'd first viewed the still form at the foot of the tree, but now, as Jed pushed him toward the waiting mounts, he hesitated. "If the man had not pressed the attack when the game should have been up, this would not have happened," he said softly, turning to look back at the tableau beneath the oaks. The doctor and Alain Corbet still bent over the crumpled figure and there was a stillness to the September air that seemed unearthly.

The frown on Jed's face cleared just long enough for him to say, "Bastard deserved it." Then he was pushing a set of reins into Adam's hand. "Come on, I'll give you a leg up."

Adam grasped the reins. He thought fleetingly of Charity. How would she take this news? In all honor he owed Charity an explanation of what had happened, but he did not know where she was, how to reach her. His insides wrenched at the vision of her face crumbling in shocked sorrow, and he staggered as he tried to turn to the horse. As always, Jed was there, steadying him. Slowly, painfully, he mounted, wondering if it wouldn't be better to ignore everyone's advice and simply go to the authorities himself right now. He swayed in the saddle, feeling the wetness seeping through the bandage at his side. He looked at the stalwart form astride beside him, and realized his instincts might be honorable, but he had more to think of than just himself. For the sake of Jed and these other men he would not go to the authorities. And for everyone's sake he would not try to find Charity. There was nothing more they could say to each other. Both their lives were in ruins for now, and an unbridgeable gulf yawned between them. Better to follow instructions and disappear.

Corbet and the doctor had been emphatic in their insistence that he return to Frederico's house and gather his belongings. They would have to admit the truth of the matter, but they wanted no part of the inquiry and unpleasantness that would follow. If he were to disappear from New Orleans with all possible haste, they would stall the news, and claim no knowledge of his whereabouts. Let the authorities make of it what they could. And Frederico, who had been helpful these past days, would be protected. No one here had known where Adam had been staying, and when it was discovered, he would be well away and Frederico none the wiser for any of the events. It remained only for them to reach the *levée* with all haste and discover what craft they could board.

From her place in the corner of the slanting roof, Charity watched the trap door lift and held her breath. Her damp hair clung in tendrils to her neck, and beads of perspiration stood out on her brow and lip. Dark smudges beneath enormous liquid eyes spoke of the hours of sleeplessness and fear that had just passed. With a rush she let go her breath as a graying head appeared above the floorboards. Bent double, she moved forward and took the bowl of gruel held up to her.

"You are all right?" Marie's quick eyes took in Charity's bedraggled condition and haggard face. The girl nodded. "I am so sorry you had to stay in this sweltering attic, *petite*. But today you will be free."

The woman climbed the last rungs of the ladder and pulled herself through the opening as Charity sat down on the dusty floorboards with a thump. "You have found some way to get me from this city?"

"I believe so. I will go in a few moments to the ship. I will claim to be your maid, and will persuade the captain to take you on board. It will not be hard, I think. Phillipe has already gone. He will try to discover the outcome of that duel you told us about."

Charity's heart thudded painfully. She did not want to think any more of that duel. She had spent the horribly lonely dawn hours picturing with agonizing clarity the outcome, and hating herself for her helplessness to prevent it. The dread of the news Phillipe might bring so filled her that she had to put down her spoon and gasp for more breath.

Marie patted her shoulder. "Death is a rare occurrence in these affairs of honor, remember."

Charity nodded. "I have tried to remember that. But Paul is a ruthless man. He as good as said he would kill Adam today." She choked and tears spilled over the long fringe of lashes onto the pale cheeks.

"It is done now, *chérie*. We cannot change what is past. We must think instead of how to get you beyond the reach of that LaRoche."

With the back of her hand, Charity brushed away the tears. "Marie, since our long talk last night, I have thought so much. I am afraid for you and Phillipe. I have a horrible feeling that Paul did not believe your story. He will have everyone out looking for me, and I must get away from here and not entangle you any further."

The narrow shoulders shrugged. "Certainly they will look. What of it? They have nothing more to learn from me. You came to the shop. I was not finished with the straw hat. You left. I brought it to you, and was sorry you were not there to approve my work. I never saw you again. That maid has told them of the shop you entered, where she stood for an hour waiting." Her face split into a wide smile at the thought. "You simply vanished, *chérie*. In this city, stranger things have happened. And no one would think to look for you here, I know. They will ask me again, perhaps. I will tell them again. They would not think to question Phillipe. And if they did, he has never seen you, only heard of the peculiar guest of the Corbets' who was so hard to please."

Her face crinkled again, and Charity tried to echo her smile. She felt better. Perhaps Marie was right; there was no way they could lay the blame at the door of this good woman. She prayed it was so. "I'm sorry about all those hat alterations. You are a very good milliner, in fact. So good, I doubt if you'll always have to work for Madame Morel."

"That is my hope too." Marie's eyes twinkled. "Now, I must go. We have talked." Her hand rested lightly on Charity's cheek. "And we have already said our *adieux*, really. We must not talk more, but act. And it will be all right. Better things await you, *chérie*."

Charity kissed the long fingers. "Who told you that? Your friend in the *vaudun*?" Marie's smile was enigmatic, and Charity almost dimpled. "It doesn't matter. For anything would be better than a life with Paul LaRoche." Or almost anything. The thought came unbidden, and she shoved it aside. If she worried about what was now in store she would lose her mind.

The long thin cloak pulled tight around her rumpled dress, the hood covering her glossy hair and much of her face, Charity stood at the rail of the ship and looked across the bustling *levée* to the roof tops of New Orleans. How she might have liked this exotic city if it hadn't been for Paul LaRoche, she thought. Then, sighing, she turned with Marie toward the companionway and her dark little cabin.

Bustling efficiently, Marie unpacked the one box they had brought on board. "You will at least be respectable in these, *chérie*. But it is such a pity that we could not think of a way to get any of your own clothes."

Charity eyed the two muslin dresses hanging on the narrow wall and smiled. "I seem to make a life's work of leaving my wardrobes behind me. It will not be the first time I have worn someone else's clothing. I am only sorry to deprive you of your best things."

"That is nothing. I hope that you may be able to alter them to fit you well." She laid out underwear on the small wash stand and stood looking around the tiny space. "It is altogether like the last voyage, is it not?"

"Yes. I too was thinking that. But I shall miss you so." Quickly she looked away. "I wonder which officer I have displaced by being taken on board? Perhaps some day I will travel on a ship equipped for passengers."

"I could wish you were on one now. There would be more safety for you among fellow travelers. But the captain, he seems a good man. If you have any difficulties, I am sure you may turn to him."

"That is reassuring to know. But I'm convinced there will be no trouble, Marie." Charity spoke with a conviction that surprised her. Those were brave words, the sort spoken by foolhardy youth who knew nothing of the real world. But she realized that they came from her own inner conviction that nothing could terrify her anymore.

"You will send me word that you are safe at this sister's home, no?" Marie's worried frown brought Charity back from her musings.

She smiled as broadly as she could. "I will send you word, dear friend. But I think perhaps I will not return to Abby's home. I do not even have news of her brother to take her, and I do not think I could bear to face her."

"Ah, Charity. It is so much too bad Phillipe could discover nothing of any duel fought this morning. It is so strange. Normally the news is all over the city before the men even return to their homes."

"Yes. It is as though I dreamed the whole thing. So perhaps Jed managed to stop it after all." She brightened perceptibly at the thought, and Marie hugged her.

"Then where will you go, *chérie*?"

Charity shook her head. "Perhaps I will return to the plans I laid in Virginia. To Philadelphia, I think, to find others like me, who have been cast out of their homes on Saint Dominque and have made their way in this new land. If they have done it, so shall I. Perhaps in Philadelphia I will find a place to call my home."

The girl's head was so high, Marie's eyes filled as she watched her. Pressing a hard little bag into Charity's lap, she touched the shining hair once. "May God go with you, child."

"And with you, Marie." Charity choked and clenched her fists. Through blurred eyes she saw the narrow door close softly. Then she felt the weight in her lap. Her tears falling on the little bag, she opened it to find what must have been the last of any savings Marie and Phillipe had possessed. With a gasp she started up. But she knew running after the former slave would be futile. Marie would never allow her to return the money. Throwing herself sideways on the bunk, she cried till she could sob no more and fell into fitful sleep broken by shouts and clankings and thumps from above.

A knock awoke her, and she sat up, wondering where she was. The knock sounded again as she stared uncomprehendingly at the rough walls. "Who is it?" she called automatically, her brain still searching for answers.

The door opened a crack and the round face of a young boy peeked around the edge. "Missus?" The boy looked puzzled.

"Who are you?"

The door opened wider and the small figure stood very straight in his knee breeches and wide blue shirt. "Billy Little, Missus. I'm the cabin boy. Cap'n sends his respec's, an' asks if you would like to join 'im in his cabin for dinner."

"Oh!" Charity's hands flew to her hot face as memory rushed back. She recalled that Marie had told her she was now Madame Boucher, traveling to meet her sick husband in Philadelphia. At the moment she felt she could not hold to the charade for an endless dinner. "Billy." She sat straighter. "Would it be possible for me to have a tray in this cabin, just this evening?"

"I guess so. I gotta take 'em to the other passengers anyway."

"Other passengers?" Charity's heart skipped a beat. Perhaps she wasn't to be alone on this ship of men after all. This was one of the few times in her life when she would actually welcome the company of another woman, no matter how vapid or uninteresting. Anything to keep her from her lonely thoughts.

"Yeah." Billy closed his mouth firmly and began to back into the passage.

"Please send my regrets to the captain, and thank him for me. And Billy...I'm grateful." Tomorrow would be time enough to find out about the others aboard.

The round face split wide in a grin and the door closed to the scurry of bare feet.

Chapter 29

Through the last of the daylight hours, and later by lantern glow, Charity occupied herself determinedly with sewing. Marie's notion box proved a treasure trove, and deftly Charity ripped seams on the taffy-colored muslin, restitched, added dark brown braid to the wide neckline, sewed matching braided buttons down the front of the bodice. Her own strong will kept her from thinking of anything but the work her fingers did, and she went on until her eyes bleared and she had no choice but to retire.

Only in the night did visions of a long, masculine form lying on muddy earth, blood soaking the curling dark hair on the chest, gray eyes staring in the blindness of death come to haunt her and make her twist in misery on the hard bunk. Waking with a start, Charity shuddered and forced herself to remember that it was more likely the dreaded duel had never taken place. If only she could have stayed in New Orleans to find out! But she knew she could not have continued to put Marie and her kind husband in danger that way. It might have been days before they could find another ship leaving the port for the eastern coast. Having Paul discover her would be even worse than this gnawing uncertainty about Adam's whereabouts. Her hands grew clammy at the thought of Paul. Was the ship clear of the river yet? Could he still discover her in some fiendish way? She'd no idea how long it would take to reach the Gulf, but prayed for sight of the sea tomorrow.

If I can just make it till tomorrow, she thought. Then I will take each day at a time. Don't look ahead. There are no plans to be made. First, look only for the ship's rounding the Floridas, then for the docking in the Carolinas, then for the more northern ports. Her mind stopped there. Think only of tomorrow. With that she drifted back into haunted sleep.

Hollow-eyed, Charity paced the confines of her cabin for most of the next day. Billy had brought her light meals, but she must not ask for another tray this evening. Perhaps by now the other passengers had roused sufficiently to go to the captain's table. But even if they hadn't, she knew she could not stay here alone much longer. When Billy knocked on her door once more to announce the hour, Charity steeled herself to follow him calmly. She'd tried to discover more about the others from him, but the boy had turned sullen at her questions and she'd given up. Perhaps these were not people she'd care to know after all.

"Madame Boucher." Captain Benton came from behind his small desk with outstretched hand. For a moment Charity wondered whom he was addressing. Then she remembered. Covering her confusion, she smiled brightly and allowed him to bend over her wrist. When he straightened she could see his surprise echoed her own. He was young for a captain of a ship, she thought, as they appraised each other. Curly blond hair, grown long at the sides, golden-brown skin and bright blue eyes made a very handsome combination too. She realized she was staring as frankly as he, and quickly she looked around the cramped quarters, to discover that there were just two other men present. One was a middle-aged man of military bearing who eyed her with incredulity. The other was a sallow-faced youth whose mouth hung slack as the captain introduced her. She discovered they were the first and second officers of the ship, and wondered anew where the passengers were. But Billy had been so secretive about their presence, she felt she shouldn't ask more questions.

"Do you find your accommodations sufficiently agreeable, Madame?" The captain's rich voice had the lilt of a southern drawl. "I'm sorry we are not better equipped for passengers."

"It is most agreeable, thank you. I am only sorry that I

must have discommoded one of your officers." She looked around and saw the youngest man flush.

"It is my privilege," he stammered.

The men were all very polite over dinner, but she found it a strain to try to recall the web of lies she must tangle around herself now. She tried to keep to a simple story she could later remember, that of being a worried wife on her way to join a husband taken ill on his trip north.

"It is so too bad your maid had to leave the ship at the last moment," Captain Benton said at one point during the evening, and Charity thought his blue eyes were growing bolder by the moment.

"Yes," she sighed. "But when I realized she had a high fever, I could not keep her aboard." She spread her hands helplessly. "I shall miss her sorely, but once I reach Philadelphia, I shall find another."

"A long journey, though, Madame." The captain raised his glass at that, but Charity did not return the gesture.

She escaped as soon as she decently could, and wondered if she had the strength to face another meal alone with these men, especially with Captain Benton. He obviously thought it odd that a young woman would require instant passage on his ship to travel alone to the North without proper luggage. He would probably try to find out more, and she wasn't sure she could keep her story straight. Anyway, his frank approval of her appearance made her nervous. Drawing the bolt on her door, she heaved a sigh and reminded herself sternly that now they were clear of the river, she should be feeling hope once again. She should consider only gratitude to Captain Benton for taking her on board at the last moment, and not look for trouble where there may be none.

By the following afternoon she knew she must brave any questions, though, because she couldn't keep to this little cabin much longer without beating her head on the boards of the door. When Billy came to take her tray, she watched his retreating figure with envy and suddenly made a decision.

"Billy, wait," she called, and jumped across the cabin to the door.

Startled, the boy looked back. "Yes, Missus?"

"Billy, do you think I might be able to go on deck for some air?"

The boy frowned at the question. "I don't know, Missus.

309

I guess the Cap'n wouldn't mind. We've never had a lady on board before, though," he added dubiously.

Charity tried to sound lighthearted. "I will not walk far, perhaps only to the door. The cabin becomes stuffy after two days, you know."

Billy nodded. "I guess it does at that, Missus. Would you like me to show you the way?" Grinning, Billy jerked his head to the left and walked quickly down the gently swaying passage. On the wide planking of the deck he hesitated. "You won't stay long, will you?" he asked anxiously, looking around.

Charity assured him she only wanted a breath of air, and watched as he scampered back to his duties. The atmosphere was heavy under leaden skies, but the sea was glitteringly calm to the far horizon. Charity filled her lungs with relief. She noticed a seaman look up from coiled rope on the deck below, and she stepped back into the shadow of the door. She would have to settle for that glimpse of water and sky, she thought, until she could obtain permission from the captain to come on deck for regular exercise at whatever hour he thought best. Reluctantly she took one last look around.

A movement at the rail almost behind her made her glance back. The captain leaned there, talking to a big man whose left arm was in a sling. She couldn't interrupt him, but perhaps when he was done ... Her thought was never completed, for her hasty look had returned to the figure beside Captain Benton, and her breath had been choked off. Falling backward against the door jamb, she gripped it till her knuckles whitened.

At the same instant the men at the rail turned and started toward her. The shock in gray eyes matched her own, and for a moment the world stood still in unearthly silence. Then Adam, too, fell back and gripped the rail with his good hand.

"Ah, Madame." The captain's blue eyes lit up at sight of her. "You have decided to leave the confines of your berth at last." He held out his hand, and Charity stared at it as though it were a dead fish. Forcing her fingers to let go the wood she clutched, she clenched them together and stood upright.

"Allow me to make another passenger known to you, Maame."

Charity felt dizzily that she'd lived through all this scene before too. Was her entire life doomed to repeat itself in painful cycles? She had no control over her feet, which had rooted themselves to the deck, no control over her face which must look idiotic, no control over her insanely beating heart which must be heard clear up in the rigging. She heard the captain's voice trail off with the name Crandall, and then Adam was stepping forward, his ashen face nearly under control.

"A pleasure, Madame," he said stiffly, and made a creditable bow considering the awkwardness of his sling.

Charity didn't know if she nodded. The other two were talking. She heard nothing. The captain grasped her elbow, asked if she was all right, but she didn't answer. The next thing she knew she was standing in her cabin, the door was closing on something the captain was saying, and she was staring sightlessly at the wall, her brain repeating, "Adam, Adam," over and over.

It had been many weeks since Charity had dressed with such nervous anticipation. Her greatest sorrow was that she could not savor the selection of a dress. Her choices were minimal now: the violet dress she'd not yet altered, the taffy muslin she'd worn all day, or the pink, much more fashionable gown in which she had run away. Washing and mending had helped that dress a great deal, and she thought it would look presentable. Anyway, the color was so becoming. A sparkle returned to her eye as she savored that word. Adam was forever telling her what was becoming. Now she would show him again that she knew perfectly well.

With a lightened step, she left her cabin that evening and stood in the passage, looking up and down the narrow confines. Where was Adam's cabin? Not that it mattered, she reminded herself with something close to a giggle, for whatever space he had was surely shared with Jed. The giggle had been a good release for her nervousness, and with more composure she went to the captain's table.

But all her efforts had apparently gone for nothing. There was no sign of Adam in the hot little cabin this night, and even the nice, middle-aged Mr. Scott was absent since he had the watch. She drank more wine than she should have, trying to hide her disappointment, and chatted inanely about anything that entered her head.

Not that she knew what she would have done if Adam had come to dinner, she reflected, staring into the dregs of her second glass. She'd come to the table in a kind of mindless fog of joy, longing only for the sight of him. The fact that he

still hated her had shown clearly on his closed face this after
noon. She could hardly have sat here and begun an expla
nation to him of all she'd gone through. Even if she could
what then? She couldn't expect him to leap for joy when he
learned that Paul had not only threatened her with marriage
but had made free use of her before they could wed. She
moaned inwardly, and by the time Billy had cleared the
dishes from the round table, she had a headache. She knew
her laughter was becoming brittle, but felt powerless to stop
it. She noticed the captain was eyeing her speculatively, and
she nearly giggled again.

"Madame." The blond head leaned toward her and his face
swam in the candle light. "I was glad to see you had decided
to take some air this afternoon. Your cabin must be very
confining. Please feel free to come to the quarterdeck when
ever you have need to escape it." Nodding, she thanked him
"In fact," the man went on, and his hand managed to find
hers on the tablecloth and covered it caressingly, "why don't
you consider a stroll right now? It's a lovely starlit evening
I would be happy to escort you."

Charity focused her bleary eyes. She would like to stroll
for she felt sure she needed air. But Captain Benton was
altogether too self-assured. "That would be very pleasant,"
she said carefully, then smiled brightly, turning her atten
tion to the pale young Mr. Renquist on her left. "If you will
both escort me, I would be very proud." She saw the watery
eyes light up at her suggestion and smiled to herself. That
should take some of the wind out of the captain's sails. Ea
gerly she stood up. "Shall we, gentlemen?"

The evening was as promised, soft and warm with a mil
lion stars twinkling overhead. Charity watched the foaming
waves beside the hull and thought of another evening, her
first on the deck of a ship, and of the man she'd been with
She turned away from the sight of the waves, and as though
in answer to her wayward thoughts, saw broad shoulders
hunched over the rail across the deck. Mr. Renquist was
trying to capture her attention, but she paid him no heed
His querulous voice reached across the space, though, and
Adam straightened quickly, turning to see who had inter
rupted his solitude.

He shut his eyes against the sight of Charity, willowy and
graceful in a pink-striped confection that he once would have
approved heartily. His fingers curled against each other
tightly as he watched her leaning on the captain's arm. That

debonair young man had certainly lost no time in taking Charity under his protection. And she, ever the faithless wench, had spared no days for mourning the loss of her husband. A film of rage seemed to come over his eyes, and he tried to convince himself it held no particle of jealousy for this man to whom Charity turned so easily. It was just his damnable luck to have been dumped aboard the only ocean-going vessel that was leaving New Orleans the day of the duel, and to find he was trapped with the one person in all the world he would have avoided. The noble thoughts he'd had of facing Charity and telling her of her husband's death had long since flown with the realization that he hoped never to see her again. Now here she was, strutting before him with that blond captain, looking glowingly soft and desirable in the lantern light. Well, he'd be damned if he was going to skulk about this ship like a stowaway because of the presence of Charity Ashton. In fact, a much greater danger was that he might throttle her if he came on her alone.

Smiling grimly now, he strode forward to meet the three.

Charity, glad at last that she'd taken pains with herself this evening, and noticing Adam no longer wore his sling, watched him bow and then begin to turn away when he straightened. Impulsively she held out a hand to him. Tossing her head so her hair swirled over one shoulder, she looked up at his face. "Surely you will join us for a stroll, sir?" she said, and was appalled at how arch her voice sounded.

Adam looked only at the men. "I have been on deck for some time, so you will forgive me." Bowing once more he left.

The girl thought her heart must be shriveling inside her, but she smiled determinedly and took another turn around the deck before pleading her very real headache as an excuse to escape.

Despite her splitting head, and despite her agony over Adam's behavior, she slept soundly that night, a sort of security, knowing he was only a few ship's timbers away, wrapping itself around her like a blanket.

She spent the next day working over the violet dress with gritted teeth. How she would occupy herself each hour once this dress was done, she didn't know, but perhaps she would discover some other way of avoiding all her churning thoughts.

Her entrance at dinner was all that she could have wished, if she'd wanted to create an effect.

"Why, Madame!" Mr. Renquist toppled his chair as he started up.

"Ah," was all Captain Benton said as she paused in the doorway, stopped by the sight of Adam standing by the stern window. His face was a mask, but she thought she could just detect a quick gleam of admiration enter his darkened eyes before he looked away. Mr. Scott was the first to recover and step forward to guide her to her place. But even in his worldly-wise eyes there was a spark of appreciation as he seated her.

The dress alteration had obviously been a success. Folding back the high sedate neck to create a deep cleavage had done wonders for the line of the top, and the addition of lace at the wrists and under the bodice had given the whole a simple elegance she knew to be eye-catching. Perhaps a bit too eye-catching, she now thought as she felt Captain Benton's eyes on her.

Trying not to notice the hesitation with which Adam seated himself, Charity looked brightly at the captain. "I must thank you for arranging such calm weather for this trip. It has been a pleasant surprise." Fleetingly she wondered if the still seas had helped Jed with his seasickness, but she couldn't ask. She wasn't supposed to know Adam, let alone his "valet."

Immediately her question was answered, though, for Captain Benton, leaning across the dish Billy proffered to him, gave her a ragged smile. "We have been lucky, Madame. But at this time of year, we cannot presume that our luck will hold." He swiveled to look at Adam. "And I gather that the ease of the voyage has made no difference to your man, Crandall. Is he still in a bad way?"

"I'm afraid so. But he shows signs of recovery at last."

Charity smothered a smile, but when her gaze met Adam's opaque look, she saw no answering twinkle.

"Well, we will hope for continued good weather." Captain Benton looked warmly at Charity. "I would not want to deliver you to your husband in anything but the best of health, Madame."

Charity flushed, realizing that Adam knew nothing of the identity under which she was traveling. She saw startlement cross his face before it was swiftly quelled. "You are marrying again, Madame?" The words seemed to have been surprised out of him.

"Again? Once is enough." Charity tried to keep her voice

314

light, but she shrank from this conversation and her eyes tried to warn Adam.

He shook his head. For a split second the thought had crossed his mind that LaRoche had not in fact been dead under the oak tree. But that was absurd. He'd seen him himself. Then what the devil was she playing at now? He might have been amused if the whole situation hadn't been so macabre. She was running straight from her dead husband into someone else's arms? By way of the handsome Captain Benton? By God, he would kill her if he had to remain aboard this ship for weeks. He began to think of ports in the Gulf where he might ask to disembark.

Charity fell silent after that exchange. She felt light-headed with the sheer presence of Adam. But she suffered with the realization that her feeling was not returned, for Adam managed to monopolize the attention of one man at a time through three courses, and never again did he even look at her, let alone address her.

By the end of the meal she was terrified she'd burst into tears in front of them all, and knew she could not possibly say anything more to the overattentive captain. Rising, she choked out her excuses, and saw Adam get up reluctantly from his chair. His eyes looked angry as he raised his wine goblet in cynical salute. "Good night, Madame, ah, LaRoche, is it?"

"Boucher," she said faintly, flushing under his contempt. Weakly she turned away.

"Allow me to see you to your cabin." Captain Benton was beside her.

"Thank you, but I know my way. You mustn't leave your guest." Her voice was little more than a whisper, and she fled from the cabin, startling the seaman outside and nearly upsetting the tray Billy balanced in the passageway. Mumbling an apology, she fled down the dark passage and slammed into her cabin. Her hands pressed to her throbbing temples, she stared at the blank walls. The cabin was hot in the breathless night, and she felt the timbers were closing in on her. If only she could *walk*. Suddenly she dropped her hands. The captain and Adam were in that cabin still. She could have a few moments alone on deck. With trembling fingers she lifted the latch on her door and listened for any sounds in the passage. The soft creak of timbers beneath her feet and the distant slap of a sail were all that met her straining ears. Slowly she pulled the door open and stepped into the corridor.

"Oh." Her hand flew to her mouth in surprise. Standing not ten feet in front of her was Adam.

His own face quenched surprise with a scowl. Then he made a perfect mocking bow. "Madame Boucher." His voice was very soft, deadly sounding. "I seem always to be startling you at inconvenient times." The big form moved toward her menacingly and she backed through her door again. "And who is it you go to meet at this hour?" He was in her doorway now, large and threatening.

"N-no one," she stammered. "I thought you were all at table still. I wanted air...walking."

"Ah, it is exercise you seek."

Charity nodded, still backing. His look was thunderous as slowly he closed her door. Her heart hammered in her throat and she thought she'd suffocate in another moment.

"Perhaps I could give you some exercise." A wicked smile pulled at his mouth, and his big hands reached for her.

"Adam." She was against the wall now, swallowing convulsively to clear her throat. He held her shoulders, and his eyes raked slowly over her. The mixture of rage and desire on his face, in his eyes, made her tremble. "Please," she choked. "Not like this."

"Not like what, Madame? You prefer the captain's broad bed, perhaps? Or the perfumed luxury of your room in New Orleans? Or perhaps the deck of a keelboat?" His hard voice took her breath away, but her heart beat even faster at the touch of his hands, angry though they were.

"I seek only my share, Madame. Your captain can wait. I've been too long without a woman, and suddenly I find myself with one who is willing to give her favors to the nearest man. You can hardly be surprised." His hand tightened on her neckline.

"Stop it," she cried, and smacked at the hand. She was amazed at the irrelevancy of her thoughts. "If you tear this dress I shall be nearly without clothes."

Adam's wicked smile curved higher. "Then we will all enjoy you the more." Both hands tugged at the neckline again, and without ripping, the material slid down her arms. Looking at her soft shoulders, the nearly exposed breasts, Adam sucked in his breath, but his face was as black as ever. Roughly, he spun her, and with a jerk he snapped the buttons down her back from their threads.

Charity clutched at her gown as he turned her again, and now the tears were coming at last. She wasn't afraid of him, she realized. Not physically. Even when he was most furious with her, he'd never made love brutally. But his deliberate humiliation of her now was almost worse than physical brutality. She loved him. She would respond to him, and he would think all the worse of her.

He jerked her hands back and she closed her eyes, trying to stem the tears. The gown fell away, and she felt rough hands tug off her petticoat. The tears wouldn't stop, and she bowed her head, quickly brushing at them as Adam let go of her and turned away to shed his own clothes. Savagely he jerked her around then and threw her onto the bunk. She huddled there, burying her face in the pillow and heard him say, "Your tears for LaRoche are a little late in coming, don't you think? Or perhaps you are crying for your missed opportunity on deck?"

Her tear-streaked face lifted then. "You are so stupid," she cried. He was standing over her and now she could see, swimmingly, the scar on his left side. She stared at it, wondering if it had been Paul's sword that had made that scar.

Adam saw her look. "Yes, I am stupid. I have been very stupid. But I will now rectify some of my mistake." His big hands jerked her hips flat onto the mattress. "You can cry all you want for your dead husband, but you will remember that you were mine first."

"Dead?" Charity's voice rose, and the hysteria that had threatened for hours surged in her.

For the first time Adam's expression changed. Surprise softened the raging scowl, and suddenly he sat down heavily beside her. "My God, you didn't know?"

With a jerk she was upright. "Know what?" she fairly shrieked.

"That LaRoche is dead?" The hard voice sounded strangled.

"Paul is *dead?*" The *vaudun!* Suddenly she didn't have to ask what had happened. She knew. That little doll on Paul's bed should have told her two days ago. Adam's sword had set her free before she ever left New Orleans. The hysteria burst then, and Charity had to cover her face as she laughed and sobbed. It was unholy, but she couldn't help it.

"Oh, my God!" Adam repeated. He was going to lose his mind in a minute. But his fury carried him on. "Then why the hell are you on this boat?" he fairly shouted.

Charity hiccoughed as the laughter gave way to tear again. "Because I love you," she said in a tiny voice. She heard the sharp intake of breath, and then both his hand held her face, forcing it up to look at him. The expression of his features was so incredulous she pushed his hands away and sat up straighter. "You *beastly* man. How could you think I care *that* about Paul LaRoche?" she cried, snapping her fingers before his wide eyes.

The scar by his cheek looked even brighter as a slow flush of color rose across his face. "What was I supposed to think you vixen? You disappeared in thin air in Cincinnati, and all trails led to that keelboat and LaRoche. And then I found you'd *married* the man!" His rage was back, but Charity's own rose to meet it.

"He was never my husband!"

Adam heard her words through a fog of fury and pain. "Never your husband?" He shook her then, as though to spill the truth on the rough sheet between them. "Then why in hell did you let me think he was?" He dropped his hands in a despairing gesture.

She was on her knees now, her face level with his, her eyes brilliant with fire. "You *assumed* it. You assumed everything; that I had happily come to New Orleans with Paul, that I was living there of my own free will." She choked, and hiccoughed again. "As for being on this boat, I was so sure Paul would kill you in that duel, and I couldn't stop it," her voice was a wail, "I ran away rather than face him again."

Adam felt as though whole years of his life were dropping away. God, he should have known, should have trusted his own instincts, should have trusted her...He stared at her lithe figure, coiled like an angry snake in front of him and a grin tugged at the edges of his mouth. He wondered if he could ever keep his equilibrium with this girl, but he didn't care. He reached for her. "Quiet, vixen," he said.

Charity had seen the twitch of his lips, and felt her own fury mount higher. She thought of all the unfair and vicious things he'd assumed about her, and she was overcome with the urge to wipe that hateful smile off. Drawing back her hand she slapped him as hard as she could, not caring if he beat her senseless for it.

His head snapped sideways and she recoiled in fear. But suddenly she was thrown backward and his face was buried between her breasts. He was shaking. She pushed at him rying to ignore the desire that welled at his touch. When he raised his head, she saw he was laughing.

"I deserved that," he choked. "And you deserve a fair throtling yourself for thinking you could disguise yourself as a boy and not be discovered, and for driving all of us half insane with worry."

"I don't," she cried. "I was only trying to find you. I was so afraid you were dead. And then those awful men kidnapped me." She shivered, and felt Adam's arms tense around her.

"Rivermen." His voice was husky, his face grim before he turned his head away.

"No," she said softly. "They did not touch me. They thought me a boy the whole trip." But afterwards. She grew cold with remembrance, and slithered away from him, huddling in the corner of the bed.

Adam's face had lightened as she spoke, and now he looked puzzled. He tried to smooth her hair, but she huddled further away. "What then, Charity?" He steeled himself for her answer, horrible images crossing his mind.

"Paul," she whispered, not daring to look at him.

The images became more tortured and Adam could barely speak. "Where did he keep you?"

"Only one night in a horrid little hotel. Then I lived with a family to be respectable before our marriage." She was crying again. "I'm so *glad* you killed him!"

Adam's relief made him lightheaded. He didn't want to know about that one night. Anyone who would kidnap a girl and drag her off to a strange city was capable of... Very gently he pulled her down on the bunk and stretched out beside her. Cradling her like a child, he kissed her hair. "My poor darling." Her eyes were wondering as she looked up at him, and he almost laughed with the sheer joy of looking into their blue-green depths again. His thought to just hold her and comfort her dissolved as her soft body moved and stirred his weeks of need for her.

His lips were on hers and Charity was dizzy with remembered sensations. Her hands came up to his hair of their own accord and her body arched to meet his. Gone were the endless days of fear and longing. She couldn't even remember what Paul had looked like. There was only Adam. His strong arms were around her again, his dark head was bent to kiss her throat, her breasts. She moaned and clung to him. Through a haze of passion she saw him lift his head, watched his eyes

319

bright with something more than desire, heard his voice dee
with excitement.

"You've done with adventuring, Charity. For I find it take
years off my life. And I have too much to do now to lose an
more time. I'm taking you back to Virginia."

"Oh yes," she breathed and touched his face.

He grinned then, in the way he used to do, and her hear
contracted with love to see it. "Our good captain will be star
tled to discover that you are changing your name yet agair
But Mrs. Adam Crandall is the last one you'll have."

Her eyes widened. "Oh. He thinks I go to meet a sic
husband," she gasped. "We will have to tell him the truth
or..."

"Quiet, vixen." His mouth covered hers and she closed he
eyes. Captain Benton didn't matter. The world didn't matter
At last she was going home.